Fury of Surrender

ALSO BY COREENE CALLAHAN

Dragonfury Series

Fury of Fire
Fury of Ice
Fury of Seduction
Fury of Desire
Fury of Fate: A Dragonfury Short Story
Fury of Obsession
Fury of a Highland Dragon: A Dragonfury Novella

Circle of Seven Series

Knight Awakened
Knight Avenged

Warriors of the Realm Series

Warrior's Revenge

Fury of Surrender

COREENE CALLAHAN

This is a work of fiction. Names, characters, organizations, places, events, and incidents are either products of the author's imagination or are used fictitiously. Any resemblance to actual persons, living or dead, or actual events is purely coincidental.

Published by Montlake Romance, Seattle

www.apub.com

ISBN-13: 9781612185057
ISBN-10: 1612185053

Cover design by Janet Perr

Printed in the United States of America

To my dad—for showing me the true meaning of courage under fire, and because I love you.

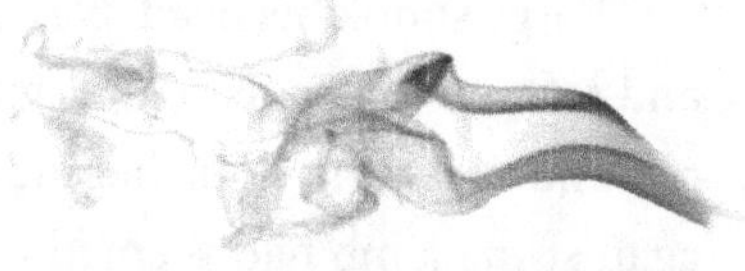

Chapter One

The buzz of halogens breathed life into the absence of sound. The silence should've bothered him. Sounded internal alarm bells. Put him on high alert. Something. Anything. The smallest response to the eerie fog of quiet descending over Black Diamond would be good. Forge glared at the precise seams of the chair rail instead, searching for flaws as he strode down the extrawide corridor.

Perfect fucking corners. Smooth, curving surfaces. Nary a chip in an ocean of glossy white paint covering the wood. Colorful paintings joined the parade, holding court, sending him deeper into the lair, pointing him toward the last place he wanted to go.

His gaze jumped from pale walls to the trio of Kandinskys hanging to his left. He scowled at the collection, the sight of even brushstrokes on priceless masterpieces irritating the hell of out him . . . for no good reason. His reaction to the sight qualified as over the top. He saw the flash 'n glamour every day. Lived in the lap of luxury inside the home he shared with the other Nightfury dragon warriors. Was accustomed to seeing the tidy show of wealth, so no need to be pissed off by it. Not today, or ever, except . . .

He didn't know how else to stem the growing tide of unease.

Like a tidal wave, worry washed in. The force of it rolled over him, slowing his pace, clogging his throat, making him yearn for the safety of his bedroom. It wouldn't take much. A quick pivot. A minute or two of walking. A solid door between him and what he'd learned to fear over the last week and a half.

Forge shook his head. Nay. No way. Not now. He wasn't a coward and refused to run. Not after forcing himself to step over the threshold and close the door behind him. The thud of the wooden edge against the jamb had seemed final. He wanted it to be *final.* Needed it to be. No more hiding. No more avoiding. No more holding it in until he thought he might burst at the seams.

Onward. Upward. To his own death if necessary.

Gaze glued to the framed Matisse hanging at the end of the hall, Forge struggled to keep his legs moving. But it was hard. His feet felt heavy, each stride taking real effort. Bend knee. Lift foot. Move forward. His boot sole said hello to the floor. A second later, the other landed.

One step, two step, three step, four.

The counting didn't help.

He muttered each number aloud anyway, walking toward the elevator that would take him into the underground lair. A few more bedroom doors to pass, and he'd be there, facing off with a steel cage he didn't want to enter. Not that he'd been given much choice, but as his footfalls echoed in the deserted corridor, a hollow spot opened behind his breastbone. The usual ache settled in and built a home, making him wonder if Myst—the Nightfury commander's mate—was right.

Forge frowned. Maybe she was onto something. Maybe he was pushing too hard. Maybe all he needed was time. A little R & R. A slice of respite, the chance to catch his breath, open his mind wider, and remember.

He fisted his hands. His knuckles cracked under the strain. The snap 'n pop broke through the quiet and—Christ help him. He hated that word: *remember*. It sounded so simple. Reach in, grab hold, and pull the information out of his mind. Easy-peasy. Nothing complicated about it. But no matter how many times he tried to retrieve the memory, he came away empty handed. Zero information. Few visual clues, a dark hole where recollection should live.

A huge problem.

Catastrophic, given Bastian needed what lay buried in a forgotten place inside his mind.

The thought landed like a bomb inside him. Mental debris scattered. Forge cleared it away, acknowledging what up until now he'd refused to admit. God forgive him, but he didn't want to do it. Didn't want to sit in that god-awful chair and allow B inside his head. Again. For the fifth bloody time, but running—leaving the lair and disappearing—wouldn't solve anything.

He had a price on his head. Had been rubber-stamped for assassination by Dragonkind elite. Why? Forge huffed. For unbelievable shite . . . a pack of fucking lies. He still couldn't believe the balls on the bastards. The Archguard high council and Rodin, leader of the entire travesty, had tried and convicted him of murder. Without Forge ever stepping foot inside a courtroom. Or touching the male he'd been accused of killing. Angela and Rikar had managed that all on their own. No help from him. Hell, he'd barely been part of the Nightfury pack at the time, never mind in the vicinity of the kill.

Not that he wasn't happy to take the blame.

Lothair had needed killing, the state of his family tree notwithstanding. The sadistic SOB might have been XO of the Razorback pack—and Rodin's second-born son—but powerful connections never exempted a male from what the universe doled out. The bastard had had it coming. The world was better off without him. Would be without Rodin too, if fate ever saw fit to deliver the Archguard leader into his claws. The instant that happened, Rodin would end up a dead dragon so fast heaven would spin on its axis as angels sang Forge's praises.

Still . . .

Last he checked, wanting someone dead wasn't a crime.

Manufacturing evidence, however, made the list of no-no's. For that, the Archguard wiggled on the hook. The original question, though, remained—why target him? Charging him for Lothair's death made no sense . . . unless Rodin was using the murder as misdirection. A distinct possibility. Clever beyond words. Particularly if Forge's missing memory unearthed something Rodin wanted to keep buried. A *something* so important it threatened the ambitious bastard's bid to become the High Chancellor of Dragonkind.

Which left one conclusion to draw.

Whatever lay locked inside his mental vault must be vital. A true threat. Potentially devastating to Nightfury enemies in Prague. Rolling his shoulders, Forge stretched taut muscles. Could be. Probably was, which meant the Archguard would never stop calling for his head. Or lift sanctions on the Nightfuries as long as his brothers-in-arms protected him.

All the more reason he needed to remember.

Endangering his new family wasn't in the plan. Protecting the males he now considered his brothers, however? Aye. Without question. Duty and devotion dictated the path. He loved the Nightfury warriors more than he did himself. Owed his brothers-in-arms everything. None judged him for his mistake—for dancing the two-step with Ivar as he considered joining the Razorbacks. Grief and the loss of his birth pack in Aberdeen, combined with a desperate yearning to belong, had driven his decision, and him right into disaster.

Thank God he'd come to his senses in time.

Ivar's endgame—mass genocide, the extermination of the human race—sickened him. The rogue leader needed his head examined. Or, mayhap, ripped off. Forge snorted. Aye. Sounded like a plan. Someone needed to take the bastard out. Dragonkind would be stronger for it, and humans all the safer. Not that Forge could do much about either. At least, not from outside the Razorback pack. He could kill rogues wherever he found them, but he was out of Ivar's inner circle now. Gone for good. Never to return.

Bastian had done that for him. Stepped up, risked his life to drag Forge out of darkness and into a strong pack, then let his warriors do the rest. A miracle to his way of thinking. He still couldn't wrap his brain around the shift in circumstance most days. The Nightfuries had accepted him. Drawn him in. Given him purpose and a best friend in Mac. Provided him and his son a home while worming their way into his heart. So . . .

No choice at all.

He would stay the course. Sit his arse in the chair. Endure the agonizing claw of mind regression. Recall all the ugly details to protect his pack. No matter how dangerous. No matter how damaging. Even if it proved too much for him to handle in the end.

Forge grimaced. Talk about terrible odds. Nowhere near comforting given his near-frayed mental state. One day he'd simply unravel. Lose it for good. Crash and burn. *Mayday, mayday, mayday, fire dragon going down.* He snorted in strained amusement. Christ, he was a mess. A total head case, and the dream wasn't helping.

Every time he closed his eyes the nightmare pounded on him, taunting him with murky imagery without ever giving him a clue. Day after day. Hour upon hour. The unholy screams picked him apart. His blood brothers' shouts for help in the dreamscape fed on him, leaving him gasping, in the grip of terror, when he woke.

He'd tried everything he could think of to stop the brutal onslaught. Opened his mind to accept the dream. Closed it off to block out sight and sound. Nothing worked. No matter what he did, his dragon half refused to relent, bombarding him with shadow memories—the blurry, indistinct details of a night long past. Now he couldn't tell fact from fiction. How much was real? What had his subconscious invented in an effort to protect him from what happened the night his family died?

Forge closed his eyes. Another terrible truth. His sire and brothers hadn't merely *died*. They'd been torn apart. Murdered by the claws of an unknown enemy.

Bile touched the back of his throat.

His feet slowed to a halt in front of the elevator doors.

Raising his hands, he gripped the back of his head. The movement locked his elbows. His arm muscles protested the tension. He didn't care. Honed by hardship, he barely felt the discomfort. Pain never bothered him anymore. Jagged sensation focused him instead, tuning him in as he stared at the floorboards between his feet. God. He was so tired of the bullshite. His dragon half needed to decide. Open his mind wide or shut it down tight. Remember everything or let him forget altogether.

The latter wouldn't make Bastian happy. His commander wanted what he carried inside his head and—

"Christ." Staring at his reflection in the steel doors, Forge blew out a long breath. "All right, then. Time tae stop fucking around."

Dropping his hands, he reached out with his mind. Magic flared in the hallway. Heat exploded around him, rushing toward the high ceiling as he called the elevator. Gears ground into motion. A hum burned through the quiet. His mind settled, accepting the inevitable. No more stalling. If he didn't get his arse into the underground lair in the next five minutes, Bastian and Rikar would come looking for him. He sensed the pair's growing impatience. Could read the worry as B prepared for the mind regression session inside the clinic.

The elevator pinged.

The double sliders opened.

A pair of aquamarine eyes narrowed on him. "About time you showed up."

Forge raised a brow.

Mac scowled. "What took you so long? I've been riding this bitch for the better part of"—his best friend glanced at his watch—"fifteen minutes."

"Stopped in tae see my lad."

"Ah, and how's G. M. this evening?"

"Hungry as hell. Growing like a weed."

"Aren't babies supposed to do that?" Mac asked, a confused look on his face.

"Apparently," he said, stepping into the elevator. Setting up shop next to Mac, he punched the down button with the side of his fist. The doors closed. The steel cage dipped before descending in a smooth glide. "Myst's got him now."

"Is she on standby?"

Forge shrugged. Maybe. Probably. God willing. The last time B mind-regressed him, his dragon half revolted. He'd overheated and gone into V-fib. Myst brought him back with a defibrillator. Three hundred and twenty volts of nasty-ass electricity. Not that he was complaining. He was alive, wasn't he? Hale and whole, not a brain cell out of place after plummeting into a downward spiral.

"I'm going in with you this time."

He opened his mouth to argue. Or tell his friend to fuck off. Forge wasn't sure which, but—

"No arguing." Mac's pissed-off tone hit him like a mailed fist. Forge drew a rough breath. Hell and a hand grenade. Trust Mac to object the only way he knew how—by putting up a fight. His presence during the session would impact everyone in the room—Bastian, Rikar, him. Maybe it would help. Maybe it wouldn't, but one thing, for sure? His friend didn't care. Mac was in protection mode, his goal clear—to ensure Forge made it out alive. "I can pull you out of trouble faster than B and Rikar can now. And you know it."

True enough. A serious point in his friend's favor.

The bond he shared with Mac deepened by the day. True friendship. A strong sense of brotherhood. Serious respect rooted in common interests, shared goals, and a deep liking of one another. Surprising in many ways, not so shocking in others. Some might call the friendship inevitable. Forge called it lucky. He couldn't, after all, take credit for Rikar's idea. The smart (stubborn, sneaky) male ensured Forge's inclusion into the pack from day one, entrusting him with an important task. One that carried significant weight in Dragonkind circles—the mentoring of a fledgling warrior.

Raised in the human world, Mac had been vulnerable after his first shift into dragon form: confused, unable to access his magic, in need of a strong warrior to guide him. The fact Rikar chose him—an unknown male and former enemy—to protect and teach Mac still humbled him. The mentor-apprentice relationship was a serious one, the responsibility enormous, forging the kind of bond that could never be broken.

Now, Forge couldn't imagine life without the mouthy SOB. Didn't want to either. He loved the male like a brother. Trusted him like no other, so . . . aye. Having Mac take part in the mind regression session made a certain amount of sense.

No one else would be able to connect with him as fast. To reach into his mind and drag him out before he seized and his heart stopped beating.

"Listen—"

"Not this time." Challenge in his eyes, Mac crossed his arms over his chest. The movement signified pure stubbornness. It also made his friend flinch, and Forge saw it—the flicker of pain, how fast Mac dropped his hands to his sides, the muscle ticking along his jaw.

Forge's brows collided. "What's wrong with your shoulder?"

Mac smoothed his expression. "Nothing."

"Bullshite."

"Come on, man. Right now isn't about me, and anyway—"

With a quick pivot, Forge reached out. Mac shifted to one side, trying to stay out of range. Too late. He grabbed hold and squeezed Mac's left shoulder. His friend cursed a second before his leg buckled. His knee hit the elevator floor. Bone hammered marble tile. The brutal crack raged against steel walls.

"Motherfuck." The ragged whisper spoke of pain.

Concern rang Forge's bell. He gentled his grip.

Head bowed, breathing like a wounded animal, Mac listed sideways on one knee. His shoulder bumped into Forge's leg. "God, that hurts."

"What the hell, Mac?" Careful not to touch his left arm, he hauled his friend to his feet. Mac swayed. Forge steadied him, waiting until he found his footing, looking him over, searching for the source of his pain. He frowned. No blood stains on his shirt. No lumpy bandages beneath the cotton. No indication he'd missed something. Or hurt Mac during dragon combat training. "What's wrong? I know you arenae injured. We haven't had a good fight in days."

"It's nothing like that."

"What then?"

"My tattoo. It's doing some weird shit."

Forge blinked. *Weird shit?* That didn't bode well. Particularly since no one understood the hows and whys of the tattoo. Least of all Mac.

Rooted in magic, the tribal image covered one side of Mac's chest, then turned north to roll over his left shoulder and mark his upper arm. Intricate, drawn in precise lines, the tattoo had arrived with the male's *change*—his first shift into dragon form. No rhyme. No reason. No explanation to be found in ancient tomes brought over from the old country. Forge should know. He, Mac, and Rikar had spent hours in the lower vault, scouring ancient texts written by Dragonkind elders, in the hopes of finding answers.

No luck. Not a single answer on the pages. No way to unlock the mystery either.

"It started glowing, Forge," Mac said, flexing his hand. "And my skin . . . shit. It's sensitive as hell."

"Show me."

Fisting his hand in the hem of his T-shirt, Mac pulled the cotton over his head. Heavy muscles flexed. Navy ink moved in concert, making his friend wince and . . . ah, hell. There it was, the problem in plain view.

"Christ."

"I know." Holding out his arm, Mac stared at the markings he'd inherited in an odd twist of fate. Color swirled inside the design, the pattern flickering like fire. The red glow started at the outer edges and bled inward, reaching toward the center as it spread. Chest, shoulder, and biceps—it didn't matter. Bright color took over, flowing through the tattoo, flaring in ominous warning, heralding the beginning of bad news. "It's like someone's holding a blowtorch to my skin."

"Does Tania help?" he asked, hoping Mac's mate took away the pain with her touch. Kept the glow at bay . . . whatever. Just as long as Tania soothed the male enough for him to sleep.

Dragonkind fledglings were fragile at first. Mac was no exception. Four months after his *change*—and the upheaval of having his dragon DNA activated—he still needed extra care. Good food. Lots of sleep. Loads of TLC.

Mac's mate gave him all he needed . . . and more.

A high-energy female, Tania connected to the Meridian in ways other women didn't. Power personified, she held a direct line to the source of all living things, tapping into the electrostatic bands ringing the planet, accessing the kind of energy most males never saw. Or got to taste. But even more astonishing, the rate of her bio-energy vibrated at the same frequency as Mac's. The perfect fit ensured his friend received the nourishment his water dragon half required to stay healthy and strong. A rare find for any warrior. A fortunate one for Mac given most Dragonkind males searched their whole lives for a female like Tania and never found one.

"Does she take the ache away?" Leaning closer, Forge examined the flickering edges of the tattoo.

"Yeah. She's the only one who helps."

"Good. Spend as much time with her as you can."

Mac threw him a "duh" look.

Forge's lips twitched. All right. Stupid advice. Bonded males didn't need an excuse to spend time with their mates. Being with their females was as natural as breathing. "Have you told Rikar?"

Mac shook his head.

"You need tae tell him."

"I will . . . after we get you sorted out."

"Mac—"

"I'm going with you. No way you're going in solo. Not after last time," he said, a lethal undertone in his voice.

The point slammed home with the force of a dagger. An answering echo panged inside his chest. Forge gritted his teeth. Bloody hell. He shouldn't allow it. Mac was hurting, less than one hundred percent on the physical front. Vulnerability came in all sizes. Small. Medium. Large, and . . . aye. Extra large with a side order of screwed up. Mac landed in the last category with the freaky tattoo shite in full swing, but . . . God. He wanted the male with him during the session. Would feel safer—saner too—with Mac standing inside the room.

Selfish. Pansy-ass pathetic. Wrong in so many ways.

He should be putting his apprentice first, ensuring Mac's safety, not worrying about himself. Or letting his unease take over. But as he held his friend's gaze, Forge went the sane route instead of the safe one and did the unthinkable. He gave in. Just rolled belly-up and let Mac win.

"All right, lad," he said without heat.

Tugging his shirt back over his head, Mac grunted. "Knew you'd see it my way."

"Donnae get lippy, Irish," he said, using Mac's nickname to soften the warning in his tone. "I'm giving you the green light, but mind your place. Let Bastian and Rikar work. No interrupting unless it goes sideways—got it?"

"Whatever you say."

Forge snorted. *Whatever you say.* As if. If only. Dealing with Mac was never that simple. The male always did as he pleased. Which meant . . . yup, screwed-up central, here he came. "You're a pain in the arse."

"Look who's talking." Raising his good arm, Mac nudged him with his elbow.

The love tap evened Forge out. Made him feel more solid inside his own skin. Hallelujah. He had a wingman, one who wouldn't hesitate to protect him if Bastian pushed too hard.

The elevator slowed to a stop.

The doors slid open, dumping him into the diamond-shaped vestibule.

Forge hung a right. The foyer narrowed into a hallway that branched in two directions. Mac at his back, combat boots doing double time, he veered left and made for the medical clinic. Circular lights embedded in the polished concrete floor threw *v*-shaped splashes toward twelve foot ceilings, highlighting chisel marks on solid granite walls. The hum of electricity swirled along the corridor. Keen for the hunt, the beast inside him stirred. His senses contracted, picking up trace energy, hunting for the slightest sound, listening for B's voice in the stillness.

A low rumble drifted into the hall.

Harsh scraping followed. Metal feet being dragged across concrete, maybe.

The scent of cinnamon swirled into his airspace.

Forge inhaled, sucking as much into his lungs as possible. He adored the smell. The spiciness tugged at his tension, smoothed ragged edges, soothed him . . . seduced him a little at a time. The entire reason Bastian used it. His commander wanted him relaxed, able to open his mind, no matter what it contained—good, bad, or ugly.

Reaching the door, Forge slowed to a stop in front of the clinic. Fronted by glass, the entrance gave him a clear view into a space with pale walls and a shitload of medical equipment. Under normal circumstances, Myst ruled the room, barking orders, running triage, sewing up the Nightfury warrior of the moment after a hard night of fighting. Not right now. Gone was the tidy workstation, no steel gurney or plastic-wrapped packages in sight, just a chair that looked like it belonged in a dentist's office. With one marked difference—the leather shackles attached to the padded arms and sturdy looking footrest. Forge drew a deep breath. The moment of truth. Now or never. Another round in the blasted chair. Or a lifetime without answers.

Mac palmed the nape of his neck. "You okay?"

"Aye," he said, voice steady, lying like an accomplished sociopath. Glancing sideways, he nailed Mac with an intense look. "Keep me out of V-fib."

"It won't come to that." His friend gave him a reassuring squeeze. "Not tonight."

"Your word."

"You have it."

Hard-core commitment in three little words. An oath between warriors.

Nothing trumped it. But as the glass door slid open and Forge stepped into the clinic, heart pounding, fear rising, uncertainty gathering like storm clouds, he started to pray. A little ask. A lot of faith, hoping he managed to walk out again unscathed. Any other day it wouldn't have mattered. Bashed up and bruised, bleeding like a sieve—who the hell cared? He owned skills, handled whatever the enemy threw at him. Tonight, however, his prowess in a fight meant nothing. The challenge he faced involved a laundry list of variables he couldn't control. The biggest of which stood across the room: arms crossed, shoulders pressed to the wall, expression neutral as he looked him over.

Forge stared back, refusing to show weakness.

Silence stretched. Bastian held his gaze. A full minute passed before his commander pushed away from the wall. He rolled one shoulder, then the other, the movement designed to break the tension as he moved across the clinic.

Not that it did the same for Forge.

Quite the opposite, in fact.

Each step B took cranked him tighter. A paradox. A real kick in the arse. Particularly since he liked the Nightfury commander. Respected the hell out of him too. Bastian might exude a brutal amount of vicious, but he was a true leader of males: cunning, caring, lethal when it counted. The closer he came, though, the harder the invisible strings pulled, making Forge feel as though he'd been stretched tight on a rack.

The chair between them, B stopped a few feet away. "Ready?"

One word. A simple question delivered in a quiet voice. Nothing threatening about it, but . . . bloody everlasting hell. Forge clenched his teeth. Nay. He wasn't ready. Never would be either.

Pride wouldn't let him admit it. So instead of telling the truth, he stepped toward the chair. "Aye."

A snort sounded to his right. "Liar, liar, pants on fire."

The remark snapped his head around. His eyes narrowed on Rikar. "Fuck off, Frosty. No one asked you."

Leaning against the prep counter, Rikar chuckled. "There he is—all fire, brimstone, and pissy attitude. Thank God. I was worried for a moment."

Teeth clenched, Forge glared at his XO. "How much time do we have, B—enough tae beat the shite out of him before we get started?"

"There we go." Frost dragon out in full force, snowflakes tumbled over his shoulders as Rikar grinned. "Now he's ready."

Bastian's lips twitched. "Afterward, Forge. I'll even hold him down for you."

"Two against one," Rikar murmured, interest lighting his eyes. "Unfair."

"But necessary." Abandoning his position by the door, Mac stopped alongside him. He treated Forge to an affectionate slap. Skin stinging beneath his T-shirt, his upper body rocked forward. The loud *whap* bounced off the walls as Mac tossed a perturbed look in Rikar's direction. "Last time you fought dirty. Nearly froze my balls off before I got ahold of you."

"I love fighting dirty," Rikar said with an unapologetic smile.

Mac growled. "Next time I'm bringing a blowtorch."

"Better make it a Flame Thrower," Bastian said, his gaze on Mac. He frowned. Mac stiffened, and Forge sensed the silent tug-of-war. The clash of wills set up shop inside the room, making the rounds, giving B's thoughts away, an argument entitled: Time for fledgling warriors to leave for safer surroundings. "Mac—"

"I'm staying."

Rikar glanced at B. After getting a nod, the Nightfury XO turned his attention to Mac. Uncrossing his arms, he pushed away from the counter. "I know you think you can handle it, Mac, but it's best if you leave. Once the session starts, we won't be able to control the magic. It'll detonate. You're not experienced enough yet to channel the whiplash. You'll end up getting hurt." Rikar gave Mac a pointed look. "Wait outside."

Mac shook his head, refusing to back down.

Bastian cursed.

Forge jumped into the breach. "Mac stays."

"Fucking hell," Rikar muttered, icy eyes meeting his from beneath lowered brows.

"He's strong enough," he said, holding his ground, wielding his authority as Mac's mentor, giving his friend a vote of confidence. Aye, it was risky. But then, danger didn't discriminate. Everyone involved risked injury—him included—considering the warriors in the room and the potent magic each possessed. The influx would be brutal, the energy blast so massive most males wouldn't be able to withstand it, but . . . too late to back out now. He'd given Mac his word and intended to keep it. "He stays—for now."

"Shit." Rubbing the back of his neck, Bastian shook his head. "Not a good idea."

"Give me a little credit, B. I know what I'm doing."

Bastian grumbled something inaudible.

Rikar sighed, but gave in. "Your call."

Aye, it was, along with setting the ground rules. "Rikar?"

"Yeah."

"He's your responsibility," Forge said, laying out his wishes. Promise or nay, he would only risk his friend so far. The second Mac faltered, he expected Rikar to do what he wouldn't be able to while deep in mind regression—shield Mac from harm. "Throw him into the hallway if it gets tae intense."

"You got it," Rikar said, cracking his knuckles.

Mac scowled. "Motherfuck."

"No arguments, Irish." Reaching out, he shoved his friend. Mac stumbled sideways. Forge walked toward the chair. "You want tae be here, you follow the rules."

Mutiny on his face, Mac nodded.

Forge tipped his chin in acknowledgment. Good enough. One pissed-off water dragon pinned down. Time to get the show on the road. Or rather, his arse in the hot seat.

Feet planted beside the chair he hated more than Razorbacks, Forge grasped the headrest. Leather whispered against his palm. A chill chased uncertainty down his spine. He pushed it aside, refusing to allow fear to take hold, and sat down. Black boots stark against tan upholstery, he settled in.

Metal creaked.

The chair groaned beneath his weight.

Taking a fortifying breath, Forge leaned forward and grabbed one of the ankle shackles. The first went on quick. The second made his hands tremble. Flexing his fingers, he finished feeding the strap through its holder. Glancing to his left, he held out his arm, offered his hand, asking Rikar for help without words. With a nod, his XO buckled him in, working with stark efficiency to secure the cuffs around both wrists.

Forge tested the bonds. Thick, smooth leather pulled at his skin. Panic threatened. His heart started to pound, hammering the inside of his breastbone. A large hand landed on his shoulder. Reacting to the slight pressure, he sat back, allowing the chair to support him, and looked up.

Serious green eyes met his.

"Easy, brother." Palm pressed over Forge's heart, Bastian gave him a reassuring pat. "I'll start slow. Close your eyes. Listen to my voice. Relax into it. It's all good. You're safe here."

Safe. Right. He wanted to argue, rip the shackles off, and call bullshite. Self-preservation told him to do it. Duty refused to let him. He'd volunteered. Forge huffed. Shite. He'd spent the better part of three days convincing Bastian it was the only way. His commander hadn't wanted to risk it but, in the end, relented. He knew what Forge did—mind regression remained the best and only way to get the information the Nightfuries needed, so . . . aye, no choice. Time to double down and trust B to control the fallout.

Fighting instinct, Forge forced his eyes closed.

Bastian started talking. About nothing important. Little things. Everyday happenings in the lair: his mate, the baby growing inside her, the son he couldn't wait to hold. The inflection of his voice remained consistent, the deep timbre smooth and even, no jagged undertones or spikes of intonation. Just the relaxed tone of one male chatting with another.

Soothing. Calming. Velvety sound mixed with a reassuring beat of blended syllables.

Magic flared inside the room.

Heat blazed a trail down his spine.

Taut muscles released.

Forge breathed out. Breathed in. Each inhalation a steady draw, every exhalation a relief. His heart slowed, thumping a sluggish beat inside his chest. Prickles crept down his arms. His fingertips twitched. A sinking feeling took hold. The chair, then the room, dropped away, leaving him floating above the floor. Words came again, sounding far away as hands slid over his nape, then settled, cupping the back of his skull.

The intrusion into his space made him flinch.

The voice murmured a reassurance.

Deep between layers of consciousness, Forge paused mid-breath to think about it: fight or accept. Push the hands away or ease into the cradle of them. The first option seemed like the best. His dragon half disliked the invasion, wanted him to shred the shackles and break free. The other half of him, however, urged him to make the leap. He knew the voice, trusted the male, and half-conscious or not—more out of it than in—Forge understood the silent message. He could let go, allow his human side to lead and the warm, soupy waves to pull him under.

Total relaxation engulfed him.

All worry drifted away.

"Good. Now . . . ," the voice said, touch growing firmer. Twin points of pressure gathered against his temples. Prickles ghosted along the sides of his head, immersing him in a cocoon of warm comfort. "You're at home, inside the mountain lair, about to fly out for the night. Your brothers are there, your sire too . . . what's happening, Forge?"

"Dragon combat," he mumbled, the words slurred. "First shift. New tae me. Need training."

The mesmerizing voice came again. "Show me."

Magic streamed into his veins.

An odd vibration exploded inside his head. The tremor gathered speed, tumbling between his temples. His mind spun away. Images flared, brightening the dark screen on the forefront of his brain. Happy times. Treasured memories of his mother: her and his sire kissing in the kitchen, the laughter and warm hugs . . . the sugary scent of shortbread cookies as she pulled baking sheets from the oven.

Forge hummed in contentment. Hmm, shortbread. His absolute favorite. He loved the treats she made. Enjoyed beating his brothers to the kitchen and—

The scene shifted.

Pictures whirled across his mental landscape. The reel stopped, setting him down in another time and place.

No longer in the kitchen inside his mountain home, he stood outside, atop a cliff, bare skin steaming in the cold, toes an inch from the edge. He leaned forward and peered over the jagged outcropping. His mouth curved. Oh aye. A thousand feet up. Nothing but the brutal bite of winter wind between him and sharp stone protruding from the ground. Exhilaration pumped excitement through his veins. God, he couldn't wait for his sire to give the word and say GO. He needed to shift into dragon form and spread his wings. Wanted to fly so badly he tasted the anticipation.

His sire whispered, "Now."

Forge transformed. His body lengthened beneath the spread of dark-purple scales. He flexed his talons, testing his claws, then leapt into the void. The craggy face of Ben Nevis stared him down. Ignoring the mountain's mood, he dropped into nothingness. Frigid air caught in the webbing of his wings, lifting his bulk into an updraft and the swirl of heavy snow.

He heard his brothers shout in approval.

Forge growled in answer, but didn't look back. No need. He knew they followed. Sensed each male's flight path, along with the one taken by his sire. Divide and conquer. Split the odds and attack from different directions. Forge bared his fangs, humming in enjoyment. It had begun—the training that would help him become a warrior. Satisfaction took hold, growing roots inside his heart as he banked hard, rocketing out of a mountain pass. Rough terrain gave way to rolling hills before meeting the edge of swampy moorlands. He scanned the horizon, hunting for his brothers, anticipating the first attack.

His sonar pinged.

Tingles streamed around his horns. The warning jarred him. His eyes narrowed. Strange, but . . . Forge frowned . . . something was off. Not quite right. The buzz in the air felt wrong somehow, nothing like the unique energy signals his brothers emitted. A shadow presence uncloaked in the corner of his mind. The dark form stepped forward and peered into the scene, trying to get a better look. Forge flinched, disliking the intrusion, but kept flying. He needed to know his brothers were safe. That whatever he sensed wasn't what it seemed—a threat, the invasion of his pack's territory. Eyes narrowed, he scanned the horizon, searching for the source.

Nothing and nobody. Except . . .

The wind died down. An unnatural stillness settled over the landscape. A torrent of energy flowed over the moor. Not understanding,

Forge drifted toward a copse of oak trees. Over there. Somewhere. He was sure the signal was—

A fireball exploded across the night sky.

His brothers yelled his name. He glanced over his shoulder, hunting for them in the gloom. His temples throbbed. The outsider inside his mind moved closer. The fireball stopped mid-flight, pausing in the middle of his mental screen. With a snarl, his dragon woke and spun full circle. Eyes aglow, the beast locked onto the intruder. The shadow presence froze. The monster inside him bared its teeth.

A male started talking. Fast words. Smooth, even tone, calling on his human side.

Forge tried to reach it. He wanted to do as the voice commanded: stay inside the dream and his own head, not succumb to the beast inside him. But it was no use. The dragon had slipped from its cage. Now he rampaged, refusing to listen, roaring with rage and brutal intent. A surging wave of magic hit. Sound went cataclysmic. The boom shattered the screen inside his mind. The image exploded like broken glass, decimating him with shards of memory shrapnel.

Pain ripped through him.

Desperate to protect him, the beast shoved him aside and took over. Inferno-like wrath bled into his veins. Claws deployed, his dragon attacked the shadow figure, trying to burn him alive as his mind whiplashed and his body seized.

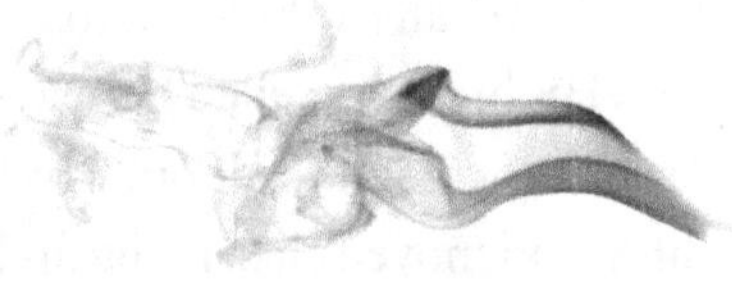

Chapter Two

Heart pounding like a motherfucker, Mac bared his teeth on a snarl. "Goddamn it, we're losing him."

Fear for his friend made his throat close and the words fade. He couldn't help the vocal lockdown or stop his mental slide into panic. Forge was in serious trouble. Flaming out. Unconscious. In agony from the torque and tear of mind regression.

Working to stabilize him, struggling to hold him down, Mac gathered his magic. The spell sped through his mind. His water dragon half zeroed in—a kind of *X* marked the spot—before unleashing the magical torrent in a raging rush. A cool wash splashed through his veins. Rain gathered inside the clinic, coating the pale walls, flowing up instead of down. Mist settled on his skin. The waterworks focused him. He tunneled deeper, trying to connect with Forge through mind-speak, his voice spiraling into his friend's psychological space.

Nothing.

No answer. No change in Forge at all.

The male plummeted into physical free fall instead, muscles seizing, heavy frame rattling, the slam-bang of his spine hammering the seat back. The chair shook, bouncing across the floor. Metal feet shrieked against concrete. The leather shackles restraining Forge groaned as he flailed. Mac cursed and dug in, tunneling deeper into Forge's mental landscape. The tattoo he didn't want, but couldn't ignore, throbbed.

Pain clawed over his shoulder. He shoved the discomfort aside. Not now. He couldn't quit now. His friend needed him and—

He pumped more magic into Forge.

His mind bled energy, forcing everything he had into his friend. The heavy chair frame shuddered. *"Come on, buddy. I'm here. Grab hold, let me pull you out."* The words spun out of his skull to invade his friend's. Forge gasped in agony. He arched in the chair, head thrown back, a silent scream locked in his throat. Mac held the line, but . . . holy shit. He needed help. A miracle or something to stop the onslaught and save his friend. Not an easy task as a seizure shoved Forge toward cardiac arrest. Exactly what he promised his friend wouldn't happen.

Motherfuck. It was a nightmare. A goddamned *nightmare.* He'd given Forge his word nothing bad would happen. Now everything was upside down and backwards, with his mentor one breath away from a heart attack.

Tightening his hold on Forge, he snarled at Bastian. "Unhook, B. Let him go."

"I'm trying. If I exit his mind too fast, I'll damage his brain." Both hands cupping the sides of Forge's head, fingertips pressed to the base of his skull, Bastian bared his teeth. Magic whiplashed, howling through the room, buffeting medical machinery. Fluorescents flickered overhead. The electrical buzz amplified, whipping into a high-pitched whine. "Rikar—he's overheating. Cool him off while I get the hell out."

A death grip on Forge's legs, Rikar murmured.

Frost rose in a crisp swirl.

Arctic air blew into the clinic, freezing the raindrops hanging in mid-air. The temperature dropped. Ice spread over the walls, cracking the plaster, frosting the sliding glass door. Mac breathed out, frigid air puffing between his lips as B withdrew—tentacle by mental tentacle—from Forge's mind. The seizure downshifted from catastrophic to chaotic. Forge shuddered, and Mac went to work, monitoring his vitals, dousing the psychological burn, keeping his heart beating and—

Thank God. It was working.

Little by little, Mac infiltrated the mental cage protecting Forge's mind. Snow swirled overhead. The chill slid like a knife over his nape. Still unconscious, Forge relaxed a little more, accepting Mac's presence inside his head. His friend calmed, then settled, collapsing against the chair, muscles trembling but no longer seizing. One hand pressed to Forge's nape, Mac attacked the leather cuffs, unshackling his wrists. "Rikar—get his ankles."

Hands working fast, Rikar undid the ankle shackles.

The second the last buckle gave way, Mac rolled Forge onto his side. Recovery position, a CPR move, the same one a lifeguard would use after saving a drowning victim.

Breathing hard, worry in his eyes, Rikar stared at Forge. "Jesus Christ."

"Fuck," Bastian whispered, the strain in his voice unmistakable. Big hands clenched into fists, he tipped his head back and stared at the ceiling.

Rikar blew out a long breath. "Anything new, B?"

"No. Same images . . . a woman, his mother, I think, and him flying. The blur of rough landscape beneath wing tips." Pale eyes aglow, Bastian dropped his head and rolled his shoulders, combating his tension. "Same as before. I can't move into new memories. His dragon half won't let me."

Mac glanced at his commander. Upset clouded B's expression, the toll of trying to extract the information he needed from Forge written all over his face. Mac understood. Bastian didn't like the mind regression sessions any more than he did.

"B," he said, a soft undercurrent in his tone. Bastian responded to the warning. Fierce green eyes narrowed on him. Holding his gaze,

Mac cranked his hands into fists and pushed to his feet. "That was the last time."

Regret in his gaze, B shook his head. "We need to know what happened in Scotland, Mac. It's important. If we can prove Rodin was involved, we can bury the bastard for good."

"I don't give a fuck about Rodin right now."

"Settle down," Rikar murmured, playing mediator, throwing him a back-the-hell-off look. "B's right. It's the only way to—"

"It isn't working," Mac said, feeling sick to his stomach. Forge might be desperate to remember—to give the Nightfury pack what it needed—but he couldn't stand any more. Couldn't handle seeing his friend suffer night after night, so it was done. Finished. No more. *No fucking more.* "We're killing him. Forge isn't going to remember this way. We need to change tack . . . look for another solution."

Bastian sighed. "What kind?"

"A simpler one. A gentler one." Grabbing a pillow off the floor, he settled it under Forge's head. His friend groaned. Bastian winced, and Mac examined a new possibility. It could work. Might be exactly what the doctor ordered. Which meant . . . now or never. The faster he got what amounted to a crazy idea in Dragonkind circles out into the open, the better for Forge. "A human one."

Rikar blinked in surprise. "Are you serious?"

Mac nodded. "We need to do something. He won't survive another round."

Bastian rubbed the back of his neck. "What do you have in mind?"

"A hypnotherapist."

"You know one?" Rikar asked.

"Yeah. A consultant for the SPD and the DA's office," Mac said. "She's good."

Bastian paced to the other side of the room, then pivoted, and came back. "How good?"

"Best I've ever seen."

"So, what?" A thoughtful look on his face, Rikar crossed his arms. "We bring her here?"

"Yeah." Eyes narrowed, Mac examined the variables. "Under controlled conditions."

Running down the list of complications, he searched for problems in the plan and headed for the bank of cabinets across the room. Set above a stainless-steel countertop, iced-up cupboard doors gleamed in the low light. He reached out and flicked one open. Frost burned his fingertips. Hinges squawked, working against frozen metal, sounding loud in the quiet. Finding what he needed, he grabbed a washcloth and whispered a command. Water bubbled from his palm, soaking the cotton. He wrung it out with his mind and returned to Forge. Brows furrowed, trying to be patient, his buddies watched him place the cold cloth on Forge's forehead. Still unconscious, the Scot muttered something in Gaelic. Mac spoke low, reassuring his friend before turning back to the other males in the room.

"Here's how it'll play out." Making a checklist, Mac ticked off the necessary boxes. Ones called cover-your-ass in the human world and . . . all right. His idea wasn't perfect, but hell, it was better than nothing. Better than putting Forge in the hot seat again. With a little foresight, he could control the outcome with a few concessions. The first? The entire Nightfury pack—females included—must agree to the plan and toe the information line. The second? Once inside Black Diamond, the therapist would be locked down, no contact with the outside world. "No talk of Dragonkind. We tell her we're a covert military outfit sanctioned by the government. That she'll be working on-site and off the grid to help one of our own retrieve a memory. No more, no less."

"Keep it simple." With a quick pivot, Rikar ass-planted himself on the countertop. Combat boots banged against the lower cabinets.

"Control the variables. Dress it up, sell the story by making her sign a confidentiality agreement."

"In other words—lie our asses off." Bastian's mouth tipped up at the corners. "No need to mind scrub her afterward."

Mac nodded. "Exactly."

Rikar's eyes narrowed. "Could work."

"It'll work," Mac said. "One small problem, though."

Bastian raised a brow, asking for clarification without words.

"I'll need Ange with me when I talk to her . . . to sell it properly."

"No," Rikar said, a lethal undertone in the denial.

Mac eyeballed his first in command. "Rikar—"

"My mate is not going out after dark." Frost gathered over Rikar's shoulders, misting the air around him. He shook his head. "It's too dangerous."

"She'll be armed with twin Glocks," Mac said, unleashing logic. Not that it helped. He knew what worried Rikar. The male would protect his mate at all costs, but well . . . hell. Talk about overprotective. Angela was ex-SPD. A sniper with serious skills and enough moxie to kill rogues with nothing but bullets and a long-range rifle. "I'll be with her. The Razorbacks are in hiding, so—"

Rikar growled at him. "No. Fucking. Way."

"You sure you need her, Mac?" His gaze locked on Rikar, B went the reasonable route, treading carefully. No one, after all, wanted a pissed-off frost dragon roaming around the lair. "The therapist won't come with you willingly?"

"It's a gamble. Hope Cunningham is smart. She's always been leery of me." He shrugged, telling the truth even though it pained him. He'd never done anything to make Hope fear him, but she did. Maybe it was the lethal vibe he carried around like luggage. Maybe it was his height and size. Could be he reminded her of someone in her past. Who knew? He'd never asked, leaving the chitchat to his partner whenever they'd needed the therapist on a case. "She knows and trusts Angela. Has worked with her countless times with violent-crime victims, so getting her to ask Hope is our best chance. She'll listen to Ange."

Silence swirled as Bastian considered him. "You really think she can help? That Forge will respond better to her?"

"I know it," Mac said, hoping he was right.

Arms crossed over his chest, B glanced at his best friend. "Ange goes."

Rikar cursed.

Mac exhaled in relief.

"But everyone goes," Bastian said, setting the ground rules. "The whole pack flies out. Mac—you and Ange take the Denali. We'll set up post around you . . . total protection detail. Myst will stay with Forge while we retrieve the female."

A muscle jumped along Rikar's jaw. "I don't like it."

"I know, but it's worth a try." Bastian pushed away from the back wall. Strides even, pace sure, he crossed the room and stopped beside the chair. Eyes closed, chest rising and falling at regular intervals now, Forge lay on his side. Unconscious. Vulnerable. So unlike his usual vicious self Mac's chest tightened. Staring down at the Scot, B reached out and cupped the back of his warrior's head. Forge's eyelashes flickered an instant before he fell into a deep sleep. An ache in his voice, Bastian murmured, "Better than this shit. Better than hurting him again."

Mac nodded. Fantastic. He had a consensus along with a preapproved game plan.

Now for the tricky part—precise execution. The kind of implementation he prayed Angela could pull off. Hope Cunningham wasn't a pushover. She ran a thriving practice. Had a busy life helping all kinds of people. Mostly trauma victims. Not an easy thing to abandon for a couple weeks. But Forge needed help, so like it or not, the hypnotherapist was coming to Black Diamond. Even if the use of duct tape and caveman tactics became necessary.

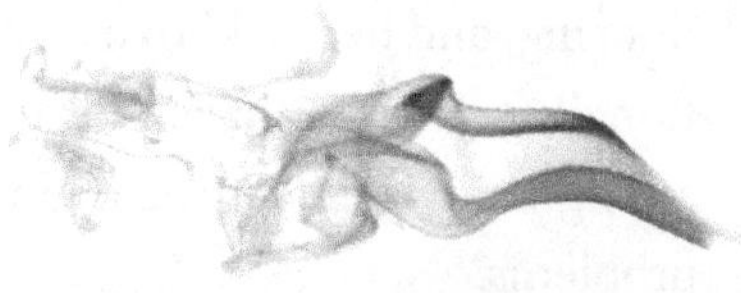

Chapter Three

Her technique was all wrong.

Hope Cunningham didn't care. She hit the heavy bag anyway. Over and over. Again and again. Slam-bang-thump. She went twenty rounds with black leather, punishing it with singular purpose. Proper form be damned. It didn't matter. Neither did the unfinished pile of case files stacked on the desk in her office. Not tonight. She needed an outlet, a way to stem the flow of recall. Of heartbreak and loss. Of guilt and inadequacy. Of playing the blame game.

Five years, and she couldn't shut it off or push it away. Same time, different year. February, twenty-eight days of god-awful. Not that her least favorite month cared about her preferences. Days away from the anniversary, the memory tortured her. Like a knife blade, recollection cut deep, sliced hard, leaving her nowhere to run. The visual played like a movie inside her head: the rapid staccato of gunfire, the terrified screams, the smell of blood in the air . . .

Her twin brother bleeding out on a library floor.

Protected by boxing wraps, her fists flew, flashing with brutal intent in the dim light thrown by crappy overhead fluorescents. Jab, left cross, uppercut. Crack-whack-thud. Sweat rolled down her spine. The leather bag swayed, reacting to her assault by swinging back toward her. Guard up, she dodged right and hammered it again. Her knuckles connected with the target zone. Pain streaked up her arm.

Violent sound shredded the quiet, banging around her home gym. Her garage, in point of fact. Decked out with free weights, rubber flooring, and her kickboxing equipment, it was a mecca for the emotionally scarred. A haven for the physically frustrated. Paradise after a long week spent sitting in an office sorting through other people's problems.

Ironic when she thought about it.

She helped others move toward emotional stability and on with their lives every day. And oh, how she loved her job. She snorted a little. *Job.* Right. Not even close. Serving others—helping people move past horrific trauma—was more calling than occupation. One she took seriously, refusing to allow her patients to shy away from difficult truths. She encouraged them to be open and honest. Provided a safe haven for each one, a place to do the hard work and face a situation head-on. What did she always say? Ah, yes. Admitting to a problem was the first step in solving it . . . to recovery and mental health. A lovely turn of phrase. Too bad she never took her own advice. She ignored her problems instead. Most of the time, she pretended they didn't exist. Her approach went something like . . .

Push the memories away and pray none ever came knocking.

The story of her life.

Her motto in a nutshell: Shut it down, turn away, bury the hurt deep.

Hope cursed under her breath. A total bullshit strategy for a psychologist who specialized in helping violent-crime victims.

Gritting her teeth, she brought her feet into play. She kicked high. The top of her bare foot slammed into the bag. Thick rope groaned. Eyes locked on her target, she spun and thrust backward. Her heel rammed into leather. With a quick pivot, she changed position, pretended she fought a real person, one in need of a serious beating. Kick after kick. Punch after punch. She brutalized the bag, making her muscles shriek with fatigue. God, how she wanted it. Needed it.

Craved the oblivion exhaustion would bring. Maybe then she'd be able to forget. Maybe then she'd be able to sleep. Maybe then absolution would come and her father would forgive her.

The thought stalled her mid-punch.

Swaying on her feet, fists raised and heart hammering, Hope squeezed her eyes shut. Wishful thinking. Nothing but a pipe dream. It would never happen. A vice admiral in the US Navy, her father didn't believe in forgiveness. He doled out discipline instead of second chances. Gave orders instead of hugs, and shame instead of support. Not that she blamed him. He was who he *was*, no changing him. And honestly, she deserved the silent treatment. All the unreturned phone calls too. For so many reasons, but mostly because she hadn't guessed. Hadn't known her brother was in trouble . . .

Or about the stockpile of weapons in his closet.

Unforgiveable. Inexcusable. Her mess from start to finish.

Her father was right. She should've known.

Palming the back of her neck, Hope laced her fingers and hung her head. Knotted muscles groaned. She welcomed the pain. It was better than the alternative—letting emotion out of its cage—but . . . God. Shame on her.

She should have known.

Adam had been more than just her twin. He'd been her best friend. They'd done everything together: gone to the same university, shared an apartment off campus, belonged to the same collegiate clubs. Her friends had been his, and his friends, hers. But that was over now. None of the old crowd talked to her anymore. No one wanted to know—or remember—the clueless girl with the homicidal sibling.

Strange, but she was okay with that.

Hope understood the reaction and her exile. Empathized with the victims. Understood and accepted the animosity of a community in mourning. She grieved too. Ached so hard, she couldn't cope half the time. Even all these years later, grief ate at her, hollowing her out, delivering loads of guilt and an extra helping of hurt. Forget the UPS man. Mental anguish was more efficient. Like clockwork, it arrived on time, the instant she opened her eyes each morning. Nothing had been the same since Adam walked into the busy college library and opened fire. Eleven dead. Twenty-seven injured. Her brother's standoff with police. The shoot-out. Her twin lying lifeless on the floor while she huddled beneath a desk one floor up, desperate to survive a mad gunman she hadn't realized was related to her.

And there it was . . . the terrible truth.

Adam had unraveled right under her nose, disappearing down a rabbit hole she hadn't known existed—and hadn't seen coming. She breathed deep, the harsh inhale half huff, half sob. Some kind of human behavior specialist she'd proven to be. Pitiful. Oblivious. Such a disappointment to the psychology faculty. Her professors had singled her out during her sophomore year, praising her talent—telling her how gifted she was, what a rarity in the realm of psychological profiling. Law enforcement agencies came calling, courting her, trying to recruit her before she finished her degree.

Leveling her chin, she frowned at the weights across the room. Color-coded dumbbells stood like soldiers, shoulder to shoulder on the black rack. Hope shook her head. So neat. So tidy. So freaking solid. Unlike her. Unlike her brother. Damn, damn, and *damn* again. She should be angry at Adam, for so many things. For pulling the wool over her eyes. For pretending everything was all right. For ruining her chances with the FBI's Behavioral Analysis Unit.

Somehow, though, she wasn't.

Despite his crime—and the body count—she loved him anyway. Missed him every day. Remembered the good times, his smiling face, before it all went so horribly wrong.

Her chest tightened. The missed opportunity—her lost career—didn't matter. It never would. A hole—Adam had left a giant, gaping *hole* in the center of her life. One she didn't know how to fill.

Sweat trickled over her eyebrow.

Hope swiped at the droplet before it reached her eye and dropped her hand. She tipped her head back. The ceiling came into focus, perfect plaster glossed over by white paint. No flaws in sight. Unlike her mess of a life. God, she needed it to stop. She wanted the guilt to go away. Yearned to be happy again, instead of—

Bright light flashed outside, shining into the garage.

Hope glanced toward the row of high windows. Quieting the thump of her heart, she turned toward the door leading outside and listened. Gravel crunched beneath tires in the driveway. A motor rumbled a moment, then went quiet. The cooling engine ticked. Two doors opened, then closed, the slams echoing in her quiet corner of Suburbia and . . . huh. Visitors on a Saturday night.

Unexpected, but not unusual.

The curse of having her office attached to her house. Nature of the beast. Par for the course. Home offices presented a myriad of problems. The biggest one? Everyone she worked with knew her home address. She'd set strict ground rules when she moved to Seattle and set up her practice four years ago. Made sure to put protections in place: serious electronic locks between her office space and home, a state-of-the-art security system, the SPD on speed dial. So far, none of it had been necessary. Her patients followed her rules to the letter, calling first, making an appointment, respecting her privacy. Colleagues, however? Not so much. Some dropped by without warning. Cops with an urgent case, more often than not.

Relief streaked down her spine, shoving her off memory lane.

Finally. At last. A distraction, one with the potential to pull her from the past. From the anniversary that dogged her every move.

From having to face what her brother had done one more time. Again, always, for the fifth year in a row.

Grabbing a towel off the workout bench, Hope looped it around her neck, then ripped the Velcro holding her boxing wraps in place. With a rough tug, she unraveled the long cotton strips, freeing her hands. Her skin sighed in relief as the pressure lessened on her knuckles. She flexed her fingers. Footfalls sounded on the flagstone walkway leading to her front door. Leaving the wraps in a pile on the floor, she pivoted toward the interior side door and crossed the garage.

Pace quick, she mounted the stairs into the house. Brushing past the open door, she strode over the threshold into the laundry room. Washer and dryer to her left, baskets full of unfolded clothes sitting on the countertop to her right. She pursed her lips, but ignored the mess—per usual. A nasty habit. One her cleaning lady scolded her for once a week, but . . .

Ah, well. Who was she kidding? She enjoyed untidy sometimes. Liked that her home felt lived in, comfortable, a little chaotic even. Her father would have a nervous breakdown if he ever visited. Why? Her place wasn't perfect. Mismatched furniture dotted the living room. She handpicked each piece herself: the sleek sofa with teak armrests, a trio of club chairs—two done up in pinstripes and dark-purple upholstery, the third in soothing chartreuse—the mirror-clad end tables, the colorful swath of silk curtains, and the pièce de résistance, a river rock fireplace between the pair of French doors leading into the backyard.

The gorgeous mix warmed her as she walked past.

All right, so the design combo was unusual. Eclectic and eye catching. Beautiful, sophisticated, and soothing. Hope's mouth curved. And just the tiniest bit bossy. She eyed the lopsided stack of magazines sitting on the Lucite coffee table. One hundred percent her style. Nothing like the stuffy, regimented household she'd grown up in.

"Take that, Dad," she murmured, running her hand along the back of the couch as she strode past. Gray suit fabric caressed her fingertips, bringing a sad sort of satisfaction. It was sick, really. Even from three thousand miles away, she tried to one-up her father. Always. Forever. A childish sort of game.

Particularly since he didn't give a damn about her anymore.

The thought made her heart hurt. She shoved the pain away. It didn't matter right now. She couldn't change it if he refused to answer her calls. Hardwood floors underfoot, she walked into the kitchen. Built in an open plan, her gourmet kitchen faced off with the living room. Light-gray cabinets with white end gables and Carrara marble countertops grounded the space, balancing color with style. Moving past the large island with tall stools, she veered right and headed for the vestibule.

The doorbell rang.

The sharp sound rippled, seeping through the quiet.

Hope upped the pace, jogging across heated floor tiles and onto the Turkish area rug. She slid to a stop in front of the antique cedar door. One hand curled around the handle, she popped onto her tiptoes and leaned right. Knowledge, after all, was power. An excellent thing to possess considering it was dark as hell, just shy of ten o'clock at night. With a quick flick, she flipped on the porch light. Squinting, she looked through the peephole and—

"Oh my God," she whispered, unable to believe her eyes. She blinked to clear her vision. It couldn't be. Just couldn't. Was completely impossible and yet . . .

She stared anyway, trying to figure out if it was a trick of the light. Maybe she was imagining things. Maybe squaring off with the heavy bag had knocked a few screws loose. Maybe stress had finally done its job and corroded her mind. No way was she seeing what she was—

"Open the door, Hope," a deep voice growled from the other side of the thick cedar. The rough edge in his voice sent shivers down her spine. "We don't have all fucking night."

Recognition slammed through her.

Her mouth fell open even as her body moved to obey.

Fingers trembling, Hope turned the dead bolt. She cranked the handle and pulled. The door opened with a creak. Porch light bled into the vestibule from outside. She stepped back, heart thumping, mind whirling, incredulity rising, and stared. An aquamarine gaze narrowed on her. She shook her head, her voice failing her as she looked up into the eyes of a man the SPD declared missing four months ago.

And was now presumed dead.

A death grip on the door edge, Hope struggled to get a handle on the situation. Cool air and the salty smell of the Sound drifted up the porch steps and into the vestibule. The chill nipped at her damp skin. She barely noticed. The goose bumps didn't matter. Neither did the open door. She needed her brain to work. Right now. Clear thinking. Deductive reasoning. The ability to focus. She required every bit of her considerable IQ working on the problem. This instant, before the whole thing got away from her. Too bad mental acuity was already gone, galloping off to some far-flung destination.

She blinked to clear away the shock.

It didn't work.

And he didn't help.

Big boots planted on her doorstep, he stared down at her, waiting like a sharp-toothed predator for her to make a move. She probably should. Moving—talking, easing into conversation—was an excellent strategy. Right up there with self-preservation, and yet, she didn't do a thing. She gaped at him instead, trying to find her voice. The traitor had gone packing—was now missing in action, just like he was supposed to be.

He'd been blown through a plate glass window. Gone missing from the hospital after the violent assault on police headquarters. Presumed dead by the SPD months ago.

Not one word of it was true.

She shouldn't be surprised. Really, she shouldn't. The SPD rarely told her everything, but . . . holy balls in a banana sack. After working with the cops for years—helping profile violent criminals and prepping witnesses for the DA—she hadn't suspected a thing. Not a single *thing*. She'd simply accepted the explanation, mourned the loss of her friends, and carried on. Heart beating double time, Hope shook her head. The magnitude of the cover-up floored her. It was huge. Bigger than gigantic. Particularly since Detective Ian MacCord, all around hard-ass, stood three feet away, looking far too alive and not nearly ghoulish enough to be a ghost.

The realization swept surprise away, grounding her in the truth.

Hope drew a shaky breath. "You're not dead."

Mac huffed. "Brilliant observation, Doc."

His tone—along with the heaping scoop of sarcasm—should've pissed her off. Under normal circumstances, it would have. Tonight, however, didn't qualify as *normal*. It fell under extraordinary. Alive. Mac was *alive*. Which pointed to an insurmountable fact. If he'd made it out in one piece, so had Angela. No other conclusion to draw. Colleagues, best friends, and partners, the pair stuck together. Some whispered behind their backs, hinting at a romantic connection. Hope knew better. Despite the rumor mill, Mac and Angela treated each other like siblings, brother and sister to the end. The duo worked as a team, watching each other's backs, and sometimes hers as well.

Tears stung the corners of her eyes.

Ending the standoff, Hope reached for him. Her hand landed on his forearm, fisting in the sleeve of his motorcycle jacket. Butter-soft leather balled against her palm and—

Static electricity sparked from her fingertips.

Heat ghosted over the back of her hand and up her arm.

Mac jumped as though she'd hit him with a thousand volts. With a muttered "motherfuck," he flexed his knuckles. Something sparked in his eyes, a something she couldn't identify before he hid it behind an intense expression. One she'd come to associate with him. The sight of it hamstrung her heart. Her chest went tight. Real . . . he was one hundred percent *real.*

"Thank God. Thank God," she whispered, her voice so thin it barely registered. "Where's Ange?"

Angela stepped out from behind her partner. Auburn hair cut pixie short, her friend twirled a key ring around her middle finger. Metal jangled as she swung the set until it struck the center of her palm. "Hey, Hope."

"Bonehead. You're such a jerk," she said, so happy to see her friend she didn't know what to do first: punch her for faking her own death. Or hug her so hard her ribs cracked. Planting her hand in the center of Mac's chest, Hope shoved him out of the way and stepped over the threshold. Her feet touched down on the wide-planked porch floor.

Angela opened her arms.

Hope didn't hesitate, opting to hug her friend instead of hitting her. "Thank God you're all right. I'm so happy to see you."

Angela laughed and hugged her back. "Good to see you too."

"Hell." Gaze glued to them, Mac crossed his arms. His lips twitched. "What am I—chopped liver?"

"Shut up," she and Angela said at the same time, voices overlapping as they turned to glare at Mac.

Hope gave her friend one last squeeze, then let her go. "Sorry. I'm a little sticky."

"Kickboxing?" Reaching out, Angela flicked the end of Hope's ponytail. Strawberry blond hair flashed in her periphery, before swinging back to brush the nape of her neck.

"Yeah. I hit the heavy bag tonight."

Mac frowned. "You been doing that a lot lately?"

Hope glanced his way and got nailed by aquamarine eyes. She tensed. He ran his gaze over her, stripping her with a look, making her realize she stood barefoot in workout tights and a too-thin T-shirt, nothing but a towel looped around her neck for protection. She stayed still, resisting the urge to squirm, refusing to give him the upper hand. Mac always made her uncomfortable. Not that he'd ever been inappropriate. He wasn't interested in her that way. No sexual chemistry to speak of, and yet when he turned his razor-sharp focus on her, she understood what trouble meant. He was too intense. Too intuitive. Too alpha in a Navy-man-SEAL-Team-6 kind of way for her to relax around him. Baggage from her past, she knew. Anything military—shades of her father—put her on guard, shields up, edge a whole lot sharper.

Not that Mac noticed.

Or maybe he did and simply didn't care. The guy enjoyed pushing people's buttons, for kicks and giggles, the fun of seeing the fallout. So no surprise, he just kept poking at her.

"You're thinner than before." The concern in his voice nicked her, sharpening her edge to a fine gleam. She didn't like it. He saw too much, too fast. Maybe he knew about her brother and the crappy month called February. Maybe he didn't, but the underlying worry in his words meant something. Especially when matched with the assessing look in his eyes. "Are you taking care of yourself? Have you been eating right?"

Did chocolate-covered almonds count? She'd been eating a helluva lot of those lately.

"Leave her alone, Mac." Angela warned her partner off with a look meant to maim. "We all have our ways of coping."

"Mine's sex." He sighed as though remembering a particularly happy session. One in which the woman in question screamed his name. "Ever try that, Doc? Great cardio. The best stress relief around, and you look like you could use a good fuck. You're wound way too tight."

"Screw off, Mac," she said without heat. No need to take offense. Mac liked to tease, but only those he considered friends. A much safer place to be in than the category he labeled *enemy*. Her gaze narrowed on him, then swung in Angela's direction. "What the hell, guys? What's going on?" Initial shock fading, her brain came back online. Questions streamed into view, taking the available real estate inside her head. "The last I heard you were both MIA. The attack on the precinct. The explosion at the rail yard. Cops up in arms. Is Captain Hobbs in on it? Why the cover-up? What—"

"Hey, hey—slow down, Doc," Mac said, holding both hands up as though she pointed a gun at him.

"We'll get to that. I'll explain everything, I promise." Angela gave her shoulder a gentle squeeze. "But first—can we come in? We need to talk and I don't want to do it out here."

Hope turned toward the door and waved her friends inside.

Angela followed her over the threshold. "It's February . . . a week away now, isn't it?"

The quiet caution—the sympathy—in Angela's voice rubbed her the wrong way.

Hope grimaced.

Frig and a fiddlestick. The anniversary, the day she dreaded with every fiber of her being. Trust Angela to remember the date along with the whole sad story. She sighed. Wouldn't you know it—a single lapse in judgment over too many vodka tonics after work one night, and she'd let her secret loose. Now her friend knew everything, every sordid detail about the shooting and her brother's part in it. Recall ripped her apart. Sorrow tightened her chest. She pressed her shame down deep, refusing to allow any to seep into her expression.

Same old, same old.

Except, in this case, not the *same* at all. *Unprecedented* described the situation better. She never talked about that day. With anyone. At least, she hadn't until Angela pressed the issue, and she'd fallen apart like a piece of week-old crumb cake. Hope exhaled in resignation. Happy hour gone wrong in a cop bar. A total cliché, and yet, she couldn't bring herself to regret it. She'd needed to talk, and Angela was a very good listener.

Crossing the vestibule, Hope glanced over her shoulder. Hazel eyes that saw way too much met her gaze. "Got something good for me, Ange?"

"I have exactly what you're looking for."

Please, God—be merciful and throw her a bone. "A distraction?"

"An interesting case."

"Perfect." Stepping out of the vestibule, she turned into the kitchen. "Beer or tea?"

"Beer," the duo said together, voices merging.

Hope's mouth curved. Fantastic. Despite the crazy coming-back-from-the-dead thing, nothing had changed. Beer it was. And a good pale ale it would stay.

Skirting the bar stools, Hope swept past the floor-to-ceiling cabinets and made for the refrigerator. Silence descended. The wall clock ticked, interrupting the hush, soothing her as her guests settled at her kitchen island. So predictable. Angela always sat in the same spot, choosing the middle stool, while Mac leaned against the island, forearms planted on the countertop, black leather jacket a blight against white marble.

Stainless steel glinted in low light, flashing beneath the row of halogens overhead as she grabbed the door handle and pulled. The fridge opened with a sigh. She glanced at the top rack, reached inside, and grabbed three bottles by the throat. Glass kissed, clinking in the quiet. Hope turned toward the island and set her bounty down on Carrara marble. Falling into routine, Mac went to work, twisting off the tops. Carbonation hissed. Beer bubbled up the bottle necks. Foam trickled down the glass, sending the sharp scent of alcohol into the air. Ignoring the froth, he placed the first microbrew in front of Angela. Another got set in front of Hope before Mac took the last for himself.

"So . . ." Raising the bottle, Hope took a sip. Cool and crisp, the ale touched the back of her throat and went down smooth. Hmm, so good. She hadn't drunk a beer in months. The last time she indulged had gone down just like this—with Mac and Angela sitting in her kitchen, about to toss an interesting case in her lap. The difference here? No file folder full of details and crime scene photos sitting on the countertop between them. Gaze moving between the pair, Hope tipped her chin. "Spill. Give me the details."

"Okay." Pursing her lips, Angela set her beer down. The bottle clinked against stone. A furrow between her brows, she glanced at Mac. "Where the hell do I start?"

Mac sighed. "Four months ago, Ange and I got caught in an investigation that led to an interesting opportunity. There's a lot of info, but the short of it is—we were recruited by an elite outfit running covert ops."

Surprise popped Hope's brows skyward. Wow. Unusual, but all right. Given the pair's badassery, she bought that. "Military or civilian?"

"Military," Ange said. "Very hush-hush."

"National security?"

Mac nodded. "Top secret, classified."

And there it was—the entire reason behind the cover-up.

So much made sense now. She knew all about Special Forces and deep-cover squads tasked by the government to clean up dirty situations. The kind no one in power wanted the public to know about. Dangerous missions. Top secret government-sanctioned activities—terrorist or otherwise. Hell, she wasn't naive. She'd grown up in a vice admiral's house where terms like *wet work* and *black ops* got used from time to time. "So, the job required that you disappear. Fall off the grid without explanation."

"No one but you knows we're alive, Hope." Expression serious, Mac eyed her over the top of his microbrew. "We'd like to keep it that way."

"Understood," she said, reacting to the authority in his voice, resisting the urge to tack a *sir* onto the word. Maybe even add a salute for good measure. Hope cringed. Crap. She kept falling into old habits. Her father had trained her far too well. "All right, then . . . that's the what and why. Now, give me the who."

"He's a good friend of ours," Mac said. "He's been through some harrowing shit and—"

"PTSD?"

Angela shook her head. "I don't think so. He doesn't act like it, but we have another problem."

She raised a brow. "What's that?"

Mac met her gaze. "He can't remember something we need him to."

"Mission gone bad?" Hope asked, mind already churning, running down the possibilities, making a mental list of potential psychological disorders. No one reacted the same way to trauma. Some internalized and shut down. Others craved an outlet, became violent or self-destructive. Some simply needed to talk and work through the issues. But in the rarest of cases, the mind reacted with such savagery it treated the memory like the enemy and closed ranks. Compartmentalized in the name of mental stability. Built a bulwark around the incident to lessen the pain and prevent the mind from splintering. "Loss of life?"

"Brutal." Hazel eyes intent, Angela frowned. "He lost his entire family in the attack."

"Hell," she whispered, knowing that was exactly what it must feel like to him. Total and complete *hell.* For his loss—the grief he no doubt suffered—with an added complication. Survivor's guilt. The condition was a powerful thing. Some never got past it.

"Yeah," Mac said, picking at the label on his microbrew.

Elbows planted on the counter, Angela shifted on her stool. "We love him, Hope. He's important to us. So is the information he's got locked inside his head. We've tried a bunch of different things to get at the memory, but he hasn't responded well."

The desperation in Angela's voice made her heart clench. The *we love him* caused her instincts to twang. Huh, interesting. Pretty rare for coworkers to feel that way about one another. Intrigued, her psychologist hat firmly in place, Hope tipped her chin. "What can I do to help?"

"You're the best. If there's anyone who can get through to him, it's you," Angela said. "We want you to treat him. Straight up therapy. Hypnotherapy. Any new treatment methods you want to try. Whatever you feel is necessary to help him."

"Is he willing to be treated?"

Mac nodded. "He's on board."

"The catch?"

"How do you know there is one?" Angela asked.

Hope snorted.

Mac laughed and tipped his bottle in salute. "Smart girl."

Angela grinned.

"All right, fun time is over," she murmured, warmed by their antics. "Tell me the rest. What else do I need to know?"

"Solid instincts." Mac huffed, a glimmer of pride in his eyes. "Not much gets past you, does it, Doc?"

"No," she said, tone even, selling the deception. God. One little word, such a huge lie. She missed things all the time. Exhibit one—her brother and the dead college students in Rhode Island. "Intuition is a powerful tool when wielded properly, Mac."

His mouth curved. A second later, he smoothed his expression and got serious again. "There are things we can't tell you, Hope. The less you know, the safer you'll be."

Great. Just perfect. It sounded like covert on top of covert. "Will not knowing compromise the work—my ability to help your friend?"

Mac shook his head. "No."

Angela set her beer down and, reaching inside her leather jacket, pulled a piece of folded paper from the inside pocket. Holding her gaze, her friend set the letter down on the counter, then slid it toward her. "You'll have to sign a waiver, a strict confidentiality agreement. The second you do, you agree to come with us. Now. Tonight. Treatment will take place on-site. You'll be blindfolded on the way and won't know where you are for the duration. Once you're done, we'll bring you home."

"And if I'm unable to help him?" she asked, gaze on the letter.

She understood the odds. Recognized difficult when it came calling. Nothing was certain. Not in the field of psychology. A one hundred percent success rate didn't exist when delving into mysteries of the human mind.

"We'll cross that bridge when we come to it." A plea in her eyes, Angela tapped her fingertip against the paper edge. "Either way, it's a week or two—a month at most—of your time. We're offering you fifty thousand dollars just to show up, and we'll triple your hourly rate. Whatever the end result—success or not—you wind up right back here. Home sweet home."

Hope drew a sharp breath.

Holy crap. Fifty thousand dollars, plus triple her fee. Jeez. The dynamic duo meant business. Not that she cared about the money. She didn't. The almighty dollar didn't motivate her. She lived to help. Wanted to serve and make a difference in someone's life. Longed to be challenged in her field of study. Those were her weaknesses, the very things that kept her going each day. And this case? She stared at the letter. No doubt about it. The unique patient psychopathy spoke to her, drawing her in as surely as changing tides called to an oceanographer. Add time away from home into the mix and . . .

No question. A change of scenery sounded like heaven.

It wouldn't take much to rearrange her schedule. A few calls, and she could disappear for a couple of weeks—perhaps a whole month. Frowning, Hope chewed on the inside of her lip. Space between her and the ordinary. Much-needed separation from the date looming like a shadow. A chance to immerse herself in a challenging case. An opportunity to help someone who really needed her. Time enough to forget and bury the hurt deep, if only for a little while.

She flexed her hands, then unclenched her fingers. Open. Closed. Twin fists shifting into open palms. It would be so good to get away. Was oh so tempting. The perfect solution to the desolation threatening to swallow her whole, but . . .

Her eyes narrowed on the pair staring at her with expectation.

Something wasn't right. Mac and Angela were hiding something. An important *something* that had nothing to do with securing her services. She sensed it. Could feel the truth seething just below the surface. The duo might be her friends, but both were smooth operators. Hope recognized the game. Knew it far too well. She'd spent a lifetime playing it with her father. And if there was one thing she'd learned, it was to take nothing for granted or anything at face value. Which meant . . .

She could only trust her friends so far.

"Listen to me—both of you." Hope paused for effect. "Before we go any further, we need to get a couple of things straight."

Plucking the confidential agreement off the counter, she wagged it at Mac, then turned to look at Angela. "I'm willing to sign the waiver and keep your secrets, but if I go with you, I'm there for him, not you. He'll be mine for the duration. No one on your team interferes with his therapy. And if at any time I need more information to help him recover the memories, you will give it to me. No questions asked. No hiding behind classified bullshit. I might be going in blind, but I won't be hamstrung by either of you."

Mac grimaced. "Shit."

"Agreed," Angela said, throwing her partner a look Hope couldn't interpret.

Not the most auspicious beginning.

Secretive buggers.

But some give was better than no take, and as she accepted the pen from Mac, signed and dated the letter, the gloom crowding her heart lifted. Not a lot, but enough. Purpose. The chance to make a difference. An adventure. She'd just been given all three. In the nick of time too. Lord knew she didn't want to face another anniversary alone.

Chapter Four

Arse planted on a stool at the kitchen island, Forge frowned into his teacup. A smooth-tasting chamomile concoction swirled inside, a soothing balm for a ragged soul. At least, it was supposed to be—what the box label advertised. A bloody pack of lies. Tea wasn't good for the spirit.

Forge lifted the mug anyway and, following Myst's orders, took another sip. The brew stuck, swimming at the back of his throat. Gritting his teeth, he forced himself to swallow. Hot liquid burned on the way down. Intense heat expanded behind his breastbone, and he waited. For the relief. For the blaze to melt the chill sitting like a chunk of ice in the center of his chest and the pain to become bearable.

No such luck.

He was frozen. A solid block of hurt and sensory overload.

Worse than the physical anguish, though, was the jumble inside his head. Two hours, and still, his mind refused to settle, dipping, diving, tumbling until his thoughts fractured, exploding in multiple directions. Now he couldn't think straight. Mental blur yanked his chain, killing his ability to make sense of his surroundings. Forge snorted. Shite, it was tragic. A total fucking catastrophe. He scowled at the tea leaves staining the bottom of his cup. The extra shut-eye inside the medical clinic should've helped. Should've been enough to smother the emotional turmoil, laying down a track of all clear on the psychological front.

The aftereffects of a mind regression session didn't work that way. The effects lingered, refusing to dissipate, leaving him so tense his skin stung and his temples throbbed. Bowing his head, Forge closed his eyes. The murmur of female voices burned across his frayed nerve endings. A tremor rumbled through him. Fuck. He was still so bloody sensitive. Cracked open. Rubbed raw on the inside. The unrelenting pressure made his eyes water.

Irritation times a million.

And it wasn't getting any better.

The longer he sat in the kitchen, the more pronounced the discomfort became, making him wonder where he'd gone wrong. And how the hell he'd gotten trapped.

Forcing his eyes open, he scowled at the countertop. He'd screwed up somewhere along the way. Taken a wrong turn. Been slow to react. Whatever. The how of the problem didn't matter anymore. Only one thing would save him now—escaping the dynamic duo before they drove him stark raving mad.

His gaze ping-ponged between Myst and Tania. He toyed with the mug handle, then spun his tea full circle. One revolution whirled into a second, and then another. Round and round. Over and over. Ceramic scraped against marble as he stared at the pair. Bloody hell. He might as well throw in the towel. It was official. He'd turned into a pansy, a male easily neutralized by the flap of feminine concern. Now he was on lockdown. Completely trapped. Cornered by two females who refused to leave him alone. No matter what he said.

Or how often he tried to make a break for it.

Forearms stacked on the counter, he shook his head. The taut muscles bracketing his neck squawked. Discomfort clawed down his spine. Rolling his shoulders, he attacked the tension. No good. Even less effective. Nothing but freedom would work, but well . . . hell. He couldn't un-ass himself and leave, now could he? At least, not yet. Not until the females messing with his chi released him.

With a sigh, Forge studied his tormentors. Such bonny lasses. Good company dressed in workout gear and high ponytails. Total terrors with iron wills and obstinate natures. Surprising, really, given the angelic expressions and pleasant demeanors each wore like body armor. Focus locked on them, he spun the mug into another revolution. The hellions standing on the opposite side of the kitchen island ignored him. Heads together, eyes locked on the blueprint spread out on the countertop, the pair studied a myriad of intersecting lines. A comment here. An observation there. Yakety-yak-yak. The two never stopped talking, shoulders bumping, soft voices drifting, often finishing each other's sentences without knowing it.

His gaze paused on Myst, then jumped to Tania. Complete opposites. One blond and slender, the other dark-haired and curvy. One unshakable with the calm confidence of a medical professional. The other a complete worrywart with too much artistic energy and an elaborate landscape to design. Both beautiful. Both stubborn. Both strong-willed, so hardheaded the number count on the obstinacy scale reached the millions.

Forge grimaced. Christ help him. The problem—and his subsequent imprisonment inside Black Diamond—was one hundred percent his fault. Bugger him, but he'd given in. Simply folded in the face of female worry after he'd woken in the clinic and found the lasses fawning over him.

More fool him.

It had been a trick. A trap sprung by wee devils with long eyelashes.

Forge huffed. Who was he kidding? No sense getting bent out of shape about it. None of the other Nightfury warriors would've faired any better. The dynamic duo disguised as innocent females made a formidable team. Witness the fact he was at their mercy—inside the bloody kitchen instead of where he wanted to be . . .

Out flying with the rest of the Nightfury pack.

Pushing away from the countertop, Forge glanced at the plate in front of him. He frowned at the piece of cherry pie. Neat slice. A lovely, tidy triangle. Baked perfection set out on expensive china—flaky crust, the ooey-gooey goodness of fruit filling, a dollop of whipped cream—out in full force. His stomach grumbled. Shoving the tea aside, he picked up his fork. Tines hovering above the plate, he stared at the artery-clogging mess. The promise of sweet decadence. Deception wrapped up in comfort food, a distraction designed for one purpose . . .

To soothe his pride.

And help him forget his failure.

Putting the fork to work, Forge squished a lone cherry. Syrupy juice squirted across bone china, obscuring the fancy design rimming the dish. The tang of baked fruit drifted into his airspace. Despite the tasty temptation, he wasn't interested. No matter how much his stomach grumbled, he couldn't eat. His appetite had bottomed out, leaving him on edge. Now pent-up energy flowed into a river of frustration. Fucking hell. Forget about the past. Set aside his family's murder for the moment. The latest lapse was much more serious than that. Shite. He couldn't remember the last few hours, never mind what had gone on before.

Forge blew out a breath. All right, so that wasn't quite true. He remembered entering the clinic and sitting in the chair. He recalled Bastian, Rikar, and Mac setting up, getting ready, strapping him down. After that, though? Flicking at the piecrust with a sharp tine, Forge struggled to draw the memory forward. He tunneled deep, searched hard, shining light into the dark recesses of his mind, hunting for answers, willing the truth to surface. Seconds turned into more, ticking into minutes.

Nada.

No flash of memory.

Nothing but a head full of jagged, shadowed images.

Pressure banded his rib cage. God be merciful, it was getting worse. Whatever poisoned his mind continued to eat away at his memories, wiping his mental slate clean. He shook his head, forcing himself to think. What was wrong with him? Why couldn't he remember the mind regression session? Why couldn't he—

"Hey, Forge?"

The soft voice broke into his thoughts. He looked up, taking his attention off the pie. Brown eyes full of uncertainty, Tania met his gaze. The specters of his past—all the dark ghosts haunting him—vanished in an instant. Simply disappeared in the face of her growing insecurity. Forge's mouth curved. Would wonders never cease? Tania was stewing, worrying about something she considered important.

Different night. Same issue. Identical results.

Tania always landed on the wrong side of worry. Mac's mate might be lovely, but her nature bordered on obsessive. She picked at a problem until the whole thing unraveled. Some nights, she worried about her sister. Most of the time, she zeroed in on Mac, her love for him overflowing into caretaking the likes of which most males never saw.

Forge swallowed a chuckle.

Oh, the joys of the female mind. He adored women. Enjoyed everything about the fairer sex: the emotional upheaval and behavioral inconsistencies, the ups and downs, the absolute challenge of a woman with a sharp mind. The game—the thrill of the hunt, the grind of a heart-pounding chase, the ecstasy to be found in a female's arms—captivated him. True challenge. Burning need. Gorgeous conquest. His over her. Hers over him. It didn't matter who landed on top as long as the female of the moment received pleasure in the end.

Not that every interaction ended with sex.

Sometimes, like tonight, it was about talking. About soothing a female who didn't belong to him . . . and never would. Myst and Tania, along with other females in the lair, existed in a different category. Each belonged to a Nightfury warrior. Which meant sex never came into play when dealing with them. Mated males were possessive. Dangerously so. Once energy-fuse and the binding spell took hold, a warrior would kill to protect his chosen female. Sometimes for the slightest infraction—a disrespectful comment, an unintended insult, or oh, say, getting too touchy-feely.

Forge never crossed that line.

The women inside Black Diamond belonged to his pack—were his to protect and shelter—not take to bed. What he'd found with his brothers-in-arms' mates went deeper than the usual surface shite. It was about kinship and support. About helping a pack member who required it. About feeling necessary to another and being included, accepted, and trusted. Heady things for a male who'd been without kin for too long.

Meeting Tania's gaze, he tipped his chin. "What is it, lass?"

Flipping a sketch pad around, she pushed it across the island toward him. "I need your opinion."

He raised a brow. "New design?"

"Yeah," she said, tone full of apprehension. "What do you think—will Mac like it?"

With a flick, Forge pushed his plate aside and reached out. Textured paper caught against his fingertips. Metal spirals holding the pad together scraped across the counter as he dragged the drawing closer. "You've not shown him yet?"

"Not this one. I want it to be a surprise. And anyway . . ." She blew out a breath. "I don't like the other designs. The lagoon's not right. None of the layouts work, but this one—"

"Is fabulous," Myst said, smiling.

"You're biased." Tania threw her friend a look of exasperation. "You think everything I draw is awesome."

"Of course I do. What are best friends for?"

"Hair-raising honesty, I hope."

"Right." Myst snorted. "As if. No way I'd survive if I told you one of your designs sucked. You'd smack me upside the head with one of your drafting rulers."

"Probably," Tania said, mischief in her dark eyes. "Sometimes violence really is the answer."

Myst huffed. Snatching a pencil off the countertop, she tapped the tip against the blueprint. "Do you see what I'm dealing with here?" She gave him a pointed look. "Tell her it rocks, Forge, and save me from getting skewered."

Forge's lips twitched. "Let me have a look . . ."

Setting the sketch pad to one side, Forge grabbed the edge of the blueprint. He tugged on the thick paper. Myst lifted her elbows, letting him drag the architectural plans across the island. With a quick turn, he spun the design 180 degrees to get a better look.

Precise lines intersected, connecting to create an elaborate landscape. Seven acres of abundant vegetation: mature trees, thick shrubbery, and flower beds full of perennials. The whorl of elegant footpaths. And near the center? A two-tiered lagoon, lush waterfall flowing from the pool above to the larger one below. He traced the lines with his fingertip, then glanced at the sketch pad. Painted with water colors, the secluded oasis leapt off the page, allowing him to picture it. Christ. What a marvel. Tania had outdone herself. Was going for gold with one goal in mind: to please her mate and give Mac—and his water dragon half—what he needed, a place to swim each evening.

"'Tis incredible, lass," he said, pride for her work in his voice. "Bloody well gorgeous. Mac is going tae love it."

Tania smiled, relief on her pretty face. "You think so?"

"Aye. No doubt at all."

"Told you so, my lady." The words melded with a thump across the room. Hinges squeaked. The door from the butler's pantry swung open and closed. With a happy hop, Daimler bustled into the kitchen, mixing paddles covered with strawberry icing in hand. "It's going to be wonderful. Everything is in order. The backhoe and bulldozer arrive tomorrow. The plants are scheduled to arrive next week."

"Wicked," Myst said, accepting a mixing paddle from Daimler.

"Perfect." Licking icing from the second paddle, Tania moaned in delight. "Thanks, Daimler."

"Shite," Forge muttered, giving the Numbai a meaningful look. "Better keep the bulldozer away from Wick."

"I've already spoken to Master Bastian." Daimler grinned, gold front tooth winking beneath bright halogens. "Master Wick will not be permitted to handle the equipment without supervision."

Handle. Forge snorted. That was one way to put it. Another would be *duck and cover . . . or die.* A sound strategy. One that made perfect sense.

Wick enjoyed throwing things. Heavy machinery topped the list. The male couldn't resist the allure of a good tractor-toss. Or KO'ing rogues with a dump truck to the teeth. Slam-bang. Poof-gone. Nothing but piles of ash in his wake. He should be grateful for Wick's predilection. The enemy didn't stand a chance when the warrior picked up a front-end loader. The problem? Whenever his friend went kamikaze with construction equipment, the Nightfuries scattered, ramping into serious flying to stay out of the way, but well . . . shite. Nobody was perfect, and Forge refused to hammer Wick for his weakness. Particularly since Forge indulged in his favorite way of killing Razorbacks all the time—by slamming the assholes skull-first into the sharp corners of skyscrapers.

Daimler cleared his throat.

Forge glanced his way.

Amusement in his eyes, the Numbai met his gaze and switched to mind-speak. *"Looking to escape?"*

"Christ save me from obstinate females. I cannae get away."

"Gage is in the garage."

Surprise blindsided him. Forge blinked. *"He didn't go with the others?"*

The Numbai shook his head. *"The youngling is still fearful. Osgard doesn't do well alone yet. He's most comfortable when Gage remains close."*

"He'll adjust."

"Of a certainty he will, but in the meantime . . ." Daimler tilted his head toward the exit. *"Off you go, Master Forge. I'll distract the ladies while you make a break for it."*

Bless him. The Numbai was straight up fantastic with a hefty helping of outstanding. *"Have I told you how much I love you lately, Daimler?"*

The tips of his pointy ears turned red a second before Daimler rolled his eyes, turned to the lasses, and murmured something about marzipan decorations. Myst and Tania both pivoted in the Numbai's direction. Talk of a triple-decker cake and the need for taste testing ensued, distracting the hellions with the promise of chocolate. Focused on the trio, Forge slid off the stool. His feet touched down on the limestone floor. He shifted sideways. Slow and steady. No sudden movements. Stealth was the name of the game. He needed to fly under the females' radar. Otherwise, the pair would pounce, and he'd be stuck in the kitchen instead of safe inside the garage.

The trifecta approached the pantry door.

Forge skirted the end of the island. The promise of freedom looming, he sped toward the exit. His heart thumped, setting a boom-boom-slam rhythm inside his chest. Dragon senses set to maximum, he glanced over his shoulder. No imminent threat of pursuit. No flap of feminine outrage. Nothing but smooth sailing. Expelling a ragged breath, he listened harder, hoping his luck held.

Nothing.

So far, so good. All quiet on the female front.

Entering the corridor, he slowed to a jog. Fantastic. He'd made it. Was almost out of range, ten feet and one turn away from escaping for good. He should've realized Gage had stayed home instead of flying out. Since his return from Prague, the warrior rarely left the lair. Some might argue Gage's capture—and subsequent torture by an Archguard death squad—had taken its toll, making him gun-shy, less willing to leave Black Diamond for extended periods. Forge knew better. Not much fazed Gage. The male was solid, the best kind of deadly. Fast in flight. Brutal in a fight. Smart with heaps of cunning piled on top. So only one conclusion to draw. His stay-close-to-home policy didn't stem from any lingering effects of captivity, but from another source altogether . . .

Osgard (the youngling he'd rescued from the Archguard) and the lad's fear of strangers.

Turning the corner, he strode toward the end of the passageway. The quiet calmed him, settling into his bones, seeping into his chest to surround his heart. Forge sighed. About time. He needed a reprieve. Longed for peace of mind and craved the comfort of camaraderie. Normally, he got that from Mac, but with his apprentice out of the lair, Gage would have to do. Forge's lips twitched. Hell. No contest there. The male, and his sarcastic, pissy attitude, was a good substitute. A battle of words—and the clash of a high-level intellect—was what he needed to feel like himself again. And well, working with his hands—helping Gage rebuild the Corvette ZR1 Tania had totaled on a midnight run outside the lair—wouldn't hurt either.

Forge's mouth curved. Christ, he couldn't wait to razz Gage about it again. Was looking forward to the argument and the male's reaction to a female cracking up "his baby." Anticipation slithered down his spine. He focused on the end of the hall. The walls dead-ended into square, precise corners, gleaming wainscoting, no seams at all. At least, to the naked eye. Eyes narrowed on one corner, he unleashed his magic. Heat flowed through his veins, fanning out behind him as he murmured a command.

Gears ground into motion. A series of locks clicked. Hinges moaned as the hidden door popped open. Forge shoved it aside, stepped over the threshold and onto the landing. He flicked the door closed behind him. Twelve steps down and he stood in the underground passageway. Wide with a high ceiling, the tunnel connected the aboveground lair to the garage, allowing movement between the two during the day.

A necessary thing. Useful too, considering Gage refused to move his bedroom into the lair. He preferred the apartment inside the garage, and no matter how much Daimler nagged—or mayhap due to it—the male remained entrenched. Forge grinned. Bad-tempered bastard, stubborn to the bitter end.

Not bothering with the light switch, Forge moved into darkness. His night vision sparked. Details jumped out at him: the grainy texture of cinder-block walls, the cobwebs hanging from unlit wall sconces, the staircase sitting at the opposite end. Without breaking stride, he closed the distance and took the stairs three at a time. His boots banged against metal treads, killing the quiet before he reached the top. He pushed the heavy door open and—

"Hand me the three-quarter-inch wrench, kid."

The deep growl spiraled across the huge space. Steel rattled as tools got shoved aside.

"Here."

Metal smacked against skin. "Thanks."

Standing behind a wall of tall toolboxes, Forge bowed his head. The grind of a socket wrench joined the buzz of industrial lights overhead. He sighed as tension seeped from his muscles. Hallelujah. Nice. Normal. The striking sound of sanity.

Another low murmur.

His sonar pinged, giving him Gage's location in the fifty-car garage.

Kicking aside a stray bolt, he sidestepped the last toolbox. His gaze swept the scene. Crumpled hood of the canary-yellow ZR1 in the background, Gage stood off to one side, beside a sturdy table with an engine mounted on it. Hands blackened by grease, the male stripped the motor, removing parts only to set each down next to its compatriot sitting on the steel tabletop. Murmuring to Osgard, Gage held up a part, explained its purpose, teaching the youngling as he went. With a look of extreme concentration, the lad nodded, took the broken piece, and placed it in the discard pile.

He stopped six feet away. "Getting it sorted?"

At the sound of his voice, Osgard jumped. Fearful blue eyes swung his way.

Forge gritted his teeth, trying to keep his anger at bay. Goddamn the Archguard. The abusive bastards had done a number on the lad. Now Osgard didn't trust anyone but Gage. He needed time, patience, and loads of persistence. Forge recognized the way forward. So did Gage and the rest of the Nightfury pack, but . . . God. He forced his fists to unclench. It was painful to watch the youngling struggle. Even more difficult not to push the lad and get involved. But Gage was right—the less pressure on Osgard, the better. Which left everyone with one strategy . . .

Respect the healing process. Wait until Osgard was ready.

Staying still, Forge waited, giving the lad time to adjust to his presence. Focus riveted to him, Osgard took a step back. A wrench in one hand, Gage reached out with the other. He grabbed the lad's arm to hold him in place. With a "Settle down, kid," the warrior glanced

Forge's way. An intense bronze gaze met his. "What the fuck do you want?"

"A safe place tae hide."

Gage huffed. "The female horde driving you crazy?"

He shrugged. No sense lying about it. "Aye."

"Stay the hell out of the kitchen, man. Safer that way."

Good advice. Next time he'd heed it and make a fast getaway. Ignoring Osgard, hoping the lad didn't spook, Forge walked to the table edge. Attention on the engine, he tipped his chin. "The ZR1's?"

"Yeah. Damn female cracked the engine block."

"Running grill first into a tree will do that tae a 'Vette."

"Fuck." Gage scowled. "Wish I could be pissed at her."

"Aren't you?"

"Nah," Gage said. "She's too pretty. Can't even bring myself to yell at her."

Forge laughed.

"Doesn't mean I won't take it out on Mac, though." An unholy gleam in his eyes, Gage treated him to a speculative look. "Might have to appease my curiosity and beat the shit out of him, see what all the water dragon fuss is about."

"Good luck with that." Forge shoved his hands into the front pockets of his jeans. "The wanker knows kung fu."

"Really?" Gage grinned. "Starting a fight just got a whole lot more interesting."

Stifling a laugh, Forge shook his head. Christ. Trust Gage to take on what most warriors wouldn't touch. Mac packed a serious punch. Toss in the fact most Dragonkind males feared water and . . . aye. A smart male knew when to quit. Or at least, stay the hell out of a water dragon's way.

Picking up a wrench, Forge cranked the socket all the way round, listening to the *zzz* the metal gears made. "Want some help?"

Gage raised a brow. "Hell, you must be hard up. Need something to do that bad?"

"Whatever you need done."

Releasing Osgard, Gage eyed the lad. "Stay put, Oz. Still need your help. Forge might be scared of a couple of females—"

Forge scoffed in feigned protest.

"—but he isn't in the habit of kicking the shit out of snot-nosed kids." Gage frowned, amusement in his eyes as he glanced at Forge. "Are you?"

"Nay," Forge said, playing along, helping Gage ease the lad's fear. "Bronze-eyed bastards, however? I make no promises."

Gage chuckled.

Osgard stared at him a second, then relaxed, the beginnings of a smile on his face. "What's next—the carburetor?"

"Good plan." Patting the lad on the shoulder, he handed Osgard a screwdriver. Gage picked up another and went back to work. One minute turned into more, the silence comfortable as the three of them settled in, pulling apart the engine a piece at a time. Time lengthened, and Forge unwound, the whisper of hands on tool handles, the clink of steel on steel, the smell of motor oil smoothing the rough edges of his mood. After a while, Gage pulled a rag from his back pocket and wiped off the pliers he held. "Heard what happened in the clinic tonight. You okay?"

"I'll live."

Gage glanced at him. "Not what I asked."

"Only answer you're going tae get."

"Fair enough, but if—"

"No need tae talk about it." Attention on the engine, Forge lifted his hand. A small screw fell into his palm. He set it aside, adding it to the growing pile on the table. "It'll get sorted . . . or it won't. Enough said."

Silence settled, whispering around the workstation.

Standing on the other side of the table, Osgard shifted his weight from one foot to the other in the lengthening quiet. Forge watched him, heartstrings pulled taut as the youngling fiddled with the screwdriver, turning it over in his hand. The movement signaled the return of nervousness, and . . . ah, hell. He wished he could take it away. Wished like hell the lad hadn't been hurt at all. But the world wasn't that kind of a place. Bad things happened to good males all the time. He should know. He lived with fate gone wrong every day. Knowing it, however, didn't make his regret any less real. Given a chance, he would shoulder Osgard's pain and make it his own.

Pressing the blunt point of the screwdriver into the pad of his thumb, Osgard lifted his chin and . . . looked straight at Forge. Pale-blue eyes met his, darted away, then came back. A heartbeat passed. Osgard cleared his throat. "Did it hurt?"

Surprise jolted through him, making Forge slow to comprehend. "What, lad?"

"Mind regression," Osgard said, tone quiet and curious. "What was it like?"

Gage raised a brow, daring him to answer.

Forge stifled a shiver. His throat closed as his muscles went taut. Bloody hell, he didn't want to answer. Didn't want to remember the session, never mind talk about it. Particularly after he'd told Gage to mind his own business. But as he stared at Osgard, he refused to do the same with the lad. He'd asked a question, a good one, braving his displeasure, offering his trust. The question played like a well-planned chess move. Most males would've scoffed at the idea. Not Forge. He recognized the game. Osgard was reaching out, testing the boundaries to see how another male—a bigger, much stronger one—would react to being put on the spot. Bridges were built that way, honesty arching into trust, so like it or nay, he needed to answer. If only to teach Osgard he had nothing to fear.

Steeling himself, Forge opened his mouth to explain.

The whine of machinery shattered the moment. The garage door opener activated. Heavy chains clanked. Lights at the far end came on, expelling the dark, as one of the heavy industrial doors opened.

"Find me later, lad. I'll tell you all about it," Forge said, focus split between Osgard and the slow rise of the garage door.

Osgard nodded.

"Good deal," Gage murmured, slapping Forge on the shoulder.

The love tap spoke of approval. The sick feeling in the pit of his stomach receded. Forge exhaled, the breath slow and measured. Shite, that felt good. Talking about mind regression might suck, but gaining the lad's trust would be worth it. Was far more important than his continued comfort, and as the black SUV rolled in, headlights flashing, oversize tires squeaking on the concrete floor, Forge let the shame of his failure go. He couldn't change it now. Or ever. Time to move on. Tomorrow would be soon enough to worry about the next step and reclaim his memories. Right now, he had a different mystery to solve. Namely? Why the hell Angela sat behind the wheel of the Denali.

Wiping his hands on a rag, Forge stepped away from the table and turned toward the SUV. Intense aquamarine eyes met his through the windshield. He scowled at his apprentice. Planted in the passenger seat, Mac raised a brow in challenge. Forge growled under his breath. Damned fool. What did the male think he was doing? He might be new to Dragonkind, but Mac knew better than to take a female out of the lair after dark. It was unsafe. A total jackass move and—

His sonar pinged.

Sensation burned across the nape of his neck.

The flap of multiple wings thumped through the quiet.

Dust kicked up in the driveway beyond the garage door.

White scales flashed, glowing in the gloom as Rikar landed outside. Dragon claws ground against gravel. Rubber squealed as Angela hit the brakes inside the garage. Engine rumbling, she put the truck into reverse and backed the SUV into its designated spot.

Forge frowned in confusion. What the hell was going on? Rikar flying in support could only mean one thing—the warrior had been on board with his mate leaving the lair . . . at night. *At fucking night.* The shift in procedure signaled trouble. What kind and for how long? Forge curled his hands into fists. Shite. Excellent question. One in need of answering, and fast. Particularly with Gage's and Mac's gazes locked on him, as though waiting for a reaction.

His instincts screamed in warning.

Something was up.

Something was off.

Something nasty with his name written all over it.

Muscles locked, Forge met Mac's gaze, glanced at Gage, then turned his attention to the driveway. Bastian landed next to Rikar, midnight-blue scales in stark contrast to the Nightfury's first in command. Rikar shifted into human form. B followed, rolling his shoulders, adjusting his leather trench coat, stomping his feet into his boots as Haider, Sloan, and Venom touched down behind him. Bringing up the rear, Wick dropped out of the sky. Black amber-tipped scales rattled in the wind rush. His huge paws slammed into the ground. A brutal cacophony of sound echoed, rumbling through the garage. Tools jumped on the workbench, steel clanging against steel, as Forge sidestepped Gage and headed for his apprentice.

Popping the door open, Mac slid out of the Denali. The truck door slammed behind him. A shimmer in his ocean-blue eyes, he hammered Forge with a be-reasonable look. "You're going to listen to me before you lose it."

The statement of fact rubbed Forge the wrong way. His eyes narrowed. "You think?"

A muscle ticked along Mac's jaw. "I know."

"What the fuck did you do?" he asked, soft tone full of all kinds of lethal.

"I brought you what you need."

Unease slithered down his spine.

Glancing at his partner, Mac tipped his chin. Already out of the truck, Angela gripped the rear handle. The back door of the SUV opened. A dark blindfold covering her eyes, a female stepped out and—

Forge lost his ability to breathe for a moment. "Bloody hell."

"I'm sorry," Mac said, switching to mind-speak. Hands raised, palms up and out to the side, Mac approached on silent feet. *"I didn't know she was high energy until I got there. It's not ideal, but she's the best at what she does. You need her and . . ."*

Mac kept talking.

The words didn't register. Forge couldn't hear a thing. His ability to focus on anything other than the female vanished. Nothing penetrated the thick fog of attraction. Fuck. Even with the blindfold covering half her face, she was beautiful. Red-gold hair tied in a ponytail. Gorgeous mouth made for kissing. Pearl-white skin with the faintest smattering of freckles. Brilliant aura glowing like a supernova. Lust clawed through his veins, hardening him so fast it was painful.

His dragon half snarled.

The sound echoed inside his head.

The noisy rush made his heart throb. One beat pounded into another. His mouth went dry. His skin grew more sensitive, sending a clear message: *get closer*. Speed would close the distance. A few strides. A quick touch. A faster taste—his mouth on hers—and he'd know. Would draw on her power, assuage ravenous need, learn what raw energy felt like against his skin and how well she would feed him.

Footsteps sounded behind him.

A chuckle drifted over his shoulder.

"Well, now. I wasn't expecting that," Gage said, laughter in his voice. "Things just got a whole lot more interesting."

Forge snarled at the bastard. Idiot male. Gage needed a serious attitude adjustment. One helped along by Forge's fist slamming into his face. He needed to pound on someone. Right now. Mac was his first choice—the meddlesome arsehole—but Gage would do, 'cause sure as shite, *interesting* didn't begin to describe the situation.

Dangerous seemed a better word.

A safer bet too considering his reaction to the female now shoving the blindfold off her head. Big green eyes blinked in the bright light. Her ponytail swung as she pivoted, small booted feet rasping against the floor, and met his gaze. Her soft inhalation of surprise battered him. Forge's stomach clenched. Bloody hell. Trouble—he was in serious fucking trouble. In uncharted territory with a female he shouldn't get anywhere near.

Mac's fault.

Forge stifled a growl. *All Mac's fault.*

Which left him with two options. Scare the hell out of the female by letting lust out of its cage. Or beat the shite out of the male responsible for bringing her into his sphere.

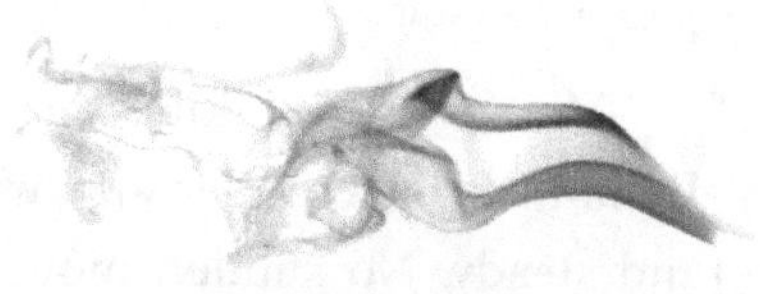

Chapter Five

Forge was going to kill him.

Mac knew it. He'd resigned himself to the inevitable on the ride home. The entire reason he hadn't argued when Angela insisted on driving. A good thing too. His mind hadn't been on the road. It had been at Black Diamond, on his best friend. After getting a look at Hope—and seeing her through Dragonkind eyes—he'd known what kind of shit storm he planned to bring into the lair. Another high-energy female on the hook, about to walk into Nightfury central and upset the balance of the entire pack.

But then, hindsight was twenty-twenty.

Knowing then what he did now, he might've altered the plan. Waited a day for his friend to recover. Brought Forge along for the ride. Had him knock on her front door. Or at the very least, told him what he intended and how Hope figured into the scheme, but well . . . shit. No way he could've predicted she'd be high energy. Or guessed how Forge would react to her. With inferno-like heat that bled into the air around him, scorching everything it touched.

Proof positive on the rising danger scale? The way Gage inched away, foot by cautious foot, shielding Osgard, shoving the youngling behind him as he retreated toward the workbench.

"Here if you need me," Gage murmured, his attention jumping from Forge to him. Serious bronze eyes collided with his. *"Careful, Irish."*

Mac nodded, taking the warning to heart as he skirted the Denali's front bumper and walked toward his best friend. Slow and steady. No sudden movements. His approach needed to be perfect. Like a zookeeper nearing a wild animal with bared teeth, otherwise . . .

Hell. Shit storm was a polite way of putting it.

Forge was more than on edge. The male was set to go off. Ka-boom. Ker-slam. Serious injury dialed up to DEFCON 5. Jesus. Mac could actually feel the violence shimmering around him. Like a living, breathing thing . . . expanding by the second as he held his mentor's gaze.

Surprise whispered through him.

He'd never seen Forge so amped up. Or upset. Until now, the male had been the poster boy for calm, cool, and collected. Mac clenched his teeth. Motherfuck. He should've expected Forge to balk and fight back. No one enjoyed being ambushed. Especially a male as strong minded as his friend. Sudden changes outside of battle never felt safe to a Dragonkind male. Status quo equaled stable, a pleasing kind of predictable. No surprises. No need to go on the alert or move to the offensive. And as he watched Forge shift, widening his stance, fisting his hands, preparing to kick his ass, Mac understood the reaction.

And acknowledged his mistake.

"I fucked up," he said, tone quiet, but contrite. Eyes glued to Forge's face, he moved left, using his body to shield Angela and Hope. An excellent strategy. A necessary one given Forge's primal reaction. One false move. Less than an instant and goodbye secrecy. Hello to a warrior in dragon form and a shitload of screaming from Hope. *"I should've warned you, buddy, but you still need to hear me out."*

Forge bared his teeth.

Mac took another step sideways, blocking his friend's view of Hope. "Ange?"

"Yeah?"

"Probably best if you get Hope into the house now."

"Gotcha." Boot soles scraped against the concrete floor. "Let's go."

"Wait," Hope said, a little out of breath. A pause. The sounds of a scuffle behind him. "Hang on a sec. Is he the one I'm supposed to be—let go, Ange. Let me—"

"Later," Angela said, a hard note in her voice.

"But—"

"Argue if you want, but move it, sister."

A huffy sound. "Fine."

"Use the front door, angel," Rikar said, moving into view with Bastian at his back, ensuring the females' safe retreat out of the garage into the driveway.

~

The second the HE female stepped from view, Forge let loose and lunged at Mac. Bad idea. His human side said so, laying down logical arguments. His dragon half didn't agree, brushing aside logic, leaving it behind to deal with a face full of *fuck you*. He could see it happening. Almost the same way a spectator witnessed a fifty-car pileup. The blood rush and deafening roar in his ears. The crumpling echo of his loss of control. The pungent smell of sulfur as he moved. Primal instinct spun into biological imperative. Rational thought ceased to exist. Stopping became an impossibility. He needed to fight. To vent his displeasure and dispel the aggression by putting a target on someone's back.

Mac shifted into a fighting stance.

Forge growled. Outstanding. A willing participant, one able to give and receive. To be as brutal as he needed. A male who would show no mercy.

He slid right.

Mac circled left, still yakking at him. "Forge, listen. I know you're pissed off, but this isn't—"

He threw a hard jab. His fist punched through Mac's guard. Knuckles cracked against bone. Pain spiraled up his arm. Mac cursed as his head snapped to the side. Shifting his feet, Forge unleashed a combination—right hook, punishing uppercut, spin, parry, and . . . wham! His elbow hammered Mac in the chest. A brutal thud rang through the garage. His friend cursed. Forge let another roundhouse fly. His fist slammed into Mac's rib cage. His friend grunted and gave ground, retreating toward the SUV.

Rage consuming him, he advanced.

"Motherfuck." Mac scowled and reset his stance. "All right, you idiot. You want it, I'll give it to you."

"Fucking hell. Mac—stand down," someone grumbled, the low voice full of icy tones. Twisting to avoid getting grabbed from behind, Forge frowned. Who the hell was that? Rikar? Bastian? "B, grab Forge. Mac shouldn't be fighting. His shoulder is screwed up enough already."

The comment made Forge pause. Something about it tweaked a memory. One that should bother him. Somewhere in the deep recesses of his mind, he knew it, but . . . shite. He couldn't unearth a reason for restraint. Couldn't think straight or force himself to stop. Concern. No concern. It didn't matter. Nothing cut through the stranglehold of anger. Not Mac's voice. Not the threat of injury. Nor the knowledge he was in deep and sinking fast, his human side drowning beneath the weight of his fury.

Purple wash stained the floor as his eyes began to glow.

Bastian pushed Mac aside. Merciless green eyes met his. "Simmer down. Back off, Forge."

"Make me," he said, all snarl, no reason.

"Take a shot at me and I don't care how rough a night you've had," B said, tone calm, the threat in his voice chilling. "I'll kick your Scottish ass and dump you in a prison cell to cool off."

Forge's eyes narrowed. Might be worth it. Could be interesting to see how far he could push the male. Sounded like fun actually. A great way to get the fight he craved, test another warrior's skill, and see who came out on top. All that with an added bonus—to start hurting more on the outside than he already was on the inside.

Shifting focus, Forge raised his fists.

Bastian sighed.

"Well, shit. That doesn't look like his I'm-ready-to-give-up face," Venom said, red eyes gleaming as he stopped beside Bastian. He jostled the Nightfury commander with his elbow. "Move over, B. I got him. Wick?"

"Here."

"You're on standby."

Wick frowned at his buddy. "You suck."

Venom hummed. "Best I can do since I want to kick the Scot's ass myself."

"Enough of the bullshit," Mac growled, rolling his shoulder backward. A grimace broke over his features. Cradling his left arm, he rotated his elbow as though trying to work out a kink and glared at Venom. "I don't have time for this crap. Tania's waiting for me."

Venom cracked his knuckles. "Perfect. Away you go, water boy, while I—"

"Shut up, Ven," Mac said, looking like he wanted to punch Venom in the face. "And Rikar?"

"What?"

"Ice him the hell up."

Rikar raised a brow. “It’ll hurt.”

“Just do it,” Mac growled through clenched teeth.

“Nike,” Wick murmured. “Love those ads.”

Ads? Forge blinked. What was the male talking about? The question prompted another as he struggled to understand. He shook his head. The fog of fury started to recede, leaving him off balance. The purple haze misting his vision disappeared. Tense muscles started to unfurl. His dragon half settled, bringing him back to himself. Standing with his fists raised in the middle of the garage, Forge glanced around. Comprehension struck. His brows collided. What the fuck was he doing? Well, besides trying to kill his best friend?

“Bloody hell,” he said, staring at Mac.

“There he is.” The corner of Mac’s mouth tipped up. “Good to have you back.”

Forge scowled, ’cause shite, it seemed like the thing to do. A superb strategy considering the arseholes were engaged in an idiotic conversation guaranteed to spoil a perfectly good fight. Gaze bouncing between his brothers-in-arms, he took in the group forming a semicircle around him. Strong. Solid. Loyal. Forge glowered at the jackoffs. “You wankers. The lot of you take all the fun out of a fight.”

Bastian’s lips twitched. “Fighting for fun’s one thing. But when you get like that? No one wants to get in your way.”

“I would’ve,” Venom said, disappointment in his expression. “Big fun when you consider he exhales *fire-acid*.”

Wick nodded in agreement.

Mac rolled his eyes.

Forge flexed his hands. “What the hell happened?”

“The female triggered you,” Rikar said, stepping alongside him. Palming his shoulder, he gave him a gentle squeeze. “Understandable. She possesses powerful energy. You were blindsided and your dragon half reacted.”

“Violently,” Wick murmured, keen amber eyes locked on him.

A niggle of worry ghosted down his spine. Bad. Very *bad*. His reaction spoke volumes. None of it good. "What's her name—Hope?"

"Yeah," Mac said.

Forge tipped his chin. "Friend of yours?"

Mac nodded. "Ange and I worked a lot with her at the SPD."

"You need tae keep her away from me," he said, his concern growing by the moment. He wasn't strong enough to avoid her on his own. The uncontrollable lust he'd suffered when she stepped from the vehicle told him resistance would be futile. "Far, far away."

"Not going to happen." Arms crossed over his chest, B leaned back against the SUV. His commander drilled him with a no-nonsense look. "You're the whole reason she's here. She's a psychologist who specializes in hypnotherapy, the absolute best the human world has to offer. Mind regression has become too dangerous. It isn't working, so we're trying something new. Hope is it."

Denying Bastian, he shook his head.

Rikar eyed him from a foot away. "She's worth a try."

"Nay." Absolutely not.

"Even if she can help you recover the memories?" Gage asked from behind him.

Swiveling on his heel, he met the male's unwavering gaze. Trapped. Cornered. Nowhere to run and even fewer places to hide. The truth of what Bastian said stared him in the face, but . . . Christ. He'd already killed one female without meaning to. How much worse would his reaction be when his attraction to Hope burned a thousand times brighter than the one he'd shared with Caroline?

Forge closed his eyes. He hadn't meant to hurt her. Would've sacrificed himself to keep Caroline safe had he known what was coming, but that didn't change the facts. He'd made a terrible mistake. One he couldn't undo or take back. The moment he realized his error—impregnating her without first ensuring his dragon half wanted her, had bonded with her, ensuring the magical match—he'd known what it meant.

Certain death for Caroline.

Another female taken in her prime.

Another motherless son in a long line of many.

One hundred percent his fault. A terrible truth to face. A hard thing to admit. The inherent difficulty, however, didn't make it any less true.

Or him any less culpable.

Memories swirled into a fog of warning, making his chest hurt. Bowing his head, Forge rubbed his temples. "There has tae be another way."

Green eyes steady, B held his ground. "There isn't. It's happening. Make your peace with it, Forge, and get on board."

"Shite. I donnae want . . ." Dread balled in the pit of his stomach. "What if I hurt her?"

The question came out strained.

"You won't hurt her," Bastian said, the confidence in his voice steadying. "Your history isn't in play here. It's over. Done. You won't make the same mistake twice."

One hip propped against the workbench, Gage twirled a wrench in his hand. "Give her a chance, Forge. She may surprise you."

"Mayhap." Mayhap not, but one thing for sure, he needed to get himself under control. Tuck all the nasty emotions away and return to his usual calm as fast as possible. Otherwise, the female brought in to help him would suffer, and he would be to blame. "When do we start?"

"Later this afternoon," Rikar said, pale blue eyes unrelenting, no mercy in sight. "Get your shit together, brother. Be ready to deal with her."

Forge sucked in a breath. God grant him grace. Some much-needed patience too. Forgiveness might be worth asking for as well.

Why? *Dealing with* Hope was the last thing he wanted to do. He had other things in mind. Erotic things. Sexy things. Terrible, filthy things that would end with him deep inside her . . . and her screaming his name.

The image took root inside his head.

Forge brushed it aside and buried it deep.

Wanting Hope was a bad idea.

High energy or not, he refused to need another female for more than an hour of mutual pleasure. Not after losing Caroline. He'd learned his lesson. He didn't deserve what the other Nightfury warriors shared with their females. Peace and connection, the bond between mates, weren't his to claim. Neither was Hope, so . . . sure. He'd honor his pack's wishes and work with her, but he'd keep his distance. No flirting. Zero physical contact. Absolute respect for the patient-therapist relationship. Sounded good. The perfect strategy. One that might keep him sane in a high-stakes game with odds not in his favor. He'd gambled once and lost. No way would he risk it again.

Chapter Six

Sweat trickled over his temple, catching on the edge of his eyebrow. Bent over the workstation in his lab, Ivar swiped at it with the back of his hand and frowned into his electron microscope. Tiny organisms swam inside a glass petri dish. The up-close, in-depth look should've illuminated the situation, marrying fact with understanding. His surroundings should've done the rest. The equipment inside his state-of-the-art laboratory was the best money could buy. High-tech perfection housed one hundred and fifty feet below ground level.

Most of the time, Ivar took pride in his new digs. He adored the lair he shared with his personal guard. Buried deep beneath 28 Walton Street, the underground living quarters lived up to expectation: safe, comfortable, beautiful. And his lab? The space screamed symmetry, functionality, every single utilitarian line dressed up in glossy white walls and stainless steel countertops. His refuge. His sanctuary, a stronghold against humanity and the banality of the outside world. The only place he lost himself long enough to indulge his passions—science, technology, experimentation coupled with complex problem-solving.

Tonight, though, couldn't be shelved under "the usual fun."

It needed to be filed under "fucked up" instead.

With a sigh of frustration, Ivar pulled away from the eyepiece and pushed his stool back a foot. Wheels squeaked against the smooth industrial floor. The soft screech made his muscles clench. Rolling his shoulders, he loosened the tension and, tipping his head back, stared at the ceiling. Under normal circumstances working in his lab calmed him, banishing stress the way a hard workout did for other males. Not tonight. The usual things—a sterile work environment, the row of glass-fronted refrigerators against the back wall, the pleasant hum of the ventilation system—didn't soothe him. He stewed instead, marinating in toxins spilling from a horrifying problem.

One he hadn't yet figured out how to fix.

Quitting, though, wasn't an option. He must find a solution. *The* solution. Do what he did best and identify the variables. Nail down the viral load and disease sequence. Isolate the contagion and eliminate it. Otherwise, he would fail . . .

And the human race would die.

Not that he cared about the annoying little insects. Half of him wanted to let the bastards roll right into extinction. The other half, however, refused to give up the fight. He needed humankind to live. At least, for a while longer. The idiots might be a pain in the ass, but they also represented a means to an end. Nothing more. No less. A way for Dragonkind to keep on breathing.

With a growl, Ivar removed his safety glasses and tossed them onto the counter. The pair landed with a bang and bumped into an empty petri dish before skidding across stainless steel. He watched the clear plastic slide, then closed his eyes and bowed his head. Taut muscles pulled. Pain streaked up his spine, colliding with the base of his skull. Not surprising. Discomfort was par for the course after hours spent bent over his microscope. Now his back ached and his head hurt.

Inhaling in a long draw, he filled his lungs to capacity. He held the air, felt the burn, then let the breath go. Goddamn virus. Idiotic fucking idea. He'd created a monster with superbug number three—a highly resistant beast that refused to slow down, infecting humans by the dozens as it worked its way south to Seattle.

Ivar pinched the bridge of his nose.

God. If that happened, if the bug reached the city—

Ivar shook his head. Jesus. Scary didn't begin to describe the situation. Catastrophic worked better considering a worldwide crisis would ensue if the virus escaped the confines of the CDC quarantine. Human casualties would jump from hundreds to thousands, perhaps even into the millions, the instant infected hosts arrived in an urban area. International airports would do the rest, ferrying sick humans all over the world, allowing the disease to go global and become unstoppable. An epidemic with far-reaching consequences.

Serious trouble for Dragonkind.

He'd screwed up when he released the supervirus. Been too eager to experiment and watch the havoc his baby would wreak. Which amounted to him rushing the initial trials.

Like an idiot, he hadn't done the usual due diligence, releasing the contagion into Granite Falls' water supply before understanding the true nature of the bug. Or how it would affect human hosts, latching onto the X chromosome pairing embedded in every female's DNA, infecting women, leaving men untouched. Now women in communities all over northern Washington State were dying, and the scientists the CDC flew in to contain the disease had no clue how to stop it from spreading.

A huge problem considering Dragonkind males needed human females. As annoying as the situation was, Ivar couldn't deny the truth. Without close contact with the fairer sex, a male couldn't connect to the Meridian—the source of all living things—and draw the nourishment he required to stay healthy. And if he didn't, he'd die, waste away in the most horrific way imaginable—gut-wrenching hunger and eventual starvation. So . . .

He must deal with the fallout and fix the problem. Fast. Before more females became infected and died.

His eyes narrowed on his workstation. Ivar flexed his fingers. The sleeves of his cotton lab coat shifted up his forearms, then settled back at his wrists. Planting his heels, he rolled the stool toward the microscope. Time to get back to work and find the cure. So far nothing he'd tried had worked. Every antivirus he produced failed. Miserably. Ivar pursed his lips. Maybe the seventh try would be the charm? He hoped so. The sickness continued to gain speed, breaking down human immune systems, ravaging families, taking mothers from children and baby girls from fathers.

At one time, the outcome wouldn't have bothered him. Death, after all, was a fact of life, but well . . . hell. Something had changed in recent months, leaving him more susceptible to the instability of his human side. A *something* he wished would change the fuck back. He liked emotional distance. Needed the numbness. Craved the cruelty his dragon half excelled at delivering. Neutrality, however, seemed to have settled in his past. Proof positive? He couldn't ignore the damage being done. Not anymore. Not with the constant stream of teary-eyed men being interviewed on the news every night.

The humans' grief left him curiously empty inside, more husk-like and hollow by the day. Every time a male's voice broke, anguish of his loss evident on his face, Ivar's gut clenched and one thought streamed into his head—his fault. He'd done that, caused all that pain, all that sorrow, all those tears and—

My fault. All my fault.

The accusation jabbed at him. Ivar grimaced and, shoving the thought aside, buried the guilt under piles of icy resolve. Emotion held no place in science. If he wanted to make it right, he must wipe the outside world from his mind and concentrate. Be better—smarter, stronger—than he'd ever been before. Looking into the microscope's eyepiece, Ivar turned a dial and refocused. He watched the microbes squirm inside the glass dish, then scowled at the contents. Too soon to tell. The cultures needed more time to mature. Six hours, maybe seven, and he'd know for certain. Would have the answer, but God, it was hard to wait.

So much lay on the line.

Fighting his worry, Ivar closed his eyes. *Please, Goddess. Let attempt number seven be the one. The right path. The cure that saves my kind.*

The request banged around inside his head. He exhaled long and hard. His breath hit the steel tabletop and bounced back. Heat puffed against the bridge of his nose, then changed direction, ghosting over his jaw. Ignoring the rush of air, he adjusted the magnification dial again. Fluorescent box lights hummed overhead as he picked up an eyedropper and added the second dose of antiserum. Sweat trickled down his back, slithering beneath his T-shirt. Sticky. Exhausted. Pissed off. *Da,* that pretty much summed up his night. But he couldn't quit. Not yet.

Only one vile of blood remained.

Just sixteen milliliters of the female's plasma confined inside a small test tube. His salvation stolen from inside Cascade Valley Hospital. Dark-red cells teeming with warrior antibodies, Evelyn Foxe's blood—the building block of his antivirus—would prove to be the answer. Or his undoing. Ivar didn't know which, but—Goddess help him. He had so little of her blood left. Hardly any at all to synthesize into a cure.

Cursing under his breath, Ivar raised the microscope lens and reached for the petri dish. Double gloved, his hands cupped the container. He turned toward the containment unit and, moving with care, walked to the end of his worktable. Grip steady, he slid his experiment into the clear box sitting on the countertop. He studied the maturing culture a moment. Perfect. One hundred percent stable so far. The location shift hadn't dislodged or damaged the bacteria.

Relief loosened his tension. Ivar flipped the lid closed, turned the heat lamps on low and—

Movement flashed in his periphery.

Knuckles struck glass. The hard rap echoed across the lab.

Ivar glanced toward the wall of windows. Four panes thick, floor-to-ceiling glass panels separated his lab from the outer chamber. Hamersveld, his new XO, stood on the other side, an unhappy look on his puss. Ivar's mouth curved. Nothing new there. Angry was the Norwegian's default expression. Well, at least, one of them. Murderous rage came a close second, gracing his friend's face more often than not.

Ivar's lips twitched.

He smoothed his expression and met Hamersveld's gaze through the glass. Ivar tipped his chin. The abrupt gesture came off the way he intended, the inherent "What the fuck do you want?" clear in the movement. Shark-black eyes rimmed by pale blue narrowed on him. Ivar raised a brow, just to mess with the male. Sad to say, but razzing his friend—tweaking the water dragon's tail—was the only amusement he got most days. With a scowl, Hamersveld flicked his fingers, the motion as impatient as the male. Ivar sighed. All right. Playtime was over. Teasing Hamersveld might be fun, but keeping the warrior waiting never made for a good plan. The warrior was as likely to rip his head off as talk to him.

With a nod, Ivar skirted the end of his workstation and headed for the exit. Motion sensors went active. The door into the decontamination chamber opened. Bright lights came on. The burst of illumination made him flinch. With a murmur, he conjured his favorite sunglasses, shielding his light-sensitive eyes, and stepped inside. The unit closed around him. A red light flipped to green an instant before a blast of air hit him. Wind whipped his hair around his head. The tail of his lab coat flapped. Head low, muscles tense, he forced himself to stay still as the machine did its job, killing contaminants carried from the lab.

The gusts increased.

He swayed inside the chamber. Cold air rushed over his skin. His fire dragon half reacted, disliking the chill. His love of all things high tech was one thing. Being cramped inside small spaces, however? Ivar stifled a shiver. It never got any easier. Counting off the seconds, he waited, trying to be patient. Fifty-seven. Fifty-eight. Fifty-nine. Sixty and—

The blower turned off.

The door swiveled right, rotating open. Not wasting a second, Ivar stepped into the antechamber and his XO's presence. He glanced at his friend.

Arms crossed, Hamersveld leaned back against the countertop housing his computer equipment. "How's it going in there?"

"Should know in a few hours," Ivar said, acknowledging the question even as he took note of the change in his friend's tone. Well, shit. Not good. Whenever the warrior's Norwegian accent thickened, trouble always ensued. Taking off his eyewear, he tossed his Oakleys onto the round table in the center of the room. The pair banged into a bowl full of apples. "What's up, Sveld?"

"Silfer's balls," the male said, shifting his ass against the counter edge, his expression growing darker. "What isn't?"

Picking over the bowl, Ivar selected a green apple. He tossed it toward his friend. He watched Hamersveld snag the piece of fruit out of the air before selecting a juicy Red Delicious for himself. "Give me the good news first."

"The first round of dragon combat training is complete."

Ivar turned his snack over in his hand. "Any standouts?"

"Some okay fighters. Most need work, but . . ." A crunch sounded as Hamersveld bit into his apple. He hummed in appreciation, then took another bite. Black eyes narrowed, he chewed, a look of consideration on his face. “Three warriors are top notch. They blow everyone else out of the water.”

“Who?”

“Azrad, Kilmar, and Terranon.” Finished with his treat, Hamersveld tossed it toward the garbage can sitting beside the double doors. The core rimmed the basket before sinking with a crinkle into the plastic bag. “Best of friends, those three. All are skilled—smart, lethal, extremely fast in flight. The trio works well together. Their fighting triangle is tight.”

“The alpha of the group?”

“Azrad,” Hamersveld said without hesitation. “Got a bit of a temper, though. Had to stop him from gutting a male tonight.”

“The warrior all right?”

“Kind of.” Amusement in his eyes, Hamersveld shook his head. “He’ll need a couple of days to recover. That’ll teach him to run his mouth and piss off Azrad.”

Ivar huffed, liking Azrad already. “Promising.”

“Yeah,” Hamersveld said. “Good choices for the breeding program. Put any one of the three with an HE female and you’re guaranteed strong offspring.”

“So they’ll place high in the competition?”

“They’ll land in the top three, for sure.”

“Good.” Eyes narrowed on his treat, Ivar took a bite of his apple. Tart and sweet, the juicy chunk melted on his tongue.

Hamersveld motioned with his hand. Ivar threw him another apple. The fleshy fruit smacked against the male’s palm. “The competition is set, and the obstacle course ready. The pack knows the rules and is eager to start.”

Ivar nodded. Dragonkind Olympics, right on schedule. Perfect. Not a moment too soon either. With the Meridian’s realignment approaching—one of only two times a year his kind became fertile—he needed to know which of his warriors held the most promise.

The top five fighters would win time with a high-energy female and send his breeding program into its final phase. Nerve racking in some ways. Beyond exciting in others, considering what was at stake—the first female Dragonkind offspring in centuries, the liberation of his kind from the human race.

In a month, the HEs imprisoned below 28 Walton Street would be thrown into service, and he'd know if the serum he'd been working on for years worked. So yeah. The competition was important. A means to an end—find the strongest Razorbacks, pair each with one of the five HE females in cellblock A, and wait to see what happened.

Lifting one boot over the other, Hamersveld crossed his feet at the ankles. "I need you in the Cascades to judge the first round."

"When?"

"Tomorrow night."

"I'll fly out with you at sunset."

"That'll do."

Ivar indulged in another bite. He took his time, chewing, swallowing, before he met his XO's gaze. "And the bad news?"

Hamersveld scowled. "That comes in two stages."

"The first?"

"Haven't found the mole yet."

Ivar swallowed a growl. More frustration. Another failure. A deadly game of cat and mouse, one with the potential to not only hurt the Razorbacks, but bring him to ground. "Shit."

"Yeah," Hamersveld said, more growl than word. "Whoever is feeding the Nightfuries information is a slippery bastard. He hides well, is patient, smart enough not to play his hand too soon."

Ivar's eyes narrowed. "Keep at it. Sooner or later, the asshole will make a mistake and—"

"We'll nail him. Make an example out of him."

"Exactly." Turning on his heel, Ivar paced to the other side of the table. A traitor. A mole inside his pack. A Razorback in the process of betraying him. His temper sparked. Pink flame flickered over his shoulders, heating the nape of his neck. Issuing a mental command, he snuffed out the fire, imagining what he would do to the turncoat. God, he couldn't wait to get ahold of the male. "In the meantime, we keep the information chain tight, tell the pack as little as possible. Any mission instructions will be given at the last minute . . . no lead in or prep time."

"Agreed."

Good enough, for now. Time would tell, hopefully by exposing the mole and giving Ivar what he craved—closure by way of life-affirming violence.

"And the second problem?" he asked, turning the half-eaten apple over in his hand.

A muscle ticked along Hamersveld's jaw. "Zidane plans to visit Seattle."

Ivar tensed, the apple halfway to his mouth. He dropped his hand back to his side. Holy fuck . . . Zidane. The sadistic bastard left a bad taste in his mouth. Not that anyone cared what he thought. Eldest son to the leader of Archguard, the male enjoyed free rein. Whatever the male wanted, he got . . . with very little effort.

Ivar rolled his shoulders, combating the sudden tension. "How solid is your intel?"

"Very. My sources are never wrong."

"Fuck." Ivar frowned, his expression fierce enough to eclipse his XO's. "Any way to dissuade him?"

His friend shook his head. "Not that I can see."

"How soon?"

"Something's going on with the high council," Hamersveld said. "Can't find out what. Very hush-hush, but the Archguard is sequestered and that can only mean one thing."

"Rodin," Ivar growled, the name leaving a bad taste in his mouth. Tossing the Red Delicious at the trash can without looking, he clenched his teeth. Not good. Nothing ever was with Rodin involved. The leader of the Archguard could contaminate a situation faster than a virus did a body. Which left him with one conclusion. The bastard was up to something, pulling strings, manipulating outcomes, meddling in things best left alone. "That asshole."

"Uh-huh." Dark eyes full of warning, Hamersveld pushed away from the countertop. "Something else too."

"What?"

"No one can find Nian."

"How long has he been missing?"

"He hasn't been seen in over a month."

Ivar frowned. Shit. That wasn't good. In fact, it was very, *very* bad.

Born into the ruling class, and as a member of the Archguard, Nian sat at the top of the food chain. His disappearance didn't bode well . . . for anyone. Particularly him and the Razorback nation. The absence signaled a major disruption in Dragonkind hierarchy. A seat left unfilled on the high council—a voice gone unheard—was a huge threat. One that could destabilize the entire upper echelon and cause powerful packs to break away from the greater group: go it alone, form new allegiances, creating the kind of imbalance that ended the status quo and threw the Dragonkind world into chaos.

Ivar cursed under his breath. Like he didn't have enough to worry about already? One superbug out of control. A mole feeding sensitive information to his enemy. Zidane off his leash and the leader of the Archguard gone renegade. Damn Rodin anyway. The male sure knew how to throw a monkey wrench into a great plan. Now all Ivar wanted to do was ditch Rodin and distance his pack from the entire mess. A lovely thought, but for one problem—Rodin was too valuable an ally to trash. He needed the male's money to fund his science experiments and the breeding program.

"Dig deeper, Sveld. Get Denzeil involved," he said, ignoring Hamersveld's grimace. He didn't care how much his XO disliked the

Razorback second in command. The pair would get along—and help each other—or he'd kick both males' asses. Ivar held his friend's gaze, a warning in his own. "Play nice. Let D assist. He's good with computers and we need to know what's going on before Zidane lands in Seattle and fucks everything up."

Hamersveld nodded. "I'll let you know what I find out."

"Do that." Stepping away from the table, Ivar headed for the exit. "I need to fly. You coming?"

"Only if you head toward the Sound."

"Done." Fucking water dragon. Nothing was good enough if it didn't involve water.

Heavy footfalls sounded behind him as Ivar punched through the double doors. Out. He needed *out*. Into fresh air. Surrounded by cold winter winds as he spread his wings, soared across open skies, and came up with a new plan. One that would neutralize Zidane and keep Rodin from ruining everything he'd worked so hard to accomplish.

Chapter Seven

Standing in one of the guest bedrooms, Hope pulled a dresser drawer open and tossed the last pair of socks inside. It landed on top of the pile and bounced off, rolling into her boxing wraps. She reached out, brushing her fingers against the cotton coil, the familiar sight helping her feel more grounded in unfamiliar surroundings. Her gaze jumped to the boxing gloves tucked into the back of the drawer. Old faithfuls, ready to be used at a moment's notice. She released a pent-up breath. Thank God she'd thought to bring the pair. Something told her she would need them before her time inside Black Diamond came to an end.

An uncharitable thought? Hope pursed her lips. Probably, but with her instincts howling, erring on the side of caution seemed the best way to go. Something about the house didn't ring true. Not that she could put her finger on what exactly, but . . .

She glanced around the room. Yeah, without a doubt. The vibe seemed off. Not bad, just odd. Powerful somehow, as though electricity escaped the outlets and buzzed in the air. The strange hum permeated the house, amping her up, making the nape of her neck tingle.

With a frown, she slid the drawer closed and turned toward her suitcase. Staring at it, she reached out to shut the top and . . . hesitated. She should close it. Right now. Zip the Samsonite up tight, tuck it under the bed, and abandon what lay inside one of the interior compartments.

"Crap," she whispered, her eyes locked on the interior pocket.

Hope sighed, the sound a manifestation of her misery. She never traveled without it. The desire to have it close, where she slept, beat on her like an ill-tempered gladiator. No rhyme. Zero reason. Well . . . she frowned . . . except for one. She couldn't wipe the memory of her twin from her life any more than she could deny her next breath. Family honor refused to let her. Her conscience toed the line, kicking up memory after memory. Now the fun times taunted her, demanding she remember the good things and let go of the bad.

Damn Adam and his selfishness anyway.

Blinking back tears, she crouched beside the bright-pink suitcase. She stared at the zipper, then gave in to the inevitable and reached out. The padded pocket gaped open, revealing the treasure inside—a barn owl made of clay, fired in a kiln in art class, painted with care by a seven-year-old boy determined to wrap something up for his sister's birthday.

A lopsided head made an appearance as Hope pulled her owl out of its hiding place. Despite the tightness of her chest, she laughed a little. She always did when she looked at its crooked feathers and big eyes the same color as her own. The same color as Adam's. Green, so green it hurt to look at them sometimes.

Hope ran her fingers over the imperfections, finding each one charming, and pushed to her feet. She glanced around. Pale blue walls, creamy wainscoting, a bed piled high with pretty throw pillows. She walked toward it, her attention on the mirrored side table. Stepping off hardwood and onto the area rug, she sat on the side of the mattress. Covered in a white duvet cover embroidered with navy stars, the thick comforter gave beneath her weight. Reluctant to let go of her owl, she slid the pad of her thumb over its feathers, feeling each contour, reliving the day Adam had handed her the T-shirt-wrapped bundle held together with pink ribbon. She forced herself to put it down. The clay bottom settled on the tabletop, reflecting her owl's face and the lampshade spread like a canopy above it.

She adjusted its position. First this way, then that.

A touch more to the left.

A tiny push closer to the lamp base and . . .

Perfect.

The second she opened her eyes in the morning, her owl would be the first thing she saw. A little something from home. A trace of the familiar while staying in a strange place with even stranger people. Or rather, men. Angela, after all, seemed okay. Nothing out of the ordinary with her. One hundred percent normal, the same way her friend had always been: tough, steady, kick-ass, with a hit of get-the-hell-out-of-my-way. A comforting thought considering the collection of testosterone that had gathered inside the garage.

"Jeepers, Bart," she said, talking to her owl, calling him by name. She couldn't help it. Her habit of naming everything—her car included (*thank you, Lucinda*)—never said quit. With a frown, she reached for the closest throw pillow. Fat and feather filled, its soft body settled in her lap as she replayed the scene in the garage. "Talk about serious firepower. You should've seen the size of them."

Bart didn't answer.

Hope didn't expect him to; one-sided conversations were a habit with him. But as crazy as it sounded, talking at him made her feel better. Helped her work through problems. Difficult ones, like what to do about the dark-haired guy who'd gone head to head with Mac in front of the SUV. Staying away from him sounded like a good idea. His lethal vibe—the intensity of his expression, the pain in his eyes, and the tension of his body—in the garage had nearly put her on her ass. Add the way he looked—tall, dark, and *GQ* gorgeous—into the mix and . . . holy crap. It was a miracle she'd managed to stay upright. Thank goodness Angela had dragged her away before she'd—

Hope shivered. God, she didn't know what she might have done. Approached him, perhaps. Told him everything would be all right. Maybe even given him a hug. God knew he needed one . . . desperately. She knew what psychological pain looked like. Had read it in his tight expression and the controlled way he moved. The observation made her heart ache. No one should have to suffer that kind of agony. She might not know him, but already, she wanted to help, to heal the wound she sensed he hid from the world.

Well, that, and maybe get closer to him.

Hope grimaced, but couldn't stymie the thought . . . or control her reaction. He was a wide-shouldered, long-legged, hard-bodied dream. In a word, her type (and every other woman's on the planet). One look, the second his gaze had met hers, and—Ka-blam! Her long-deprived libido jolted awake.

And now stood at attention along with her hormones.

Dumb things. So inconvenient. The worst timing in the history of mankind. She wasn't here to hook up, especially with a super-hot guy who might end up being her patient.

The thought rattled her.

She shook her head. *Bad Hope. Bad, bad idea.* Lusting after Mr. Dreamy, sleeping with him—

"Strike that thought." Hope scowled at Bart, fighting a shiver of appreciation. No. No way. She wasn't that girl. No chance in hell would she allow her mind to wander in that direction. In *his* direction. She was here to help a wounded warrior, not to get her rocks off.

A great game plan along with excellent advice.

Something to strive for and stick to, but wow, her inner alley cat wasn't going to make it easy. Military men tended to tick all of her I'm-attracted-to-you boxes. More shades of her past, her father's fault too.

He'd taken her to visit the SEAL training facilities once, during March break her first year of high school. Talk about memorable.

She'd never seen anyone—never mind an entire group—work so hard before, be so dedicated, take protecting others so seriously. The experience opened her eyes, leaving her with a greater appreciation of the men and women her father commanded, sent into danger, every day. After witnessing that kind of commitment, she came to some immediate conclusions about Angela's friends. She recognized an elite fighting unit when she saw it. A lifetime of watching the vice admiral provided insight. Sharp instincts laid out the rest, leaving no doubt. The men Angela and Mac worked with operated at a whole other level, a higher one, a place only the upper echelon of covert ops ever reached.

Which could pose problems on the therapy front.

Mac and his buddies weren't the type to open up. Men like that preferred to stonewall, avoid, deny any and all problems. Forge, whoever he was, would no doubt react the same. He'd put up a fight. Talking to a psychologist wasn't easy for anyone, but for a silent, stoic, self-contained man? A solider with serious prowess and even more pride? Hope pursed her lips. Breaking through his barriers—getting him to trust her, no matter how great her skill—would be difficult. Nearly impossible.

Excitement sparked in the pit of her stomach.

Butterflies erupted, shoving her into the kind of nervousness professional athletes suffered before a big game. Finally. A challenge. Someone she could truly help. A way for her to make a difference. But first, she needed a therapy treatment plan. A flexible one, something she could adjust mid-session and on the fly, a strategy that would come alive and grow roots the instant she met her patient. So . . .

Time to get creative.

No more playbook. Toss out the operating manual and—

A knock echoed through the room.

Pushing off the side of the bed, Hope pivoted toward the door. "Come in."

The door swung wide.

A blond carrying a baby stepped over the threshold. Hope assessed her with practiced eyes. Pretty. Young, mid-twenties maybe. Standing with the easy confidence of a woman who knew herself well.

"Hey there." The blond paused halfway into the room. Her eyes bounced from the empty suitcase to the dresser before landing on the nightstand . . . and Bart. "Oh good, you're settled in." Perched on the blond's hip, one tiny fist shoved in his mouth, the baby gurgled something unintelligible. He grinned at her around his knuckles. Hope smiled back. She couldn't help it. The sparkle in his eyes warned of future mischief. God, he was so cute with his chubby cheeks and dark Mohawk-styled hair. Her visitor adjusted her hold on him, kissed the top of his head, and met her gaze. "I'm Myst. This little guy is G. M. Did you get some rest?"

"A little." Four hours to be exact. Too much to be considered a nap, too little to be labeled a full night's sleep. Enough, however, to wipe away the blur of fatigue. Surprising, really. Most nights she needed a full eight hours to feel rested. Hope glanced at the perfect collection of throw pillows, the ones she replaced after her nap, then at the digital clock on the nightstand. Five thirty-five a.m. Earlier than she normally crawled out of bed. Somehow, though, half the shut-eye had done the trick. She felt rested and ready . . . for anything. "Are you the welcome wagon?"

"Part of it," Myst said. "Hope you don't mind, but I schooled Ange so I could meet you first. Beat her at rock-paper-scissors for the chance to come by and say hi before all hell breaks loose."

"Hi . . ." Hope blinked as the last of her greeting sank in. Ah, crap. That didn't sound good. "All hell breaks loose?"

"Yeah. I mean, none of the guys are easy, but Forge can be . . ." Myst treated her to a look of consideration. "How should I put it?"

"Difficult?" Hope said, helping her out, the lion with a thorn in its paw analogy front and center in her mind. "A hard-headed asshat?"

Myst huffed in laughter. “Exactly. Super stubborn.”

“Kind of figured that after what happened in the garage.”

“Intense?”

Hope held her index finger and thumb an inch apart. “Just a tad.”

“You don’t scare easily, do you?”

“Nope. Got the kickboxing certifications to prove it.”

Myst’s mouth curved. “You’re going to fit right in. The other girls are going to love you—and oh, don’t worry. If you’re as good as Mac says, Forge won’t stand a chance. You’ll get through to him.”

“I hope so,” she said, not knowing what else to say.

“The room okay?” Myst asked.

“Great. Really beautiful.” Almost as pretty, although not nearly as colorful, as her bedroom at home. She pointed to the open door leading into the en suite bathroom. “I have everything I need. Ridiculously soft towels included.”

Myst chuckled. “Daimler goes a little overboard with the fabric softener. Something about our delicate skin.”

“Daimler?”

“He runs the show around here. Makes sure the house is clean and stocked,” Myst said. “You’ll meet him in a bit. He’s a chef, cooks to-die-for gourmet meals. Cakes and cookies too, chocolate upon chocolate.”

“Your favorite, I take it.”

“You got me pegged.” Expression sheepish, Myst propped her baby-free hip against the side of the bed and dangled a set of plastic keys in front of G. M. The baby latched onto the ring, shoved it into his mouth, and started chewing. “Just wait until you try his triple-decker fudge cake. You’ll melt into a messy puddle of gratitude.”

“Sounds amazing.”

“He is. It is,” Myst said, turning toward the door. “I’m salivating just thinking about it. How about we go and see if he made some last night.”

Sidestepping the bench at the end of her bed, Hope grinned. “We going to steal a piece?”

“Total covert operation. But fair warning . . .” Myst glanced over her shoulder, eyes full of devilry. “If we get caught, I’m putting it on you.”

“Oh sure.” Hope grumbled, making a show of it, playing along, liking Myst already. “Throw the new girl under the bus.”

“All’s fair when stealing chocolate.”

Her lips twitched. “I’ll remember that.”

“You should, with all the girl power PMSing in this house.” Stepping into the hallway, Myst turned left.

Trailing behind her new friend, Hope followed her over the threshold. Wide hallway. Dark hardwood floors. A multitude of honey-colored doors with white trim marching down the corridor’s length. Her mouth dropped open as she got a load of the painting hanging to her right. A Jackson Pollock? The next one over—Robert Falk? Knockoffs or originals? Her gaze danced over brushstrokes and swirling lines. Jeepers. She couldn’t tell, but . . . wow. The pair sure looked like the real deal.

Ignoring the artwork, Myst kept walking. “A word to the wise, Hope. If you aren’t quick enough, you’ll be blamed for every cookie that goes missing before mealtime . . . and Daimler will ban you from the kitchen.”

“Bad mojo.”

“The worst. You’ll go into serious sugar deprivation before he lets you back in.”

She passed a painting full of ballet dancers. Hope blinked. Holy crap. That one was a Degas, no question. “Sounds like Daimler’s the hard-ass, not Forge.”

“When it comes to pilfered desserts?” Myst threw her a warning look. “Believe it.”

Well, all right then. First lesson learned: when stealing sweets, don't get caught. Or at least, be quick enough to eat the evidence and blame someone else for her crime. Got it. Welcome to the house of hard-core operatives and covert cookie wars. No problem. Throw out her scruples. Her sense of fair play too. Never let it be said she wasn't a good sport. Or a total sugar addict, jonesing for her next chocolate fix.

"Hey, Myst?"

"Yeah?"

"I've got a few questions."

Myst slowed to walk alongside her. "Shoot."

"How many on the team?"

"Nine. Although . . ." She paused mid-step, switching G. M. to her other hip. "Nian's here now, so I guess that makes ten. Five of the guys are married and—"

"Black Diamond is home base?"

"Yeah."

"And all the wives live here?" she asked, the oddity setting off her internal sensors.

"Yup."

The casual affirmative confirmed her suspicions. Black Diamond landed nowhere near the norm. For one, the group was bigger than she expected. Most special ops units had six or seven members. Ten guys pushed the envelope, but the whole living with their spouse thing . . . inside a mission base? Weird. She'd never heard of covert operatives doing that before.

When she stayed silent, Myst continued. "Bastian's commander of the pack. I'm his mate."

Hope's brows collided. *Pack commander? His mate?* The strange phraseology tweaked her psychologist antennae. Her feet slowed, brushing against the hardwood floor. Myst stopped beside her. Hope stared at her escort, trying to figure her out. Myst blinked as though surprised by what she'd said and . . . bull's-eye. Right on target. She was right. Something was off. Brain in overdrive, she chewed on the inside of her lip. What the hell was the crew at Black Diamond hiding?

Reacting to her confusion, Myst cleared her throat.

G. M. dropped the ring.

Plastic keys rattled as the colorful collection hit the floor. An adorable frown on his face, the baby squawked. With a soothing murmur, Myst crouched, grabbed the toy, and wiped it off. Handing it back to G. M., she pushed to her feet.

"Listen, Hope," she said, tone reasonable as she backtracked. Hope could see it happening, the furious pedaling of a woman about to gloss over what she'd let slip. "We do things a bit differently here. What I meant to say was—wife. I'm Bastian's *wife*. The pack thing? Well, the guys use that because each one has a specific role to play, like in a wolf pack."

A lie. A nice juicy one. And an excellent try.

Not about Myst being married. She believed that, but the rest was well-spun fiction. How could she be sure? Part of her job entailed separating lies from the truth. Body language. Inflection and tone of voice. How a person's eyes moved while interacting with others. She'd spent hours studying people—the microexpressions most missed—and could spot deception a mile away. The kind that, right now, was written all over Myst's face.

Uncomfortable under her scrutiny, Myst shifted the baby to her other hip. "Anyway, you'll meet everyone in a bit and—"

"Oh hey, you found her," a woman three doors down said after poking her head into the hallway. Tall and curvy, the brunette rounded the doorjamb and headed their way. She held out her hand. Hope took it and shook, getting the greeting underway. "Tania. I'm married to Mac."

"Mac's married?" The news jarred her. Surprise made her drop Tania's hand. "Seriously?"

Tania laughed. "I know . . . shocking. He was a total commitment-phobe before I got ahold of him."

"I'm in awe of you."

"You should be," Tania said, brown eyes twinkling. "You have no idea what I went through to nail him down."

Myst snorted. "She chased him all over the lair."

"Did not." Tania frowned at her friend, the expression more playful than pissed off. "I made that man come to me."

Hope swallowed a huff of amusement, imagining Mac begging for the brunette's attention. It wasn't hard to do. Tania seemed kind, and given her witty comments, possessed a wicked sense of humor. She was also beautiful, the kind of woman magazines put on their front covers, so . . . ding-a-ling-ling, someone ring a bell. She was exactly the kind of woman that drew Mac like bears to honey.

"For that snarky comment . . ." Tania turned to Myst and held out her arms. "You lose the prize. Gimme. I need a snuggle."

"Oh, all right." Myst rolled her eyes, but handed G. M. over. "Enjoy him while you can. The second Forge sees him, you'll lose him."

Wives *and* babies living in the house? Surprise made Hope's mouth drop open. Who were these guys? "G. M. is Forge's son?"

"Sure is." With a hum of enjoyment, Tania nuzzled the baby's cheek. Small hand flying, G. M. grabbed a fistful of her dark hair. He tugged on the long strands. Tania squeaked in discomfort, her head tilted sideways as the baby babbled a happy greeting. "Gorgeous, isn't he?"

Hope nodded, but glanced at Myst. "I thought you were married to Bastian."

The blond raised a brow. "I am."

"But . . ." Hope opened, then closed her mouth.

Tania laughed. "No need to be polite. Forge is a single dad. We all take turns mothering G. M., but Myst runs point. She's the one he'll call 'mama' the second he can talk."

"Oh," she said, sounding dumb, feeling outgunned, but . . . well. She couldn't help it. Curveballs kept getting thrown her way, the kind she had yet to hit.

After untangling her hair from G. M.'s grip, Tania raised her head. Her gaze met Hope's, then jumped to Myst. "Ange and J. J. are already in the kitchen. We need to pick up Evie on the way by."

Myst's mouth curved. "You mean drag her out of the office."

"Probably." Tania shook her head and started down the hall. "Never seen a girl who loves numbers as much as she does."

Keeping pace with the pair, Hope piped up. "Maybe we can bribe her with triple-decker fudge cake."

Tania smiled. "Good plan."

"Might work." An unholy gleam in her eyes, Myst chuckled. "Otherwise, we'll sick Venom on her."

Hope frowned. *Venom?* Jeepers. Another curveball. What kind of name was that? And who did it belong to—their dog? Could be. A good guess considering where she'd landed. Elite Special Forces units took highly trained dogs on ops all the time. Toss in the fact guys gave their pets strange handles—names like Killer and Cujo and Fang—and well, *Venom* fit the bill. Although, getting him involved didn't sound like a good idea.

For anyone. Least of all Evie.

A minute later and a bunch of doors down, Hope understood the problem. Standing on the threshold of an office with more filing cabinets than floor space, she shook her head. Her gaze trailed over book-laden chairs, then ping-ponged to the floor-to-ceiling bookcases jammed full of accounting ledgers, only to land on the winding trail between stacks of paper that led to the rear of the room. At the end of the paper path, a woman sat behind a huge antique desk piled high with file folders. Mocha skin glowing in the lamplight, an expression of extreme concentration on her face, Evie ran her fingertip down a page, tracing the entries in a ledger. Dark eyes narrowed on a computer screen, her other hand flew over the number pad on the keyboard.

Myst called her name.

Grumbling to herself about messy accounts and Daimler's "pain-in-the-ass chicken scratch," Evie continued on, oblivious to the world around her.

"Throw something at her," Tania said. "I'd do it, but I'm holding the baby."

Myst growled at her friend. "Chicken."

"Darn right."

"Here. Let me." Picking up a pencil lying on the stack next to the door, Hope took aim. One finger bob. Two finger bobs. Three . . . She let it fly, eraser end leading the way. The clickety-click-clicking of the keyboard cut through the quiet as the HB no. 2 hurtled end over end. "And . . . touchdown."

The pencil landed with a smack next to the ledger.

Evie jumped a foot. "Holy crap!"

Myst fist-pumped into the air. "Nice shot."

"Bull's-eye." Tania crowed in delight, making G. M. laugh.

"God, you two," Evie said, her scowl fierce enough to start a fire. Nowhere near advisable considering all the paper lying around.

"Actually, it's three." Flush from her pencil-toss victory, she waved at Evie from the doorway.

"Oh gosh." Evie blinked once, then popped to her feet. The leather chair bobbed as she skirted the desk and, navigating the paper trail, came toward her. "You must be Hope. Venom told me you were coming. I'm married to him. So nice to meet you."

Hope opened her mouth to reply.

Hooking arms with her on the flyby, Evie dragged her into the corridor. "Time for the morning meal, I guess. Have you met everyone yet?"

"Ah, no, and . . . wait. Venom?" Not a dog, but a man? "You're married to—"

"Yes. He's awesome. Totally hot." Still towing her along, Evie winked at her. "You'll meet him and the rest of the gang this morning. Don't worry, though. Everyone's super nice. Well . . ." She glanced over her shoulder at the other two. "Except for Wick."

Tania and Myst uh-huhed behind her.

Evie took up the baton and explained. "Don't get me wrong. He won't hurt you or anything, but when in doubt, it's best to stay clear of him."

"Or scream for J. J.," Tania said.

Hope threw a confused look over her shoulder.

Amusement in her eyes, Myst shrugged. "Wick and J. J. are married. He turns into a pile of mush around her."

Hope considered the tip. Okay. She bought that. It made sense and . . . lesson number two underway. File "scream when unsure" under strategies to employ. Also, underline the heading "Tough Guy Turns to Goo in Presence of Wife."

"Super strategy." Evie nudged her and, eyeing Tania, picked up the pace. As the distance between them and the others grew, she yelled over her shoulder. "If you're a wimp."

"Hey!" Her eyes narrowed, Tania pretended to pursue. After a few steps, she gave up and slowed to walk beside Myst. "You're lucky I've got G. M., otherwise . . ."

Tania let the threat hang in the air.

"She'd have to catch me first, and just between you and me . . ." Evie bumped shoulders with her. "I'm pretty fast."

"Run, Forest, run."

Evie sputtered in laughter. "There's the spirit. I like you already."

The feeling was mutual. God. What fun. The girls were a blast, and for some reason, Hope fit right in, better than she had with her old college friends. Instant acceptance. A sense of belonging. Already included in the club. She liked everyone she'd met so far. A lot. The second Evie pulled her out of the corridor and into the kitchen, however, Hope changed her mind.

The air thickened, then stalled in her lungs.

Holy ka-smoly. Forget the fabulous layout and design-fueled perfection of the room. Glossy white cabinets and miles of marble countertops were the least of her concern. The guys standing around the massive kitchen island, however? Oh boy. That might prove to be a problem. Her gaze settled on one man, then skipped over to the next. Good lord. Just look at them. Not an ugly face in the group. Suddenly, Evie's *totally hot* comment made a heck of a lot more sense. And no wonder. Some had dark hair, some light, but all stood well over six feet tall. Add well-built, muscular, and wearing vicious vibes the same way wolves wore fur and . . . yikes. Looked like she'd found where the Murderers R Us support group met. Either that or she'd hit the special ops lottery.

Holding up one end of the island, a blond guy with freaky pale eyes frowned at her.

Hope's stomach clenched.

Then again, maybe *lottery* was too strong a word. *Dead* might be a better one. *Run* seemed like the best choice by far. Hope took a step back. And then another. She bumped into Myst and—

A dark-haired man stepped into her line of sight.

His purple gaze captured hers. "No need tae run, lass. We're all friends here."

His voice rolled over her, rich as vanilla cream in the perfect cup of coffee. A wave of heat washed in to surround her. Taut muscles loosened. Hope released a pent-up breath and leaned into relaxation. Another burst of warm comfort flowed around her. She sighed. Oh wow, that felt good. Much better than the stress she'd suffered for weeks now. First the approach of the dreaded anniversary, then the trip here, into the unknown. But looking at him made her forget it all.

Banished the tension. Pushed aside her despair. Made her feel more like herself than she had in, well . . . ages.

"Hi." Hope stepped forward. Screw professionalism. She wanted to touch him. Just once. A simple handshake. A quick how-do-you-do. Nothing to get too excited about, and really, what could it hurt? Excellent question with only one answer. Getting close to him was a bad idea. She knew it even as she moved, but the urge was too strong to deny. Walking between the island and wall cabinets, she stopped a few feet away and extended her hand. "I'm Hope."

"You certainly are," he murmured, his gaze on her face. His thick Scottish brogue stroked over her senses, making her shiver. One corner of his mouth tipped up as he accepted her greeting along with her hand. His much larger one engulfed hers. Heat poured from his palm. Her skin prickled, sending sensation spiraling up her arm, jolting her into a strange kind of recognition. "Forge, lass. Seems as though we'll be spending some time together."

His name spun her out of infatuation. The mental whirlwind blew her back into reality. Her hand still in his, Hope blinked. Ah, crap. Of all the rotten luck. Forge of the gorgeous face and rock-hard body. Mr. Dreamy in all his masculine glory. Her patient for the next couple of weeks. The realization hit like a bullet shot from a .357 Magnum. The impact made her flinch. She tugged her hand away. He let her go, but it was too late. Her libido was in hyperdrive, and she was already neck-deep in trouble.

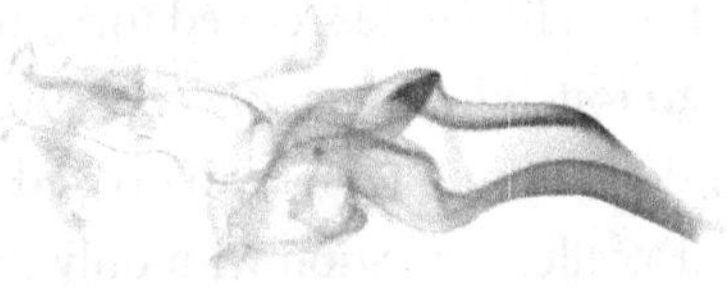

Chapter Eight

No need tae run. What kind of advice was that?

Forge bit down on a curse. The worst kind . . . the very *worst* a male could offer. He flexed his fingers, struggling to forget the feel of the female's hand in his, the decadent spark of her bio-energy against his palm along with the delicious scent of her.

Unable to help himself, he drew another deep breath.

Tempting and sweet, her fragrance invaded his lungs. His skin started to heat. Prickles sparked across his fingertips. Oh yeah. Give him more. She smelled amazing, like hot cinnamon and shortbread cookies, his favorite of all treats and . . . bloody hell. Not good. He was in serious trouble. She was practically edible.

Forge frowned at the female standing a few feet away. Too close. Far too close. With no effort at all he could reach out and cup her cheek. Learn the texture of her skin. Run his fingers over the smattering of freckles on the bridge of her nose. Feel the zap of her energy as he connected to the Meridian, took what he wanted and—

Fuck.

It was official. He was an idiot. A double-damned arse for touching her in the first place. For letting her get so close. For making her feel welcome too. He should be scaring the shite out of her, making her *run*, not encouraging her to stay.

Or sound happy about all the time they'd be spending together.

God. What the hell had possessed him?

The question banged around inside his head. Forge didn't bother answering. He couldn't. He was too busy reacting, backpedaling, resisting errant urges. Out. He needed to get *out* of the kitchen. Away from her, back to some semblance of himself.

Unclenching his hands, Forge told himself to move. His muscles tensed in preparation. His boots stayed planted on the floor. He snorted in disgust. Hell, that wasn't true. He wasn't stuck. He was moving . . . in the wrong fucking direction. Small increments. More lean than true displacement, shifting by degrees toward the female instead of backing away. Stupid. Ridiculous. One hundred percent brainless given he didn't know her. Had barely talked to her. Had only touched her once.

Which led to an irrefutable conclusion.

Her presence obliterated good sense. Hope-of-the-mouth-watering-energy scrambled his wits or something and . . . God. Someone please put him out of his misery. Shoot him. Hang him. Draw and quarter him. The method of his demise didn't matter, just as long as his interest in her died before it exploded into full-blown obsession. Too much to ask? He clenched his teeth. Probably, considering he couldn't take his eyes off her.

Waging an internal war, Forge forced strength back into his legs. His feet shifted.

He started to back away from her.

His dragon half balked, snarling a denial, rooting his feet to the floor, being an uncooperative arse. Prompted by predatory need, his inner beast inhaled, seeking more of her scent. Sweet as Highland heather, it reached him. His nostrils flared again. Saliva pooled in his mouth. Primal instinct detonated, then spiraled into territorial drive. Forge swallowed, fighting to stay in control.

Unaware of her peril, Hope held his gaze and, with a graceful flick, pushed the end of her ponytail over her shoulder. The red-gold strands swung, catching the light, the sparkling sheen enhancing the gorgeous glow of her aura. His body tightened. He lost ground and shifted toward her. Fucking hell. It wasn't fair. Everything about her called to him. A serious problem considering his new just-made-up plan—all-out retreat before he reached out, grabbed hold, and stripped her naked.

In the middle of the goddamn kitchen.

Before God and all his comrades.

The thought set him straight. His control came back online, allowing him to put a leash on desire and back away from her. One step turned into two. Hope frowned at him. He dragged his focus away from her face. Mac met his gaze. Forge's eyes narrowed. His friend raised a brow, the message clear: man-up, buddy.

"I'm going tae snap you in half, Irish." Forge scowled at his apprentice. The traitor. Sneaky bastard. Wanker of the first order. Whatever. Pile on the names, make each one count 'cause . . . shite. Some best friend, throwing him to the wolves—or rather, a bonnie lass—without warning. *"Then gnaw on your bones."*

Mac's mouth curved. *"I won't taste good."*

"I don't give a shite."

"That's going to be fun to watch," Venom said, running his mouth . . . per usual.

A nasty gleam in his eyes, Wick leaned his elbows on the countertop. *"Big fun."*

"We need to make a poster. Get some artwork going—water boy versus fire-acid asshole." Venom glanced at Mac and raised a brow. *"You think Tania will draw it up?"*

Mac snorted.

Gage chuckled.

Rikar shook his head. *"Before or after she guts you like a Razorback?"*

"Before." Wearing a shit-eating grin, Venom bumped shoulders with the Nightfury first in command. *"I want to see the poster first."*

Laughter made the rounds inside the kitchen.

"All right. Enough screwing around," Bastian said, amusement in his voice. Tilting his head toward the dining room, he slid off his stool and, grabbing Myst's hand, dropped mind-speak. "I'm hungry. Time to eat."

"Good plan." A sharp snap ricocheted as Sloan closed his laptop. Grabbing the high-powered computer, the male headed for the timber-beam archway on the other side of the room. "If it gets cold, Daimler will kick our asses."

The comment caused a mass exodus.

The thump of multiple boot soles echoed off white cabinets, pale walls, and marble countertops. As the kitchen cleared, Forge waved Hope forward. "After you, lass."

She hesitated, gaze glued to the group stampeding beneath the archway. After a moment, she nodded as though making up her mind, murmured "Thanks," and put her feet in gear. A few steps behind her, Forge told himself not to look. He really did, but his eyes didn't listen. As if possessed by a libidinous poltergeist, his gaze slid down her back. All the blood left his brain, rushing south as he traced her frame. Trim waist, curvy hips, long legs and . . . he stifled a groan . . . her arse filled out her jeans to perfection. He hardened behind his button fly. Christ on a pogo stick. Had he said *not good* earlier? Well, he'd meant *devastating*. The view of her going was as compelling as the one of her coming.

Taking a fortifying breath, Forge dragged his eyes from her arse and strode into the dining room. Polished to a high sheen, the long mahogany table gleamed beneath a huge chandelier. Taken from a palace in Europe, centuries-old crystal hung like icicles from a gilded frame, reflecting light, sending rainbows arcing across the coffered ceiling. He heard Hope's breath catch and understood her reaction.

The room was anything but ordinary. Casual in some ways (from the double-sided stone fireplace and laid-back artwork on the walls), fancy and sophisticated in others (well-padded Louis IX dining chairs, the size and scope of an Old World table that sat thirty with ease), the room embraced history, yet epitomized family.

A welcoming place.

A gathering place.

The place the Nightfury pack assembled each day to spend time together, sharing meals along with the latest news.

"You know," Rikar said, standing behind his fancy-ass chair, looking thoughtful. "I PVRed the game. The Blackhawks played Dallas last night."

"Blackhawks?" Nian asked, plate and utensils in hand. "What the hell is that?"

Every gaze snapped toward the recent addition to the Nightfury pack.

Forge stifled a laugh and watched his brothers-in-arms' reactions. Nian held his ground, refusing to hide his curiosity. His lips twitched. Brave lad. Ballsy stance, considering the warriors in the room, and the male's precarious welcome inside the lair. Born into the aristocracy—the youngest member of the Archguard high council—Nian remained an unknown variable. Haider might have saved his life in Prague, pulling him out of a kill room and Rodin's reach, but no one knew whether or not to trust the male.

The jury was still out in Forge's mind.

The lad seemed solid enough. Smart. Strong. In search of a home—the same way he had a few months ago. Just like him, Nian needed a second chance. Forge wanted to give him one, despite Bastian's reservations—and the fact Gage wanted to kill him. Shite. The warrior asked B for the green light and Nian's head almost every day. Some leeway with Nian, though, would go a long way. The male longed to be part of a pack, with warriors who valued him. Forge understood the need for acceptance, empathizing with the male's search for a place to belong.

He'd been in the same position just months ago. Cut off from his birth pack. Alone in the world. So lonely he'd thought he might die. And just like Nian, the condition had been of his own making.

After the murder of his family—and waking in a swamp, buried nostrils-deep in water and mud—he could have gone home. Reached out to his cousins. Stayed safe inside the Scottish pack. Suspicion had kept him from it. Someone inside his birth pack had given the enemy his family's precise location on the moors that night. A harsh conclusion to draw? Maybe, but Forge didn't think so. Nothing else explained the ambush and subsequent attack. Both had been too well coordinated, no simple one-off for the bastards leading the charge. The rogue pack had done what they'd intended to do—kill his sire, murder his brothers, take out the entire branch of his family tree in one well-planned assault.

Surviving his family hurt. His inability to protect his brothers and sire still bothered him. A warrior now, he could see the array of options from which he could've chosen. Pick one. Follow through. His sire's words, but in his inexperience, he hadn't considered a single one. Forge swallowed a curse. He never should have retreated. No matter how shaken, or badly wounded, he should've stayed and figured it out. Found the traitor. Avenged his family. Killed all those involved—cousins included. The shame of leaving it undone weighed on him. His family had died on his watch. Through some stroke of fate, he had not. Now he couldn't imagine returning to the place of his birth, to the memories or the dragon warriors who called Aberdeen home.

Which had left him adrift in the wilds of humanity.

He refused to see the same happen to Nian. No matter his history, the lad deserved better than exile and abject loneliness. Dragonkind males didn't do well in isolation, and well, if B required a concrete reason to keep the lad around, Forge could offer one. His rationale wasn't all hearts and roses. He recognized faster than most how things changed for the worst. No one knew what the future held. So aye, having a member of the Archguard in their back pocket could only amount to a good thing.

"I can't believe you don't know who the Blackhawks are," Rikar said, staring at Nian as though he'd grown a second head. "Where the hell have you been—under a rock?"

Nian shrugged. "A close second—in Prague. I had businesses to run and Rodin to watch. No time for fun."

"That needs to change. How about we start right now?" Devilry in his mercury-colored eyes, Haider glanced at Rikar. "A hundred bucks says Chicago lost."

A rabid hockey fan, Rikar scowled at the male insulting his beloved Blackhawks. "Too easy, Haider. You don't want your money? I'll take it."

Haider scoffed. "The only one losing money tonight, Rikar, is you."

"It's on." Moving with stark efficiency, Rikar reached for the food dishes. Ceramic lids clinked as they hit the tabletop. He grabbed two plates. A stack of pancakes covered with maple syrup went on one. A mound of eggs and bacon topped with five pieces of cinnamon toast got piled onto the other. Giving the caloric nightmare disguised as flapjacks to Angela, he leaned in, kissed his mate on the mouth, and handed her utensils. "Come on, angel. We're eating in front of the TV."

Sloan reached for his computer. "I could tell you who—"

"Don't," Rikar growled.

Haider glared at their resident computer genius. "You'll ruin the bet if you tell us who won. Butt out, man."

Rolling his eyes, Sloan set the laptop down.

"See ya." With a laugh, Angela turned from the table and followed her mate.

"I want to see this." Snagging a couple of plates, Gage passed one to Osgard. "Load up, kid, and be quick about it. Rikar and Haider might beat the shit out of each other during the game. No way I'm missing that."

A rumble of agreement rose around the table.

Standing to one side, Forge watched the other Nightfuries dig in, loading up plates, feeding their mates, grabbing cutlery before hightailing it out of the dining room. As Wick and J. J. disappeared around the corner of the fireplace, he glanced at Hope.

Laughter in her eyes, she shrugged and, flatware in hand, made a beeline for the pancakes. "I don't know anything about hockey, but I'm game to learn. You grab the—"

Bastian shoved a chair against the table. The hard rap echoed. Hope froze mid-stride, her attention locked on the Nightfury commander. "Hope, I'm Bastian, Myst's mate. Welcome to Black Diamond."

"Thank you, ah . . . sir," Hope said, standing military straight, hand twitching as though she fought the urge to salute.

Forge didn't blame her. B might be reasonable—most of the time—but he looked lethal. Flat-out scary to anyone who didn't know him. To be expected. A commander of warriors, he wore intimidation like a second skin. And a female meeting him for the first time? Aye. No doubt at all. Anyone—male, female . . . the groundhog nesting in the yard outside—would do well to stay wary with B in the vicinity.

The hard-core attitude served Bastian well. Was one of the reasons he led the Nightfury pack with efficiency. Strength, honor, and razor-sharp intelligence rounded out his virtues, making him a male to be reckoned with. Warriors respected him. Their enemies feared him. Everyone listened when he spoke. Even so, B's tactic with Hope bothered him. He didn't like the uncertainty on her face. Or the idea another male stood so close to her. Close enough to touch, a fact his dragon half refused to accept.

Bastian ran his hand along the back of the chair and took another step, closing the distance.

The urge to plant his fist in his commander's face grabbed hold. Forge shifted to stand beside Hope, lending his support, willing to shield her with his body. "Careful, B."

One side of Bastian's mouth tipped up. He switched to mind-speak. "*Watch yourself, Scot. You're getting awfully territorial.*"

"*Fuck off,*" he said, borrowing Wick's favorite expression. Bastian raised a brow. He ignored it in favor of getting back on track. It was either that or let loose and knock his friend's teeth down his throat. "We'll fill our plates and join you in the living room."

"No, you won't. Not you two." The last to leave, B picked up his plate and started for the exit. "Stay here. Eat. Talk. Get to know one another."

Forge tensed. Oh Christ, nay. Alone in a room with Hope. Nothing and no one to stop him from touching her again. Shite. His stomach flip-flopped. Anything but that. The female turned him inside out without even trying. No way would he survive sitting across a table from her without his control slipping. Or suffering a serious case of blue balls.

Panic rose at the thought.

Looking for a way out, Forge challenged his commander. "Is that an order?"

Bastian paused mid-stride, green gaze level, expression full of don't-fuck-with-me. "Do you need it to be?"

He scowled at his commander. Arsehole. Clever, clever bastard. Bastian was too smart by half. The male had outmaneuvered him, leaving him between a rock and a hard place. Stay or go? Courage or dishonor? Be a warrior and accept his fate or rail against his future for the next few weeks. Forge rolled his shoulders. It seemed foolish to fight, but God, he wanted to start one. Bay at the moon. Let his fists fly. Complain at the unfairness of it.

Bastian waited for an answer.

Forge shook his head, answering without words. No sense prolonging the inevitable. Hope was here to help him recover his memory. Mac said she was good at her job. He prayed for his sake his apprentice was right. He needed a breakthrough. Craved answers. Longed for the pain to end more than he wanted to avoid a female that made him feel too much. But as B left the room and he looked at Hope, Forge knew whatever experiment/therapy she planned would end in disaster. For him? With absolute certainty. For her? No way around it. Now only one question remained. The fifty-million-dollar one—could he keep it professional and stay out of her bed? Good question, given he'd spent less than five minutes in her company and already wanted to lay Hope across the dining room table and treat her like a meal.

Chapter Nine

Worrying blew . . . big time. So did being hungry every minute of the day. Toss in the fatigue that always accompanied his near-starved state and—yeah. It sucked to be him.

Sitting on the sofa in the great room, Mac tried to watch the game. One–nothing Blackhawks. He didn't give a shit. Unusual to say the least. He enjoyed hockey. Got a kick out of Rikar's obsession with the game and all the body contact. His mouth curved. Hell, those guys could hit. Sometimes with enough force to break bones.

Always fun to watch.

A plate balanced on one knee, Mac picked up his fork. Eggs. Bacon. Crispy potato wedges. All of it smothered in maple syrup, the real kind, one hundred percent authentic. Mouthwatering aromas rose on a curl of steam. He frowned at his stack of pancakes. The commentator droned on about a penalty—a stick infraction, some kind of shot to the head. Mac sighed. Enough stalling. Might as well get on with it. No sense beating the issue to death. He might not be able to stop worry from eating him alive. He could, however, fill the bottomless pit he called his belly.

His stomach growled.

Frustration tightened his muscles.

An awful ache bloomed beneath his skin. Nothing new there. Every time he moved, the discomfort reminded him he wasn't normal.

Hell. Mac huffed. He was always in the dark. Left to flounder, a male without any idea of his origins or what the ink etched into his skin signified. He hadn't signed up for it. Hadn't sat in an artist's chair or picked it from a book full of example tattoos downtown. The damn thing arrived with the *change*, his first shift into dragon form. Still, he wished he knew what it meant. Or that one of the other Nightfury warriors did. Information, a boatload of knowledge, would go a long way to easing his worry right now, but . . . no dice. None of the other Nightfuries owned a tattoo or had the first clue why navy-blue ink covered one side of his torso.

Rotating his elbow, Mac stretched his muscles, causing himself pain just to be contrary, and stabbed a forkful of eggs. With more determination than enthusiasm, he shoveled the load into his mouth. Chew and swallow. He took another bite. And then another, making steady work of the abundance on his plate. He'd go back for seconds. Maybe even thirds before his hunger subsided and let his appetite rest.

"Good?"

The last bite halfway to his mouth, Mac glanced to his left. His heart skipped a beat. Damn thing always did when he looked at Tania—his mate, his love, the only woman in the world for him.

Seated beside him, she nibbled on a piece of bacon.

Her gorgeous brown eyes met his.

Meal forgotten in a blast of molten lust, he reached out and gripped the nape of her neck. Thick and luxurious, her hair caressed the back of his hand. Mac leaned in. He couldn't resist. Didn't want to either. He needed a kiss, a little taste, a lot of contact . . . everything she had to give. Touching her—making love to her—was his manna. Pleasing her never got old. She nourished him in ways he couldn't explain, and didn't want to do without.

His mouth met hers. He licked in, seeking her tongue. She opened and, fingers buried in his hair, gave him all he asked and everything he needed.

"Yum. You taste like pancakes and . . ." Her lips brushed his again. She flicked him with the tip of her tongue. "Hmm, sex."

"Insatiable woman."

"When it comes to you? Absolutely." She leaned away. A twinkle in her eyes, Tania raised a brow. "Are you complaining?"

"No way. I can't get enough of you, *mo chroí*."

"I know." Tania grinned and came in for another kiss. Mac groaned into her mouth. She tasted delicious, the perfect combination of smart, sweet, and smoking-hot female. "You've got that look. Finish eating, and we'll go."

To bed.

She didn't say it. Fuck, she didn't need to. Mac knew what his mate wanted. What she needed, craved—all the explosive pleasure he adored giving her. He wasn't any better. His yearning for her surpassed normal. Each day. Every night. He wanted her with a fervor that bordered on insanity. A state of being that troubled him a little. He was so needy, and his female was a giver. Tania never said no. Most males would've been happy about that. Mac worried instead. He fed every day, activating energy-fuse, connecting to the Meridian through her, drawing the nourishment he required to stay healthy and strong.

Sometimes, though, Mac worried he took too much.

As a general rule, Dragonkind males fed once a month. Some of his kind could go much, much longer without finding a human female with strong enough energy to feed. Not him. His hunger never abated. It gnawed on him with steely teeth instead. Normal, Rikar assured him, given his abrupt transition into Dragonkind. He was a fledgling—a warrior in training—and what his pack called a late bloomer. A male who'd experienced his first shift years later than usual. Why his dragon DNA had lain dormant was anyone's guess. But the second he'd encountered his own kind—by way of being attacked by an asshole Razorback at his old SPD precinct—the transition began. Scary at the time. Still disconcerting months later, considering he had yet to find his footing.

Mac scowled. Fucking tattoo.

"Don't worry." Wrapping her arms around him, Tania snuggled into his side. His whole being sighed in relief. Taut muscles relaxed. He closed his arms around her before the thought to hold her even occurred to him. "Forge is going to be fine. I like Hope. She seems okay. I'm choosing to trust her with him."

"I hope you're right. Forge is pretty pissed off."

"He'll get over it," Tania whispered, nestling her head beneath his chin.

"You sure?"

"Yup."

"How?"

Tania snorted, the inelegant sound conveying better than words she thought he was an idiot.

Mac lifted his head to peer down at her. "I know that look . . . pure mischief. Tell me how you know, honey."

"Well," she said. "He seems quite taken with her."

"So?"

"I have a feeling he'll forgive you the second he gets her into bed."

Surprise overrode mental acuity for a second. He frowned. "She's not here for that. He isn't supposed to—"

"What—screw her?" Tania snorted. "Oh, that's going to happen. Forge won't be able to keep his hands off her, and Hope won't be able to resist him. He's got that whole Highlander thing going on. Wicked hot."

Mac opened his mouth. Words escaped him. He closed it again. *Wicked hot?* Seriously? What the hell was Tania thinking? He gave his mate the stink eye.

The love of his life rolled her eyes. “Oh please. Put the jealousy away. Just because I can appreciate Forge’s hotness doesn’t mean I want him. You’re the only guy who gets me hot, Mac.”

And wet.

Again, she didn’t say the words. No need. The meaning was implied. All of a sudden, Mac felt better. Excellent. Ego salvaged. Male pride soothed. Jealously tucked back where it belonged. Just in case, though . . .

He nipped her bottom lip, tasting her again. “Let’s go. I need to fuck.”

Tania blushed. “Mac!”

“How many orgasms do you want?” he asked, teasing her as she glanced around to see who might’ve overheard. Gage met her gaze and grinned. Tania went from rosy to bright red. Mac chuckled and, dipping his head, nuzzled her ear. “I’m going to make you scream my name. Everybody’s going to hear.”

“Oh my God! You—”

He kissed her hard, interrupting her mid-scold.

She gasped in outrage.

Setting his plate aside, Mac grasped her hand and pushed off the couch. A quick tug brought his mate to her feet.

Glaring at him, Tania laced her fingers with his. “You are so bad.”

“You love it.”

“Don’t know what it says about me, but . . . yes, I do.” She sighed. All show. How did he know? The blistering heat in her eyes told the tale. She wanted him as much as he needed her. And yeah—he smiled—talking dirty turned his female on. “Come on, Lover Boy. Let’s get you looked after.”

“And you thoroughly fucked,” he said, keeping his voice low, for her ears alone.

Tania turned an even brighter shade of red. She cursed him under her breath. Mac laughed. Bewitching. Beyond beautiful. He adored the way she reacted—with feminine disapproval and an overwhelming dose of lust. He could see it on her face, in her eyes, in the shift of her scent. White-hot arousal, pure and simple, gorgeous and full bodied. A few well-placed words, and his female went from simmering to wild and ready.

God. He loved that about her.

Her hand clasped in his, he pivoted toward the door. Time to make a quick getaway. Wick and J. J. were already gone, behind closed doors, sweating up the sheets, no doubt. And Venom and Evelyn? Mac glanced toward the wall of windows east of the big screen and the row of wide-assed armchairs. He huffed. Shit. Those two weren't shy. Mouth fused to Evelyn's, hands cupping her ass, Venom lifted his mate onto the lip of the pool table. Evelyn wrapped her legs around his waist. Venom groaned in appreciation and settled in, inhaling his female as though he might die if he stopped kissing her.

No one paid attention.

Different day, same story.

Venom couldn't keep his hands off his mate. Hell, the male didn't even try.

Mac snorted in amusement. As if he was one to talk. He was just as bad. A real sex addict when it came to Tania. And speaking of which . . .

He headed for the exit, his mate in tow.

A few feet from the archway, a wave of heat rippled over his nape. Someone hissed his name, the voice more static than substance. *"Exshaw—Exshaw is coming."* The words echoed inside his head. Mac paused mid-stride. Tania stopped beside him. He glanced around. Nothing out of the ordinary. Game on screen. Chairs arranged in a semicircle in front of it. Half-empty plates perched on his brothers' laps.

Mac frowned.

The low hiss came again. *"Exshaw—Exshaw is coming."*

Prickles tightened his scalp. He glanced toward the windows. Weird, but it felt as though something approached. Something fast.

Something furious. Something unstoppable. Transfixed by the sensation, Mac tried to get a bead on it. His tattoo pulsed. Pressure built behind his eyes, then funneled, whirling through his mind before coiling around his rib cage. Pain knifed along his spine. Heat slithered beneath his skin, then spread, pushing an inferno through his veins. His vision blurred. His mind hazed. He blinked, trying to focus, to beat back his confusion, but . . . seething red fog rolled in, swamping his senses, stealing his air.

He swayed on his feet.

"Mac?" Coming from far away, Tania's voice reached through the thick mental sludge. Cold hands touched his face. "Mac? Talk to me. What's wrong, baby—tell me what's happening."

"I can't breathe." Sucking wind, he doubled over. A second later, he hit his knees. Bile touched the back of his throat. His stomach heaved. His windpipe contracted. He lost his breakfast in one violent, muscle-torquing go.

"Oh God—help! Rikar, help! I need—"

"Step aside, Tania. Let me see him."

Mac threw up again.

"Christ." Rikar's voice. Tania crying out in concern. Strong hands, bigger than Tania's, bracketed Mac's head. "Gage, get some water. Haider, get to the clinic, start a salt bath. He's too hot."

"Fuck," B said, palm pressed against Mac's forehead. "He's burning up."

"Get him downstairs," a female said, tone full of command. Still on his knees, tears in his eyes, Mac fought through the mind-fog. He knew that voice. Not Tania, but . . . Myst, maybe? "He needs fluids. I want to get an IV going."

Pain turned a corner, rushing into unbearable.

Mac cursed. His skin—the tattoo—throbbed. Needle-thin, razor-sharp points ripped over his ribs. His muscles cramped. The debilitating burn arched his spine. Twisting in agony, Mac fought the hands holding him down.

"Get it off. Get it off!" Clawing at his T-shirt, he tried to pull it over his head. "Jesus fuck—get it off!"

Rikar yanked the cotton over his head. "Holy shit."

Bastian dropped another f-bomb. "Myst—get moving. Sloan—go with her. We'll be right behind you."

As B rolled him onto his back, Mac opened his eyes. Rikar's face jumped into focus, then blurred. His lungs clogged as he looked down at his chest. Poker hot, the tattoo glowed bright red, lighting up his skin, throbbing like a psychotic heartbeat.

Mac groaned. "What the fuck?"

"Good question." Bastian's even tone gave him hope. His commander wasn't freaking out. Which could only be a good thing . . . right? Mac frowned. *Right*. Excellent deduction, except for one problem. B never got too worked up about anything. Calm as hell. Steady as a rock. The guy never panicked. Was always cool under fire, especially when bad shit went down. "Let's get you upright and mobile, then figure it out . . . yeah?"

"Yeah," Mac rasped, trying to move his legs. But God, it hurt and . . . motherfuck. There wasn't enough air. "Tania?"

"I'm here, baby."

"Need you."

"I've got you," she said, the worry in her voice almost killing him.

Mac didn't want to cause her pain. He was supposed to take care of her, not the other way around. She shouldn't have to worry about anything, least of all him.

"Mo chroí . . ."

"Easy, my love. I'm right here."

Cool hands touched his abdomen and slid up, over his skin. Powerful energy sped from her fingertips, sinking into his bones, soothing him, helping his muscles unlock. His chest expanded. Oxygen filled his lungs.

He refocused, desperate to see her face. "Stay with me."

Tears in her eyes, Tania leaned over him. "I'm not going anywhere. Now—get up."

A command from his female.

Mac redoubled his efforts. His dragon half responded, lending him strength. Sweat trickled over his temple, the slow, wet slide registering an instant before his body cooperated. With a grunt, he rolled and, using Rikar and Bastian as crutches, struggled to his feet. His head bobbed on his shoulders. His brain sloshed inside his skull. Gritting his teeth, he reached for Tania. His fingers brushed her hair and—

A wind gust blew into the room.

The sizzle beneath his skin intensified. A chant started up, the beat hammering his temples. *"Exshaw—Exshaw is coming."*

Mac turned toward the windows.

Blinding light exploded through the highest pane.

Like a long-tailed comet, the horrific glow rocketed across the great room. An unearthly shriek echoed. Mac sucked in a breath. The fireball slammed into the center of his chest. Air exited his lungs. Fiery tendrils attacked his tattoo, burrowing into the tribal markings. Pain ripped him apart as the shock wave threw him backward. In full flight, Mac hit the wall. Gypsum cracked behind his back. Two-by-fours shattered as his shoulders smashed through wood. The big screen exploded, hurling shards of glass toward twin billiard tables.

Tania screamed his name.

His brothers-in-arms shouted in alarm.

Mac slid to the floor with a thud, his body failing, the world sinking beneath a veil of darkness.

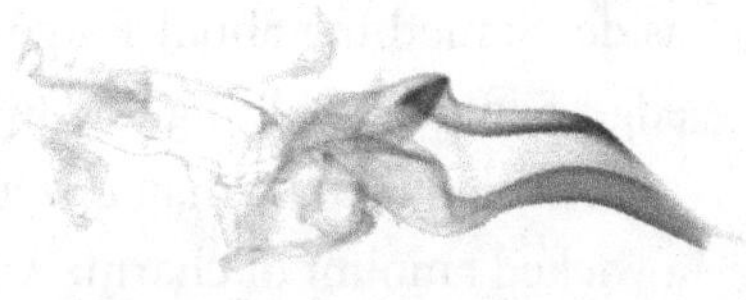

Chapter Ten

Sitting at the table across from Forge, Hope stared at him, searching for flaws. She needed to find a whole bunch. Pages full—right now, but well . . . her strategy wasn't working. Luck and intellect had abandoned her half an hour ago. No matter how good the argument, she couldn't deny his appeal. Her gaze drifted over his face. The strong line of his jaw, the sculpted cheekbones, the color of his eyes, and dark day-old stubble—each feature pointed to one god-awful conclusion. He was gorgeous. Pure male beauty. The kind no woman on earth could ignore.

Or resist.

Bad news for her. Even worse for professional ethics. The longer she looked at him, the less her brain worked. Now she didn't know what to do—keep talking to him or push the pancakes aside and kiss him senseless.

The urge startled her. Worried her a whole bunch too. She'd never been attracted to one of her patients before. Never sat across from anyone meant for her therapist's chair and wondered what he tasted like . . . or if he was any good in bed.

The thought made her choke on a strawberry.

As she coughed, Hope tried to make sense of her reaction. Why Forge? Why now? What about him shoved her beyond the limit of her usual calm? She never had these kinds of problems.

Compartmentalizing her thoughts and feelings came naturally. No matter the client, no matter the issue, she managed to put each one aside. Something about Forge, though, unbalanced her. Put her on edge. Sent her skidding uncontrolled into the danger zone.

All right, so the man oozed sex appeal. Sexy. Strong. Smart with a wicked amount of charm. And his mouth. Holy God. It should be illegal. Or at least on the most wanted list. Every time he opened it and that delicious accent rolled out, she got a little hotter. A little hornier. A little more imaginative about the best way to wrap herself around him.

Hope shifted in her seat.

Stupid brain.

Stinking libido.

Both were in overdrive, putting unethical thoughts in her head. Now all she could think about was how good he'd taste. Like maple syrup and man, no doubt. Sweet and sultry. Hot as all get out. Dark and delicious. Erotic with a debilitating dash of just-do-me-now. Stabbing another berry with her fork, Hope indulged in a silent redirect. She needed somewhere else to look. Something else to focus on. And while she was at it? A way to shield herself from the vibe he emitted like pheromones would be advisable too.

Help.

She was here to *help*, not jump into bed with him.

But oh, wouldn't that be nice? Oh, so *nice*. The best way to scratch her itch, assuage the growing ache, and get some relief. It had been ages. Hope pressed her knees together beneath the table. Far too long since her last man-induced orgasm and—

"Are you all right, lass?"

"I'm fine." She put her fork down. Grabbing her napkin, she wiped her mouth and waved her hand. "Just a little sex on the brain."

Fork poised over his pancakes, Forge blinked.

She drew a shallow breath. Oh crap. Bad brain. Bad, *bad* mouth. Had she really just said that out loud? "I mean . . . I didn't mean . . ." Cheeks flushing hot, Hope sputtered, struggling to find words. The ones that would backpedal her right out of the situation.

One second ticked into another. Nothing came to her rescue. No great epiphany. No humorous just-laugh-it-off comment. Nary an interruption in sight.

Silence throbbed through the room.

A look of consideration on his face, he raised a brow.

"God." Planting her elbows on the tabletop, Hope palmed her forehead. So much for professionalism. She'd just blown it sky-high, imploding any chance of hiding her attraction to him. She pressed her thumbs to her temples. Dear God. She needed a reset, a do-over . . . whatever. Just as long as it wiped out the past thirty seconds and put her on firm footing again. "I can't believe I said that. Talk about awkward."

"Why?" he asked, setting his utensils down. The knife and fork clinked against fine china as Forge sat back and stretched out his legs. He nudged her foot with his beneath the table. "I want you too."

Surprise brought her chin up.

He met her gaze, pure challenge in his.

Hope froze. "You do?"

"Aye. I have from the second I saw you."

"Oh well . . ." She trailed off as her libido raised its unruly head. Butterflies took flight, fluttering in her belly. Hope shut that crap down, refusing to be pleased. It was a dumb reaction. She shouldn't be happy Forge wanted her. She should be finding something to say instead. Something intelligent. Something that didn't start with "Where's the nearest bed?" and end with her unbuttoning his jeans. "Guess it's good we got that into the open."

"Mayhap. Mayhap not." Wiping his mouth, he tossed the cloth napkin beside his juice glass. Unruffled, he shoved his plate aside, set his forearms on the table, and leaned toward her, one hundred percent comfortable in his own skin . . . and the topic at hand. "But now that it is, we need tae decide what tae do about it."

"Ignore it?" she asked, hoping he agreed.

"Or we could follow our bliss and fuck ourselves silly while you're here."

"Not a good idea."

"Why not, lass?"

She scowled at him. "I'm a professional. I don't sleep with patients."

"Good tae know," he said, sounding pleased . . . with her. Hope squirmed in her seat. Weird. His approval did something for her, warming her inside, making her want to please him again. Do anything to hear his sexy Scots voice deepen into a rumbling purr one more time. "But we've a problem, you and I."

"You think?" A huge understatement. Colossal, really, given her inner sex addict adored his suggestion. Was lapping it up like a kitten would cream. "Serious issues."

"Simple tae fix, Hope."

Her eyes narrowed.

His mouth curved. "You're here to help me regain my memory. 'Tis unlikely to happen with both of us suffering."

"Really," she said, whipping sarcasm out like a sword. "Big ego, much?"

He huffed, the soft sound full of laughter. "Nay, not really, but something needs tae be done. The attraction will come between us. Make things more difficult in the long run."

"So what—we screw like rabbits?"

"It'll take the edge off." An untrustworthy gleam sparked in his eyes. He bumped her with his foot again. "Be a helluva lot of fun too."

Well, at least he was honest. In an unthreatening, playful kind of way.

The psychologist in her appreciated the first. The woman in her enjoyed the second. Despite his outrageous suggestion, she liked him. Was enjoying the conversation along with the man, but . . . sleep with him? Cross professional boundaries? Break rules she always adhered to, no matter what? Chewing on the inside of her lip, Hope entertained the notion for a moment. Really thought about it, imagining how much fun she could have with him. How much pleasure he would give her. How well he could help her forget what her brother had done.

The thought stopped her cold.

Damn it. She was better than that, more responsible.

Using Forge to bury the pain was a bad idea. It wasn't right. She deserved better, and so did he. "I'm not in the habit of using people."

"Neither am I, lass." His brow furrowed. "What would make you say that?"

Holding his gaze, Hope hesitated before answering. Should she deflect or be honest? Dodging his question would be easier. A helluva lot less painful too, but as she held his gaze, instinct warned her to tell the truth. Honesty could be a weapon, an effective one when dealing with grief, pain, and trauma. Intuition told her Forge would respond best to a little give and take. The more she shared with him, the more he would with her.

All of a sudden, she knew what to do. This was her strategy, how she would get through to him, how he would learn to trust her, and—despite her aversion to sharing her past—it was the best way to begin their first session together.

Taking a fortifying breath, she sat straighter in her chair. "I lost my brother. He was everything to me, my whole world. Now that he's gone I tend to . . ." Without mercy, old memories surfaced. Happy times. Challenging times. All the times Adam shielded her, taking the brunt of their father's anger. Her heart started to hurt. Hope swallowed past the tight knot in her throat. Sweet, sweet Adam, loyal despite his troubled end. "I don't know . . . I guess I bury myself in work, distract myself to keep from thinking about the fact he's never coming back."

"I'm sorry, Hope." Concern in his eyes, Forge reached across the table.

Hope moved her hands and leaned back, getting out of range. She didn't want him to touch her. Not right now. Fragility had set in, unearthing vulnerability, making her feel brittle and broken, tainted by a past she refused to let go. "Thank you, but I'm not telling you because I need sympathy."

"Why, then?"

"Because I want things to be clear between us and . . ." Fighting to find the right words, Hope stared down at the place mat. Tiny dragons, embroidered on the fabric, made her mouth curve. Such a pretty sight, unlike her messy confession at the moment. "I thought you'd understand. You know what it's like to lose someone you love."

"More than just someone," he said, dark shadows in his eyes. "Everyone."

"Then I'm sorry too."

He murmured a "Thanks," accepting the gift of her comfort. Silence descended. Seconds ticked into more. Forge shifted in his chair. Hope resisted the urge to do the same and waited him out. She'd opened her heart, entrusting him with a piece of her life. The next move needed to be his.

A line between his brows, Forge picked up his orange juice. He took a sip, set the glass down, then turned his attention back to her.

Dark-purple gaze full of pain, he tipped his chin. "What was his name?"

The question, softly spoken, startled her.

After a second of surprise, Hope answered. "Adam. Fun-loving, generous Adam . . . until he walked into a library with a semi-automatic and killed eleven people."

"Christ."

"Yeah, I know. Shocked the hell out of me too." Fighting tears, she cleared her throat. "I blame myself for not knowing he was in trouble. I think that's probably why I can see you're doing the same."

Forge's hand flexed around his napkin. "Different situation."

"I'd like to hear about it." She paused, backed off a little, giving Forge the space she sensed he needed. "Whenever you're ready."

"Is that how this works?"

"It can," she said. "All I ask is that you be honest with me. Surrender to the process, Forge, and tell me the truth. I'll keep your confidences. Whatever you choose to share with me, stays with me."

Taking a deep breath, he nodded. And she didn't push.

With the groundwork laid, he needed a chance to process. To think things through and decide what he wanted to bring to the table. Fair play, after all, was her strong suit. So was honesty, which meant she couldn't stall any longer. Forge needed an answer to his outrageous proposition, the one that landed her in his bed.

A shiver ghosted through her.

Hope breathed through the tremor and . . . crap. Much as she wanted to, she couldn't accept his offer. Sleeping with him was a terrible idea, for so many reasons. For one, sexual intimacy would muddy the waters—for her, for him, for everyone counting on her to do her job. And two? Her integrity meant something. She couldn't cross into uncharted territory and hope to find her way back to a place where professionalism lived and values mattered.

"Listen, Forge, I—"

"Donnae decide now," he said, cutting her off. Hope eyed him. He raised a brow, as if he expected her to challenge him. She wanted to, almost opened her mouth and told him where to stick his gorgeous accent. At the last second, she decided against it. His mouth curved in approval and . . . weird. It was almost as though he could read her mind and knew what she wanted to say. "Think on it. Take all the time you need, lass. I'm not going anywhere."

Hope smothered a snort. There went his ego again . . . along with the deepening of his sexier-than-sin voice. She grimaced. Wrong thought. Not at all helpful given the gorgeous man seated across the table. Her gaze drifted to his lips. Full. Perfectly shaped. A mouth made for kissing. She swallowed her dismay and dug deep to unearth her resolve. No way would she give in to her urges. Her inner alley cat was not running the show. She repeated that to herself, pointing a mental finger at her out-of-control libido. *Not*—she shook her imaginary finger again—absolutely *NOT* in charge, no matter how much the bitch whined.

"I don't need time." To emphasize the point, she treated Forge to her best no-nonsense look. "I'm not going to change my—"

A loud crack split the air.

Bright light flashed, bleeding in from the living room. The house shuddered around her. The table shook, dancing across the hardwood floor. Covered dishes clanked. Glassware clattered, spilling juice onto expensive place mats.

Male voices shouted.

"Holy crap," Hope said as Forge leapt to his feet. "What is it—an earthquake?"

Already on the move, he spun toward the living room. "Stay here, lass."

The house shook again, rattling picture frames on the walls.

A man roared in agony.

Shoving away from the table, Hope shook her head. "Not on your life."

Forge didn't hear her. Arms and legs pumping, he sprinted past the fireplace, under the archway, and into the living room. Shoe soles scraping over the hardwood floor, Hope lunged after him. She skirted the end of the table as he disappeared from sight. Nuts. Freaking guy.

Where did he think he was going without her? Nowhere, she hoped. Being alone while powerful tremors tore the house apart wasn't a great idea. She might end up buried alive with no one to help her. And standing in the open under a timber-beam ceiling? List that under things she refused to do. She didn't know much about earthquakes, but obeying Forge didn't seem like a smart play.

She remembered something about taking cover in doorways. Or hiding under tables, but neither of those options felt right. Forge seemed like the safer bet. Despite his fast exit, she knew—without proof or complete understanding—he would protect her. Maybe it was instinct. Maybe it was insanity. Maybe she'd somehow come to trust him, just a little, while sharing her past—and denying him sex—but none of that mattered. Only one thing held sway . . . following and finding him.

Picking up the pace, Hope hightailed it after him. She rounded the base of the enormous stone fireplace. Cursing erupted from the living room. She ran beneath the arch, down a short corridor and—

Straight into chaos.

Her brain took a quick snapshot: a huge hole in the wall, shattered glass on the floor, Mac prone, covered with a blanket, and unconscious. Tania on her knees beside him, tears running down her face. Bastian holding his legs down while Mac's body shook, Rikar checking his vitals. Forge knelt on the floor at Mac's head, using his hands to keep his neck from moving. Classic CPR maneuver. An indication of injury. Alarm jolted through her. Her heartbeat ramped into a full gallop as concern punched through. It looked serious. Really bad and . . .

Hope took a steady breath and pushed panic aside. Mac was hurt. He needed help, not her freaking out. Fighting to stay calm, Hope slid to a stop beside a sectional sofa, bumping into its leather side.

"What happened? Is he all right? What can I do to help?" she asked so fast the questions ran together.

Forge's focus snapped toward her. "I told you tae stay put."

"I didn't listen," she said, stating the obvious. He scowled at her. She flexed her hands and stepped forward until she stood a few feet away. The earthquake subsided. The house settled. The rattling stopped as she fought to contain her worry. "What can I do? He's my friend too, Forge. Please, give me a job."

His hard-ass expression softened. "Ange went tae get the stretcher. Go help her." Hands steady around Mac's head, he tipped his chin toward a door leading into the kitchen. "Through there. Take a right into the main corridor."

She nodded. "Okay."

"Good lass," he murmured, his gaze locked with hers.

Hope told herself to turn and go. She needed to help Angela, be useful, but . . . Forge wouldn't let her. The heat in his eyes held her immobile. His irises started to shimmer as he stared at her. The purple glimmer expanded into a simmering glow. A warm current rolled in on a strange wave. Tingles washed over her shoulders and down her spine, relaxing tense muscles. Her heartbeat slowed. Her eyelids grew heavy. Her mind ceased its rapid racing. Hope blew out a long breath as panic receded.

The corner of his mouth tipped up. Forge looked away, breaking eye contact. The shimmer disappeared, releasing her, making her question whether she'd seen it at all. "Off you go, *jalâyla*."

The odd endearment whispered through her.

Hope shivered and, remembering her task, hurried toward the door. But not before she looked back one last time. She couldn't help it. That glow. So strange. A trick of the light? Conjured by a flight of fancy? Or something else entirely? She frowned. Crazy thought. Nothing but her unruly imagination hard at work. But as she rushed through the kitchen, past glossy cabinets and marble countertops, intuition told a different tale. Black Diamond was not all it seemed.

Something odd was going on.

Something intriguing.

A something she couldn't explain.

The situation, each inconsistency, roused her curiosity, prompting her need to know. She loved a good mystery. Enjoyed the hunt and chase of unearthing an interesting story. She did it with her patients all the time, asking the right questions, reading between the lines, revealing the truth anchoring their lives. She wanted to do the same with Forge, but more than that too. The urge to figure out what made Angela's friends different hummed in her veins. The idea sparked her interest. Irresistible. Undeniable. A secret waiting to be uncovered. A dangerous game given the men who called Black Diamond home.

Chapter Eleven

Shoulder blades pressed to the rear wall of the viewing chamber, Forge stared through the glass separating him from his best friend. The barrier rubbed him the wrong way. He should be in there doing . . . well, something. What, exactly? He frowned. No bloody idea, but God, the waiting. He hated waiting—along with the MRI surrounding Mac, the *human thing* keeping him from his best friend's side. Damned machine. Crossing his arms, he scowled at it and told himself to be patient—for the umpteenth time—but . . . shite. It was hard to do. Hard to wait. Hard to watch. Hard to feel so completely helpless.

His stomach dipped.

Forge smoothed away his unease and forced himself to remain still. Perfectly fucking *still.* Pacing wouldn't help. Wearing the floor out never worked. Neither would putting his fist through the wall, considering Mac lay unconscious, stretched out on the patient table, his tattoo glowing red against the walls inside the cylinder. Bright lights blinked above the round opening, painting pale walls with green flashes. A throbbing beep butted against the floor-to-ceiling windows as the medical unit worked, treating Mac to a full body scan.

Forge swallowed a growl of impatience.

Fear tightened his chest.

He couldn't stand it. He needed to move. Find a target. Kill the threat. Make it right and Mac well again. Forge blew out a breath, then reversed course and inhaled. His chest rose. He held the air, counting out the seconds. Five, four, three, two, one—breathe out, breathe in. Repeat, release, begin again.

The breathing technique didn't work either. Forge flexed his hands and shifted against the wall, adjusting his stance. Twenty feet. Less than ten strides from here to Mac. From being able to help a male he loved like a brother. "How much longer?"

Seated beside Myst, Tania flinched. Drawn by his voice, she glanced over her shoulder. His heart sunk lower in his chest. He hated seeing her like this. She looked lost, so hopeless and hollow eyed. So scared for her mate, her bottom lip trembled.

"It's going tae be all right, Tania," he murmured, trying to soothe her.

Tears filled Tania's eyes. "Why isn't he waking up?"

"He will," Myst said, reaching out to take her hand.

"I need to touch him," Tania whispered, clinging to Myst, her desperation almost killing him. "I need to hear his voice."

Struggling to contain his own fear, he prompted Myst again. "How long?"

"I don't know." Dragging her attention from Tania, Myst refocused on the double screens. "Half an hour? An hour? I've been taking courses online, reading about MRIs since getting the machine, but it's my first time running it, so . . ." She shook her head, the uncertainty in her eyes telling. "I just don't know."

Christ. Not what he wanted to hear, but well . . . hell. None of it was Myst's fault. Despite her hesitancy, he trusted her with Mac. She knew her way around medicine. Had stitched him up after a night of fighting more times than he cared to count. Which meant he needed to butt out and let her work.

Shoving away from the wall, Forge raised his arms and, cupping the back of his head, pressed his chin to his chest. Taut muscles screamed in protest. He held the stretch, welcoming the discomfort before raising his head. He glanced at Mac, then pivoted and strode toward the exit. Fuck it. Forget staying still. Watching over Myst's shoulder wasn't helping. He couldn't stand inside the viewing room an instant longer.

"Find me when you're done," he said, tapping Myst on the shoulder as he walked behind her chair.

She nodded.

Reaching the door, Forge grabbed the handle. He twisted, yanked, and—

Tripped over Rikar.

"Fucking hell," the male grumbled from his seat on the floor.

Forge stepped around his XO's outstretched legs. The other males camped out in the hallway shifted. Clothing rustled. Boot soles scuffed across the floor. His throat went tight. What a welcome sight. They were all here, each Nightfury warrior, waiting to hear about Mac.

Their concern thrummed in the corridor, filling the narrow space like a drumbeat. The show of solidarity lent Forge strength, easing his pain. Rock-steady, his brothers-in-arms never let him down. He hadn't been with the pack long, but he was a bona fide Nightfury now. One hundred percent on board. No doubts. No questions about his loyalty. Just full-on trust. Joining Bastian and the lads had been the best decision he'd ever made.

Rolling his shoulders, Forge met each warrior's gaze in turn, gratitude in his own, and . . . frowned. What the hell? He'd given Bastian explicit instructions—keep Hope in sight and stop her from snooping. The lass wasn't stupid. He stifled a snort. Shite. The female was the complete opposite—smart, canny, far too curious for his peace of mind.

Bastian might not know it yet, but Hope represented a threat.

One he could read from a mile away.

He held a unique talent among Dragonkind—the ability to read intention. Forget the way a person talked. Disregard the emotion disguising the truth. Intent drove action. And Hope's? Forge huffed. Christ. Hers was anything but pure. He sensed her mind, knew her questions and the suspicion that gripped her while in the living room. She recognized a mystery when she encountered one. Now, thanks to a plethora of inconsistencies, Mac's strange illness, and Forge's glow show—stupid fucking eyes—she was determined to solve it. So aye. Allowing her to wander around the lair unsupervised? Not a great idea.

His temper showing, he scowled at Bastian. "Where's Hope?"

"Relax," B said, amusement in his eyes. "She's not off unearthing Dragonkind secrets."

Rikar's cheek creased. "She went with Angela and Evie."

"Ange was losing her mind." His back to the wall, arse sitting on polished concrete, Venom crossed one combat boot over the other. "Evie and Hope are keeping her busy so she doesn't freak out about Mac. They're in the clinic, filling the big tub. The second Mac's done with the MRI, the salt bath will be ready for him."

Forge nodded. Okay. Good. Mac's water dragon needs taken care of and on track. Hope nailed down. The secrets of Dragonkind safe for the moment, so . . .

Time to go on the offensive.

Dodging the collection of male bodies, Forge headed for the end of the hall.

B tipped his chin. "Where are you going?"

"Archives."

He needed to take another look. Mayhap he'd missed something the first time around. If he got lucky, he'd find the information required to save Mac's life. He hadn't paid close enough attention to the most ancient tomes. The answer might yet lie buried in an obscure passage. On a single page of text. In one of the gilded pictures drawn by the elders of Dragonkind.

"Good idea," Rikar said, the determination in his tone mirroring his own.

"I'm going with you." Bastian pushed from his lean against the wall. "The wait is killing me. I need something to do."

"All hands on deck." Unwrapping a lollipop, Venom cracked the candy with his teeth. The crunch echoed in the hallway. Tossing away the empty bitten-to-shite stick, he pulled another sucker out of his pocket and shoved it in his mouth.

Haider rolled to his feet. "The more eyes the better."

"Let's go." Gage popped off the floor. With a quick shift, he grabbed Nian by the scruff of the neck. "That means you, namby-pamby."

"Hands off, asshole." Nian rotated his shoulder, brought his arm around, and broke the hold. Planting a hand in the center of Gage's chest, he shoved him backward.

Feet sliding on smooth concrete, Gage bared his teeth. He raised twin fists.

Rikar stepped between them. "Ease off, boys. Move your asses."

One eye on the potential scuffle, Bastian glanced toward a recessed alcove. "Sloan, you coming?"

"Not yet. I'll wait here in case Myst needs me." Sitting cross-legged, gaze on the tablet he held, Sloan flicked his fingertip, scrolling down. Text whirled across the small screen. The visual onslaught made Forge blink. Sloan didn't bat an eye, making him worry about the lad's retinas. He might not know Sloan well, but the male needed to lay off the electronics. Get out of the lair more. Enjoy the night sky and some female company—instead of the Internet—every once in a while. Looking up from the screen, Sloan met his gaze. "But I'll keep digging online. Some packs have set up chat rooms on the dark net. I ask the right question of the right male, and I might get lucky."

"Let us know," B said.

Sloan uh-huhed.

Wick left without a word, walking toward the vault and the library.

Forge's heart beat a little faster. God, he loved his new pack. Each warrior considered Mac his brother, and Nightfuries never abandoned one another. No one ever got left behind. And as Forge turned into the main corridor of the underground lair, leading the males who protected his back, he prayed the library held the answer. Otherwise he'd be forced to do what he'd sworn he never would—call home. Revisit his past and reach out to his former pack—cousins left behind years ago—with the hope the Scottish archives contained the information Mac needed to survive.

Call home.

Shite. The idea presented a problem. A major one. A potentially life-threatening one, given he suspected a male inside the Scottish pack of helping to murder his family, and his cousins thought he was dead.

~

Seated in the underground library, the scent of old parchment in the air, Forge set a heavy tome aside and picked up another. A quick glance made him clench his teeth—another volume full of everything but what he wanted to know. He opened it anyway. Musty paper rustled. Tiny dust motes drifted up, glinting in the low light as he scanned the first paragraph and moved on to the next. His fingers kept flipping. Page after page. Chapter after chapter. Hour after bloody hour and . . . nada. Zilch. A big fat zero on the information front. Nary a clue to Mac's condition.

Or any mention of water dragons on the seldom-read pages.

Lifting his hands from the treatise, he set his elbows on the stainless steel table. Piles of books lay strewn across its long, sturdy surface. Thick tomes. Thin volumes. Some leather-bound, others covered by vibrant linen overlay. Blue. Green. Red, beige, and gold. Every color of the book rainbow present and accounted for. An intellectual feast spread out in front of him, a taunt of the worst kind.

Fingers laced, palms pressed together, Forge stared at his knuckles. Weariness rose, eroding his will to continue searching, allowing hopelessness to float to the surface. Slumping forward, he put his head down. His forehead touched the back of his forearm. The move shoved his chair backward. Wooden feet scraped across polished concrete as he exhaled in disgust and closed his eyes. The buzz of dimmed lights hummed overhead, swirling in the relative quiet.

God, he was tired. So fucking tired of hunting for information that didn't exist.

Or at least, he couldn't find.

"Forge."

Raising his head, he sat back in his chair. "Aye?"

"Time to call it a day."

"Nay, B. Not yet." Grit scraped the inside of his eyelids as he opened his eyes. Seeing nothing but blur, he blinked a couple of times. Bastian snapped into focus. Tired green eyes met his a second before his commander placed a thick volume back on its shelf. Ignoring the order to quit, Forge nudged his chair closer to the desk. "I've got a couple more hours in me."

Framed by tall bookcases, B shook his head. "It's past mid-day, brother. You're fried. You need to sleep. We all do."

We. The word stuck in his throat.

The warriors had done better than average, pulling a third of the books off the shelves, riffling through old documents in the archives before calling it quits. The bonded males—Rikar, Wick, and Venom—had left first in search of their mates. Not far behind, Gage, Haider, and Nian packed up, promising to renew the hunt after getting some much-needed shut-eye. A wise choice. Exhaustion wasn't good for a male. Forge knew it, but couldn't make himself leave. He wanted to stay, just a little bit longer. Mac needed him. He needed to help, so . . .

"One more tome, B, and I'll shut it down for the day."

A muscle jumped along Bastian's jaw. "If you think I'm leaving you alone here, think again."

"But Mac—"

Sloan snapped a book closed. "Is alive."

Forge glanced to his right, meeting Sloan's gaze. "Has he woken?"

"No, but his vitals are strong. Tania is keeping him stable," Sloan said, using medical jargon he'd learned somewhere in Texas, under the watchful eye of a human doctor.

How he'd managed to get a college degree in the human world Forge didn't know. Sloan never talked about his time down south. Not that Forge blamed him. Rumor had it, he lost a female along with his newborn son during his time in the Lone Star State. No one knew much, or anything for sure, but after experiencing the joy Mayhem brought to his life, Forge understood the male's grief. So nay, he wouldn't be asking anytime soon. Bringing it up—poking at Sloan's wound to assuage his curiosity—didn't seem like something a smart male would do and hope to keep his head on his shoulders.

Setting a thick hardback on top of the pile beside him, Sloan rolled off the floor and onto his feet. With a grunt of discomfort, he stretched out the kinks and crossed to the door. "She's feeding him the energy he needs."

"For how long?" Concern tightened his chest. Forge breathed through the lockdown, holding panic at bay. "She can't feed him indefinitely. The longer Mac's unconscious—the more he takes—the closer she'll come tae energy deprivation. She won't last, Sloan."

"Mac and Tania are mated, Forge. The marriage ceremony is done. Their life forces are joined," Bastian said, regret in his eyes, real worry on his face. "If he dies, she dies. No way around it. The best we can do now is let her feed him and keep hunting. Pray like hell we find a cure for him—and help her—before it's too late."

Forge snarled in response.

Sloan growled a curse, seconding his unspoken opinion.

"I know." Bastian flexed his hands, his whitened knuckles standing out in stark relief against his skin. "It's fucking frustrating, but we'll screw up . . . miss something important . . . if we're too exhausted to see it. So, get a few hours of sleep. We'll come back after the evening meal and look through the remaining tomes with fresh eyes."

The practical approach made Forge feel sick. How could he leave, give up the hunt without finding a single clue, when Mac lay unconscious in a recovery room? While Tania's life hung in the balance? He couldn't lose another female. Couldn't bear the idea of Tania joining Caroline. Of her entombed in a casket and being lowered into the cold, dark—

"Forge," Bastian said, a warning in his voice.

"Bloody hell. All right." With a quick shift, he stood. The chair slammed into the table behind him. The wooden seat back clanged against stainless steel a second before it tipped sideways and hit the concrete floor. Throwing his commander a dirty look, Forge left his seat where it lay and, walking past half-empty bookcases, moved toward the door. "I need tae see my son anyway. Is he with Myst?"

Hot on his heels, B rolled in behind him. "I tucked my mate into bed hours ago. She needs her rest."

Another thing that made perfect sense.

A pregnant female required three things—tons of time with her male, good food, and plenty of sleep. Bastian ensured Myst got all three. Stretching out sore muscles, Forge shook his head. The two were fun to watch. Myst kept her mate on his toes. She enjoyed pushing B's buttons . . . and his boundaries. His commander, though, never wavered—no matter how often Myst insisted she needed M&M'S to survive. Not that Bastian cared about the amount of chocolate she ate. Or didn't know Daimler played a role in her sugar addiction, supplying enough sweets to keep her happy. The skirmish had nothing to do with her health, and everything to do with the enjoyment a male took in teasing his mate.

Forge stifled a snort and rounded the last corner. Stairs led up toward a single door. He took the treads three at a time and, unleashing his magic, punched in the security code with his mind. The electronic lock disengaged. The door into the main corridor of the underground lair swung wide. He stepped over the threshold, turned right, and walked toward the elevators. Daimler, the sneaky bastard played along. The Numbai was hard-core, pretending to deny Myst whenever Bastian stood in earshot. The secret chocolate stash he hid in the pantry, however—for what he called "emergencies"—told the real tale, keeping Myst and the other hellions well stocked no matter the circumstances.

Five females strong. A force to be reckoned with.

A concept Daimler grasped with ease.

Amusing most days. Dangerous sometimes too, 'cause . . . aye. The second Myst discovered her mate's game, Bastian would be in trouble, and all hell would break loose in the lair. And speaking of which . . .

He glanced over his shoulder. "Myst isnae with my lad?"

Bastian shook his head. "Hope offered to put G. M. to bed . . . and stay with him."

Forge's brows collided. Shite. "Stay with him." Translation: in close proximity, within easy reach, nothing but a sliding door between Hope and his bedroom. The realization shoved good sense out of the way. His mind blanked. Lust-fueled fantasies sped into the void, offering a slew of terrible suggestions. Bearing down, Forge fought to bring his brain back online. No such luck. His imagination remained mired in a savage place full of mental pictures—Hope on his bed, her body bared, her red-gold hair a tousled mess, her lips swollen from—

Christ help him. He was in so much bloody trouble.

Mouth gone dry, Forge swallowed. "I am so fucked."

Bastian laughed. "Go with it, brother. Why fight it? You want her—take her."

So simple. Beyond dangerous.

Forge knew himself well. Naught but trouble lay in that direction. After learning about her brother, he recognized her vulnerability. Just as he had with Caroline. Aye, she was different, stronger willed than the female who'd borne his son, but that didn't mean he couldn't hurt her . . . and send them both spinning into disaster. So aye. Like it or nay, sleeping with Hope—pleasing her, loving her—would be wrong. So bloody *wrong*. Instinct joined his conscience, sending a clear message. He needed to leave her alone. She'd told him no. He ought to respect her wishes. Forget about seduction, abandon the field, and retreat to safer ground.

Excellent notion.

Honorable intentions.

Slight problem with the plan.

He wanted Hope with a desperation that shook his resolve. She made him feel things he didn't understand and couldn't begin to control. It was odd and aye, even a wee bit scary. He shouldn't be feeling anything for her. His reaction wasn't safe or prudent. But as desire rumbled through him, his dragon half fixated on her. Awareness prickled through him. Need boiled beneath his skin. Hunger rose like a tidal wave as he glanced toward the ceiling. She was up there, just seven floors above him, naught but a short ride away.

Rolling his shoulders, Forge slowed his pace. He stopped in front of the elevator that would carry him to the aboveground lair—closer to the female on his mind. With a murmur, he issued a mental command. Heat rushed along his spine. Gears ground into motion, bringing the cage to his level.

A ping echoed inside the diamond-shaped vestibule.

Double doors slid open.

Forge remained rooted to the floor. Getting onboard was a bad idea. He should turn around and walk away. Head deeper into the underground lair until the rest of the Nightfuries got up for the evening. Use his brothers-in-arms as a buffer. Do the right thing and spare Hope the furious nature of his need. He stared at his reflection in the mirrored wall inside the elevator. A second of hesitation and . . .

He stepped inside.

Well, hell. So much for restraint. Uncage the beast and get out of his way. Lust ruled him now, shoving him toward the need to know what touching Hope would feel like. She was a powerful pull, and as the elevator ascended, Forge acknowledged his weakness along with his downfall. He needed her. Longed to experience Hope in all her glory. Be fed by her energy. Be held in her arms and surrounded by her warmth. Nothing less than full surrender would satisfy him. So . . . soft and sweet or a hard, fast loving? One hundred percent her choice. Forge didn't care how it happened, just as long as she said yes and he mastered her in the end.

Chapter Twelve

Holding G. M. in her arms, Hope waltzed across the nursery. Thick area rug underfoot, the scent of baby powder in the air, she hummed Vivaldi, moving to the concerto of violins playing inside her head. She counted out the beat, twirling between each step. An easy three count: one, two, three—pivot, slide, spin into a gentle turn. One, two, three—sway with the baby cradled against her, keeping him happy and herself content.

Pulled free of a ponytail, her hair swung loose. The soft strands brushed across her shoulders as she sidestepped the end of G. M.'s crib. The Winnie-the-Pooh mobile bobbed. Eeyore nodded at her. Ignoring the encouragement, Hope danced by the toy box full of stuffed animals, skirted the changing table, then whirled around the rocking chair.

Sucking on his thumb, G. M. sighed in contentment.

Joy bubbled up, settling into her bones, invading her heart. God, what a pleasure. It had been ages. Way too long since she'd held a baby.

Her gaze on her temporary charge, Hope watched his eyelids grow heavy. He was so cute. Such a beautiful little boy with violet eyes and a dark head of hair. Cuddling him closer, she nuzzled his cheek and hummed more of her song. He blinked, a slow up and down, then gave in and closed his eyes. She slowed her pace. His eyes popped back open. He frowned at her. Hope smiled back and kept dancing. Almost there. It wouldn't be long now. One more circuit. Another turn or two around the room, and she'd have him right where she wanted him—fast asleep in her arms.

Stubborn little guy.

Hope shook her head. Such a difficult customer. She'd been at it for an hour, but he was all cried out now, so tired he struggled to keep his eyes open.

He squirmed, whimpering, still fighting sleep.

"I know, handsome boy," she whispered, rocking him in her arms. Hope understood his upset. She felt the same way, couldn't shake the memory of Mac lying unconscious on the floor. Or the sense that something terrible was about to happen.

The tension in the house backed up her theory.

Not great for her. Even worse for G. M.

Babies were sensitive, often reacting to the emotional state of those around them. The upheaval wasn't good for him, and Black Diamond had been unsettled for hours. All the guys jacked-up. All the women in the house worried. Nowhere near the kind of vibe G. M. needed right now.

Humming more of her song, she patted his bum and added a jostle to the dance. "Shh, it's all right. Close your eyes and go to sleep. It's all right now."

He seemed to take her word for it.

The instant he relaxed and slid into sleep, her own fatigue rose, making her aware of the aches and pains from the hour spent soothing him. Hope rolled one shoulder, then the other. Sore muscles protested. The twinge nipped along her spine, then spread to her arms. She stifled a groan. Man, she really needed to work on that—do more bicep curls, work in an extra set of push-ups . . . hold a baby more often. Her mouth curved. A little angel in her arms every day.

Wonderful plan. The idea ranked high, right up there with making time for an afternoon nap.

Stifling a yawn, Hope glanced at the clock hanging by the door.

Nearly one in the afternoon.

She looked down at G. M. Still sucking on his thumb. A furrow between his brows. Not in a deep sleep yet. He needed a few more minutes. A little more cuddling. A gentle jostling rhythm. Just enough to ensure he didn't wake when she laid him down.

Bypassing the crib, Hope headed for the rocking chair. A smooth about-face, and she sank onto the padded seat. Grabbing a throw pillow off the floor, she shoved it between her elbow and the armrest. Her biceps relaxed. She sighed in relief as the cushion helped support his weight, allowing her to adjust her hold, settling him at a more comfortable angle in the crook of her arm. Pressing her toes into the rug, she pushed off. The chair rocked. Back and forth. To and fro. Over and over. Again and again.

Minutes passed. The sway rolled into a soothing rhythm.

G. M. snuffled in his sleep.

Exhaling long and slow, she leaned into the chair back. The cushions cupped her nape, supporting her head, letting her float. Another minute, maybe two, and she'd go. She couldn't sit much longer and stay awake. G. M. was almost ready. Her room wasn't far, just a few doors down the hall. Hardly any . . .

Her eyes drifted closed.

"Hope?"

The voice came from far away, through a tunnel of thick fog. A few things registered. Deep voice. Scottish accent. Delicious, woodsy scent. "Forge?"

"Aye, lass."

Hope tried to open her eyes. A no-go. Her eyelids refused to cooperate. Some idiot had glued her eyelashes together. "What—where?"

"Shh, now. Donnae move," he murmured from somewhere close by. Above her? Beside her? Hope frowned. She couldn't tell. It felt as though Forge was inside her head, each word a faint echo, soothing her back to sleep. Something brushed over her temple. The gentle stroke moved across her cheek, then turned to tuck her hair behind her ear. "Stay just as you are, *jalâyla*. You've naught tae worry about. I've got him."

Him? Him-who?

Half-aware, so tired she couldn't open her eyes, Hope let the question go and drifted back toward slumber. A warm weight lifted from her arms. Muted footfalls moved away. A rustling sound. A masculine murmur. More footsteps. A big hand cupped her shoulder, another slid behind her knees. The feeling of weightlessness as her body left the comfort of chair cushions.

Hope jerked.

"Easy." Strong arms tightened around her. "Curl into me, Hope. Put your arms around my neck. Let me care for you."

She hummed. Oh, how nice. A rare gift—someone who wanted to care for her. A man who enjoyed being in charge.

Unable to resist, Hope turned into his embrace and snuggled closer.

He rumbled in her ear, the sound full of approval. "There's a good lass."

"I'm so tired."

"I know. Poor me," he said, but despite his words, he didn't sound disappointed. He seemed amused instead. "'Tis a crying shame."

"Why?"

"I had plans for you this eve."

Oh well. Guess that explained it. Nestling her face against his throat, she sighed. "Sorry."

"I'm not," he said, laying her down on something soft.

A mattress? Cotton sheets? Hope murmured in pleasure. Sure felt like it, but honestly, who cared? Forge had set her down somewhere comfortable. Somewhere safe. No need to investigate further.

Turning onto her side, Hope snuggled into the pillow.

"That's right, *jalâyla*—sleep. There'll be time and plenty for what I need later."

His words rang an unfamiliar bell. As it tolled inside her head, her eyes opened. She frowned. Nothing but blur. She closed both again.

What he needed. Later.

Right. Okay, good. Whatever he said and—

The mattress dipped.

A warm weight settled behind her. Forge's muscled arm arrived next, crossing over her belly, drawing her into the curve of his body. Her back pressed to his chest—spooning, her favorite position, the perfect one to indulge in while sleeping with a man. Cuddling with her, he rubbed his face against her hair. Hope grumbled, but let it happen, enjoying his heat and strength while telling herself she shouldn't. Wanting Forge was foolish. Letting him get too close was a mistake. She knew it. Felt it. Was aware of the danger on a visceral level but . . .

To hell with it. Tomorrow would be soon enough to figure it out.

She would set him straight *tomorrow*. Put her foot down. Take him to task. Outline their relationship in clear terms and get back on track, 'cause . . . yeah. Being held by him felt too much like heaven, and his *later* sounded too much like a promise.

Awareness arrived like sunlight through heavy storm clouds. In chaotic bursts and rapid-fire flickers. Thin light bled through darkness only to fade away, into a black sea of nothingness. Another bladed burst. More searing prickles. Hope flinched as the flash struck, sharp, insistent, lightning bolt bright, dragging her out of shadows.

It didn't hurt. Not really. The rush was more jarring than painful, and yet . . .

She frowned. It was odd. Unnatural. Beyond the realm of reality. She recognized the place. She hovered on the edge of sleep, warm and foggy, in the layer where slumber transformed into dream. Vivid imagery swirled over the screen inside her head, painting her mental landscape, making her senses swim and her mind sharpen. She hung on the horizon, gliding, flying, soaring through frigid night air, beneath a dark blanket of pinpoint stars. Satisfaction trickled down her spine. Contentment burned through her veins. Hope hummed and, spreading her wings wide, pitched into a slow roll.

The temperature dropped.

The wind picked up.

Frost slid over her scales, holding her like a lover.

An updraft lifted her into the cascading spiral and . . . God. So good—it felt so damned good, exhilaration edged by ecstasy. Shift, flip, angle into the next turn. Avoid that mountain peak. Dip into a descending valley. Not a care in world, save one: she wanted it to go on forever, to stay in the moment and cling to the blood rush.

The wrong decision.

Nothing but bad mojo wrapped in the promise of future problems.

Hope knew it, but didn't care. The weightlessness wooed her. The rush sped through her veins. And the dream?—soul-searing perfection. Reality need not intrude. Not here, and never now. None of it seemed important. Not the soft press of a mattress beneath her shoulder and hip. Not the big body curled around her, warming her back, keeping her safe as she soared in the dreamscape. Nothing but the open sky mattered. She was safe. He—whoever the hell *he* was—would see to it. No reason to be alarmed. No direct action required. Nothing left to do but spread her wings and fly.

"Jalâyla."

Roughened by sleep, the voice pierced through the mental fog. The strong body surrounding her shifted, pulling her closer. Warm breath caressed the side of her neck.

The prickle of sensation derailed her for a moment. Hope shifted focus. Weird, but . . . she knew he was there, flying alongside her, invading her mind until her emotions melded with his. Now she registered what he thought, how he felt, what he expected. She hummed. Oh baby—Forge. It couldn't be anyone else. She recognized his scent, the sound of his voice, his pleasure as her scales rattled in the blackening night sky. Hope frowned. Knowing he flew with her felt odd. Strangely right, yet somehow wrong. Her mind split, maintaining both realities—staying with the dream while she soaked up his heat. The twin mental tracks highlighted the duality: he was outside her body, but inside her mind.

The idea should've scared her. Made her stir. Forced her to move. Prompted her to wake and roll away from him. But as the velocity increased, reality fractured, dropping her into the rush, propelling her toward the need to go farther and fly faster.

"Go," she whispered, making room for Forge inside her head. Accepting his reality as her own, she snuggled into his embrace. "Let's fly."

Forge growled in agreement. His arm tightened around her.

Hope bared her fangs and, sharp tail whipping through frosty air, rocketed past a steep outcropping. Shale tumbled down the stone face, rumbling as her wing tips brushed the sky. Her sonar pinged. Tingles flowed over the horns on her head. The spikes ridging her spine rattled, unearthing delight as she checked her position. Longitude and latitude? Right on target. Speed? Batshit crazy. The tumble of winter air currents over the jagged rise of soaring cliffs? Breathtaking.

The perfect night to fly above Cairngorm.

The location registered on a sensory level. Scotland, north-northwest of Aberdeen. Hope didn't question how she knew that. Tapped into Forge, information arrived on demand, informing her, calming her, making the experience feel right. Turning her head, Hope studied a rocky ledge as she flew by. She glanced up, taking in ice-capped peaks. The mountain looked like many others, jagged, craggy, inhospitable. Somehow, though, she knew exactly where she was—the Highlands, home of fierce clans and bitter, age-old feuds.

Delight fizzed through her. She'd always wanted to visit Scotland, take in the history, walk the land, talk to the locals . . . buy a tartan. Maybe some tasseled argyle socks too. The thought made her snort. Ridiculous. Completely stupid given she could order a pair online anytime she—

A prickle swept her temples.

The wind shifted. She scanned the sky.

No one on the horizon.

Not a soul behind her either.

She checked her position again. All good. Nothing to get worked up about, but . . . her eyes narrowed. Instinct set off her internal alarm. Her heart picked up a beat, thumping hard, pumping adrenaline through her veins. Something wasn't right. The feeling of being followed grew stronger by the second. She couldn't stay here. It wasn't safe. Something nasty shadowed her and . . .

Hope snarled. Time to break out some evasive maneuvers.

Dropping into a free fall, she banked hard, ducking around a cliff face. A spark flared in her pupils, blinding her before a switch flipped inside her head. Perception expanded. Her focus narrowed. Black became red as her vision shifted from normal to infrared, allowing her to see in the dark.

The sky flexed.

Her sonar pinged.

Shadows burst onto her radar.

Braced for impact, Hope rotated into a flip as two dragons rocketed from behind a jagged outcropping. Hope sucked in a breath. *Dragons. More dragons,* like her in the dream. Except, not quite. Her muscles tightened. She flexed her talons, feeling the interlocking weave of rigid dragon skin.

Purple . . . her scales were deep purple with metallic blue flecks. Zeroing in on the approaching threat, she stared at the lead dragon. Dark green with yellow-tipped scales. Her gaze jumped to the second beast. Yellow scales muted by purple speckles. She frowned at the pair. Spiked tails. Horned heads. Webbed wings silvered by moonlight. She braced as the duo flew in to surround her. One on her left, the other on her right. She held still, maintained a steady glide, and waited while questions circled. What did they want? What did their appearance mean?

Hope glanced at the yellow dragon from the corner of her eye.

Raising a brow, he thumped her with the side of his spiked tail.

Pain nipped along her rib cage.

She scowled at him.

"Bloody hell," she said, all snarl, zero patience. Hope blinked. What the hell? She didn't sound like herself at all. She sounded Scottish and . . . male. *"Get the fuck away from me, Conn."*

Fangs flashing in the gloom, Conn grinned. *"Where's the fun in that?"*

"Hit me one more time and . . ." She raised a paw and clicked her razor-sharp claws together. *"You'll find out."*

"Och, now." Amusement in his eyes, Conn glanced at the green dragon flying off her left wing tip. *"Watch out, Droztan, little brother's in a bad mood."*

Droztan chuckled and bumped her from the other side.

She hissed in warning.

The idiots laughed, swung into a tight turn and—

"Lads." Like a wraith in the dark, a black dragon with white-tipped scales rose in the gloom. Ahead of the pack, the male glanced over his shoulder and, eyes narrowed, gave Conn and Droztan stern looks. *"Behave yerselves. We've much tae do tonight and teasing Forge is not one of them."*

"Aw, come on, Da," Conn said.

"No bloody fun," Droztan murmured, tone disgruntled.

The group banked, movements synchronized, heading for open moors.

Hope followed, her body obeying the shift, but . . .

Her mind refused to discount the information.

She stalled inside the dream. The older dragon had called Forge by name. Reality intruded for a moment. Confusion circled a second before understanding dawned. Hope took another look at the pack flying for distant fields. Different-colored scales, but . . . yeah. No doubt about it. The resemblance was striking. All big. All dangerous. Definitely related. Forge's family, his brothers and father . . . inside her dream. How bizarre was that? Very. Beyond perplexing, but even as she turned to examine her discovery the dream pulled her back in, blocking the revelation, running her up against a dead end.

She flexed her hands, trying to push past the barricade. A no-go. Instead of answers, more questions arose as her fingers morphed into talons tipped by black claws. She stared at the razor-sharp tips, then at her wings, fighting the mental blockage. The dreamscape dipped. The pack banked around a towering cliff face, derailing her brain, upending her search, caging her inside the dream.

Hope glanced ahead. Open moors lined by tangled trees tumbled across a frost-laden terrain. Snowflakes swirled on an updraft. The frosty dance pulled her deeper, blanketing her in slumber, making her snuggle into Forge. He murmured in his sleep. Turning to face him, she wrapped herself around him, pressing her face into the curve of his throat. Tingles swept over her skin. The invigorating rush held her high, pulled her close, strengthening the tether connecting her to him. Puzzle pieces snapped together, making her one with him.

The blur of a craggy landscape whirled past as she descended through wispy clouds. The ground approached. Cold mountain air warmed. Slowing her wing speed, Hope exhaled hard. Sparks swirled from her nostrils, melting the frost coating her scales. As ice chips fell in her wake, Hope leveled out above the widening terrain.

"All right, here's as good a place as any." Rotating into a flip, Conn pointed to a plateau overlooking a farmer's field. Wind swept across the plain, making tall grass sway like seaweed in water. *"Time tae put you tae the test, little brother."*

"Let's see what you've learned," Droztan said, an unholy gleam in his eyes. *"Only one rule."*

Hope raised a scaly brow. *"What's that?"*

"No hiding behind Da."

She snorted in disgust. *"The only one in need of hiding is you."*

"Cocky, aren't you?" Conn smiled, baring huge fangs. *"No mercy, then. Prepare tae have your arse kicked, you wee whelp."*

Hope wanted to scoff at the insult. *Wee,* her arse.

Curling her lip, she showed fang, banked right, and headed for higher ground. So be it. Let the games—and dragon combat training—begin. She was ready. She'd been studying—practicing—waiting for a chance to prove her worth. So, screw it, bring on the bravado. All the nasty tactics and fancy flying too. Let them try to ground her. To push her into making a mistake and—

A strange vibration buzzed between her temples.

"Shite." Spiked tail whipping overhead, Conn spun around, flying in behind her. *"Droztan—do you feel that?"*

"Aye. 'Tisn't friendly."

"Break it down."

"Not sure. Outlaws, mayhap. Could be Wanderers." Dark eyes shimmering, Droztan scanned the horizon. *"From across the North Sea."*

"Denmark?" she asked, without knowing why. For some reason, though, the location made sense. Something sinister grew by the day in Denmark. Knowledge of it seemed solid, even though she couldn't name the source. *"Or farther inland?"*

"No way tae know," Conn said. *"Bloody Archguard is always a threat."*

Flipping up and over, Droztan closed ranks, settling into a protective position above her. He tucked his head under, his gaze no longer teasing. *"Make for the cliffs, little brother."*

Rebelling at the order, Hope held the line, refusing to back down. Deep-seated need took root inside her. She didn't want to go. She needed to stay, to help, to protect her family and be a part of whatever unfolded. Holding Droztan's gaze, she stayed on course, keeping pace with the pair.

Conn snarled a warning.

"Lads—incoming. Right flank." The guttural growl rolled in on a gust of wind. *"Forge, listen tae your brother. Take cover. Hide among the rocks, son."*

Hope shook her head. *"But Da—"*

"Nay, laddie. You're still in training, not yet ready tae fight," her father said, taking lead position in the fighting triangle. *"Now, go. We'll come for you after—"*

Fireballs exploded across the sky.

Her brothers cursed.

Hope dodged, torquing into a spine-bending spiral. A blaze of poison gas rocketed past. The tail end of the inferno grazed her side. Heat blazed across her scales. The spikes along her spine clanked as pain lashed her, driving spikes through her rib cage. Shite . . . acid. The enemy had just jammed her up, hitting her with enough neurotoxin to down multiple dragons. Gritting her teeth, Hope ignored the poison eating her scales and banked into a tight turn. She needed to get into position and help the others.

As she swung around, Droztan snarled. *"Run, Forge. There are too many. Get the fuck out!"*

The words registered.

Hope hung in mid-air, torn, hesitating, wanting to listen, not wanting to leave. But it was too late. She was here, in the middle of the moors, no time to fly back, little choice but to move forward. Music to her ears. Strength in numbers. Solidarity in spirit. Her brothers needed her and—

Enemy dragons uncloaked and . . . oh shit. A platoon, every color of the rainbow, flying hard, moving in fast to surround them. Hope twisted into a side-winding flip. She needed to circle around, get behind her brothers, and cut the enemy off in order to protect their flank. A massive dragon materialized out of thin air. Orange with brown-tipped scales, the male hung in mid-air directly in front of her. She calculated the distance. One hundred yards, give or take a yard or two.

Good for her.

Very bad for the bastard eyeing her brothers as the enemy pack closed ranks.

Gaze fixed on the orange dragon, she spread her wings and slammed on the brakes. Her muscles stretched as the webbing caught air. Her flight slowed. The male hadn't seen her yet. And given her position? Keeping him in the dark until it was too late made for a good plan.

Narrowing her focus, Hope slipped in behind him. She flexed her talons. Timing was everything. Quick and quiet. Move fast. Hit hard. Show no mercy. All precepts of an effective blitz attack.

She lined him up.

She leveled out.

She raised her razor-sharp claws.

The bastard spun to face her. Glowing black eyes met hers. He bared his fangs. She attacked, rocketing into his orbit. Tucking his wings, the warrior somersaulted. Orange scales flashed. Her claws caught air. Shit. She'd missed. Fucked up her chance. Lost the element of surprise. Now, it was anyone's game. The big male swung around. Hope dodged. He struck, nailing her with his spiked tail. Her head whiplashed. She lost sight of the horizon and tried to adjust: bank fast, regain her equilibrium, avoid—

Sharp talons dug into her side. Jagged teeth tore into her back. Anguish clawed through her. Flailing, she lashed out, desperate to break his hold. The bastard bore down. Her scales cracked. Bone snapped. The brutal sound echoed as a fireball lit up the sky. The stars blurred. The warrior tearing her apart snarled. He hit her again. And again. Another strike. A second set of sharp claws raked her side. Blood rolled down her belly. The male dug in, shredding her muscles, burning her flesh.

More pressure. Too much pain.

Hope roared in agony. Droztan shouted Forge's name. But it was too late. She was already gone, a scream locked in her throat, the world going dark as the bastard let go, and she plummeted out of the sky.

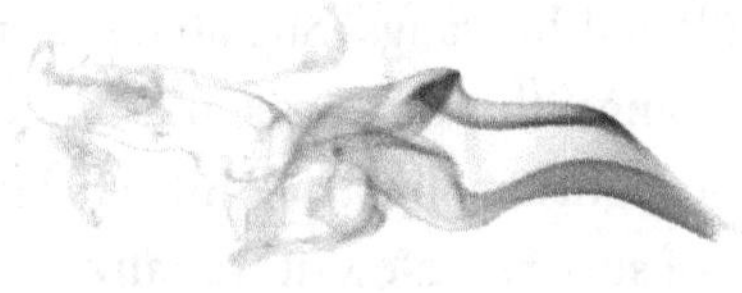

Chapter Thirteen

The dream tightened its hold, driving Forge into thick fog. Swiping at the ashy swirl, he struggled to find his way through the smoke: to level his wings, to feel the rush of air and bring the landscape into focus, but . . .

He growled through clenched teeth.

Zero visibility. Nothing but gloom and shadows.

Pushing forward, Forge narrowed his view and tried again. His vision wavered. Light flickered behind the fog and—goddamn it. He couldn't see a bloody thing. Indistinct images flashed in his mind's eye, then faded, lost forever in the mounting chaos.

He knew it was coming. Had cataloged every detail of the memory/dream each time it invaded his sleep . . . though it never picked up in the same place. Sometimes it started inside the mountain lair, with him sitting in the kitchen eating his mother's shortbread cookies. Other times, the dream began as he leapt from the cliffs. Or like now, as he approached the moors, wings spread wide, winter wind in full bluster.

He felt the rise and fall—the prickle across his scales, the ping of his sonar, the call to arms—as his heart raced and the enemy approached. Different sleep cycle, same frustration. Each time he reached Conn and Droztan, and the banter began, his mental screen went blank, as though someone had turned off a TV. Hit the abort button. Made everything go black. Leaving him flailing, without any idea which way to fly. Or how to protect his brothers.

Fucking hell. He despised the blindness, the utter darkness inside the dream. Oh, he heard the words well enough. Knew he talked and his brothers answered, but his mind refused to provide a visual. Just when he thought he might get something new, recall escaped down a black hole, holding the truth out of reach. Goddamn the blankness. He needed to remember the attack. Tunnel deep enough and unearth the memory of what happened the night his family died. Maybe then he would understand. Maybe then the pain would stop. Maybe then peace would find him and stay awhile.

But as the ash continued to swirl, desolation battered his defenses. No matter how hard he fought, he couldn't clear the mind-fog. Couldn't shift inside the dream or find a better view.

Why he kept trying, Forge didn't know. Force of habit maybe. Pure stubbornness more than likely, but . . . shite. It was useless. Impossible. The important details beyond his ability to grasp. Bile churned in his stomach. His throat went tight. Forge swallowed past the awful burn. It never got any easier and . . . Bastian would be disappointed.

Again.

Like always.

Still more asleep than awake, Forge hugged his pillow tighter. The downy feather-filled body squirmed, tweaking his senses before the dream dragged him back under. He inhaled, letting his lungs fill to bursting before exhaling again. In. Out. Breathe, hold, release. The extra oxygen centered him. He fine-tuned his focus. One more time. Another try. A harder push, just a minute or two, then he'd give up. Admit defeat. Accept failure. Let the day wake him fully and—

The pillow twitched again.

Forge frowned in his sleep as confusion set in. What the hell was that? Something new? A detail not yet unearthed, surfacing inside the dream? Could be, but . . . huh. Odd. He could swear someone lay beside him, pressed up against his chest. Long hair brushing his face. The softest skin imaginable. The quiet rush of a feminine sigh. Which was, well . . . wrong. Females never showed up in his dreams. Chaos, murder, and pain arrived instead, torturing him with glimpses of his past. Still, despite the idea he must be mistaken, he couldn't shake the sensation. He focused harder. She inhaled, then exhaled. Her chest rose and fell, keeping time with his.

Forge drew her closer.

Hmm, nice. A dream girl to keep him company, one who felt lust-revving real.

Arms wrapped around her, he shifted his hips. A curvy body wiggled against him. His body reacted, hardening so fast Forge tightened his hold. *Mine, all mine.* The words whispered through his mind. Hmm, aye . . . *his*. His to hold. His to keep. His to fuck anytime he wanted. The thought set him in motion. His hand ghosted up her rib cage. The T-shirt she wore bunched against his forearm, rising as he explored. Soft skin slid beneath his fingertips. He reached her breast and played, stroking the underside of her gorgeous curve before turning his hand to cup her. Bliss poured through him. Bloody hell. Just right. A perfect fit, a round, flawless handful. He brushed his thumb over the top, learning her shape, caressing her skin, sharing his heat.

She purred.

He stroked her again.

Powerful bio-energy flared as the Meridian woke, opening a channel deep inside him. Electrostatic current spilled into the void, rising like a tidal wave. His dragon half snarled. Ravenous hunger blurred his focus, making him burn and . . . *crave*. God. He was starving, so needy he couldn't think straight, never mind stall his reaction. Something, though, told him he should. Instinct, maybe. A strong sense of integrity, perhaps. The need for more information, without a doubt. An honorable male would ask himself questions—Was he still dreaming, was she real, should he be tapping into her energy stream without asking first?

Valid concerns. All good points.

But as his dream girl welcomed him, shifting closer, flooding him with sensation, Forge lost all sense of himself. Right. Wrong. Who cared which side he landed on? He was hungry, and she tasted fantastic, her essence so compelling he couldn't get enough. He needed more. All she gave him. Every last drop.

Giving in to his beast, Forge set his mouth against the side of her throat. Pleasure exploded through him, fizzing up like a bottle of shaken soda. With a moan, she raised her chin, granting him access, encouraging him to feed. Baring his teeth, he bit down gently, scraping her skin, holding her immobile against him. She shivered and linked in, strengthening the connection, zapping him with white-hot energy. He groaned and drank deeper, pulling mouthfuls from the source that fed his kind. Life-giving nourishment flooded him. His dragon half hummed in approval, enjoying the rush as magic crackled in his veins. The current whiplashed, turning full circle, forming restraints, shackling him to the female in his arms.

With a groan, he took another sip.

She turned her head, rubbing her cheek against his. Delight spun through him. Such open affection. Perfect acceptance. Had a female ever felt so right? Suited him so well? Or fit so beautifully in his arms? A resounding NO thrummed through his head, shaking his slumber. Forge sighed. What a shame. He didn't want to acknowledge the truth—or wake up yet. He wanted to stay with her longer. Forever. All day, if possible, and wallow in her presence. A lovely thought. The perfect strategy, but for one thing. His mind was coming back online, turning him toward an important fact—she couldn't be real. *The dream.* He was dreaming, letting his mind invent a fantasy female to protect him from the truth.

A good hypothesis given he always slept alone.

And yet, he refused to let her go. Just a few more minutes. Another sip of her energy. More of her intense vibe. He thumbed her nipple, waking the small bud and . . . aye. Forge sighed. More of touching her as well.

With a rumble of contentment, he buried his nose in her hair. Thick strands brushed his mouth. Her scent swirled around him. His lips curved. She smelled delicious, like the cinnamon buns Daimler baked for him each afternoon. He growled against her temple. The female jerked against him. A tremor shook her small frame. She turned her face away. Her legs jumped, bumping into his, bringing him closer to awareness. His brow furrowed. She twisted in his arms. The jagged movement jolted through him.

He flinched.

The dream fractured.

He woke in a rush, but stayed still, warrior senses seething as he absorbed his surroundings. Dry air. The hum of electricity inside walls. No threat detected. Without moving, he opened his eyes. A dark room greeted him. His night vision sparked. A wing chair came into focus, and two things registered at once. One, he lay in his bed, safe inside his room. And second—his dream girl was in his arms. Warm. Real. All woman. Surprise whipped through him. Forge tightened his embrace, surrounding her completely and . . . oh aye. Talk about perfect. Hope Cunningham, she of the gorgeous energy, here in his arms, her hair a glorious strawberry blond tangle around her head.

A startling turn of events. One that paralyzed him for a moment. Hope, in his bed. Him, wrapped around her. Holy shite. How had that happened? Last he remembered, she'd been telling him no—saying no . . . to everything.

Restless, she shifted in her sleep, legs and arms twitching.

Levering himself onto one elbow, he stared down at her. Recall tripped into motion—the nursery, his son, her exhaustion. Ah, aye. All right, then. He remembered now—how he'd carried her into his room, tucked her into bed, and lain down beside her. Satisfaction curled through him. His mouth curved. Beautiful. A lovely surprise so early in the day, except . . .

Forge blinked. Oh hell. She'd fed him. He'd taken from her.

The repercussions registered a second before the Meridian surged. The powerful cascade streamed through him. His heart kicked, reminding him where his hand rested. His fingers twitched around her breast. She arched into the pulse. The current intensified. Forge bowed his head as heated prickles slithered down his spine. He groaned and tried to stem the flow—he really did—but . . . oh Christ. Being fed by Hope shattered his resolve, setting him on fire for her. Now all he wanted was more. More of her energy. More of her nourishing heat. But mostly, more of her skin against his.

Urgency dug its claws in.

With a curse, he yanked his hand from beneath her shirt. His palm left her skin. His dragon half snarled at the loss, demanding he strip her bare. Stroke her some more. Taste her in far more intimate ways. His stomach dipped. Bad idea. Continuing to touch her would only make things worse, although . . . he drew a shaky breath . . . how much worse could it possibly get? The bond between them grew by the second, taking on a life of its own, forcing reality down his throat.

Jesus help him—energy-fuse.

He shook his head, denying the connection. It wasn't happening. It simply couldn't be, but even as he rejected the conclusion, the bond solidified. Rock solid. No way to avoid it. Not with his dragon half on board and . . . fuck. The territorial bastard inside him didn't waste a second, unleashing a torrent of possessiveness, marking Hope as his own.

Wonder shuddered through him.

Forge raised his hand, brushing the hair away from Hope's temple. She frowned. He changed tack, tracing the edge of her eyebrow with a fingertip. So warm. So soft. So crazy beautiful. His mate, the female meant for him, the one he'd longed for all his life. A powerful yearning welled inside him. Fear for her followed, dimming his pleasure.

Most males would have rejoiced. Done a happy dance. Wrapped her up and refused to let her go. Forge couldn't bring himself to celebrate.

Dread gripped him instead.

What the hell was he going to do with her? He couldn't keep her. Couldn't mate her, never mind marry her in the way of his kind. Not while the Archguard hunted him. The instant it became known he'd taken a mate, the high council would put a price on her head. Send death squads to find her. Use Hope against him, hurt her in ways Forge refused to contemplate. He'd be forced to counter with a move that would ensure her safety—lock her down, curtail her freedom, infringe on her God-given right to choose in order to keep her safe. A catch-22, the worst of all possible outcomes. A damned-if-he-did, damned-if-he-didn't kind of scenario.

He might not know Hope well yet, but he knew she wouldn't react well to lockdown. Raised in the human world, she valued her freedom. As well she should, but it left him in an awful spot. The sum of which pointed to an indisputable fact: a female of his own would translate into a huge problem. One that would place them all—him, Hope, and his brothers-in-arms—in serious jeopardy.

Energy-fuse might be important, but his pack deserved better from him. He must remain steadfast. He needed to remain focused and on task. Protecting Bastian and his new brothers (along with his son) remained paramount. What he wanted didn't matter. Which placed Hope off-limits. She wasn't his, not to touch or taste or—

"Bloody hell," he grumbled as an image of her wrapped around him took hold. He killed it quickly, leaving it dead inside his mind, like roadkill on a deserted highway. Scrubbing his hand over his face, Forge shook his head. "Keep it together, arsehole. Remember her purpose."

Aye. Exactly. *Her purpose*. He must remember her role inside Black Diamond: to help him recover lost memories, not warm his bed.

Or steal his heart.

With a sigh, Forge glanced at the digital clock sitting on his nightstand: 3:39 p.m. Time to wake Hope and face the day. He needed time . . . and a shitload of distance. Enough to get his head screwed on straight. A solid plan. A foolproof way forward. A way to fight his escalating need to have her beneath him.

With a gentle hand, Forge palmed her shoulder.

Still fast asleep, she bared her teeth on a growl.

Sliding his hand to her elbow, he jostled her. "Hope?"

"No!" Balling her hands, Hope raised her fists.

Her vehement denial burst through the quiet. Forge sucked in a breath. What the hell? She looked ready to fight, already halfway into battle. Gaze on her face, he studied her expression, trying to figure out what to do. Yell at her? Shake her? Neither option appealed as he watched her. Muscles taut, body ready, she turned her head on the pillow. Her eyes moved behind her eyelids as though searching for a threat. Air rasped from between her parted lips. She twitched, twisting away from him. Energy-fuse flared. Her distress registered, streaming through the connection and . . .

Jesus.

She was panicked. Afraid. In full flight, fighting demons in her sleep.

Hoping to calm her, Forge murmured her name. With a quick shift, she lashed out. The white points of her knuckles came toward his head. He reared. Her fist swung wide. She launched the second. He dodged the punch, but missed the backlash. Her elbow slammed into his chest. He grunted. She snarled, the lethal sound full of intent as her guard came back up. Fingers shaped like claws, she struck out, aiming for his face.

He ducked.

She screamed, the battle cry raising the hairs on his nape.

"Hope!" His voice rang out. Her fist stalled mid-punch, halting an inch from his face. Chest heaving, she quivered, rustling the sheets, breaking his heart. "Good girl. There's my lass. 'Tis all right, *jalâyla*. You're all right."

He murmured again and again, using his tone to good effect. He needed to open her mind and ease her fear. Without causing her more pain. God knew he hated being shaken from a bad dream. Somehow, being jarred awake made it worse. Instead of fading, the violent imagery stuck around, infecting his mind, infiltrating his body, making him tense for days on end. And shite, he didn't want that for her. Waking Hope too fast might frighten her more. Coaxing her from the nightmare—banishing the imaginary monsters in her mind—seemed like a better option.

Fists raised and at the ready, Hope tilted her head, following his voice.

Focus riveted to her, he got ready to dodge and, raising his arm, closed his hand over her fist. Her knuckles pressed against his palm. She hissed. Shifting sideways on the mattress, he gave her more room and rolled her onto her back. "Wake up, luv. 'Tis naught but a dream, a bad dream."

She flinched, jerking away from his hold.

He stilled. She settled. Waiting another heartbeat, he stroked her collarbone. His fingers turned north, skating over her throat. "Hope, it's Forge. You're safe. Open your—"

"Bastard!" Her head snapped to the side. "Get away!"

Arching in agony, she thrashed, kicking out with her legs. Her heel rammed into his thigh. Forge cursed as she pivoted on the sheets and . . . wham! Her knee slammed into his temple.

Ears ringing, he blocked another punch. "Good Christ."

"Move it! Get out of there. Break for cover!" Spinning on the mattress, she surged onto her knees. Eyes shut tight, buried inside the dream, she lunged toward the end of the bed. "Oh God, where's

Conn? Droztan, where are you? I can't feel him. I can't—Droztan! Conn!"

Forge froze as she yelled names he hadn't heard said aloud in fifty years. Surprise struck. His mind went blank. In the heat of battle, Hope slid across the mattress, shouting instructions to imaginary warriors. He opened his mouth, closed it again. What the hell was happening? How did she know his brothers' names? What the . . . how the . . . Jesus fucking Christ. He couldn't think. He stared at Hope instead, the shock so thick he couldn't move. He watched her flail, yelling things he'd yelled, fighting a battle he'd fought, but couldn't remember.

Oh nay. No, no . . . no. He recognized himself in the words she screamed. He'd shouted each one the night his brothers died. Goddamn energy-fuse. The bond worked in terrible ways. In sharing his energy with Hope, he'd started something he couldn't stop. The Meridian had reacted without mercy, bonding her to him, sharing too much, too fast.

Proof rested in the nightmare.

"Oh, Hope," he whispered, watching her struggle. He wanted to go to her, wrap her up tight, offer her comfort, but guilt held him in a death grip. She dreamed his dream, the one he suffered every time slumber dragged him under. "I'm so sorry, luv."

On her knees, tangled up in the sheet, Hope whimpered. Arms hugging her chest, she favored her right wrist, listing to one side as though injured. "It hurts. Oh God, it hurts. My wing's broken. I can't fly. I can't fly anymore."

Tears burned the back of his throat.

"Help. I need help. Someone please help me." Tears rolling down her cheeks, she fell backward, tumbling off the mattress.

As she hit the floor with a thud, shock released him. His muscles unlocked. Desperate to reach her, Forge lunged forward. "Hope!"

Reaching the edge, he catapulted over. Lying on her back on the braided rug, she cradled her arm to her chest. He landed on his knees beside her. The thump made her jump. Gasping, hurting, she cried out in her sleep. He called her name again. A furrow appeared between her brows. Almost awake, but not quite.

Shoving the sheet aside, he straddled her hips, leaned forward, and cupped her face. She shuddered beneath him. Thumbs brushing her cheekbones, he called on the bond he shared with her now. The Meridian rose. Energy sparked, arcing from him into her. His fingertips tingled as the stream gathered speed and . . . skin on skin. Both palms cradling her face. The rush of connection between them. Heaven. Hell. Shite, he didn't know which place described it best, but as the electrostatic current grabbed hold, Forge couldn't deny his satisfaction. He wanted to feed her—soothe her, protect her, be the male she counted on . . . for everything.

"He's dead." Her voice broke on a sob. "They're all dead."

"I know, *jalâyla*, I know. But it's okay now," he said, holding his own grief at bay to banish hers. Feeding her healing energy, he coaxed her out of slumber, asking her without words to trust him. She calmed under his influence, accepting his touch, making him feel like a male worthy of her. "Wake up now. Please open your eyes."

The firmness of his voice roused her. Her eyelashes flickered, then rose. Green eyes swimming with tears met his. Her pain bled through, becoming his. His stomach clenched, but he took it all, funneling her anguish, carrying the burden, trying to wash away the hurt. Another sob escaped her. The ragged sound tightened his chest, making his heart ache.

"They're everywhere," she whispered. "*Everywhere.* I can't get away. I can't . . . please, help me."

"I'm here—*right* here." Holding her gaze, he drew gentle circles on her temples. "I've got you. Nothing bad is going tae happen. It wasn't real. You were dreaming."

Incomprehension fogged her gaze. "Dreaming?"

"Aye, lass. Just a dream."

"It felt real—so real." A tear spilled over her lashes. He watched it roll over her temple, calling himself every name he could think of for causing her distress—for forcing her to share his pain. His fault, from start to finish. He should have walked away. Left her untouched, asleep in the rocking chair. But oh no, not him. He'd been selfish, wanting her close. Now it was too late. He couldn't retreat. Couldn't change it. He was stuck. Mired neck-deep as his dragon half insisted Hope belonged to him. *With him, always.* "It hurt. They hurt me."

"Aye, I know, but it's over now," he murmured, closing his eyes, shutting out the sight of her beneath him. She looked amazing there, just right and . . . God, he was a bastard. And in big trouble. Screwed by a good plan gone wrong. All he'd wanted was a few weeks with her—some intense bed play, loads of mutual pleasure, to hear her scream his name as he made her come. Opening his eyes, he recaptured her gaze. "You're safe."

She drew a shaky breath. "Safe."

"Aye—*safe*," he said, emphasizing the word, reassuring her. Pressing his cheek to hers, he caged her in his arms, surrounding her with his strength. "I will never allow anything bad tae happen tae you, lass. I will protect you at all costs."

Fresh tears flooded her eyes and fell. "Thank you, but—"

"No buts, lass."

"I don't understand."

"You don't need tae understand. 'Tis a fact now, plain and simple."

Plain and simple.

Forge stifled a snort. Someone needed to yell "bullshite." Nothing could be further from the truth. The situation was as complicated as hell. And yet, he couldn't bring himself to regret Hope's presence inside his home, or his heated response to her. A screwed-up reaction? Absolutely, but energy-fuse didn't lie and couldn't be ignored.

Stronger males than him had tried and failed. So . . . no help for it. He might know walking away was the right thing to do, but the bond he now shared with Hope told a different story. The Goddess of All Things didn't indulge in flights of fancy. She wove an intricate plan, knitting multiple threads in a vast universe, encouraging the greater good. Somehow, for some reason, she'd chosen him, gifting him with a female so stunning, so precious, his dragon half refused to turn away. No matter the danger, or cost to his pride.

Which left him with little choice.

He wanted Hope. The goddess believed he should have her, so forget about walking away. He'd take what *she* offered. Stake his claim. Make Hope his. Pray to God he didn't hurt her and it all worked out in the end.

Arm throbbing in agony, Hope hovered on the edge of panic. Any moment now, she'd plunge back in—freak out, scream some more, and run. Only one thing stopped her flight back into terror—Forge. He held her steady, hands cupping her face, nose an inch from hers, eyes the color of amethysts grounding her as seconds ticked into minutes.

It felt like hours instead. As though time had stopped, suspending her in hell.

A shudder raked her, making her teeth rattle.

She couldn't shake the chaos. Could still smell the scorched scales and burning flesh. Could still hear the shrieking battle cries. Still felt pain across her rib cage with every breath she took.

Horrifying images bombarded her. Like a well-shot horror movie, gory pictures winged across her mind. Death. Destruction. Blood. Oh God. Fresh tears welled. There had been so much blood. Hers. Forge's. Hope didn't know anymore. She couldn't keep anything straight. The screenshots kept merging, preventing her from splitting the experience into two distinct halves. She couldn't separate herself from the whole. Or tell where she ended and the dragon began.

Hope squeezed her eyes shut.

More tears fell.

"Eyes on me, Hope," Forge murmured, tone firm, yet somehow gentle. The combination cut through her fear, cleaning the suffocating stench of sulfur away. "Look at me."

She obeyed and met his gaze.

"There's my lass. Stay right here with me, okay?"

"Okay." Excellent plan. Particularly since he was right. She was safe here . . . with him. How she knew that, Hope couldn't say. Nothing proved the assertion. Empirical evidence had yet to surface, and still, she understood it was true. Forge equaled safety, at least for her. "Forge?"

"Aye?"

"I don't like this," she whispered, her voice hoarse.

"I know, *jalâyla*," he said, anchoring her in reality, interrupting the pain. "Take a deep breath for me."

For him. His request thumped on her mental door. Hope swallowed past the lump in her throat and . . . okay. Good enough. Despite the lockdown and her inability to move, she could do that, try to obey, do as he asked and—

He encouraged her with a murmur.

Her chest expanded. Air filled her lungs so fast the infusion of oxygen made her lightheaded for a moment.

"Good lass. Now—another."

She took a second breath.

With a hum of approval, Forge continued talking to her, praising her efforts, wiping her tears away, the sound of his voice becoming a lifeline in the quiet. Another breath. More life-sustaining oxygen. Her mind sparked, pushing panic aside. Flat on her back on the floor, blinking into the gloom, Hope forced her eyes to adjust in the dark. The surroundings bled through the edge of awareness.

Faint light.

The rise of shadowy bedposts.

Forge straddling her hips, crouched above her and—

An odd shimmer sparked in his eyes. The glow expanded, cascading like twin waterfalls through his irises. Hope frowned. Strange. Extraordinary. All kinds of beautiful, but . . .

She raised her hand. One hand gripping his wrist, she set the other against his face, touching the corner of his eye with her fingertip. "You're glowing."

"Trick of the light."

"I don't think so."

The corner of his mouth curved. "You think I'd lie tae you?"

"In a heartbeat," she said, voice soft, but full of conviction. "Especially if you thought you could get away with it."

He huffed. "You've had a shock, lass. You're imagining things."

Possible. Her mind, after all, remained mired in the dream. She shivered. "It was awful. I've never had a dream like that before."

"I know. I'll make sure it doesnae happen again."

"How?"

"Trust me."

Trust him. Hope frowned. Was she really ready to do that? All right, so she already felt safe with him, but *trust*? Such a big word. A huge leap as well, one that required both faith and courage in equal measure. "I don't know if I can."

"Bullshite. Of course you can. Who's the therapist here anyway?"

Amusement trickled through her. She snorted. "I study psychology. Never said I was any good at it."

He laughed.

The corners of his eyes crinkled, enchanting her, disarming her. As though the slight release of tension signaled her surrender, Forge pressed a soft kiss to the tip of her nose and leaned back, giving her more space. He didn't leave her, though, or shift position.

He played instead, one hand stroking her hair as he lifted the other from her cheek. His fingertips caressed her jaw before slipping beneath her head. He cupped her nape, his grip firm enough to hold her attention. Heat poured from his palm. A strange buzz erupted between her temples. Prickles raced along her scalp, then turned tail to ghost down her spine. Chasing the odd vibration, Hope turned into his touch.

"That's it, *jalâyla*," he murmured. "Feel the flow, take all you want."

Peace washed in like the evening tide. Rush and retreat. Roll in, pick up the slime coating her insides, push back out again. With each pass, the current intensified, taking out mental trash, rinsing her clean, shaking the nightmare's grip. Her heartbeat slowed. Fear uncurled its claws, losing the power to hurt her.

"Feels so good." Hope sighed. "Like a hot spring."

"You want me tae run you a bath?"

"No. Just keep talking."

His eyebrow hitched. "About what?"

No clue. Didn't matter. Let him figure it out.

Hope didn't want to think anymore. She wanted her brain to switch off, to float in the sea of feel-good while Forge held her. She drew in a shaky breath. God, he was something. Gentle. Comforting. So warm his body heat tunneled into her muscles, invaded her bones, sending prickles of relief through her. The mesmerizing wash eased her tension. Her mind blurred. She blinked, a slow up and down as coherence fled, becoming a distant memory and . . . huh. Wasn't that odd? The question shimmered on the periphery of her mind.

She tried to nod in agreement.

Her body refused to cooperate, closing her eyes, making her go boneless beneath Forge. So relaxed. Not a care in the world. She was past fuzzy-headed, as though she'd been downing tequila shots for hours. Which was—Hope smiled—pretty darn nice. Slaphappy drunk. Sloshed. Hammered. Blitzed . . . whatever. Label the condition and get her another glass full of awesome. The buzz was bliss filled. Fantastic and fun. Pure perfection.

Someone should really figure out a way to bottle it.

Wanting more, she sank into the stream, immersing herself in the current.

"Lass?"

"Such a great accent," she said, her voice slurring as relaxation dragged her deeper. "I love the way you sound."

He paused mid-caress. A heartbeat passed before he stroked her again, fingers moving over her in light passes. "Anything in particular you want tae talk about?"

The amusement in his voice registered.

Hope meant to answer. She really did, but well . . . crap. She didn't know how to react—be annoyed he laughed at her or grateful he kept touching her. A total toss-up. A real quandary. One that might, on some level, involve her pride. Hope pursed her lips. She should probably do something about that, but honestly—what did it matter? The slow glide of his hands soothed her. And every word he spoke, the timbre of his baritone, set her adrift, widening the distance between her and the dream.

"Hope?"

Her eyes drifted open. "Hmm?"

His lips twitched. "I'm still waiting for a topic."

Confusion broke into her bubble. "A topic?"

"Aye. If you want me tae talk, I need a topic."

"Oh well . . . anything. I could listen to you for hours." Releasing her grip on his wrist, she lifted her hand. So heavy. Her arm weighed a ton, as though cement had replaced the marrow in her bones. After what seemed like forever, her fingers touched down, grazing over day-old whiskers before reaching Forge's mouth. She traced his bottom lip. "Totally kissable. Bet you taste good."

Surprise lit in his eyes. He drew a quick breath.

Tilting her head, she considered his need for a topic. An idea flashed through her mind, lighting her up like a lightbulb. Oh yeah. She smiled. Awesome. Best plan ever. "Read to me. You got any books in here?"

Expression serious, he shook his head. "*Architectural Digest.* A tome on fine whiskeys."

"Ugh," she said, disappointed. She'd been hoping for something more interesting, like say, *The Bourne Identity*. "You like whiskey?"

"Love it. I'm building a cellar for my collection in the underground lair."

"Can I see it?"

"Aye, if you like."

"In the meantime, we still need a book."

His gaze dropped to her lips. "I have something else in mind."

"Something I'll like better?"

"Absolutely."

Oh wonderful. Excellent, in fact. "What?"

"This."

Cupping her chin, Forge dipped his head and invaded her mouth. Shock held her still. She sucked in a breath. His tongue slid over her teeth, flicked at hers, urging a response and . . . holy Mary, mother of God. She'd been wrong. So completely *wrong*. He tasted better than good. He was delicious, pure delight buried inside an impossibly gorgeous man. One who felt far too right.

The thought sent alarm bells clanging inside her head.

She should stop him. Right now. This instant. Before she went too far, allowed too much, and couldn't pull back. And yet, she didn't turn away. She welcomed him instead, opening wider, kissing him back, letting her hands roam and her libido out to play.

He groaned her name.

She whispered back, caressing his shoulders, burying her hands in his hair, asking for more. For everything, all he wanted to give her.

Bad plan. Big, big trouble.

Making love with Forge was a terrible idea. The worst, a fifteen on a scale of one to ten.

Hope knew it. Deep down where propriety lived, all the reasons to say no bubbled to the surface. A long list—practically endless—one she should heed, but . . . nope. Not today. She didn't want to listen. She wanted to wallow instead—burrow in, accept the pleasure, and make a home in his arms. She longed for him. His acceptance of her need. Hot, hard, unapologetic lust. Desire at its most ferocious. And as Forge offered it to her, she surrendered, giving him everything he asked, addicted to the rush in her veins—the unshakable sense of connection—as he settled heavy against her.

His weight pressed her into the rug.

Hooking her knee over his hip, Hope hung on hard, allowing him to settle between her thighs, scraping her nails over his scalp, egging him on without words. Forge deepened the kiss. She moaned in delight. More, she needed *more*—harder, faster . . . naked. Yes, please, *naked*. It couldn't happen fast enough. She needed to be skin-to-skin with him—to touch and taste, to serve herself up for his pleasure and reap her own in return. It had been so long, *too long*, since she'd given herself to a man. Since she'd wanted so much and been held so well, so . . .

Forget about *right*. Here, right now, was all about *wrong*.

Forge desired her. She craved him. So yeah. She would take what she wanted. All the reasons it was a bad idea would have to wait. She was jumping in feetfirst. To hell with the consequences.

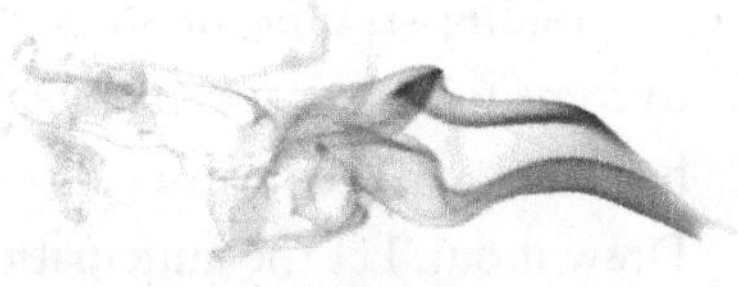

Chapter Fourteen

Forge needed to stop kissing her. He shouldn't be holding her. Shouldn't have his hands anywhere near her gorgeous arse either. And caressing her petal-soft skin? Oh, so not a good idea. He ought to be shot. Drawn and quartered. Hung from the nearest rafter. Or something. Maybe then his brain would kick over and order him to do the right thing. Wanting her wasn't the issue. Taking her—making Hope his—didn't qualify as the main problem, but . . . good Christ. He shouldn't be doing it like this, with her reeling, punch drunk from the healing energy his dragon half continued to feed her.

An honorable male would back off.

Think.

Assess.

Sit her down and talk it out.

Which made it official. He should pull away, explain the way things worked while he made his position clear and let her decide. Only two options existed for females in his world—accept his dragon half, become his mate, or run like hell. Clear cut. Concise. No room for misinterpretation. And yet, as her tongue tangled with his and lust unfurled, Forge wanted to ignore the rules. Screw the handbook and the arsehole who'd written it. He wanted to be selfish and remain where he was—on top of Hope, hips cradled between her thighs, chest pressed to her breasts, mouth fused to hers.

With a groan, he shifted to one side.

He needed access. More of her body available to him.

Taking his time, he stroked her, each touch light, giving her time to come to her senses and push him away. His fingertips ghosted over her stomach, then paused, hovering above her skin. Wait a moment. Draw it out. Let the anticipation of his next caress build as he lifted his lips from hers. Questions must be asked and answered. He needed to make sure she wanted him as much as he did her before—

"Please," she whispered, desperation in her voice.

"I know what you want." Goddamn. Did he ever. Energy-fuse gave him a direct line to her thoughts. Erotic images floated through her mind, invading his and . . . God have mercy. Talk about X-rated. Her imagination outdid his, pushing into porn star territory. She wanted to be naked in his arms, spread open, on display, her body available for whatever he wanted, just as long as he mastered her in the end.

Eyes closed, Hope arched, begging for his touch. "Please."

"Donnae worry, luv." Dipping his head, he licked her bottom lip. "I'll give you what you need."

Eager to keep his promise, he slid his hand beneath her shirt. Soft skin brushed his palm. Cotton rose, baring her midriff, bunching against his forearm. Wanting to look, but needing her mouth more, he kissed her again. And again. Over and over. Light caresses. Deeper possessive forays. A game of taunt and tease, gifting her with his taste, treating himself to hers, arousing her as he tried to get his fill. It would never happen. He knew it without proof. One kiss, and she'd ruined him for other females. Corrupted him with her sweetness. Destroyed him with her willingness to please him.

With an impatient whimper, she twisted beneath him.

Turning his hand, Forge stroked over her hip, the dip of her waist, slipping over her rib cage, worshiping her curves before releasing her mouth. He grabbed the hem of her T-shirt, and with a hard tug, pulled it over her head. Her hair caught on the fabric, then broke free, tumbling over her shoulders. His breath caught. Holy shite. He should've realized. No bra, which left her bare, on display in the low light. Exposed to his gaze. Ready for his hands. In need of his mouth to warm her in the cool air.

He traced the underside of her breast.

Color bloomed in her cheeks. Her lips parted on a moan as she rose to meet his next stroke. So pretty. Incredibly sensitive. A gorgeous, round handful, the perfect fit for his palm. Watching her face, he played, cupping her firmly, letting her feel him before brushing his thumb over her peak. Her eyelashes fluttered. A shiver shook her. Pleasure rumbled through him. Hot. Needy. Beautiful in his arms. Hope was a dream come true, his siren song, the one he'd been waiting for all his life. The female he needed above all others.

The thought registered.

His sense of fair play squawked, splitting his attention. Shite. Again with his ethics. Bloody scruples. Terrible fucking time to be interrupted by principles.

With a growl, Forge steeled himself, preparing to pull away. No matter how incredible Hope looked in his arms—or how much she made him feel—making love to her was wrong, the absolute worst way to start a relationship. Forge knew it. And even if he didn't, his conscience refused to let him forget. The bloody thing kept screaming—stop, stop . . . STOP! The warning flashed like a neon sign inside his head. Not hard to guess why. Hiding the truth from her would only lead to problems later on. Honesty was a factor. His need to protect her from all comers—himself included—was another. She needed to know about Dragonkind before he claimed her. Which meant he should tell her everything, starting with—

His dragon half stirred, waking from pleasure-bound oblivion.

The beast snarled in warning.

Forge flinched and turned his focus inward. A steely-eyed glare met his and . . . ah, hell. Not good. Terrible, in point of fact, given his territorial side didn't agree with the plan. The greedy bastard despised principles. Cared even less for honesty. Or that Hope wasn't quite herself at the moment. The beast wanted what it *wanted*—to claim his female, bind her to him so hard and fast she'd stay even after she learned the truth.

Bad idea. His conscience told him so.

He must refocus . . . fast. Things needed to go a certain way. Hope deserved the truth. All his consideration. Every bit of his patience. She needed to be clearheaded when he took her the first time. Not fucked up, drunk on his essence, deep in the pleasure of her first energy feed. Great thought. Absolutely right. Being up-front, giving her a choice, was the decent way to go. Forge nodded. All right, good. Problem solved. Now all he needed to do was stop kissing her.

Easier said than done with his dragon half AWOL.

The bloody bastard was running for the fences, refusing to listen. Baring its teeth, the beast broke the chains, escaping lockdown, and ambushed him by opening the floodgates. Unquenchable need poured out. The torrent of lust rushed through him. His mind blanked. Good intentions vanished.

Both hands buried in his hair, Hope breathed his name.

Her plea rammed through his crumbling defenses. His control detonated. The explosion ripped through what remained of his honor. Forge cursed. Fucking hell. He needed help, some kind of rescue. He couldn't resist her any longer. Not with his dragon half on the rampage and Hope half-naked beneath him.

Flat on her back underneath Forge, Hope lost all sense of herself. Self-control was a thing of the past. Her body had grown a mind of its own, wrapping her legs around his waist, fisting her hands in his hair, demanding he kiss her deeper, harder, and hmm yes, longer. A purr of satisfaction rumbled through her and . . . oh yeah. Absolutely. No question about it. He was desire personified. It was the only explanation for her reaction. His mouth acted like a drug, delivering a lethal dose of dear-God-more. She crumbled in seconds. In less than an instant. Time split as the intensity of his kiss turned her first taste of him into an addiction. And now she knew—finally understood the depths to which obsession could sink. How her patients became addicts in the face of driving impulse. How quickly someone succumbed to vice with the right impetus.

Forge qualified as the catalyst—the launchpad, the lash into wicked behavior.

At least for her.

He was a force unlike any she'd ever encountered . . . and she'd seen a lot. Had helped countless people beat the odds—unearth emotions long buried, deal with unresolved hurt, and overcome addiction—and now she wondered if she'd ever truly understood. If any of her advice was rooted in reality. Hope moaned as he drank deep. God, he tasted amazing. Was a high she couldn't ignore and refused to temper. He gave so much, bombarding her with delight, whipping her frenzy so high that ecstasy beckoned, whispering her name.

Her body throbbed.

Her libido begged.

Her professional ethics didn't make a sound.

That ship had sailed, and far too easily. Without a peep of protest.

The realization should've pissed her off. Hope wanted to scowl. She kissed Forge back instead, abandoning her scruples. The wrong thing to do. Somewhere in the part of her brain that still worked, she acknowledged the mistake. The sensible side of her screeched in outrage. Lust brushed the objection aside. She needed what Forge fed her. Wanted the pleasure, craved the connection along with the man.

Her reaction to him didn't make any sense. For once, Hope didn't care. She let her analytical side sink to the bottom, burying it deep inside her. Just once. *Please, just once.* She'd be good later. Do the right thing, but . . . not now. Not yet. She needed to loosen the reins, let the rigid ethics she lived by slip from her fingers and—

"Da!" The unhappy cry came from the next room. "Da, da, da . . . da, da!"

"Shite." Forge raised his head, releasing her mouth. She made a sound of protest. With a growl, he returned to nip her, then turned his head to glance at the digital clock sitting on the bedside table. "Three fifty-three p.m. Right on time."

He sighed, the sound full of frustration.

Hope squirmed beneath him, so needy she throbbed in discomfort. Gosh darn it all. So unfair, but babies couldn't wait. G. M. was the priority, and as Forge's gaze returned to her, she knew she wouldn't be getting what she needed from him—the body-banging orgasm she craved.

Amethyst eyes shimmering, Forge dipped his head. She lifted her chin, meeting him halfway. He licked over her bottom lip, delivering his taste, making her shiver and ask for more without words . . . like an addict would her dealer.

Forge treated her to another gentle kiss. "Sorry, *jalâyla*. Bad timing, but my son—"

"Da!"

Amusement sparked in his eyes. "Isnae the most patient of lads."

"He's hungry?"

"Aye." His lips twitched. "He's always hungry."

"Growing boys usually are."

"Uh-huh," he said, pushing away from her.

Hope resisted a moment, then let him go. No sense broadcasting her neediness, but God, it was difficult to release him. She did it anyway, unwrapping her legs from around his waist, removing her hands from his hair, allowing him to push to his knees. Cold air washed over her skin, raising goose bumps as he skimmed her face, her breasts, and lower, over her belly. Her nipples tightened. His eyes heated an instant before he dipped his head and licked one pebbled peak. Heat sped through her veins. Bliss arched her back, offering him more, begging for the pleasure.

He growled against her skin. "Donnae move, lass."

"But—"

"Stay exactly as you are." He sucked her nipple hard, the pleasure-pain made her whimper before he released her to turn his attention to her other breast. His mouth surrounded her, the suckle and draw forcing a groan as he bit down, holding her between his teeth with gentle pressure. "We'll finish what we started when I get back."

"I don't think—"

"Good. Donnae think when you're beneath me—that's my job." Gaze dark with desire, he gave her a warning look before rolling to his feet. Heading for the door connecting his room with the nursery, he glanced at her over his shoulder. "Five minutes. Get naked, lass. Be in my bed when I return."

Get naked. Be in bed—NAKED and waiting for him.

The words shivered through her. A lovely set of syllables when combined and . . . oh man. Time to be honest—Forge hadn't just used words, he injected each one with command. An order not to be disobeyed. His tone said it all, and Hope wanted to obey. Her body leapt up and down at the idea, going preschooler with its need to please. Or maybe it was the promise of pleasure he offered. The thought made Hope pause. Common sense came roaring back. She blinked. What the hell was wrong with her?

Something serious.

Something in need of adjustment.

Something she must kill . . . dead, immediately.

The realization prompted her get-up-and-go. *Get naked,* her ass. No way, no how. Without Forge touching her, her brain came back online. The therapist—the one with principles and sense enough to panic—raced to the rescue. Yeah. Absolutely. *Going* had just become priority number one. Hiding until she formed a plan was a close second. Hope snatched her T-shirt off the floor and popped to her feet. Dragging it over her head, she turned toward the door—the one leading into the hall. But more importantly, the one Forge hadn't just disappeared through.

Time to escape.

Her libido wasn't happy with the idea. Forge wouldn't be either. But as she listened to him talk to his son in the other room—his tone so pleased and loving—her heart quaked, then cracked, the fissure reaching a place inside her she'd thought long dead. God, this man. What was it about him that called to her, compelled her, made her want to break all the rules? Hope didn't know, but one thing for sure, the return of her faculties—along with a healthy dose of self-preservation—dictated the course.

She needed to run: hard, fast, and—she glanced toward the double doors on the other side of the room as she scurried toward the exit—very, *very* quietly. She didn't want him to catch her. The last thing she'd survive was a confrontation. The second Forge touched her, she'd cave. Her body still hummed. Need and sexual frustration weren't far away, so . . . you betcha. New plan. She needed to find a quiet spot to think. To regroup, put the train back on the tracks, and figure out a way to resist him before she ended up naked in her new client's bed.

Chapter Fifteen

Krkonoše mountain range—Czech Republic

Ancient treetops rocked as Zidane flew overhead. On a collision course with warriors hidden amid inhospitable cliffs and low-lying mountain valleys, he banked into a tight turn. Twin streams whistled from his wing tips. His brown, orange-speckled scales rattled. Snow spun in his wake, the mad rush matching the rise of his fury. A yellow glow sparked in his dark eyes. His gaze swept east, the citrine glow staining the washed-out winter landscape in front of him.

He needed a target. The mock battle—dragon combat training with the crew he'd chosen as his personal guard—might not be real, but at least it was something. The perfect remedy. A way to focus his rage, the promise of a fight that would leave him bruised and more than a touch bloody.

It was either that or explode.

Not a great plan considering his firepower in dragon form. An ill-advised explosion was the last thing his father's physician would prescribe. The flammable poison he exhaled would burn him from the inside out, leaving his throat raw, his scales scorched, and him with a terrible case of indigestion. Zidane snorted at the thought. Sure. Right. Never again. He'd already done that last week, swallowing his fire along with the impatience riding him. Not that he could help it.

The impulse to move before sanctioned—before being given permission to get his ass across the Atlantic—was more than he could bear.

Stupid Archguard.

The high council moved slower than snails.

Inch along. Stop to ponder. Backslide into indecision.

The political bullshit never ended. It went on ad infinitum, forever and forever amen. Thank God his sire dealt with all of the discussion and discord. No way he could handle it. He was a fighter—a killer of warriors—not a political animal. Which explained his need to break rank and fly free. A tempting thought, but not something he could do. At least, not yet. He needed the green light from his sire and the Archguard, the *go* that would put him and his warriors on a plane to Seattle. The second he landed in Nightfury territory, he would pick a fight . . . and the war would begin.

Zidane bared his fangs. Payback. He wanted a reckoning, a chance to even the score and take out the entire Nightfury pack. Maximum pain. Complete annihilation. Merciless extinction of the males responsible for murdering his brother. Zidane's chest tightened. *Hovno,* he missed Lothair. Missed his voice. Missed the weekly calls. Missed the teasing verbal skirmishes and easy acceptance. His little brother had deserved a better death. An honorable one and a fitting burial. So had Ferland, his best friend and pack-mate for the better part of three decades. Both males lay dead now, ashed out and forever gone, two holes in his heart that would never be filled by anything but fury.

His rage grew by the day, expanding until his chest ached and his head hurt.

The delays weren't helping.

Neither was his imagination.

Images of what he would do to the Nightfuries filled his mind. Gage topped his hit list. The insolent male deserved nothing short of brutality. The kind Zidane longed to deliver. He clenched his teeth on a growl. He wanted to shred the male. Could hardly wait to get his claws on the asshole. He'd kill Gage slowly: cut him up, watch him bleed out, enjoy every ounce of his suffering. But first, the Archguard needed to get off their asses. Grow some brains and get the vote out. One or the other. Either would do, just as long as the status quo changed.

With a curse, Zidane corrected his flight path. Frost kicked up, chilling the weave of his interlocking dragon skin. The scales along his side ruffled, clicking into place beneath a faint glimmer of moonlight. His sonar pinged. He hummed. Excellent. Contact off his right wing, three miles out and flying in fast. Night vision pinpoint sharp, he scanned a ridge of rocky outcroppings. He was seconds away. Just moments from another round of dragon combat training. From ripping his warriors new—

"Zidane." The deep voice cracked like a whip, opening a channel into mind-speak.

Zidane grimaced. *Kristus.* Seriously? Now? Just when he was about to get some action? He sighed. His sire had the worst timing. "Da, *Father?"*

"Come back to the pavilion. I need you here."

"Is it done?"

"Almost," his sire said, the eagerness in his voice unmistakable. A good sign. An excited Rodin meant one thing—victory for Zidane, *Xzinile* (exile and sanctioned assassination) for the Nightfury pack. *"We're tallying the votes."*

"How's it looking?"

"Five for, three against, with four more to count."

Zidane curled his lip. Frigid air ghosted over his exposed fangs. So close. So very close to being unleashed. *"On my way."*

"Make it quick. I will win this round."

"Are you sure?"

"Da," he said, Russian accent thicker than usual. Another excellent sign. Confidence rang in his sire's voice. *"The instant the vote concludes, I will anoint you commander of the kill squad."*

"I'm twenty minutes away."

"Perfect. And son . . ."

"Yes?"

"Dress accordingly—ceremonial robes only."

Excitement skittered through him.

The jagged spikes riding his spine rattled. Hmm, *ceremonial robes*. The words echoed inside his head. Zidane smiled. Goddess bless him, he was more than close now. He could practically taste victory. If Rodin wanted him and his warriors dressed in formal robes inside the Archguard's sacred chamber, it was a done deal.

Success assured.

Somersaulting into a sideways flip, he hissed. Finally. At last. Real action along with a firm target. The idea took shape and form. Zidane let his imagination go, allowing the violence to expand inside his mind. Baring his fangs, he roared in triumph. His battle cry echoed through mind-speak and across distant mountaintops, signaling his personal guard. Six strong, the soon-to-be-sanctioned kill squad answered the call, shifting course mid-flight to meet him. Time to leave the wilds behind. Prague beckoned. A pavilion full of Dragonkind elite and his sire awaited his return. He must enter the real world once more. No time to waste. He had a plane to catch and a pack of Nightfuries to kill.

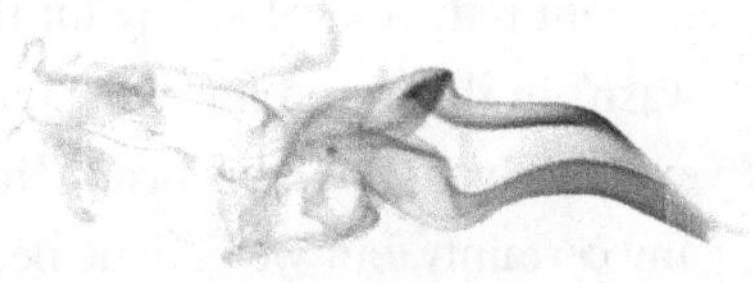

Chapter Sixteen

Cursing his bad luck, Ivar leapt off the third-floor balcony. The violent free fall blew his hair back. Frigid air burned over his cheekbones. Focused on the ground, he bared his teeth and timed his landing. The blackness was absolute. No porch light on behind his aboveground lair. No glow from streetlights bleeding into his backyard. No moon to break through the murky thread of midnight. Just stony silence and the abysmal threat of another fucked-up night.

Suppressing a snarl, Ivar called on his magic. His night vision sparked. Frozen grass came into focus, the brown, bladed edges sharp and battle worn in the darkness. One Mississippi. Two Mississippi. Three—

He let his fire dragon loose.

Pink flame licked over his skin. Heat blasted through the cold. His body lengthened beneath the spread of blood-red scales and the crack of razor-sharp claws. Winter wind snapped at the spikes adorning his tail. Brick facade of 28 Walton Street blurring in his periphery, Ivar spread his wings. The webbing caught air as an inferno raced along his spine and warm, humid air coiled around him. Ignoring melting icicles on newly repaired eaves, he tucked into a spiral, rising above building tops and human filth to turn north.

City lights fell away.

A thicker quiet descended.

Storm clouds rolled in as suburbia gave way to dirt roads and ancient forests. His attention on the roughening terrain, he scanned the stretch of giant redwoods, looking for threats, longing for a fight, knowing he wasn't in the mood for either. He needed—his brow furrowed—what, exactly? Ivar shook his head. The hell if he knew. He couldn't say with any certainty, but well . . . he needed *something*. Anything to quiet the unease buzzing between his temples. The swath of woodland should've done the job. Settled his nerves. Soothed his worry. Made him happy something on the planet remained healthy, despite humankind's best efforts to kill everything.

It didn't. Not much could at the moment.

Ivar growled. Fucking number seven. Turned out, it wasn't the charm. Seven attempts, seven failures, zero relief. The answer—the cure, the antidote, his salvation—remained out of reach. Nothing he did came close to the answer he sought. Dipping low, Ivar got up close and personal with a copse of Douglas firs. His tail whiplashed. Enormous treetops rocked, swaying violently in the dark. He pursed his lips. Such bad luck. The worst, when he considered the latest failure inside his lab. He'd always liked the number seven. Even considered it one of his favorites, but . . .

Not anymore.

Seven sucked. So did eight. Perhaps nine would bring him better luck.

Gaze narrowed on the jagged peaks of distant mountains, Ivar exhaled. Sparks exploded from his nostrils, lighting up the night. Fingers crossed his latest attempt would work. Maybe it would. Maybe it wouldn't. Time would tell—the incubation of the newest drug hours away from completion—but not soon enough. Human females were dying too fast for him to stop. And where was he—in his lab concocting the next round of antivirals? Bent over his microscope testing the supercharged immune cells in Evelyn Foxe's blood? He swallowed a snarl. Not even close. He was seventy-five miles away from the most important scientific discovery of his life, stuck judging the first round of Hamersveld's Dragonkind Olympics.

Frustration pumped impatience through his veins.

Ivar sighed. He wanted to rip his XO in half, but really, what would that solve? He only had himself to blame. The competition seemed like a good idea at the time. Perhaps it still was, but—Jesus. He didn't need the added aggravation. Too many things had gone wrong in the last month. Now, he didn't know where to turn. Or how to fix the things he'd fucked up. The list kept getting longer, which didn't bode well for the future, never mind his peace of mind.

The realization spun him toward the only thing that ever calmed him. A picture formed in his mind's eye, one of Sasha Cooper: blond hair messed up, gaze dark with desire, gorgeous mouth his for the taking. Floating on an updraft, Ivar closed his eyes. God. The feeling of her wrapped around him always turned his thoughts from the negative. Her presence inside his head, the very image of her, carried him toward contentment. He'd loved every second of the night spent in her arms. Despite the danger—and the fact she'd nearly killed him—he wanted to do it again. And again. Tap into the sex kitten side of her and soothe the raging side of himself. Love her over and over until all the stress and worry melted away.

He knew Sasha could do it.

Her bio-energy—the way she'd fed his dragon half—more than proved her efficiency. At least, when it came to him. Still, he hesitated to repeat the experience. Sinking inside her might be heaven, but the risks involved unnerved him. Her grip on him wasn't natural. The intensity of his reaction to her made no sense. He couldn't explain it, which left him wondering what the hell was going on. She wasn't a high-energy female. Would never draw males with the power of her connection to the Meridian or cause warriors to fight over her.

Excellent argument. Perfect logic. No need to explore further.

And yet, she drew him like a magnet to metal.

His yearning to see her caused him to stare out the window of his aboveground lair, eyes fixed on the house across the street. Day after day. Night after night. He couldn't stay away from that damn window. Or quell his relief when she pulled her beat-to-shit Jeep into her driveway, arriving home safe every evening. Wheeling around a steep cliff, Ivar frowned. What was it about her? Why was he still thinking about her? What would it take to expel her from his mind?

The questions circled.

No answers arrived to snuff out the mystery. Which meant one thing. He must brave the effect Sasha had on him and see her again. Wings spread wide, Ivar rocketed over a narrow valley and toyed with the idea. Touching her again carried risks. The kind a wise male wouldn't ignore, but he couldn't subdue the idea. Or stop the excitement skittering down his spine. Eagerness followed, lighting him up from the inside out.

He huffed in exasperation. Guess that answered *that*. No reason to doubt what his dragon half wanted—the blond temptress living across the street. Primal need wasn't something he could ignore. Neither was curiosity. Both demanded he approach her again. Screw the danger. Fuck all the questions. The only one that mattered was how Sasha would react when he banged on her door a second time and—

"Ivar." Edged by a Norwegian accent, the voice vibrated through mind-speak. *"About time you got here."*

Jarred by the interruption, Ivar refocused and . . . realized two things at once. First, he'd arrived at his destination. Second, he had no clue how he'd gotten there. He couldn't remember a thing about his flight north. He stifled a curse. Talk about stupid. He needed to pay more attention. Otherwise, he'd end up dead, without ever having registered the threat.

Flexing his talons, Ivar cracked his knuckles, enjoying the snap as brisk winds died between the rise of serrated mountain peaks. *"Had things to do in the lab."*

"Any progress?"

"Nyet," he said, but he was close. So fucking *close*. A whisper from unlocking the viral sequence and killing the disease for good. *"I'll know for sure by morning."*

Night vision sharp, Ivar fine-tuned his infrared and flew over the last rise. The forest retreated, giving way to sheer granite faces before dipping into a deep *V* between mountaintops. Snow blew from the ragged peaks as a nasty northeasterly picked up again. Ice crystals melting on his scales, he scanned the rocky ledge to his left.

His gaze narrowed on the waterfall cascading over the cliff face. Steam frothed into the frigid air.

Ivar resisted the urge to roll his eyes. Of course. He should have known. A perfect paradox—hot, flowing water in the heart of winter. The equation wasn't that complicated: water times an unexpected place equaled Hamersveld. Every. Single. Time.

Ignoring the wet chill, he went wings vertical and circled back around, searching for his XO in the mist. Nothing. No ping. No nasty water dragon vibe. Zero visual aids. Ivar scowled and searched the outcropping again. *"Where the hell are you?"*

Hamersveld chuckled. *"Here."*

Like a theater curtain opening onstage, the waterfall parted.

Ivar blinked. *"You have got to be kidding me."*

"Now, why would I do that?"

Ivar didn't have a clue, but well . . . shit. Finding his friend in human form, shoulders deep in a hot tub dug into solid rock—steam rising, hot water bubbling around his bare chest, an unapologetic gleam in his black, blue-rimmed eyes—surprised him. Why? Ivar huffed. The hell if he knew. Hamersveld didn't follow rules of any kind. If anything, the male excelled at breaking new ground . . . literally, judging by the uneven edges of the stone whirlpool.

Slowing his flight, Ivar hung above the ledge. His back talons touched down, scraping over granite. Pebbles jumped, then rolled, somersaulting over the cliff edge. Stone cracked against stone, echoing across the valley as he folded his wings in a fast tuck. Air rushed from beneath the webbing. The blow back ruffled one side of the cascade. Water sprayed upward, splashing over wet rock. A snarl reverberated, bouncing off the cliff face, joining the pitter-patter of falling water. Raptor-sharp white teeth flashed in the gloom. Ivar's eyes narrowed and—

A flinty, yellow-eyed glow sparked in the low light.

Ivar clenched his teeth. Lovely. Just perfect. Foul-tempered miniature dragon at one o'clock, perched in the jagged rock above the whirlpool, guarding his master's back.

"Good to see you too, Fen," Ivar said, sarcasm out in full force.

Fen curled his scaly lip, then looked away, dismissing him like dog shit on a sidewalk.

Ivar resisted the urge to squash the little bastard. One flick of his tail. A single thump of his talon and—bye-bye birdie. No more singing for miniature dragons. He imagined it a moment, enjoying the high-pitched squawk, the flow of the wren's blood, but—Ivar quashed the impulse. Killing Fen would be the height of foolishness. Hamersveld would never forgive him for hurting his wren. His XO might thrive on violence, but he loved Fen more. A pity. Dissecting the wren—learning the subspecies of Dragonkind's secrets one scalpel slice at a time—would almost be worth the grief of losing a friend.

Glancing away from the perpetually pissed-off wren, he refocused on Hamersveld and raised a brow. *"Enjoying yourself?"*

"Absolutely." Gaze leveled on him, Hamersveld smirked. *"What's the point of being out here in the middle of butt-fuck nowhere if I can't have a little fun?"*

Ivar glanced around, taking in the terrain. Pretty desolate. One hundred percent inhospitable. Ivar tipped his head, making his horns tingle. Huh. Guess Hamersveld had a point. He eyed the hot water.

Bet that would feel good. Might even help him unravel from all the time spent bent over a microscope. *"Got room in there for two?"*

"Hop in," Hamersveld said, dropping mind-speak.

With a nod, Ivar shifted from dragon to human form. He didn't bother with clothes. Instead, he stood naked in the moonlight, skin steaming, and pressed his chin to his chest. Sore muscles squawked. He gritted his teeth, embracing the pain before switching tack and rolling his shoulders. Tight knots released. Relief wormed its way into his joints as he tipped his head back. The waterfall roared from a hundred feet up, splashing down, beading on Fen's pale scales, making the rock slick and the air cooler. Mist collected and rolled down his spine. Wiping water from the back of his neck, he walked toward his friend.

Rough stone scraped the bottoms of his bare feet.

Ivar ignored the discomfort and, reaching the edge of the tub, stepped in. Heat engulfed him as he sank into the pool opposite Hamersveld. Hot water bubbled up, frothing into white ribbons around him. Sitting on a smooth granite ledge, he stretched his legs out. Nice and comfortable. The perfect size and temperature, a magic-driven spa in the middle of nowhere. Ivar sighed and—

"Better?"

"God, yeah." Groaning, Ivar slid deeper, immersing himself to the chin, before tipping his head back. Uneven stone cupped the back of his neck. Warm water lapped over his shoulders. The failures of the day fell away. He closed his eyes, enjoying the heat, then cracked one lid open. "Status report."

"All set. The competitors are in place." Stretching his arms out, Hamersveld set his elbows on the edge of the whirlpool. "Show's about to start."

Glancing right, Ivar looked out over the valley floor. Shaped like a bowl, the spines of parallel mountain ranges tapered, giving way to a braided river surrounded by huge evergreens. "I assume this is the best vantage point."

"Why do you think I chose this ledge?"

Why, indeed. Ivar smiled and let the last of his tension melt away. God, it was heaven. The absolute best. He might have to tell Hamersveld he loved him.

"Now, now . . ." An amused gleam in his eyes, his XO shook his head. "Don't go getting all gooey on me."

Ivar laughed. "You going to get it started or what?"

With a huff, Hamersveld fired up mind-speak. *"Azrad—you're up. Get moving. The rest of you—get ready."*

Surprised poked at Ivar. He blinked. What the hell did *the rest of you* mean? He treated his friend to a sidelong glance. "You sending Azrad against the entire pack?"

"Nothing so harsh." One side of Hamersveld's mouth creased. "Azrad will have help from Terranon and Kilmar—one fighting triangle against twelve of our best fighters."

Four to one odds. Pretty fucking harsh. What was Hamersveld trying to do—get his most skilled warriors killed? He scowled at his XO. "What the hell do you think you're—"

A green, yellow-tailed fireball exploded across the night sky.

Singing with violence, the inbound missile rocketed across the valley. Treetops caught fire. Tendrils of smoke seethed, writhing over the river's edge. The smell of diesel mixed with burning wood and the pungent scent of napalm.

"Ah, the sweet smell of Terranon." Hamersveld hummed, the fireball highlighting the anticipation in his eyes as he glanced Ivar's way. "Hold tight, brother. Here we go."

The high-speed missile struck the cliff opposite them.

Rock shrieked.

Green goo exploded, spraying in all directions.

Expanding like lime-colored foam, the acidy-ooze raced over the rock face before catching chemical fire. An unearthly shriek ripped through the valley. Multiple dragons broke cover and took to the sky.

Ivar sucked in a breath. Holy hell. Getting out of the way sounded like a great plan. He'd have done the same to avoid touching the mysterious green muck. The stuff looked nasty and smelled even worse, and as Ivar watched the carnage unfold, he couldn't help but feel hopeful. The battle was shaping up. His warriors looked strong, ready to fight, better prepared than the last time he'd supervised dragon combat training. The improvement seemed promising. He hadn't expected anything like—

Another fireball roared through the darkness.

More yellow than green this time, the noxious mass streaked toward the other end of the canyon. Several warriors shifted mid-flight. Flying in formation, three males uncloaked, cutting the pack off before they could regroup. Growls filled the air. The trio went wings vertical, splitting the larger pack in two. Claws shrieked against scales. The scent of blood filled the air. Males screamed in agony.

Ivar shivered. Holy shit. It was like watching a train derail—in slow motion. Gooey green fire burning across cliff faces. Rock shrapnel flying. Half a mountainside destroyed. Twelve Razorbacks in complete disarray. One fighting triangle in control.

Without slowing, the trio banked right. Azrad broke from the group. Black scales glittering, spider tattoo glowing red on the side of his neck, he went after his next target solo. He struck hard, the crack echoing off sheer granite faces as he peeled the male like an orange.

Blood spilled over pale-blue scales.

Azrad swung back around, slicing another warrior open with his quadruple-bladed tail.

Ivar's mouth fell open. "Jesus."

"Told you."

"He's going to kill everyone."

"No, he won't. Maim a few, sure, but he never quite kills them," Hamersveld said, reassuring him as Azrad sideswiped another male.

Ivar flinched as the warrior howled in pain. "Settle in, brother. Enjoy the show. It's only going to get better."

No doubt. Proof flew a few hundred yards away, making mincemeat of his pack. Gaze riveted to Azrad, Ivar watched him take on three males at once. Quick shifts. Fast spirals. Tight turns. The acrobatics were nothing short of amazing. Awe inspiring in some ways, disconcerting in others. Something about Azrad didn't sit right. Ivar took another look, staring openmouthed as Azrad gutted another male and . . .

A strong sense of déjà vu hit him.

Ivar frowned. What was it about the warrior? He shook his head and tracked Azrad as he swung around. Shift. Parry. Strike and . . . weird. With his black scales, smooth moves, and strange markings, Azrad seemed familiar somehow. As though he'd seen the big male somewhere before.

His eyes narrowed. Azrad sent a fifth warrior spinning before latching onto another. His newest victim squawked. Covered in dragon blood, Azrad's talons sank deep a second before he released his captive. His longer-than-usual claws pulled free of the male's rib cage. Still alive, but badly wounded, the bleeding warrior's wings folded. He plummeted out of the sky. Ivar leaned forward in the hot tub, wincing when his warrior hit the ground with a crunch.

Baring his fangs, Azrad chased down another.

The sense of recognition grew stronger.

Ivar tightened his grip on the edge of the whirlpool. Jesus. The male was aggression personified, an excellent candidate for his breeding program, the perfect warrior to pair with an HE female. But first, some vetting needed to be done. One way or another, he must discover why Azrad looked so damned familiar.

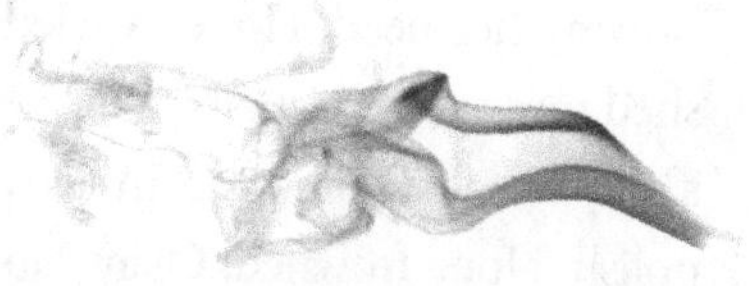

Chapter Seventeen

Sitting with her back to the wall inside her temporary bedroom, Hope turned the rolled boxing wrap over in her hands. Slap a sticker on her that read "Cooked" and call it a day. She was in big trouble, the kind of screwed that left her wondering when and where she'd lost her mind. She snorted. *When* and *where* weren't the issue. The *who*, however, remained a serious problem. One unlikely to go away anytime soon.

Stay put, he'd said.

No way she could've done that, not after . . .

Hope frowned at her knuckles. *Screwed* didn't quite describe what she was at the moment. Or rather, what she was doing.

Hiding might be a better characterization.

In full retreat was an even better one.

The fact she was doing it while wedged between her bed and the night table with her butt planted on the floor summed up her situation nicely. Hope cringed. All right, best add *pathetic* to the heap of shame and get on with her day.

Cursing under her breath, she examined the Velcro holding the boxing wrap closed. Nice. Neat. All the tidy edges lined up. No chaos in sight and . . . yeah. She ought to be like that, more in control, less of a mess. Bumping the boxing wrap against her bent knee, Hope stared at the cloth roll a moment, then tossed the tight coil onto the bed. It bounced across the comforter, a quick tumble that led her gaze to the wall opposite her.

She saw the framed mirror, but not really. Nothing had come into complete focus since she picked herself off the floor and fled Forge's room. Bowing her head, Hope exhaled a long, measured breath. All right, so she'd messed up. Crossed a line. Been blindsided by a gorgeous guy with a sexy streak a mile wide. In no way her fault. Picking at her chipped nail polish, Hope frowned. Okay. Not true. It was at least half her fault, and all the excuses in the world wouldn't fix it. Which meant she needed to man-up and stop hiding like a frightened kitten under a piece of furniture.

It was disgusting, and . . .

Sad to say, but her usual MO.

Despite encouraging others to tackle issues head-on, Hope retreated when faced with her own. She liked to hide until she thought things through and figured out how best to deal with the problem. Not the most mature way to move through life, but . . . God. Rapid change and inconstancy frightened her. Which made all kinds of sense given the man responsible for her upbringing. Her father might be good at his job, but he'd sucked as a parent, leaving her and Adam floundering in a sea of uncertainty most days. Still, running away when she felt unsure didn't make the cut.

Not that she could've done what Forge asked.

Naked, naked . . . naked in his bed. The idea turned on its axis, spinning her back to Forge's bedroom—to waking in his arms, to being surrounded by his heat, to hearing the rumble of his oh-so-sexy baritone.

Hope swallowed a groan. God help her. The way he affected her was unnatural. She never acted like a cat in heat with anyone before, but no matter how she looked at it, her reaction to Forge felt like that—wholly combustible.

Closing her eyes, Hope pressed the pads of her thumbs to her temples. The pressure didn't help. A headache hung in her periphery, banging on her mental door, demanding she let it inside her head. She wanted to do it, open the floodgates, welcome the distraction, flip the covers back, crawl into bed and never come out. But burying her head in the sand—or rather, under cotton and feather-down—wouldn't solve anything. She had a job to do, one that didn't include getting kinky with Forge.

An excellent argument.

Her body protested, squawking in disagreement.

"Goddamn it. I need my head examined." Fighting the ache, she rubbed her forehead. "Or maybe a libido-ectomy."

Hope tipped her head back and stared at the ceiling. Perfect solution. The complete removal of her wanton-sex-switch might be the only thing that saved her. Particularly with lust still raging through her veins.

"Freaking guy," she muttered, trying to forget his touch and the heat of his hands, but—balls in a banana sack. Nothing worked. Every time she thought about Forge, pleasure unfurled beneath her skin, making her teeth clench and her principles waver.

Hope snorted. So much for professional ethics. Hers had gone the way of the winds. Now she felt battered by the storm and in need of an outlet. Fisting her hand, she examined her knuckles. Perfect white points waiting to be used. She needed to hit something. The heavy bag in her garage whispered her name. Longing grabbed hold, making her itch for her small house in the suburbs. Safety lived there, the promise of a normal, everyday routine, the perfect hideaway, the only place in the world that made sense . . . and her attraction to Forge didn't exist.

Wishful thinking, no doubt. The cat-in-heat was already out of the bag. It was far too late to put it back. The past couldn't be erased. History, no matter how recent, always circled back around, looking for easy prey. So . . .

Her eyes narrowed. Only one thing left to do—move past the embarrassment and figure out how to avoid a repeat performance.

Kissing Forge couldn't happen again. Touching him was out too. A big no-no. The memory bubbled up to taunt her—the feel and taste of him, the strength of his body, the gentle way he'd handled her and—

A tingle streaked across her lower belly.

Need threatened to overwhelm her.

Hope squeezed her eyes shut. She pressed her knees together. Heaven help her. Bad, bad psychologist. "Stop it right now."

Her voice spiraled out into the empty room. The instruction settled the heat in her veins. Her libido whined like a horny feline.

"Shut up," she whispered as a picture of her inner alley cat popped into her head. "You don't get a vote."

A creak joined her words, disrupting the quiet.

A soft thud followed.

Her head snapped toward the door.

A man stood in the open doorway, one shoulder propped against the jamb. She flinched and pushed to her feet. He stayed put, letting her adjust to his presence as she tried to place him. Big guy. Dark hair. Intense bronze eyes.

Her gaze stroked over his features. "Gage, right?"

"Good memory."

"I try." Keeping the bed between them, she tipped her chin in challenge. "Are you in the habit of intruding on people?"

He shrugged. "I knocked."

Hope blinked. Crap. Not good. She needed to pay more attention to her surroundings. If she wasn't careful Forge would sneak up on her too, which would be—she shivered as the words *sexy*, *hot* came to mind and . . . dear God. What was she thinking? Having the gorgeous Scot slide in behind her would be the kiss of death. With her guard down, she'd give in to the attraction for sure.

Her focus on Gage, Hope banished her libido to the back of her mind. "Sorry. Didn't hear you. I was working something out."

"Uh-huh," he said, amusement lighting his eyes.

Blocking the exit, Gage shifted his attention from her to the room. Watchful and alert, he scanned every corner. Hope's brow furrowed as she looked around, following his visual sweep of the space. What was he looking for—a threat, a fight . . . both? Then again, maybe he was stalling.

A strong possibility given the way he stood.

He looked casual enough—ready but relaxed—and yet Hope read the hesitancy in his body language. Tilting her head, she focused on his face, his eyes, the set of his shoulders. Yup. Absolutely. Tense. Uneasy. Uncertain. All hidden behind a barricade of feigned indifference. The good-old-boy facade was effective, but a total farce. Gage was worried about something. A *something* important enough for him to seek her out.

Her first instinct was to talk, break the ice, and ask what was wrong. Years of experience stopped her, quelling the impulse. He'd come to her, which meant she must let him talk in his own time. Trust couldn't be rushed, and as silence gathered, spiraling between them, Hope tried not to twitch. But holy mother, it was hard. Standing idle while faced with a problem wasn't one of her strong suits. Neither was facing off with a guy radiating a crazy amount of lethal. And Gage? The guy practically vibrated with it, vicious piled on top of vicious. For all his strength, though, she didn't feel threatened. Wary? Sure. Watchful? Of course. Scared? Not even a little. Gage might be big, bad, and imposing, but she got the feeling he saved every scrap of violence for the enemy.

Finished examining the room, he returned his gaze to her.

Crossing massive arms over his chest, he raised a dark brow. "You always talk to yourself?"

"Depends."

"On what?"

"How much trouble I'm in."

He laughed. "So not multiple personalities then, just a pep talk. Forge giving you that much trouble already?"

"None of your business."

"Touchy."

"Not at all," she said, lying through her teeth. "Doctor-patient confidentiality."

"Call it whatever you like, but . . ." Tilting his head to one side, he sniffed the air. "I smell him all over you."

Her mouth dropped open. "You cannot."

A wicked gleam in his eyes, he grinned, leaving her hanging, letting her imagination spiral out of control. Her brow furrowed. The jerk. He couldn't possibly know that she—that Forge, that they'd . . .

Irritation rolled through her. Planting her feet, she crossed her arms. Enough patience. Time to move the conversation along. "Is there a reason you're here?"

"Definitely touchy."

"Not yet, but I'm headed in that direction."

Straightening her shoulders, Hope stepped around the corner of the mattress. Too aggressive of a move, maybe, but she didn't care. Gage was poking at a sore spot, looking for a reaction, hiding his worry by trying to get a rise out of her. She skirted the bench at the end of her bed, moving toward confrontation instead of away. A necessary evil. She needed to start as she meant to go on, and a guy like Gage understood one thing—strength. Show him weakness, and he'd go for the jugular. Every single time.

She inhaled past the knot lodged in her throat. "Either tell me what you want or I drop-kick you back into the hallway. You decide."

"Feisty," he murmured, laughter in his voice. "I like that in a female."

Her eyes narrowed on him.

"All right, all right." He held out his hands, palms up, in the universal sign of surrender. "Got a problem. Thought you might be able to help."

"Got a funny way of asking for it."

"Each to his own," he said, a rumble of disquiet in his tone. Dropping the tough-guy act, Gage exhaled, the rush of air slow and easy. After a second of silence, he palmed the back of his head. His chin met his chest. "Fuck—didn't think this would be so hard. I don't know what the hell I'm doing."

Her stance—along with her heart—softened. Taking a step back, she sat on the edge of the bed. "What's going on?"

A muscle along his jaw twitched.

"Look," she said, her focus sharpening. "I know I'm here to help Forge, but that doesn't mean I can't help you too. If you've got a problem, I'll talk it through with you."

"Never been to a shrink before."

"First time for everything."

Nerves getting the best of him, he cracked his knuckles.

"One word at a time," she said, tone soft, encouraging him.

"It's not about me . . ." He paused, frowned, then shook his head. "Actually, it is, but not directly."

She waited.

He cleared his throat. After rolling his shoulders, he found his voice. "I have a son—Osgard. Pretty new situation. I didn't sire him, but he's mine. I adopted him a month ago, pulled him out of an abusive home."

"How bad?"

"Nasty fucking shithole."

"Physical abuse?"

Gage nodded.

"Sexual?"

"He won't talk about it, but yeah, I think so," he said, rage in his eyes, a growl in his voice. "Here's the thing—I've never been a father before. I don't know what I'm doing or how to help him."

"How old is he?"

"Not sure. Sixteen, maybe seventeen. We don't have his birth records, and he doesn't remember celebrating a birthday."

A teenager. Tough. Particularly since most adolescent boys avoided heavy-duty issues in favor of bravado. "Is he the kid I saw at dinner?"

"Yeah." Stepping into the room, Gage grabbed the armchair in the corner beside the door. He dragged it over the hardwood floor toward the area rug. He set the chair down in front of her. Wooden feet thudded against the carpet. He scowled at the seat cushion, then flexed his hands, and sat. "First time he's agreed to come inside the lair, for a meal or otherwise. He's terrified of males."

And Black Diamond was full of them. Big, strong men with enough confidence to sink an armada of battleships. Which meant a man had abused Osgard. The observation made her heart pang. So many bastards in the world, not enough time to kill them all.

"If he's afraid of men, it's normal for him to be uncertain," she said, reassuring Gage as her brain pulled snippets of memory to the forefront of her mind. Osgard—tall kid, though not full grown. Dark hair, blue eyes, the handsome boy hiding behind Gage at the table. Scared kid, for sure, but . . .

Hope met Gage's gaze. "You're doing okay with him."

"How do you know?"

"He trusts you. He wouldn't have come into the house at all if he didn't." Resting her heels on the lip of the side rail, Hope set her elbows on the tops of her knees. Fingers laced, she leaned toward Gage instead of away. "I noticed he stayed close to you, allowed you to shield him from the others. That's huge, Gage. A great first step."

"You think?"

"I know," she said. "It may not feel like it, but you're making headway."

"He won't sleep in his own bed." His brows furrowed, Gage mirrored her pose and planted his elbows on his bent knees. "He has his own room in my apartment over the garage. Nice and comfortable, lots of space, and yet when I wake up each day, he's curled in a ball beside my bed. On the fucking throw rug."

"And that bothers you?"

"Of course it bothers me." He looked at her as though she'd lost her mind. "He's a youngling. He needs a good night's sleep."

"So move his bed into your room."

Gage blinked. "What?"

"He's in a new place with new people. Pretty scary for a teenage boy who's been hurt that badly. Think about it, Gage—when is Osgard at his most vulnerable?"

Gage frowned. One second rounded into two before understanding struck. "Shit—when he's sleeping."

"And where does he go when he needs to feel safe?"

Pushing away from his knees, wonder bloomed on Gage's face. "To me."

"Yes. To you. His father, the one man he knows will protect him. So screw convention—move his bed into your room. Stick it in a corner, up against the wall. Put your bed between his and the door. He'll feel safe enough to close his eyes, and you'll feel better because he's getting the sleep he needs to stay healthy. Easy fix."

"Okay," he said, breathing a little easier. "For how long? Is there a time limit? How long do I allow him to sleep there?"

"Give it a month and reevaluate. Once he gets to know the other guys and trusts they won't hurt him, he'll be ready to sleep in his own room."

"Good enough."

Hope smiled as relief and hope sparked in Gage's eyes. Her sense of purpose rebounded. Damn, that felt good—to be needed, to be useful, to have made a difference in someone's life. Pride thrummed through her, wiping out her earlier misstep with Forge. "Baby steps, Gage. No one heals from trauma of this magnitude overnight. It'll take time. Lots of patience. Lots of coaxing. Lots of talking it through when he's ready.

Take it one day at a time. As long as he's moving forward—no matter how slowly—consider it a win."

With a nod, Gage stood. "Thank you."

"Anytime." Following his movement, she slid off the edge of the mattress. As her feet met the floor, one of her boxing wraps rolled off the bed. She bent to pick it up.

With a quick dip, Gage scooped it off the floor. He looked from her to the coiled length of cloth and back again. His mouth curved. "Need to hit something?"

She huffed. "You have no idea."

"Grab your shit." Pivoting, he headed for the open door. "We've got a gym downstairs. I'll show you how to get there."

"Any kickboxing stuff?"

"A whole roomful."

Grabbing the second hand-wrap, Hope plucked her boxing gloves off the comforter. Equipment in hand, she hurried after Gage, following him out of her room and into the hallway. Hallelujah. About time, and not a second too soon. She needed to get herself under control and out of the libidinous danger zone. Before she did something stupid and slept with the one guy her ethics insisted she couldn't.

Shoulders propped against the wall, hands shoved into the front pockets of his jeans, Forge watched Mac sleep from across the recovery room. Halogens set on low, light cocooned the king-size bed, putting his best friend in the spotlight and him in the shadows.

Fine by him.

The dark corner suited his mood. And no wonder. Nothing had gone right since the moment Mac collapsed in the living room. Problems kept piling up, adding more trouble to the bottom of his tally. Case in point? His best friend still hadn't woken up. No matter how many tests Myst ran, she hadn't found out why he remained unconscious. Second on the list of Screwed-Up—the Archguard sharpened the hunt, calling for his head, going global by broadcasting his "crime" (and the charges) to Dragonkind packs worldwide, and Forge still couldn't remember a fucking thing. Last but never least . . . Hope. He glared at the end of the bed. Hospital gray, the metal footboard gleamed in the low light, framing Tania wrapped around Mac on the bed. An image of Hope spread beneath him popped into his head.

Forge gritted his teeth.

Shite. He'd messed up in serious ways with her—pushing too far, too fast. A bad move. One she made plain when she fled his room earlier.

His brow furrowed. Had he scared her? Maybe. He growled, his frustration loud in the quiet of the room. No *maybe* about it. She'd run like a frightened rabbit, and he was to blame. Problem was, how did he go about fixing it? Lines couldn't be uncrossed and . . . hell. He didn't want to *uncross* them. He wanted her in ways he'd never imagined. The softness of her skin, the taste of her mouth, the sound of her voice still hummed in his veins. A constant reminder of his yearning. Even now, hours later, he burned for her, craving her nearness.

Bowing his head, he stretched taut muscles, welcoming the discomfort. His reaction to her baffled him. Who would've thought he—a warrior born and bred—could be derailed by desire. All right, so Hope was spectacular, but . . . bloody hell. So little of it made sense to him. Being upended by a wee lass with big green eyes was absurd. Surreal. So far outside all his considerable experience, he wanted to hit something.

Mac would've been his first choice. The male always gave as good as he got in dragon combat training. Fast in flight, his friend maneuvered like a male twice his age, and was ten times as vicious. Which made battling with him a hell of a lot of fun.

Forge frowned at his friend. He wanted to yell, "Wake up!" Shake him. Curse at him and trade insults. Not grieve the male he loved like a brother. But even as he told himself to buck up, fear crept into his center. He couldn't lose Mac. Watching another brother die while he stood powerless to help . . .

Forge's throat went tight. Nay. Never again. His mind—his heart and soul—rebelled at the idea.

Which spun him back toward Hope.

He needed her right now—to soothe the ragged edges, to calm his dragon half and, as stupid as it sounded, tell him it would be all right. Forge frowned. Bugger him, how old was he anyway—five? A small child in need of soothing? He shook his head. How she held that kind of power over him in so short a time, he couldn't understand. But sometime during the night, wanting her had turned to needing her. She'd become his anchor in the heart of the storm the moment he'd wrapped his arms around her. A state of being he should no doubt question—and reject—but standing in a recovery room with Mac down for the count, Forge couldn't bring himself to let go of the lifeline.

God, he wanted to see her.

The impulse throbbed through him. Forge inhaled, filling his lungs to capacity before exhaling, and throttled back the urge. He couldn't seek Hope out. Not yet. He must stay a while longer, flesh out his idea before he presented the crazy-ass plan to Bastian.

Eyes narrowed, he ran his gaze over Mac again. No improvement. Nothing had changed in the hour he'd stood at the back of the room.

Tattoo glowing bright red, curled up in the center of the bed, his best friend twitched, muscles seizing, his expression one of pain, mind mired in whatever hell had taken hold of him. Every once in a while Mac groaned and Tania's breath hitched. Hugging her mate, she stroked his bare skin, murmuring soft words, wrapping herself around him, feeding him more of her life-sustaining bio-energy. The

Meridian rose in waves, rolling in before receding, crackling inside the room, supercharging the air.

His skin prickled. Pain danced across his temples. Forge rubbed his shoulders against the wall, absorbing the discomfort.

Mac moaned again.

Tania whispered her mate's name, trying to soothe him and herself.

The sound wrenched his heart.

What the hell was wrong? Virus or contaminate? Fixable or not? So far, no one knew. Lots of testing. Tons of back and forth. Nary a clear result. No leads either. His hands curled inside his pockets. Denim pressed against the backs of his knuckles, keeping him from putting his fist through the wall. He stared at the smooth expanse of pale paint next to him, zeroing in on a spot between two studs hidden by drywall and—

"Bloody hell," he growled through clenched teeth.

Putting a hole in the wall wasn't a good idea. If he KO'd anything else today, Bastian would kick his ass, then line up the rest of the pack to take a shot at him. So, time to take a step back. Damaging shite might be satisfying, but enough gym equipment had suffered.

The first casualty had been a weight bench, which now lay twisted inside the workout room. Total pretzel territory. The steel frame, though, had fared better than the exercise balls in the bin beside the basketball court. At least metal could be straightened. The balls, however? Forge cringed. No hope there. He'd popped the entire collection like popcorn . . . with nothing but his mind. First negative thought—pop! Second one—pop, pop! The third bout of brooding—pop, pop . . . POP!

The sound had been fantastic, if less than mature. Another bad move. One hundred percent selfish considering the potential backlash. The females in the lair used the colorful collection during Pilates classes and . . . shite. Myst would be up in arms. Totally pissed he'd left the ladies with a pile of plastic confetti instead of bouncy balls. Still . . .

The destruction had untangled the worry knotting his chest.

Absolutely worth the eventual scolding.

Taking another deep breath, Forge pushed away from the wall. He needed to get his thoughts together. Standing in the recovery room with his thumb up his butt wasn't helping Mac. Or Tania. The female might be doing her best to keep her mate stable, but time would win out. Without the reciprocation of healing energy from Mac, Tania would give too much and weaken. A dangerous state for a female. Eventually, she'd reach a tipping point and fall into energy deprivation. Major organs would start to shut down. Her brain would follow, pushing her into a coma and the inevitable slide toward death. So . . .

Forge squared his shoulders.

Time to figure it out.

Even if it meant proposing something radical. A strategy that might get him grounded by the Nightfury commander. But God, anything was better than waiting—than watching his best friend die one breath at a time.

Dragging his gaze from the bed, he headed for the door. His boots scraped over the industrial-grade floor.

"Forge?"

He glanced over his shoulder.

Arms wrapped around Mac, Tania raised her head off a pillow. Tired brown eyes met his. "Heading out?"

"Aye, but . . ." Hand curled over the door handle, Forge tipped his chin. "Donnae worry, lass, I'll be back. Eat something, and try tae get some sleep."

"Okay. You too. Grab something at the evening meal, Forge. Mac's going to need you when he wakes up," she said, unrelenting conviction in her gaze. Admiration for her grabbed him by the balls. She was magnificent. So fucking strong, exactly what Mac needed and everything his friend deserved. "Promise me you'll take care of yourself."

Throat so tight he couldn't answer, he nodded.

With a flick of his wrist, he opened the door and stepped into the hall. Heavy-duty hinges went to work behind him, hissing as the door met its frame. The electrical charge in the air disappeared. Quiet descended. Bowing his head, Forge stretched tense neck muscles, working out the kinks, and turned toward—

"Any improvement?"

His head came up. Intense green eyes stalled his forward progress. His stride slowed. Feet planted in the middle of the hallway, he took in Bastian's terse expression and shook his head. "No better, no worse."

B flexed his hands. "Fuck."

"Christ." Standing behind B, Rikar rolled his shoulders, the worry in his eyes telling. "What the hell is wrong with him?"

Good question. A fifty-million-dollar one.

"No clue, but . . ." Trailing off, he tipped his head toward the doors at the end of the hall. A conversation was in order. Time to roll out his idea, set the plan he'd been stewing over in motion, and pray Bastian agreed. He couldn't wait any longer, and judging by the worry on the pair's faces, neither could they. "We need tae talk, but not here. I donnae want Tania overhearing."

Mac's female didn't need to know. The mission was dangerous enough. No way he wanted her worrying about anything other than her mate.

Brushing past his comrades, Forge made for the double doors. Without waiting to see if the duo followed, he pushed both open and stepped into the clinic. The scent of antiseptic soap assaulted him first. The low buzz of overhead fluorescents came next, joining the visual rush of medical equipment. He walked toward the row of cabinets lining the sidewall. As he skirted the warrior-size operating table, memory flooded him, making him remember past injuries, highlighting the risks of his plan.

Electricity crackling in his wake, B strode into the clinic. "What's up, Forge?"

"I have an idea."

"About time someone did," Rikar said, snowflakes tumbling above his shoulders, broadcasting his upset as he cleared the door.

"First, I need tae know if you've heard from Azrad."

Bastian frowned at the mention of his younger sibling. "Nothing yet, but it's early. He won't break cover unless he's got solid intel to share."

"Shite," Forge murmured, wishing B's brother would hurry the hell up and find something to say. Not that he blamed the male for being cautious. Embedded inside the Razorback pack, Azrad played a dangerous game. One that involved hiding his true identity while he spied on Ivar for the Nightfury pack. The intel he'd given so far had been invaluable. Too bad there wasn't going to be any more forthcoming tonight. "I'd hope tae learn what's happening inside the Razorback pack, before . . ."

He trailed off. Rikar raised a brow. "What?"

"Information about rogue movements might've come in handy tonight."

"What are you thinking?" Bastian asked, moving across the clinic toward him. "What's the plan?"

Framed by cabinets behind him, Forge blew out a breath. "You arenae going tae like it."

Focused on Forge, B tipped his chin. "Tell me anyway."

"It might be, well . . ." Searching for the right words, Forge stepped back and, with a hop, planted himself on the countertop. Ass cheeks cooling on stainless steel, boot heels banging against lower cabinets, he ignored the bump of the top cupboards against his shoulders and eyed his comrades. "Crazy."

A fatalistic light entered Rikar's eyes. "A little or a lot crazy? Please tell me it's the latter. I haven't killed anyone in weeks."

Bastian grunted in agreement.

His gaze moved from B to Rikar and back again. "My plan leans heavily toward the 'a lot' side of the equation."

"Fantastic." Nudging a rolling cart out of his way, Rikar cracked his knuckles.

Leaning on the edge of the operating table, B crossed his arms over his chest, and his feet at the ankles. "Tell me what you've got in mind."

"Not a what," Forge said. "A who."

Rikar frowned.

B stared at him a moment, speculation in his eyes. One second ticked into more before the big male followed his line of thought. He sucked in a quick breath. "Fuck me. You want to go after Hamersveld."

Forge nodded. "Capture and cage him."

"Holy fuck," Rikar murmured. "Bring him to ground like we did you in the shipping yard."

"Aye," he said, suppressing a shiver. The powerful Taser they'd used to bring him down had hurt like hell. Knocked him out cold. He'd woken hours later, deep underground, inside an energy-infused prison cell with a magic collar full of explosives around his throat. "Pretty fucking effective. Pump the bastard full of enough electricity, and we'll bring him down and shove him into a cage before he wakes up. After that, the fun begins."

Bastian raised a brow. "Torture."

"If necessary," he said, not an ounce of remorse in his voice. He didn't like the torture route. Hit hard, kill fast was his claim to fame . . . under normal circumstances. But with Mac's life on the line, all things decent took a backseat. "We need answers. I think Hamersveld has them."

"You think the bastard knows what's wrong with Mac?" Rikar asked.

"Stands to reason," B said, his eyes narrowed. "He has similar markings to Mac, and given our boy's tattoo is glowing—"

"Bright red," Rikar said, voice deepening with the beginnings of hope. "The sickness is linked to the tattoo."

Staring at the wall above the row of medical machinery, Bastian shook his head. "Tricky, though. Hamersveld's a water dragon, and without Mac to keep him in check . . ." He paused, mind working overtime. "We'll have to amp up the voltage."

"To compensate for the damping effect of his magic?" A thoughtful look on his face, Rikar's eyes narrowed. "Makes sense. It's risky but—"

"Doable." Raising his hand, Bastian scraped his fingernails against the stubble on his jaw. "Not easy. Dangerous as hell, but doable."

Forge breathed a sigh of relief. "It'll get bloody."

"Shit, I hope so. But first we need to find the asshole." Thumping him on the shoulder, Rikar brushed past him on his way to the exit. "I'll talk to Sloan. Have him get into the database, see if he's got anything on Hamersveld in his files, then gather the others."

"Good. I'll speak with Gage about the Taser. He built it, so he'll know how to amp it up." B pushed away from the operating table. "Meet back here in an hour. We need a plan and everyone on board before we fly out."

Motion sensors went active.

The glass door slid to one side.

Moving like a male on a mission, Rikar jogged into the hallway.

Following Rikar's retreat, Bastian strode across the clinic. A second before he reached the exit, he glanced over his shoulder. "Oh, and Forge?"

"Aye?"

"See to your female before we leave."

His female. Forge blinked. Did he mean Hope? The question swirled inside his head before setting in. Hope—*his . . . all HIS.* Shite, that sounded good. Seemed right, even though it shouldn't. He needed to deny it. Should set Bastian straight before he got any bright ideas.

"She isn't mine, B."

"Keep lying to yourself." Amusement in his eyes, Bastian's mouth curved. "Sucks for you, but it's going to be fun for me to watch."

"Arsehole."

Halfway out the door, B laughed.

Forge growled, the nasty sound spiraling into empty air.

"She seemed a bit upset last I saw her," B said, poking at him, making concern rise and the need to soothe her course through his veins. "She's got good form, though. Sure knows how to hit a heavy bag."

Heavy footfalls echoing, Bastian disappeared from view.

The urge to go after him—to beat the shite out of the teasing bastard—grabbed hold. His dragon half buried the impulse, fixating instead on the one thing guaranteed to get him in trouble. Hope was in the gym, working out. She'd be hot and sweaty and . . .

The visual dug its claws in.

Longing blasted through him.

"Goddamn it," he said, fighting the attraction.

He lasted less than a second before his dragon half took over. Need swamped him, rushing in like a fast-moving current and . . . ah, hell. Screw it. He might as well admit it. He was cooked. Finished. Undone by the mere thought of her. Now he couldn't resist. She was just down the hall. Less than a hundred yards from where he sat. One hallway and a couple of doors away. Abandoning his perch, Forge hopped off the countertop. His feet touched down, but didn't stay put. Her pull on him was too strong. He wanted to see her, and it needed to be now.

Chapter Eighteen

Raising her fists, Hope kept her guard high and pivoted around the heavy bag. Footwork perfect, her bare soles skimmed over the hardwood floor. Shift right. Dance left. Keep her opponent in her sights. Rope creaked. The black bag swayed from her last strike. Muscles pulsing with energy, she flexed her hands inside the sparring gloves and, timing her punch, hammered the sucker again.

The violent thump echoed across the weight room.

The impact jolted up her arm.

Satisfaction hummed through her as her biceps squawked in protest.

Ignoring the discomfort, she struck again. And again. Jab right, a quick left cross before powering into an uppercut, moving in a rhythm that would make her trainer proud. Over and over. Again and again until her surroundings fell away. Concrete walls nothing but blur in her periphery, she brought her feet into play. Kicking high, she slammed her foot into the target zone. Black leather groaned. The heavy bag rocked sideways. Sweat rolled down her spine as she swung into another turn and, snapping her knee, slammed her heel into the imaginary bad guy.

Pivot. Spin. Slam-bang . . . do it over again.

Her heart pounded, each collision increasing the throb behind her breastbone. Now all she heard was blood rush. Not that she cared. Heart-attack, smart-attack. She needed the release, wanted the pain, longed for the mental shift into weariness. Feet and fists flying, she upped the pace until her chest heaved and her body ached, fatigue making her mind haze and . . . oh yeah. Thank God. About time. She'd hit the sweet spot, sliding down the slippery slope into exhaustion.

Maybe now she'd settled down.

She needed her brain to stop whirling long enough to formulate a plan. Execution was everything. At least, when it came to Forge. If she couldn't get her act together—and her attraction to the gorgeous but annoying Scot under control—she'd fail to keep him at arm's length, a safe distance away.

Squeezing her eyes closed, Hope pulled her punch mid-swing. She staggered back a step, wobbling on her feet, all of her hurting, and shook her head. What to do—what to do? The question knocked around inside her head, scattering neat ideals like bowling pins. Gosh darn it all. When had she lost the ability to think? Sometime in the last twenty-four hours, for sure. Now, for the first time in her life, she didn't have a clue what to do. Couldn't begin to understand how to help Forge—how to treat him, help him recover his memories—without becoming a nymphomaniac.

Opening her eyes, she frowned at her hands. Well used and worn in place, the red gloves didn't offer a solution. Hope sighed. Having a libido sucked sometimes. Particularly when it came to Forge. The second he got anywhere near her, she became one great big throbbing urge, the kind that tossed her into needy so fast it made her head spin.

And her body sing.

Hope huffed. "How the hell am I supposed to combat that?"

Good question. Another to add to the growing pile.

Not that it mattered.

Existential ponderings could wait for another day. The only thing that interested her now was Forge—and how to deal with him. She frowned. Or rather, herself. Forge wasn't the problem. She was to blame, responsible for her own actions, not the pointer of fingers.

What she required was a straightforward plan of attack. A strategy that was not only viable on paper, but achievable in real life, so . . .

Job one—murder her inner alley cat.

Task two—hit the bag hard enough to obliterate the lust Forge inspired.

Mission three—get her head screwed on straight and grow a backbone.

Sounded like a plan. Not perfect, by any means, but reasonable nonetheless. Now, if only she could—

Movement flashed in her periphery.

Hope spun toward the exit.

Forge stood in the doorway. So tall his dark head brushed the lintel, he looked her over. His gaze heated, darkening with desire, then wandered down, caressing her face, stroking over her body, and Hope shivered. A bead of sweat trickled down her back, pooling at the base of her spine, sensitizing her skin. The tank top and shorts she wore made it worse, cupping her like a lover, holding the heat in, making her throb with the pressure.

He stepped into the room.

The space contracted. The air warmed. Her senses narrowed, seeing only him: the width of his shoulders, the size of his hands, the hard planes of his face. God, he looked good enough to eat. She wanted to touch him, lick him like a lollipop, have the taste of him on her tongue again and—

Wrong thought. The worst really, given the plan she was trying to hatch. Figured, didn't it—that he'd show up before she implemented job one and task two? And crap, forget about mission three, its achievement so far out of reach Hope wanted to scream at the unfairness.

The realization sparked her temper. Swiping a damp chunk of hair off her forehead, she pointed her boxing glove at him.

"You've ruined everything. I'm supposed to treat you, not want to sleep with you, and now . . ." Knowing she sounded like a spoiled three-year-old, she huffed. God, talk about irrational. She shouldn't be blaming him for her weakness, but with him standing there looking so hot she could hardly stand it—her brain ceased to function at normal levels. Now she devolved, spiraling into unreasonableness. "And now, I'm so mad at you, I can't think straight."

"I know."

Surprise dropped her guard. Arms at her sides, she scowled at him. "You're not supposed to agree with me."

Amusement sparked in his eyes. "Nay?"

"No—you big jerk."

"Donnae call me names, *jalâyla*," he said, tone soft with warning as he moved into the room. "It'll get you in trouble."

"Trouble? I'm already in trouble." Baring her teeth, she snapped at him. "I'm not your plaything."

"You could be," he said, voice rough with desire. "I would love you for a playmate, lass."

Hope blinked. Temptation tugged at her. Thick yearning rose, tightening her chest, clogging her throat and—the self-serving, gorgeous idiot. He was baiting her, egging her on, hoping she gave in to the attraction and . . . God. She wanted to do it. Needed him so much, she actually considered it.

Her eyes narrowed on him. "Come any closer, and I'll punch you."

Halfway across the gym, he slowed his pace, but didn't stop. He ghosted left, making her shift with him. A sly move. The perfect strategy. She huffed. Talk about a smooth operator. He knew how to maneuver, pushing her buttons, pulling her strings, moving her across the hardwood floor like a master puppeteer.

He walked closer.

Hope sidestepped the heavy bag, maintaining distance between her and the man stalking her across the gym. He was bigger than her—stronger, faster, no doubt smarter in a fight too. She hated to admit it. Disliked the advantage he held, blocking the only exit, but

Hope refused to deny the facts. Forge moved like a dream, forcing her to pivot, ensuring she mirrored his movements. All of which opened her stance, leaving her more vulnerable by the second.

Angling her shoulders, Hope raised her hands, threatening him with her boxing prowess. "I mean it, Forge."

"I believed you, luv." His lips curved.

"Don't laugh at me."

"I'm not, but . . ." He trailed off, leaving the sentence unfinished.

Silence built like a wall, expanded out and up, touching the high ceiling, dripping down the concrete walls, making her itch with curiosity. No doubt his plan—the sneaky Scot. Which meant she shouldn't ask. She really shouldn't. Hope knew it, told her mouth not to open even as she heard herself say, "But what?"

"You willnae do much damage with those on." He flicked his fingers toward the gloves encasing her hands. "Bare knuckles are always best, lass."

"Like I said—jerk."

He growled, the sound soft yet ominous, the amusement in his eyes gone. Fine hairs on the nape of her neck stood on end. "I warned you, *jalâyla*. Now you pay the price for insulting me."

The threat echoed inside her head.

Anticipation shivered through her.

Wrong reaction.

Job one! Job one! her mind screamed. *What in God's name happened to job one?*

Excellent question.

Particularly since her inner alley cat appeared to be alive, well, and in heat.

Hope tried to scold it. Sleeping with Forge was a bad idea. She needed to remain impartial, ethical, and in control of her responsibilities. Terrific argument. Nothing wrong with her grasp on reality. Too bad her alley cat didn't care about consequences. The beast wanted what it wanted—now—allowing desire to override the system.

Her mind said one thing—move, shift, say something to stop him. Her body refused to comply, leaving her standing in the open, feet rooted to the floor, as Forge stalked across the gym. He strode past a freestanding weight rack. Her mouth went dry. He sidestepped a mangled workout bench. Air caught in the back of her throat. He skirted a pile of exercise mats. Her skin tingled, anticipating his touch.

Pay the price. Pay the price.

What the hell did that mean? A few feet away now, he growled her name, and Hope knew she was about to find out.

Closing the distance took a handful of seconds. Between one stride and the next, Forge reached her. A quick tug pulled Hope into his arms. His senses contracted. His magic flared, speeding through his veins as it wrapped him in pleasure. Hmm, lovely. Exactly where he wanted her—curvy body flush against his, gorgeous green eyes wide with shock, thick ponytail coiled around his fist—and . . . all right. It hadn't taken a few seconds. It had taken less than three—one, two, and . . . bam. Easy as pie. More satisfying than any dessert he'd ever eaten. A helluva lot tastier too.

And he'd barely touched her yet.

Her gasp puffed against the underside of his chin. She brought her hands up. Red boxing gloves bumped against his shoulders. Eyes locked with hers, he waited, giving her a choice, letting her decide, but . . . surprise, surprise. For all her bravado, Hope didn't try to hit him. She softened instead, conveying her need, broadcasting her level of want, asking without words to be taken. Beautiful female. Gorgeous beyond measure. A precious gift he didn't deserve, but wanted anyway.

Tightening his grip, he wound her hair around his hand, inhaling the delicious, dewy scent of her. Slick with sweat from her workout, she smelled amazing, like spicy cinnamon sticks and sunrise, the fragrance more addictive than the finest aphrodisiac. He growled in welcome, the beast in him scenting its mate as Hope tipped her chin up, parting her lips, unconsciously begging for his kiss.

He wanted to give it to her. Hand her everything. Every last microspeck of his focus. But not yet. A smart male started as he meant to go on, and Forge wasn't stupid. Ground rules needed to be set. A strong female, Hope would fight his tether, assert her will, and try to dictate the play.

Not going to happen.

A dominant male, he required a certain amount of control in the bedroom. Outside it, her opinion carried as much weight as his; everything was up for discussion. Inside it, however, she would give him what he needed—total submission in the sexual arena.

Twisting his hand, he pulled her head back a touch farther. Not enough to hurt, but enough to put her on her tiptoes. Body taut, dragon half barely contained, he shifted against her. Her back arched. The press of her breasts against his chest shook his control. He bared his teeth and bore down, asserting his will, unwilling to let his dragon half lead. Disaster lay in that direction. Denied earlier in the day, he'd get rough. Might end up hurting her. Something Forge refused to do and—

Hope quivered in his arms. She whispered his name, the uncertainty in her scent palpable as she reacted to his tension and . . . bloody hell. Not good. The last thing he wanted to do was frighten her. Once today was quite enough. But with his dragon half knocking against the cage door, begging to be set free, he struggled to hold himself in check. Unprecedented for him. He never lost control with a female. Hope, though, was different. His need for her crossed boundaries, into primitive and primal. A dangerous place to land, considering the territorial beast inside him demanded he take what it needed—Hope, in whatever position put him inside her the fastest.

Bearing down, Forge fought the urge.

"Hey." Bumping his shoulders, Hope refocused his attention. His gaze returned to her. Forest-green eyes full of concern, she patted him with her boxing gloves. "Are you okay?"

"Not really."

"What's wrong?"

"I want you too much. You threaten my control," he said, being honest, hoping it reassured her.

She blinked, surprise in her eyes. "Oh. Well . . ."

Her words dried up.

Worry churned inside his chest. Shite. A quiet Hope wasn't a good thing. He needed her talking, voicing her concerns, tackling her uncertainty head-on, not avoiding it. Otherwise, he'd never get what he wanted—her back in his bed. "Made you speechless, have I?"

"No. I mean, not really." Rubbing her lips together, she tilted her head. The move so adorable lust almost overwhelmed him. Again. Like always whenever she drew near. His dragon half didn't help. The impatient bastard kept pressing his agenda. One that insisted he take Hope now. Turning inward, he snarled at his beast. Hope blew out a long breath. "It's just . . . I'm trying to decide how I feel about your—"

"Need for you?"

"Jeez." She huffed, but Forge could tell she wasn't upset. The gleam in her eyes directed him, telling what he needed to know. The more honest he became, the more favorably she responded. "You don't pull any punches, do you? Do you even know what tact is?"

"'Tis naught but a waste of time. Blunt is better."

She rolled her eyes.

Unable to help himself, Forge slid his hand down her back. Spreading his fingers, he touched as much of her as he could and dipped his head. Hope met him halfway, parting her lips, humming in welcome, setting his body on fire. A shudder racked him. He stroked deeper, needing her taste in his mouth. She mewed, the sound so sexy he kissed her again before pulling away. "Hope?"

"Yes," she whispered, panting now, so breathless he hardly heard her.

"Do you want me?"

Her brow puckered. The movement wasn't much. Barely anything at all, but Forge understood the message. He read her like an open book, one full of tips to understanding body language. The slight frown, the way she shifted her weight from one foot to the other, the fact she looked away—all of it told a story. Hope didn't want to answer. She was afraid to face the question, and what her response would reveal. So she shied instead, searching for a way to deny him.

Forge refused to let her. He knew the answer before asking. Was attuned to her hunger, and the stark quality of her need. "Be honest with yourself, Hope. Tell me true."

She swallowed. The graceful column of her throat bobbed. "I shouldn't. I really, really shouldn't. Being with you . . . like this . . . is against everything I believe, but . . ."

As she trailed off, Hope closed her eyes, shutting him out, fighting herself, before opening them again. Conflict showed in her expression, and Forge understood. Acknowledging her desire for him was one thing, admitting it out loud was quite another. So he waited—silent, patient, worried as hell—for her to work it out, hoping she gave him the answer he craved.

"You've been honest with me, so it's only fair I be honest with you." Straightening her shoulders, Hope nodded. "I want you, Forge. I do. So much it hurts and . . . God. What does that make me?"

"Normal. It makes you *normal*, luv." Gentling his grip, Forge tucked her against his chest. He hugged her close, enjoying the way she snuggled against him, seeking comfort in his embrace. "No shame in admitting it. Guilt will never be a part of this."

"This?" Braving his gaze, she lifted her cheek from his chest. Her eyes glinted green through her lashes. "What is *this* exactly, Forge? I've lost my bearings here. I don't know what the heck I'm doing anymore. I came to Black Diamond with a clear mission—to help you regain your memory. So far, all I've managed to do is almost sleep with you."

"I like what you've accomplished, except for the *almost* part."

She snorted. "Do you have an off switch?"

"Nay. Not when it comes tae you," he said. "We're in the same place, Hope—wanting without getting. That's not going tae change unless we do something about it, so . . . time tae decide. What's it tae be, lass—me or weeks of sexual frustration?"

"Nice," she said, dry tone full of sarcasm. "Nothing like slanting it your way."

One hand flat against her back, he cupped her nape with the other. Holding her still, he lowered his head. Hope sucked in a quick breath, and he invaded her mouth. He didn't give her time to retreat. He conquered instead, taking possession, tangling their tongues, forcing a moan from her throat. Such a sweet sound. He wanted more of those, all of her sexy mews. Preferably while buried deep inside her.

Retreating a little, he gentled the kiss. She protested, trying to grip him with her boxing gloves. Half-drunk on her taste, he took her under again, fanning her need, feeding his own, nibbling on her bottom lip before releasing her mouth. Lips a hair's breadth from hers, he pressed his erection against the curve of her belly. Her breath hitched. He rocked into her, providing a preview of all he wanted to give her.

"How's that for incentive?"

"Stunningly good." A flush spread over her cheeks.

Her eyelashes rose, and Forge tensed as Hope met his gaze. She stared at him unblinking, examining him as though she'd never seen him before. He gazed back, refusing to break eye contact. His dragon half stirred again. A connection bloomed, calling forth his magic, sending delight zipping through his veins. Multiple streams of consciousness snaked into his mind. Like a braided river, the magical rills diverged, taking separate paths only to merge once more, connecting him to Hope, allowing him to read her intentions. Forge felt her mind spark. Wheels turned behind her eyes and . . . clever, clever female. Even overcome by desire, she assessed first and acted second. A fine attribute, one he couldn't help but admire.

"Forge—"

"Please, *jalâyla*. Let me love you." Tucking a stray lock of hair behind her ear, he cupped her cheek. So soft. So smooth. So pretty with the blush of arousal pinking her skin. Caressing her, he ran his thumb over her bottom lip. The tip of her tongue peeked out, licking over his skin, and . . . please God. Let her agree. He wanted her acceptance more than he needed his next breath. "No guilt. All pleasure."

"I could use that combination right now," she said, the yearning in her tone so thick his heart jolted.

"Is that an aye?"

"Yes—it is."

"*Yes.* Bloody hell, I love that word."

She smiled. "Especially coming from me?"

Forge growled. "Especially then."

Good Christ, she was beautiful. A veritable goddess with her strawberry blond hair a mess and green eyes full of mischief. He liked that best of all. Her trust humbled him. Her fortitude amazed him. And her need? Hmm, aye. Hope's hunger matched his own. She was a perfect fit—the right female . . . finally—and as he stripped the elastic from her hair and kissed her deep, Forge let go, unleashing a side of himself no woman ever saw.

Dangerous, mayhap.

Foolish, perhaps, to give so much of himself.

A warrior never exposed his flank, and emotional entanglement was never a good idea. But as he walked her backward across the gym, looking for a place to lay her down, Forge didn't care. Fuck convention. The threat of vulnerability too. Hope deserved the best of him, and he planned to give it to her—one mind-blowing orgasm at a time.

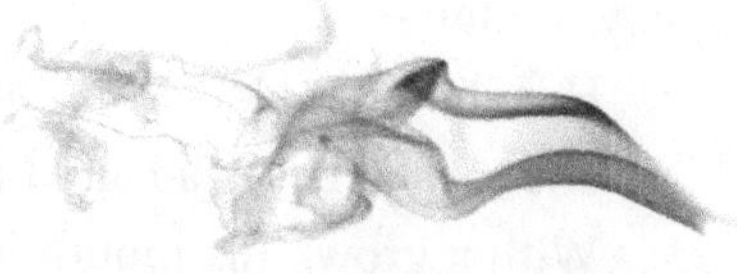

Chapter Nineteen

He tasted like fine whiskey and hot sex. A combination she loved. Nothing wrong with a single malt after work. Probably something wrong with having hot sex with Forge. But with his mouth on hers as he backed her across the gym, Hope couldn't bring herself to care. She didn't try to look behind her. She didn't ask where he was taking her. Or what he intended. None of it mattered. The moment he kissed her, the outside world fell away. All that remained was him—the wild taste of him, the heady feel of him, the delight as he dragged her so far under she couldn't catch her breath.

The idea of rethinking her decision disappeared.

It was done.

Over.

A lost cause. Ethics thrown under the bus along with her ability to say no.

She'd gone and done it. No second-guessing necessary. Hope didn't want to change her mind. She'd already tossed caution to the wind and said yes. Might as well commit. Might as well go with the flow. Might as well enjoy the ride and reap the reward.

Tangling her tongue with his, she pressed her breasts to his chest. The shift and rub drove her higher. She opened her mouth wider, took him deep, her skin so sensitive she tried to get closer. His big hands roamed the length of her back, fingers seeking the skin left exposed by her tank top. The fabric shifted. Damp cotton stuck to her skin. Hope frowned. Crap. Her workout. She was a mess, the opposite of sexy, a total—

Her shoulder blades bumped against the cinder-block wall.

She turned her head and broke the kiss. "Wait."

With a growl, his mouth jumped her throat. Day-old whiskers brushed over her collarbone.

"Forge, wait." Struggling to catch her breath, Hope gripped his biceps with her boxing gloves. "I'm all sweaty. I need a shower before—"

"Nay, I love you this way—hot, wet, and sticky."

Caging her with his body, he licked the side of her throat. Delight chased chills across her skin. She shivered as he did it again, humming his enjoyment, making her tip her head back to give him more access. Teeth pressed to her jugular, he suckled her pulse point. His tongue stroked her again before he settled in and drew on her skin. The slight pinch made her jump. He sucked harder, long enough to leave a mark.

Pinned in place, she gasped, uncertain whether to be delighted or outraged.

He tongued the underside of her chin. "You taste fantastic. Fucking gorgeous. I cannae wait tae spread your legs and lick you."

Forget outrage. Delight won out. "Forge, now. I need it now."

"Such impatience."

"It's been so long," she whispered without the least bit of shame. He needed to know she wasn't sexually active. Hadn't been for a very long time. Unwise, maybe, to give him that kind of ammunition. He could, after all, use it to tease her beyond what she could endure. Somehow, though, she didn't think so. Forge wanted to please her. She could see it in his eyes, felt it in the way he touched her, in the depth of his caring. Breathing hard, she undulated against him. "I'm on edge. I can't wait."

He raised his head to look at her. "I'll not rush my first time with you."

Panic nipped at her. She pushed against his chest with her boxing gloves. "I can't wait. I know it's stupid, but I can't."

"Easy." Reacting to her urgency, Forge gripped her hips and ran his gaze over her face. She squirmed, the pulse of desire so strong she couldn't stay still. "Does it hurt, Hope?"

"Yes," she said, her bottom lip trembling. She needed him, skin on skin, right now. Waiting would kill her. "I don't know what's wrong with me. I've never . . . I'm not usually this—"

"Needy?"

Her cheeks heated. *Needy* was a good word for it. The maximum kind of horny—extrasensitive—might be better ways of describing it. She'd never experienced anything so ragged. Her body throbbed. Her mind blurred, the burn jolting through her as though she'd been plugged into an electrical socket. Amped up. Voltage at dangerous levels. Supercharged and now ready to explode. No matter how hard she fought, Hope couldn't control her reaction. Heat buffeted her, rolling like whitecaps, frothing up desire, pulling her under until she was drowning in it.

He murmured her name.

She whispered, "Please," the plea in her voice bordering on pathetic.

With a quiet curse, he laid his palm to her breastbone, flattening her against the wall. Calloused fingers cupping her jaw, Forge tipped her chip up. Her gaze met his. His eyes started to shimmer. Muted at first, the glow intensified, the violet hue so mesmerizing time fell away, leaving her floating inside her own head. Hope blinked, a slow up and down. Her heart rate slowed. Her body calmed, powering down, moving her away from panic. Arousal banked but still burning. Muscles relaxed but still ready. The hum in her veins—the hot, hard edge of need—more manageable.

"There we go. Better. Breathe for me, Hope." The rise and fall of his voice washed over her.

Her chest expanded. "There's something wrong with your eyes."

"Is there?" He raised a brow. "Look again."

She did and . . . blinked. Weird. Whatever she'd seen was gone. What had done that to his irises—a trick of the light, long-denied pheromones, her somewhat scrambled brain cells? Had she imagined it? Her brow furrowed. She must have. No one's eyes glowed that way. Well, perhaps in the movies, but that was all computer generated, so—

"Jalâyla."

His growl dragged her away from the thought-she'd-seen-something dilemma. Tucking the mystery away, she refocused on Forge.

Staring at her from beneath his brows, he leaned away. "Arms up."

Hope startled. "What?"

"You heard me," he said, the angles of his face sharpening. "Arms. Up."

His voice deepened. The command in his tone made her move. Both her hands shot above her head.

"Good lass." The rumble of approval made her heart do a happy hop. "Now, hold still."

"Okay."

Movements measured, he reached up and grabbed her wrists with one hand. Holding both against the wall, he tugged the Velcro on the wrist-lock boxing gloves away from the cuffs. Slow and sure, he pulled until he held half of each wide strap in his hands. Hands still encased in her gloves, half the Velcro still locked around her wrists, Hope watched him tie the trailing ends together. She stared at the strong knot and frowned. What the heck was the point of that? The gloves needed to come off. Knotting them together didn't make—

Watching her closely, he looped the knotted length over a hook embedded in a cinder block above her head.

Her eyes widened. "What are you doing?"

"Restraining you. Pleasing myself."

The straightforward answer made her quiver. Oh God. Makeshift handcuffs. She tugged, testing her theory. No give. The microfiber held. The knot didn't slip. Her heart stalled, hanging behind her breastbone a second before starting up a driving rhythm. Tied up and trapped. Completely at his mercy, and oh, the things he could do to her. Naughty things. Delicious things. All the best kinds of things, and now, she couldn't do anything to stop him. Surprise dropped away. Excitement took its place, raising goose bumps on her skin.

One corner of his mouth creased. "Enjoy that idea, do you?"

Mouth gone dry, Hope swallowed. "Maybe."

"Scared?"

"A little, but . . ." She tugged on her wrists again.

He ran his hands up her arms. Checking the tension, he caressed the hollows on the inside of her elbows, the soft, tantalizing touches designed to drive her wild. Strung up, body on display, arousal rising, Hope trembled. He stroked her over and over, ever patient as he waited for her to continue.

She searched his face. Solid. Steady. Not an ounce of artifice in him. Forge would never hurt her. It wasn't his way. The realization steered her toward confidence. Worry leached away. "I trust you."

His breath caught. His hands stilled as he leaned in to kiss her. Once. Twice. A third brush of his mouth. "Sweet lass, you honor me."

Tears pooled in her eyes. Hope kissed him back, each soft caress as soothing as it was arousing. She shouldn't cry. Not now, in the face of desire and in front of a gorgeous man who wanted her. Too bad her heart didn't care. His compliment tunneled deep, digging up old wounds, exposing past grievances, laying her bare. Hope told herself to stop it—to be sensible and strong—but as her eyes burned and her chest ached, she couldn't stem the growing tide of emotion.

Such simple words. Each one, though, touched a place deep inside her.

No one had ever called her sweet before, certainly not her father, the one person who should have loved her no matter what. As strong as her father had always been, he couldn't hold a candle to Forge. He was the best kind of different—everything the vice admiral wasn't—and as she gazed up at him, heart in tatters, Hope absorbed his compliment like a plant denied water for too long. Oh, to be accepted and valued, to be found sweet instead of lacking, was incredible.

Inconceivable. Confusing too.

After years of playing second fiddle to her brother, she'd never thought anyone would truly *see* her. Not just the facade she presented to the world, but her—the flesh-and-blood woman behind the mask. In one sentence, Forge changed all that. She sensed it in his kiss. He liked her just as she was, making her feel cherished and important, *seen* in a way she'd never been before and . . .

Hope flinched. Whoa. Hold your horses, lady. Far too heavy a thought.

Swallowing the lump in her throat, Hope nuzzled the stubble along his jaw. Rough whispers scraped her skin, helping her regain her bearings. Thank God. Serious thoughts needed to wait for a more serious moment. Sex with Forge was supposed to be fun, not world altering. Which meant she needed to lighten the mood. Now. Before things got out of hand and she lost her heart to him for good.

Wiggling, Hope threw him a playful look. "You planning on torturing me?"

"Only a little."

Well, that sounded ominous. "Why am I not reassured?"

He chuckled. "Fuck, you're fun."

"Well, then, reward a girl, would you?" Wanting to get to the good stuff—like him naked and over her—she tipped her chin up and offered him her mouth. "I'll take as many orgasms as you care to give."

"Would you like each on a silver platter?"

"No," she said. "Just fast."

"There's that impatience again." His mouth curved. "But you'll have tae wait, *jalâyla*. I intend tae enjoy you first."

"Selfish."

"Ask me if I care?"

"Mean too."

Amusement in his gaze, Forge slipped his hands under the hem of her tank top. Strong fingers drew circles over her belly. Calloused palms slid over her rib cage. Without breaking eye contact, he found the bottom edge of her sports bra and pulled. The heavy elastic band obeyed the tug, the slow draw of fabric baring her an inch at a time. Cool air attacked her damp skin. Tugging on her bound wrists, Hope arched, begging him without words to touch her.

Forge didn't disappoint. Shoving her clothes up her arms, he cupped her breasts, big hands holding her secure, surrounding her with his heat. Her nipples furled tight. He rolled each one, pinching them between his fingertips.

Pleasure throbbed through her. "God, that's good."

"We've barely started, lass."

She twisted, trying to get closer. "I want your mouth on me."

With a growl, he dipped his head and nipped a tight peak. The tip of her breast pulsed. He licked the small hurt away, then suckled, drawing her into his mouth, bathing her in heat, making her breath catch. Closing her eyes, Hope tipped her head back. He bit down, pressing her between his teeth. She moaned. He sucked harder, taking her to the edge of pain and . . . glory, glory hallelujah. He was unbelievable. Just right, giving her what she craved: the firm hand of a skilled lover.

Arching into his touch, Hope keened in encouragement, egging him on.

Please, please, please, her mind screamed.

More, more, more, her body added, as urgency overtook her, zipping through her veins, glowing bright, pushing her into imprudence. She should do as Forge asked and be patient. He wouldn't leave her hanging. He'd please her in his own time. Hell, the pleasure would no doubt be better for it—explosive even—but as an insistent throb settled between her thighs, thinking became history. She didn't want a slow, gentle exploration. She wanted him hard. She wanted him fast. She wanted him inside her *now*.

Using the makeshift restraints as leverage, Hope fisted her hands and, with a quick lift, wrapped her legs around his waist. Hot and hard, his erection settled against her core. Shoulder blades pressed to the wall, she rocked her hips.

Forge released her breast. His head came up as he grabbed her bottom. She moved again. He shoved her backward, meeting her stroke for stroke. Her back bumped against cinder block. The Velcro holding her prisoner rasped in the quiet as Forge rolled into her, stroking her through her shorts. He snarled her name. Bliss blurred her surroundings, making her move with him, enslaving her a stroke at a time.

He shoved forward again.

The pleasure mounted. God, she was close. So very close. Almost there. Just a little more and—

Forge ripped the Velcro imprisoning her wrists open. The bindings gave away, freeing her hands.

"Oh yes, please." Curling her fingers in his hair, she offered him her mouth. He bared his teeth, snapping at her. The click of his molars echoed inside her head. "Sorry. I'm sorry. Go slow next time. Please, Forge—I need you right now."

With a soft curse, he grabbed the outside of her knee. "Unlock."

Thigh muscles quivering, she obeyed and opened, unwrapping her legs from around his waist. The second her feet hit the floor, he knelt and dragged her shorts down her legs. Tossing the thin fabric over his shoulder, he curled his hand over her bare hips, leaned in, touched his nose to the curls protecting her core, and inhaled.

"God, you smell good." Nuzzling her, he caressed the back of her thigh and kept going, moving down until he grasped her ankle. Applying gentle pressure, he lifted her foot off the floor. Her knee bent. He pushed it sideways, opening her to his touch. "Bet you taste even better."

Without giving her a chance to answer, he bent his head, spread her open, and licked between her folds. His tongue lashed her. The heat of his mouth scorched her. Delight whiplashed, sending her spinning into the abyss. Pleasure blasted through her. Forge growled and, tasting her deep, brought his fingers into play. Wanting more, she opened wider, baring all, giving him everything. Slick with need, her sex welcomed him. He slid in with ease, caressing her with one fingertip, then two. Back and forth. Rub here, stroke there, return for more as he learned what pleased her. Circling her entrance, he played, dipping in before retreating, only to come back and do it again.

Soft touches.

Slower caresses.

Mind-blowing pleasure.

The kind that left her hanging over a precipice Forge refused to push her over. Another light flick of his tongue. More gentle thrusts of his fingers. Her knee wobbled. He firmed his grip on her bottom. Muscles deep inside her clenched, released and . . . God. She couldn't take any more.

"You're so wet, lass. So hot." Flicking her with the tip of his tongue, he drew circles around her clitoris, exposing the bundle of nerves. Hips canted forward, Hope gasped, then groaned when he licked her again. "Like that?"

"Yes!"

"Want tae come?"

"Please!"

"Go on, then. Come for me."

His lips firmed. His fingers found her entrance and thrust deep—once, twice, a third time before he sucked . . . hard.

Hands buried in his hair, Hope came screaming.

The explosion rocked her world, sheeting white behind her eyes. Her legs gave out. Forge didn't give her time to recover. Still throbbing inside, unable to feel her toes or fingertips, Hope didn't object when he laid her down on the hardwood floor. She lay limp instead, fighting to catch her breath as Forge kissed her curls one more time and rose over her. His biceps bunched. She shivered, mesmerized by the hard flex of muscle when he fisted the back of his T-shirt and yanked it over his head. His heat hit her first, rolling over her belly to caress her breasts and . . . God be merciful. Look at him: so big, so strong, so beautiful he made her heart hitch.

Unable to resist, she set her hands on his chest.

He growled her name.

Hope whispered back, asking for patience. She wanted to explore, to make him hers one touch at a time, to enchant him even as he did her. Caressing him with her fingertips, she stroked over his shoulders. His nostrils flared. She ventured down, roaming over his chest, skimming his abdomen, following the dark trail until she reached the waistband of his jeans. She played with the buttons holding him behind his fly. He froze, chest pumping, muscles tense, as her hand slipped beneath denim. She played a moment, fingers dancing over his skin and—

Forge bared his teeth on a curse.

Hope hummed and, with a tug, popped open his button fly. One button, then two. Three, four, and five followed. Her gaze on his face, she curled her hand around his erection and . . . oh wow. He was incredible, velvety-soft skin over hot and hard. Wonder filling her, she explored his length, giving him pleasure, taking her own. "You feel so good."

"Bloody hell, lass." Eyes half-closed, he rolled his hips, seeking more of her touch. "Tell me you want me. Tell me tae—"

"Take me," she whispered, arching beneath him. "I need you inside me."

"And you'll have me—so deep, so fucking hard you'll scream my name." Taking her mouth, he forced her to open wide, take more of him, and taste herself on his tongue. The kiss lasted forever, yet not long enough, and when he lifted his head, Hope tried to follow. With a snarl, he nipped her bottom lip. "You're mine, Hope—*mine*. Every gorgeous inch of you. Donnae forget it."

His. All his.

The assertion should've scared her. Belonging to someone had never been big on her list of things to encourage, but somehow . . . for some reason . . . Forge's claim lent her power. The power to choose. The power to agree. The power to claim him in return. Strange in some ways. Just right in others. She didn't understand it. Couldn't explain it. Didn't care to either. Right now, all that mattered was Forge—pleasing him, seeing to the needs of the only man who'd ever claimed her as his own.

The idea settled deep.

As it found a home inside her, Hope trembled beneath him. Poised above her, balanced on his elbows, Forge nuzzled her cheek. Day-old whiskers burned over her skin, layering on sensation as he settled between her thighs. In no hurry, he stroked her out of afterglow and back into arousal: strong fingers playing over her skin, hot breath against her ear, sharp teeth grazing the underside of her chin. Such gentle touches. So generous in his attentions. So unbelievably hot, Hope burned brighter with each new caress.

His chest brushed over her breasts. She moaned. Intense violet eyes met hers. Her bottom lip trembled. He kissed her again. She opened her mouth wider, accepting his claim and staking her own. Craving the heat of him, Hope raised her knees and tilted her hips.

The rasp of his jeans brushing her inner thighs, he notched against her core. Big hands in her hair, he held her still, pressed in, thrust deep, possessing her with one hard stroke. Pleasure, more intense than before, arced through her, arching her spine. Lips parted on a silent scream, arms holding him tight, she tumbled off the edge and into ecstasy, trusting Forge to catch her.

~

Flat on his back in the middle of the sparring gym, Forge played with the thick ends of his female's long hair. Half on top of him, cheek pressed to his chest, Hope lay at ease in his arms, lost to the world after a long, intense loving. Raising his head off the floor, he watched her sleep a moment, then readjusted her, moving her head to the hollow of his shoulder.

A pucker appeared between her brows. She grumbled in protest.

Drawing a circle on her temple, he soothed her with a soft rumble.

The sound of his voice settled her. Her breathing evened out, warming the spot above his heart as he lay back and closed his eyes. God, she was sweet. Beyond beautiful. So bloody responsive she surpassed spectacular, burning hotter than any female he'd ever touched. His mouth curved. Not a bad tally when it came to Hope and sex. Throw impatient into the mix. Pencil in demanding—and peevish when she didn't get her way—onto the bottom of the list and . . . aye. Sounded about right.

Recalling the extent of her need, Forge hummed.

Christ, she was something. A female who enjoyed sex hot, hard, and fast. Every male's fantasy, the complete package, his absolute dream girl. Grinning like an idiot, so content he could hardly stand it, Forge stroked his hand over her back. The gentle caress kept him content, but didn't wake her. Up and down. Around and over. His palm roamed curves covered by the blanket he'd tucked around her.

He wanted to do more. Pull the thick fleece away. Bare her body for another round of loving. Wake her, take her, until she satisfied the ever-present need inside him.

His body stirred at the idea, readying him for her.

Forge blinked. Shite. Seriously? Again?

He'd already loved her twice. Had come so hard inside her the second time he'd feared for his recovery. Glancing down, Forge looked at his fast-growing erection. Demanding prick. It had the worst timing. He couldn't stay, was already fifteen minutes late for the meeting. Even now, the pack gathered, waiting for his arrival inside the clinic. Which meant he should get up and go. Now. Before Bastian and the boys came looking for him.

He stroked the backs of his fingers over her cheek.

She sighed.

"Hope?" Slipping his hand beneath the thick fall of her hair, he palmed the nape of her neck. His fingers went to work, massaging in gentle circles. "Time tae wake up."

She whined, the soft sound full of complaint.

"Come on, luv."

Her eyelashes fluttered open, tickling his skin. Stretching, she undulated against him, cranking him tight as she raised her head and set her chin on his chest. Sleepy green eyes peeked up at him. "Wow. I fell asleep."

"Aye, you did."

"How long was I out?" she said, covering her mouth with her hand when she yawned.

"Not long. Twenty minutes or so." Just long enough to make him late.

Knowing he needed to go, but unable to release her, Forge picked up a lock of her hair. The thick tendrils slid over his palm, glinting reddish gold under the glare of industrial-grade lighting. Fascinated by the color, he twirled the strands around the tips of his fingers and . . .

hell. He was in danger of acting like a pansy—one of those males who refused to leave a female—instead of the warrior his brothers-in-arms expected him to be.

Any other time, he would've said screw it and stayed. But not now. Not tonight. Mac's life took precedence over pleasure, but God, he hated to leave Hope after loving her so hard. When she was still so warm and cuddly . . . and looking at him as though he mattered to her. The soft acceptance in her gaze taunted him. Made him yearn for something he knew he had no right to think. Not that it mattered. The unruly questions refused to be ignored, circling inside his head, firing his imagination, making him ask what it would be like to be needed each day, accepted every night, but most of all loved by the female fated to him.

A mate for him, a second mother for his son.

The possibility swelled, taking root inside him. Pictures flashed in his mind's eye—a snapshot of Hope holding Mayhem, the sight of her growing round with his bairn, the idea of him creating a family of his own. And as he held her gaze, he wanted it so badly his arms tightened around her.

"Hey." Shifting to rest more fully on top of him, Hope folded her arms on his chest. "You all right?"

"Aye and nay."

"Give me the bad news first."

"I need tae go."

"Oh, well . . . okay." She glanced away, breaking eye contact, but not before he saw hurt glint in her eyes. Gathering the blanket, she shifted away, preparing to leave him. "No problem. I'll just . . . go."

Her voice cracked on the last word. She pushed to her knees.

With a muttered oath, Forge grabbed her waist, lifted her, and, sitting up, set her astride his hips. She gasped in surprise. He pressed down, nestled her core against his erection and her bottom on his thighs. The blanket slipped from around her shoulders, leaving her glorious and bare. Lust lashed him, urging him to lay her back down. An iron grip on her, he kept her in place and shoved desire back into its box, reasserting his control.

Unable to move off his lap, a blush spread over her face. She grabbed for the blanket.

Forge growled. "Leave it."

Hope froze, the blanket halfway up her back.

"Drop it, lass."

She hesitated a second, then let the heavy fleece fall. Soft and full, the folds pooled over his thighs and around her hips. With Hope naked in his arms, he looked his fill. Her nipples pebbled. Her color heightened. The hot flesh pressed to his groin grew hotter, slicker, sliding over him as she shifted in his lap. He groaned. She whimpered. Fucking hell. He needed to regain control of the situation. Fast. Without delay. Otherwise, he wouldn't be going anywhere, and Bastian would get an eyeful when he came to drag him out of the gym.

Inhaling deep, he exhaled smooth, throttling down. "Hope—look at me."

Leveling her chin, her gaze met his.

"When we're together like this, you donnae hide from me. No retreating. No running away. No jumping to conclusions either," he said, tone firm as he set more ground rules. He might have blundered by stating his intention to leave without an ounce of tact, but that didn't matter. She needed to understand he planned on keeping her, to have her in his arms for as long as the fates allowed. "Now, ask me for the good news."

"What's the good news?" she whispered, white teeth worrying her bottom lip.

"I donnae want tae leave you. If I could, I would stay, but I cannae. Not tonight," he said, hoping to reassure her.

He understood her reaction, and the insecurity that drove it. Women were complicated. No matter how confident, a female required reassurance after sex, kindness and cuddles, all the kisses she could handle. Under normal circumstances, he wouldn't care. The females he slept with understood he never stayed afterward. He gave each one what she asked—maximum pleasure in a minimal amount of time—then left.

No strings. No love words. No need for the softer side of things.

Hope, however, was different. For the first time in his life, he wanted to stay and give her what she needed. Forge huffed. Hell, he craved the intimacy too—the kind of closeness that would permit him to lounge in bed with her all day.

Holding her gaze, he traced her lips with his fingertip. Swollen from his kisses, her mouth parted, letting him push inside. Sucking on the pad of his thumb, she rolled her hips, sliding her slick heat against him. The muscles roping his abdomen tensed. "Bloody hell, lass."

"Sorry to be leaving?"

"Aye, bad girl, I am." Cupping her bottom, he stopped her from moving again and leaned forward. Hope met him halfway, returning his kiss before he pulled away. "Will you be all right until I get home?"

"Of course," she said, reacting as expected, like a strong female who'd had her independence questioned. His lips twitched. Her eyes narrowed. Forge swallowed a chuckle, knowing laughing at her would get him in trouble. The kind he might not survive given the fierceness of her expression. He clenched his teeth to keep from smiling. Fuck, he adored her spirit. "I'll be fine. I've got lots to do. I still need to plan our sessions."

"Good enough," he muttered without cringing.

A miracle. A true testament to his control. Christ, he deserved a gold star for hiding his uncertainty. *Hypnotherapy.* Forge swallowed his distaste. Shite, the word sounded as unappealing as the treatment. Not that he knew much about it. Mac said it would help. Forge wasn't so sure. Hope might be skilled, but nothing he'd tried rebuilt the memory. That night remained a black hole, the missing piece in a puzzle he couldn't complete. Bastian hadn't been able to help. Returning to the scene of the attack years after it happened hadn't worked either. Maybe he was a lost cause. Maybe hoping was a waste of time. Maybe the memory would never come back. But as he pushed to his feet and set Hope on hers, Forge wanted to give the female in his arms the benefit of the doubt.

"Keep the home fires burning, lass." One last kiss. A brief nuzzle against Hope's cheek. A quick pat to her bottom, and Forge turned toward the door. The holes in his memory would have to wait. The next few hours were about Mac, not him. About getting his best friend what he needed to survive whatever continued to attack him. "I'll be back for you later."

Wrapping the blanket around her shoulders, Hope rolled her eyes. "You are such a caveman."

Pausing on the threshold, Forge grinned at her. "*Jalâyla*, you have no idea."

She laughed.

The sound lightened his heart and cemented his resolve. He hadn't lied. He would be back for her. Would have her flat on her back in his bed when he got home. He consoled himself with the image and, footfalls thumping on the hardwood floor, left the sparring room and crossed the gymnasium. The buzz of industrial lights hummed, following his progress as he conjured his clothes. Magic flared. His favorite jeans and T-shirt settled on his skin. Leaving his feet bare, he walked across the basketball court toward the double doors.

Time to put his plan in motion and join the others.

Attuned to the chatter, he listened to his pack-mates talk, picking out the individual voices drifting in from the hallway, and sent a quick prayer heavenward. A quick word with the goddess, a ritual of his, one he observed each time he flew out of the lair. Life was short. Especially for a warrior in the heart of war. No matter how carefully planned, a mission could go sideways without warning. Tonight's op would be tricky, the raid more dangerous than most. A potential clusterfuck in the making. Downing any dragon without killing him was difficult. Caging a powerful water dragon would be even more so. So instead of shrugging off the ritual, Forge took solace in his routine, murmured each of his brothers' names, asking for safety and mission success.

Superstitious, maybe.

He didn't care.

Every little bit helped. And praying never hurt.

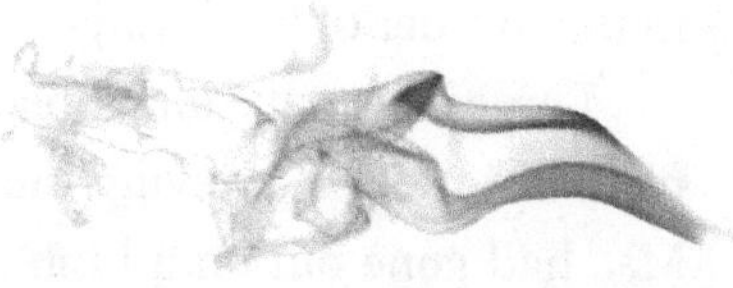

Chapter Twenty

Stretching out his shoulders, Forge turned left into the corridor and strode toward the clinic. Hardwood floors gave way to smooth concrete floors. The high polish gleamed dark gray as the round lights embedded in the floor threw splashes of light onto granite walls. Chisel marks stood in stark relief against the pale paint, reminding him of home and his painful history. Bowing his head, Forge cupped the back of his skull. He pressed down. His chin touched his chest. Taut muscles squawked. He kept his feet moving, knees bending, bare soles whispering in the quiet, pace steady despite his tension. Goddamn history. The past never left him alone. As unrelenting as a hungry wolf, it circled, making him recall the good times, taunting him with the bad.

Not that he could remember all of it. Which made him want to forget all the more.

A picture of Hope rose in his mind. Forge shook his head. Guess forgetting wasn't an option anymore. No sense turning away from the truth. Sooner or later, his female would dig it out of him. Supposition? Guesswork? Not even close. His time with her spotlit an unshakable truth: energy-fuse. His dragon half accepted her. Nay. More than that, the beast craved her now—wanted her close, needed her touch, longed for the sound of her voice. Combine that with the fact she gave new meaning to the word *skilled* in her field of study and . . . aye.

Sooner rather than later, Bastian would get what he needed: Forge's memory—the intel everyone hoped would implicate Rodin in the murder of his family—signed, sealed, and delivered by Hope.

Forge blew out a long breath. The idea shook him a little. Which pissed him off. Retrieving the memory was the whole point. Why Mac had gone out on a limb and asked Hope to help. And yet, he wasn't sure he wanted the memory dug out of his head anymore. Remembering—seeing his family die all over again—would hurt like hell. *Torn* . . . he was torn by the thought. Stretched taut between needing to help his new pack and protecting himself from the inevitable pain. Although, this time around, he wouldn't be alone. Hope would be there to help him pick up the pieces in the aftermath. He frowned. At least, if she chose to stay with him, instead of fleeing the second she learned of Dragonkind.

The possibility cranked him tight.

Fucking hell. He didn't like the direction of his thoughts. Bastian was right. Hope was his female . . . *HIS*. Every stunning inch of her.

She belonged to him.

He was meant for her.

Only a fool would deny it now.

The idea scared him. With the Archguard out for blood, he had a target on his back. Which meant if he mated her—performed the ancient ceremony joining his life force with hers—the bull's-eye would expand to include Hope. Dropping his arms to his side, Forge flexed his hands. He wanted her. He really did, but fuck, the optics sucked. If Rodin came for him, it would be a fight to the death. One winner. One loser. His mate caught in the middle. As a mated male, if he died, so would his female and—

He slammed into something.

The *something* shoved back.

Jarred out of his thoughts, Forge rocked back on his heels. His head came up along with his fists.

"Forge—pull your head out of your ass, man." Ruby-red eyes flashed in irritation. With a growl, Venom batted Forge's fist out of his face. "Watch where you're going."

"Shite," he said, taking a step back, giving his friend room to breathe. His gaze bounced around the hallway. Crowded between the chiseled walls, eight males stared back and . . . hell. Talk about inattentive. The entire pack was assembled, living large in the corridor outside the clinic doors. Rubbing the back of his neck, Forge cleared his throat. "Sorry. Lost in thought."

Venom snorted. "I noticed."

B chuckled. "The right female will do that to a male."

Gage raised a brow. "What—make him stupid?"

"Worse," Rikar said, a shit-eating grin on his face. "Relocate his brain behind his button fly."

"And keep it there," Wick said, serious amber eyes leveled on him.

"Bloody hell." Forge scowled, fighting the urge to adjust the insatiable beast inside his jeans. "Does it get any better?"

"Nope," Venom said with such glee Forge wanted to punch him. "Get used to it, buddy."

"Lovely." Forge sighed. No relief in sight—ever. Such a terrific way to start the night.

Stepping alongside him, Bastian threw him an amused look. The unsaid "I told you so" rubbed Forge the wrong way. B might be right about him and Hope, but that didn't mean the arsehole needed to grind salt in the wound. He glared at his commander. Unperturbed by the warning, the big male slapped him on the shoulder. The love tap reverberated down his spine and out through the soles of his feet.

"We've got a plan," B said, dropping the subject of females. "Ready to hear it?"

Unease transformed into a sense of purpose. Forge exhaled in relief. Good. Better. The best, in fact. He appreciated the save. Particularly since he wasn't ready to talk about Hope—and her startling effect on him—yet. Glancing around the room, seeing the serious faces, Forge nodded. "Lay it out."

"Three teams," B said. "Venom, Wick, and Sloan will take the north side of the Sound. Gage, Haider, and Nian, the south. You, Rikar, and I will set up on Bainbridge Island."

Nine warriors. Three groups. Multiple locations.

Doing the math, Forge tilted his head. "Roughly, what—five miles apart?"

"Yeah." Rikar turned toward the map taped to the wall. Three *X*'s marred the glossy surface, pinpointing the triangulation. The Nightfury first in command drew a circle around Puget Sound. "Outside the three-mile marker. Far enough away to avoid detection, close enough to close the gap quickly."

Great plan. Thorough, well thought out, but . . . Forge's brows furrowed. "How do we know he'll show up?"

"He won't be able to resist."

Glancing sideways, Forge looked at the speaker. His focus narrowed on Nian. The male didn't flinch. Standing shoulder to shoulder with Haider, the Archguard prince met his gaze head-on. Forge's mouth curved. Well, all right, then. About time, actually. He'd been waiting for Nian to assert himself and get involved. Contributing—adopting the warrior values of the Nightfury pack—was the only way to win his brothers-in-arms' respect.

Tipping his chin, Forge kept his attention on Nian. "Tell me why."

"I know Hamersveld. I had dealings with him in Prague." Eyes shimmering like multicolored opals, Nian rolled his shoulders. The stitching on his bomber jacket stretched. Leather creaked, joining the faint sound of rushing water. "The bastard's a creature of habit. He swims between three and four a.m. every night, in the biggest body of water he can find. No exceptions. The ocean—all that salt water—will draw him. He won't be able to stay away from Puget Sound."

"All right," Forge said, accepting the intel as fact. "How many volts do we hit him with tae bring him down?"

"A shit-ton, times two," Gage said, setting his boot on the huge black case at his feet. "Wick and I will wear the Tasers."

He raised a brow in surprise. "We have a second one?"

"Another prototype. More powerful than the first one I built." A nasty gleam in his eyes, Gage grinned. "It'll zap the shit out of Hamersveld. The asshole won't know what hit him."

"Perfect." And it was. The more painful the encounter for Hamersveld, the better. "Let's go."

A rumble of agreement sounded in the hall.

As one, the pack shifted toward the wall dead-ending the corridor. Boots scraped against concrete. Heavy footfalls pummeled the quiet. Magic flared, raining down like sparks in darkness as each warrior banged on the portal, asking the force field that protected Black Diamond—hiding the lair from humans and Dragonkind alike—to open the doorway into the landing zone.

Faced with nine warriors, the magic-born beast didn't balk.

Solid stone went wavy, then cleared.

Arched at the top, the door stood tall, leaving a clear pathway to follow. Musty air blew in from the LZ. Forge reached the portal first and stepped through. Smooth concrete transitioned to rough granite. Like giant fangs, stalagmites rose on either side of him. Ignoring the show of teeth, Forge ramped into a run and sprinted toward the cliff edge.

Magic throbbed in his veins.

Gravel crunched beneath his boot treads.

Wind whipped at his face. The rush spread like a shock wave. Light globes against the high ceiling bobbed, raining dust motes as Forge transformed. Hands and feet turning to talons, his body lengthened, dark-purple scales clicking into place. Armored up and buttoned down, he bared his fangs and, claws scraping over stone, leapt beyond the lip of the LZ. His tail whiplashed. The spikes along his spine rattled. His wings caught air, lifting his bulk as he banked hard and rocketed into the underground passageway. The rumble of falling water echoed against jagged rock walls. He heard his pack-mates take flight behind him.

Forge didn't slow.

He increased his velocity instead, blasting through the waterfall hiding the entrance, and launched himself into the night sky. No time to lose, even less to waste. The faster he downed Hamersveld, the sooner Mac got what he needed, and Forge would have Hope in his arms once more.

Chapter Twenty-One

Standing in the antechamber connected to his laboratory, Ivar tapped his fingertips against the keyboard space bar. The bank of monitors mounted to the wall woke up, the prompt for his password an island surrounded by an ocean of blue screen. He stared at it a moment, worry sitting like a hair ball in the pit of his stomach.

He'd landed less than five minutes ago.

The instant the timer on his watch went off, and the first round of Dragonkind Olympics had concluded, he'd dragged Hamersveld out of the hot tub and flown home. The male wasn't happy. Ivar didn't care. His XO needed to get his head screwed on straight. Choosing males to breed his HE females when the Meridian realigned might be important, but the development of his antiviral drug took precedence. Females were dying—babies, toddlers, teenagers, mothers or not. The virus he'd released in Granite Falls didn't discriminate. Which meant, as much fun as the competition was turning out to be . . .

Playtime was over.

The need to know had pointed him home. Upon arrival, he hadn't hesitated. His feet had taken him across his backyard, up the stairs of 28 Walton Street, into the elevator, and down to his underground lair where the test results waited. Hamersveld on his heels the whole way. Now, his XO stood at the back of the room, shoulders propped against the wall, arms crossed over his chest, a frown on his face.

Ivar clenched his teeth. Jesus be good to him, he needed his current attempt to work. Otherwise, the warrior standing at his back would doubt him, along with every male in the Razorback pack. Not the best place for a leader to find himself. Military coups started that way—when dissatisfaction turned to frustration, and anger into action.

Disquiet jangled his already-frayed nerves.

Ivar scowled. Enough of the bullshit. The unease chattering inside his head needed to shut the hell up. What the males he commanded thought of his efforts—and lack of results—didn't matter. Time, however, did. The longer he delayed examining the results, the more females would die.

Fingertips striking the keyboard, he tapped in his password and slid his thumb over the trackpad. The cursor landed on the video file he needed. One click and—

"Son of a bitch," he whispered, staring at a computer screen full of dead virus. Raising his arms, he cupped the back of his head. His chest tightened. Tears pricked the corners of his eyes. After all this time. After all his attempts. After all the frustration and failure. "I did it—I fucking did it."

His quiet words spiraled into the room. A beep sounded as the video ended. The computer screen shifted back to blue.

A large hand landed on his shoulder.

"Jesus!" Fists raised, Ivar swung around.

Hamersveld took a giant step backward, moving out of striking range. "Sorry. Thought you heard me."

Ivar scowled. "The hell you did."

The sadist SOB smirked, then tipped his chin at the screen. "It's done?"

"Almost. The antiviral works. Now—"

"Thank God," Hamersveld said, the tension in his face relaxing.

Ivar nodded, the same kind of relief taking hold. "I need to make more of it—prepare individual doses."

"How long will that take?"

"Minutes." A fast timeline. Unheard of—hell, undoable—in the human world. But now that he knew the basic compound, he could use his magic and replicate the antiviral drug in a fraction of the time. Storing it wouldn't be a problem either. The vault in his mind held more than enough room to transport the required dosages to the CDC quarantine center in Granite Falls. "Five at most, and I'll have everything we need."

"How long to dose the infected females?"

"A couple of hours."

Hamersveld glanced at the clock hanging above the door. "One a.m. Ten-minute flight time, a couple of hours there, another ten to get home." Thoughts churning behind his eyes, Hamersveld cocked his head. "We still have time to make it to the hospital and do what needs to be done tonight. Get a move on, Ivar. If you're fast enough, I'll get a swim in before dawn."

Ivar raised a brow. "Thought you got enough in your homemade hot tub earlier."

"That wasn't a swim, man," Hamersveld murmured, a wicked gleam in his blue-rimmed, shark-black eyes. "Just fun."

His lips twitched. Crazy water dragon. The male never quit. Or stopped asking for time in Puget Sound, a favorite watering hole of Hamersveld's. Ridiculous most nights, but . . . the warrior spent more time submerged than in open air. It was amazing the male wasn't permanently pruned. Not that it mattered. With the cure in hand, Ivar had bigger fish to fry. His antiviral needed to be made without delay. Closing his eyes, Ivar fisted his hands and bowed his head. Centered inside his magic, he called on his beast.

His dragon half rose.

Inferno-like heat streamed into his veins.

The compound took shape and form inside his mind. Calibrating each dose, Ivar manufactured one vial after another. A stockpile grew inside his mental vault. Stack after stack. Crate after crate, while he sent countless thank-yous to the goddess. Without divine intervention, he never would've found the antidote in time. Without her grace, human females would continue to die, dragging all of Dragonkind down with them.

The last time he left Cascade Valley Hospital, Ivar vowed never to return. He'd done his job. Completed the task, only to discover the disastrous results later on. Tonight, though, would be different. It wasn't about wreaking havoc, but fixing what he'd broken.

Righting wrongs. Mending ruined lives. Healing human bodies.

White streams trailing from his wing tips, Ivar banked into a tight turn, circling the building from above. Oh, the irony—him playing the hero to humankind. The situation bordered on laughable, but as he returned his attention to the flat roof, he didn't laugh. He got ready instead, sharpening his senses as his personal guard flew by and fanned out, taking up protective positions around the hospital. Tucking his wings, he dropped out of the sky as the pack settled and Hamersveld landed behind him.

Huge talons thumped down on frozen grass.

His friend shrugged his shoulders. Once. Twice. A third time.

Ivar's mouth curved as the male's wings caught air. Rolling gusts rushed down the street. Cars rocked on tires. Leafless tree limbs swayed as debris blew down the street. His friend shifted from dragon to human form. He followed suit, conjured his clothes, and stomping his feet into his boots, stepped off the curb.

Hamersveld tipped his chin. "You all right?"

"Never better," Ivar said, his attention on the front doors.

A pause. The sound of cracking knuckles.

Ivar glanced over his shoulder. Seeing Hamersveld's expression, he raised a brow. "What?"

His XO's focus jumped from him to the building, then back again. "I think I should come in with you."

He threw his friend his best what-the-hell look. "You hate hospitals."

"I know, but . . ."

He waited—and waited, and waited some more—for the male to spit out whatever was stuck between his teeth. Total silence. Nothing on the enlightenment front. Nary a peep from a male who enjoyed being blunt and never pulled his punches.

Hamersveld pursed his lips. "I hesitate to mention it."

Ivar lost his patience. "Just tell me, already."

Scratching the blond stubble on his chin, Hamersveld glanced at the hospital again. "Last time you went in there, you blew a hole in the side of the building."

Ivar scowled. "Not on purpose. Venom ambushed me."

"Still—"

"Nyet," Ivar said, cutting off his friend. He'd screwed up, lost Evelyn Foxe—a valuable HE female—in the fray, and started a global pandemic. He clenched his teeth. Jesus. Like he needed reminding. Holding his friend's gaze, he shook his head. "Stay here. Keep an eye out. If any Nightfuries—"

"Bastards," Hamersveld growled.

"—show up," Ivar said, rolling over the interruption. "Start a fight first, let me know second."

"I hope they do. I need to kill someone."

Ivar's lips twitched. "Stay sharp."

"Uh-huh." Eyes aglow, Hamersveld stared at him, then shook his head, and shifted back to dragon form. Magic expanded and contracted. Water blew into the air, coating his clothes in a fine mist.

Smooth gray scales glinting in the low light, his friend lifted off, jagged sawtooth spine rippling as his webbed paws left the ground. Wing tips even with the building top, his friend glanced down and switched to mind-speak. *"Get it done, Ivar. I don't want to be here all night."*

Giving Hamersveld the one-finger salute, Ivar put himself in gear. No sense arguing with the bossy male. His XO was right. He hadn't flown all the way from Seattle to stand around all night. Time to get a move on.

Five minutes and some fast walking later, he stopped outside the CDC's quarantine area. Ivar glanced at the electronic keypad on the wall beside the door. Disengaging the lock with a thought, he swung the door open and stepped over the threshold into a makeshift prep area. Plastic tables to his right. A myriad of medical supplies shelved to his left. Not a human in sight. Perfect. Just what the scientist ordered: no pesky witnesses, zero interruptions. Reaching into his mental vault, Ivar grabbed the first antiviral. Already filled and ready to go, the syringe settled in his hand, and he moved, pushing through the sheeting separating him from a long stretch of hallway.

The stench of sickness hit him.

Moments later, the misery registered.

His stomach clenched in protest. Fucking hell. Never in his wildest imaginings had he envisioned this—so many in such terrible pain. Women lay dying everywhere: on beds lining the corridor, in large rooms with open doors, on gurneys by the high-countered nurses' station. The female on the cot he stood next to moaned.

She grabbed his pant leg. Brittle nails scratched against his jeans. "My baby . . . Emma. Please check on her. Can you—"

"I will," he said, soothing her before he thought better of it. Rotating the syringe in his hand, he fit the needle into the notch on her IV and pushed the plunger, sending medicine into a tube attached to her arm. One down, a shitload to go. "I'll check on her."

She whispered a weak thank-you.

With a quick swivel, Ivar turned away without responding and entered a hospital room. Boots planted just inside the door, he scanned the windowless space, taking in the rows of narrow beds. The sound of crying tore open the stale air. Ivar frowned and, ignoring the plaintive whimpers, stopped beside the nearest cot and delivered the second dose. One after another. Female after female: young and vibrant, old and crooked; he didn't discriminate, making steady work, leaving the hospital nursery for last.

Not the brightest idea.

He should've done the infants first. Gotten it over with, but . . . Jesus. He didn't want to go in there and see a host of babies suffering.

Bracing himself, Ivar stepped inside the nursery anyway and . . . almost balked. Good Jesus, just kill him now. So many little girls, each one suffering alone, without the comfort of her mother or sire.

Ivar blinked as the thought snaked through his mind.

Hamersveld would scoff at his show of tenderness. The male would tell him he'd lost his mind along with his hard edges, maybe even call him weak. Months ago, he would've done the same and labeled human suffering well deserved. But as minutes passed and he reached the last crib, Ivar couldn't discount the experience. Or how settled he felt after soothing the little girls, most now fast asleep in their beds. He loved science. Adored working in his lab. Enjoyed the challenge of discovery and busting through new frontiers. But as he stared down at the final infant he needed to help, his gaze on the tuft of red hair nearly the color of his own, something fundamental shifted deep inside him. The crack in his defenses widened. Emotion spilled through the fissure, forcing him to confront a profound truth long forgotten.

He hadn't always been an uncaring male.

Somewhere along the line, he'd shut out his human side, relying on his dragon half to carry him through difficult times. Half human, half dragon—the building blocks of his kind. Two halves of a whole, a combination of species spliced together by the Goddess of All Things. One he'd spent most of his adult life ignoring instead of—

"Ivar."

The deep voice cracked through mind-speak, jarring him.

The infant flinched, whimpering in distress.

Ivar cupped her tiny rib cage. Responding to the gentle touch, she settled, making his lips curve as he answered his XO. *"Da?"*

"Almost done?"

"I just gave the last dose."

"About time, now—" The click of claws tumbled through mind-speak. *"Get the hell out of there. It's already three-oh-five."*

"Take off, Sveld. Go for your swim, but do something for me first."

"Aw, hell. I'm not going to like it, am I?"

"Take three of my personal guard with you."

Hamersveld growled. *"Unnecessary."*

Very necessary. An unavoidable precaution. With the Archguard sequestered, Zidane on the loose, and a traitor inside his pack, his XO's nights of flying off alone were over. *"I don't give a fuck if you like it or not."*

"I don't need guards," he said, sounding affronted.

"You are a part of my pack now, Sveld. I will not risk you or Fen," Ivar said, tightening the noose, bringing Hamersveld to heel, using his wren against him. *"No one flies out alone. Not anymore."*

Hamersveld muttered something nasty in Norwegian.

Ivar ignored him. *"Rinner, Gillis, Syndor—go with him. Make sure he returns home in one piece."*

"Yes, commander," the trio said in unison.

"Good," Ivar said, approval conveyed in one word. *"The rest of you wait for me. I'm coming out."*

The remaining four guards murmured in assent.

Hamersveld cursed again.

Ivar severed the link, cutting his friend off mid-grumble, and headed for the exit. Another problem solved. Now on to the next, the one he couldn't get out of his head. Sasha Cooper, the female forever on his mind. He wanted to ignore her. To forget she existed and move past the night she'd nearly killed him, but . . . hell. His dragon half refused to let him, so . . . yeah. No more putting it off. Time for a late-night visit and an in-depth chat.

Chapter Twenty-Two

Crouched atop a ridge on Bainbridge Island, Forge looked out over Puget Sound. City lights winked in the distance. Waves crested and rolled in the bay, merging with unseen undercurrents before flowing past Seattle and out to sea. The icy swirl threw damp tendrils into the air, coating his scales with water, obscuring his vision with fog, making his unease keep time with frothing whitecaps. Refolding his wings, he adjusted his stance for what seemed like the thousandth time.

Raising a paw, he flexed his talons. Black, razor-sharp tips gleamed in the moon-glow. The show of strength didn't temper his worry. The relentless shift and shuffle didn't settle him either. Step closer to the edge of the cliff. Climb to the row of boulders above the beach below him. Hop back down. Resettle once more. No matter what he did—or how often he changed position—nothing eased the disquiet. Not surprising in the grand scheme of things. Waiting always set his teeth on edge.

So did sitting in a human's backyard.

Not that the female could see him.

Hidden by a cloaking spell, Forge glanced over his shoulder. Clad in cedar siding, the bungalow stood like a ghost against the night, a pale swath in the pitch black and . . . yup. Still there. Still burning the midnight oil. Still oblivious to his presence less than fifty yards away.

Framed by a large picture window, the female stood at a tall table, hands busy making something, a solitary lamp the only light on in her workshop, her bronzy aura burning like a ring of fire around her. A beacon in the darkness. A gem hidden in the wilds of a winter forest.

Naked tree limbs creaked above him.

Rough bark brushed against one of his horns.

Sinking lower into his crouch, Forge shuffled sideways.

"Pretty little night owl." Ice-pale eyes locked on the high-energy female, Rikar leapt onto the huge boulder behind him. White claws grazed over stone like nails on a chalkboard.

Forge gritted his teeth. He took a deep breath, exhaled in a slow rush, tried to relax, but . . . Christ. It was impossible. With his patience shot and his nerves frayed, he couldn't stand the scrap of extra stimuli. Everything—his pack-mates included—irritated the hell out of him.

"Hard at work tonight."

Ruffling his scales, Forge dragged his focus from the female. As the clickety-click-click of his interlocking dragon skin settled back into place, he scanned the Sound, hoping for trouble—nay, strike that. Make it, *needing trouble*—and a whole pack of rogues to kill. *"Aye, she is."*

"Tempted?" Hanging from the cliff face, Bastian poked his horned head over the edge.

"By her?" Forge huffed. No chance. Pretty as the female looked, powerful bio-energy aglow behind her windows, she didn't interest him. He already had a female. A gorgeous one with an unwavering spirit, an abundance of brains, and a mouth that never quit. The memory of her back talk made him smile and . . . fuck. He'd left her half-naked at home, beautiful body on display, ready for another round of loving. Goddamn his bad luck . . . and Mac's illness. *"Not even a little."*

"Spoken like a bonded male," B murmured, hammering him with the truth again. *"Well and truly caught."*

"Would you stop that shite?"

Peering down from the boulder, Rikar cocked his head. *"What?"*

"I already know I'm screwed," he said, letting his pissy mood out of the box. *"I donnae need you two reminding me."*

Ignoring his wishes, Rikar poked at him. *"So . . . you going to claim her?"*

"I want tae, more than anything, but . . ." Searching for the right words, Forge frowned. *"It isnae that simple."*

"Yes, it is, Forge." Talons digging into rock, Bastian jumped up onto the ridge. Midnight-blue scales flashed through the fog. Shale tumbled down the cliff face and onto the beach, rumbling through the quiet as B settled beside him. Green eyes intent, his commander bumped shoulders with him. *"You want her, take her. Nothing so simple as that."*

He already had—twice. It hadn't been enough. He wanted to make love to her again. And again. Over and over until satiation set in and he found a modicum of peace. But even as the thought surfaced, Forge recognized the lie. He would never be satisfied. Not with a quick affair. Not when it came to Hope. He needed more from her and . . .

Goddamn it. *Simple* couldn't be further from the truth.

What he felt for Hope wasn't simple at all. Complicated as hell seemed more accurate. Messy and dangerous too given the bull's-eye pinned to his back. Stupid Archguard. Goddamn Rodin and his idiotic schemes. The male didn't know when to quit. Forge scowled. Selfish bastard. The urge to cross the pond and cut the leader of the Archguard down a notch nudged him. His eyes narrowed. Then again, why stop there? Might as well take him out completely while he was at it.

Squash him like a bug.

Skin him like a snake.

Leave him scaleless . . . ding-dong, the lead dragon's dead.

A lovely plan. Advisable too given what Forge faced in the future—exile along with a hit squad bought and paid for by Dragonkind nobility. Confronted by those facts, claiming Hope qualified as sheer idiocy. He should leave her alone. Cooperate with the hypnotherapy, then send her home—safe and sound, none the worse for wear.

The idea made his dragon half stand up and shake its head. All right, so no agreement from that quarter. Come to think of it, his human side despised the notion as well. Which made him crazy in more ways than he could count, and yet, even knowing he might endanger her life, he desired Hope for his mate anyway. Longed to come home to her at the end of every night. Dreamed of sleeping with her in his arms each day. Craved the family—and any future bairns—she might give him.

It was foolishness.

Madness at its most lethal. But as he looked from Bastian to Rikar, searching for a reason to say no to B's insane suggestion, he couldn't find a single objection. Wanting her felt right. Being with her felt right. *She* felt right, more true than anything he'd ever known and . . . shite. He was caving, considering, hoping to have a chance to win Hope's heart.

Snow flurries drifting in his wake, Rikar hopped from the boulder. His paws thumped down. The ground shook, raising the scent of wet dirt and old leaves. "*The challenge lies in making her want to stay with you.*"

"*How do I do that? How did you convince Angela and Myst tae stay?*" he asked, curiosity running rampant. His brothers-in-arms held the key. Each one knew the secret. Could answer the question most on his mind: how to not only claim Hope, but keep her happy for a lifetime as well. Some males would scoff at the idea. Forge found himself enthralled by it. He wanted what the mated Nightfury warriors had found—love, connection, acceptance from their chosen females. *"Hope has a life beyond our pack. An important one. She helps people heal, guides them past extreme trauma into healthier lives. The world needs more like her, not less."*

Bastian raised a brow. *"Who's to say she can't continue to do that?"*

Surprise rolled through him before the idea caught fire. As the blaze grew in the center of his chest, understanding added to the inferno, giving him hope, providing him with an incentive that might entice his female. *"You mean, keep her practice?"*

"It's not ideal, but . . ." Rikar paused as though wrestling with his own demons. *"Angela leaves the lair during the day several times a week. She's a born investigator with an inquisitive mind. Keeping her from what she loves would be wrong. Cruel even. I would never do that to my mate."*

"It's dangerous," Forge said, turning Rikar's arrangement over in his mind.

"It is, but necessary too," Bastian murmured. *"And Ange is not alone. Myst and the other females go to the movies all the time. And Daimler takes them shopping at least twice a week."*

"Fucking Numbai. The male loves that shit." Lips twitching, Rikar shook his head. *"Point is, Forge—I don't like it when Angela leaves the lair without me. It drives me crazy. I worry when she's gone, but I also trust her to follow the rules. As long as she stays inside the lines and is home before nightfall, she gets all the freedom she needs."*

"Then I have a chance."

"Buddy," Rikar said. *"You've got more than just a chance. You've got nature working in your favor, 'cause—"*

"If you've bonded with her, Hope's sure as hell bonded with you." Pushing out of his crouch, Bastian straightened and, sitting like a cat, wrapped his spiked tail around his front paws. *"Energy-fuse is a marvelous thing, my brother. Use it. Talk to her, touch and please her, strengthen the connection until—"*

"She yearns for you," Rikar said, a predatory gleam in his eyes.

Liking the plan, Forge smiled. *"In other words—play dirty."*

"All's fair in love and war," Venom said, breaking into the conversation.

Forge cursed under his breath. Wonderful. Just terrific. All his dirty laundry aired in front of the entire pack. Freaking Venom, nosy little prick. *"You wanker—you've been eavesdropping."*

"Well, duh," Venom said, an eye roll in his voice. *"Now, if you love-birds are finished with the Dr. Strangelove routine, we've got incoming."*

Gage laughed.

Wick growled.

Haider sighed. *"Focus, guys. The enemy is seven miles out."*

"All right," Forge said, half grumble, half snarl. *"But I'm beating the shite out of Venom when we get home."*

"Perfect," Gage said. *"I'll watch. Haider—you bring popcorn."*

Venom snorted in amusement. *"You can try, but . . . Mac's been teaching me kung fu."*

Mac's name sobered everyone in a hurry.

Silence fell as Forge refocused.

"Bastian—is Hamersveld among them?" Nian asked, interrupting the mental shuffle, wanting his theory confirmed.

Firing up his magic, Bastian put his talent to use, reading the enemies' strengths and weaknesses from a distance. *"Four rogues in the group. Two fire dragons, one acid breather, and . . . bingo. Water dragon flying point. Armor-up, boys. We're good to go."*

A zap sizzled through mind-speak as Wick and Gage powered up the Tasers.

"I'm on point, lads. Donnae break cover until I do."

A round of agreement came through mind-speak.

Forcing Hope from his mind, Forge leapt over the cliff and unfurled his wings. Winter wind blasted over his scales. The beach rose to greet him. His webbing caught air, lifting his bulk as B and

Rikar took flight behind him. As the rattle and shake got going, he banked hard and flew for the tip of the island. He needed to reach the rim of the outer harbor and circle around without being detected before the rogue pack broke through the three-mile marker. The second he reached the target zone, Nian would add to his cloaking spell and throw up an illusion shield, blocking the unique energy signal Forge emitted in dragon form. The extra camouflage served one purpose—to hide him from the enemy long enough to bring Hamersveld to ground.

Great strategy.

The perfect game plan.

Now all he needed was precise execution and a shitload of luck.

~

On point, Bastian and Rikar at his back, Forge wheeled over the north end of Elliott Bay. Whitecaps kicked up, misting the underside of his belly. Frost snaked over his scales. His fire dragon annihilated the chill, melting the ice before the fury of his flight blew it off his skin. Focus cranked to maximum, he fine-tuned his radar. Eyes aglow, his night vision sparked, throwing purple wash out in front of him as the cityscape jumped into sharp relief. Urban lights winked in the distance. Waves rolled into the Seattle shoreline, washing under piers and into concrete breakers, making ocean vessels rock on deep keels.

With a quick flick, he adjusted his sonar and sent out an exploratory ping. Magic warped the air around him. Raindrops ceased falling. The wind stopped blowing. Surrounded by silence, Forge flung his net wide, hunting for his quarry in the distance. The magical rush spilled over the terrain beyond the Sound, coating everything in its path: waterfront and skyscrapers, suburban homes and parklands . . . the forest beyond the city limits. Nothing remained untouched as he gathered the spellbound threads in a mental fist and pulled.

The slow draw made his senses tingle.

The information he needed arrived on the forefront of his brain.

He hummed in satisfaction. Almost in range. Less than four miles away. So close to breaking through the three-mile limit and into his circle.

Impatience poked at him.

His heart thumped faster, knocking against his rib cage.

Wheeling wide, gaze locked on the perfect spot to intercept his prey, Forge shook his head. Time to slow it down. Wait-and-see was the name of the game. Hamersveld wasn't an idiot. A warrior in his own right, the male understood tactics and knew how to fight. Which gave him one shot at the bastard. The second he realized his peril, Hamersveld would turn tail and run. So . . . one chance to get it right, a thread-the-needle kind of mission.

Not optimal given the stakes.

Screwing up—missing his opening—wasn't an option. Answers to the illness killing Mac couldn't wait. He needed to bring the big bastard to ground . . . fast. Time the attack. Cut off all avenues of escape. Force the warrior to fight instead of flee. Keep him in the pipe long enough for Gage and Wick to arrive and unleash the nasty-ass Tasers.

Smart plan, if it worked.

Forge clenched his teeth on a curse. He despised lopsided odds. Hated gambling even more. And this shite? Hell, it had casino written all over it.

Taking a calming breath, Forge pocketed his aggression and forced himself to wait. Nothing to it. Tight and tactical. Patience and perfection. All four would get him what he needed—the enemy pack inside the kill zone. Each Razorback must cross the three-mile marker before he made his move. The instant the final rogue flew inside the Nightfury net, he'd close ranks and unleash hell.

Sensing his unease, Bastian knocked on his mental door. *"Steady."*

"Put a leash on it, Forge." Flying off his right wing tip, Rikar glanced at him sideways. *"Wait until Nian—"*

"Shield up. The illusion is stable," Nian said, voice quiet in the wind rush. *"Stay in the seam, Forge. He won't be able to detect you there."*

He nodded even though Nian couldn't see him, searching for the magical break in the cloud cover. He spotted the narrow opening within seconds. His mouth curved. God love Nian. The male was a veritable genius. And as the seam grew, descending from the heavens like a tear in the fabric of time, Forge sensed the shift in perception. An envelope formed, creating a narrow crease in the sky where reality warped into illusion.

A nifty trick. Clever sleight of hand. Duplicity at its best.

Nian excelled at the art, fooling males into believing nothing existed where danger stood firm. Only Haider, a silver dragon—a Metallic and master at detecting deception—could see through the seam and what lay hidden inside it when the Archguard prince stepped into full illusion. A circumstance which rubbed Nian the wrong way. Forge huffed. Completely understandable. No Dragonkind male enjoyed having the veil stripped away and his magic exposed. Some secrets needed to stay where they belonged—cloaked in shadows.

"Forge, what the hell are you—"

"Hang on tae your knickers, lads. I'm going dark," he said, cutting Venom off mid-scold. *"Thirty seconds. Gage, Wick—get ready."*

Both males growled.

Forge went wings vertical, rocketing into the seam at full velocity. Tall and narrow, the crease tunneled into space, creating a new dimension, a place between here and there. Blue swirls undulated on the walls, breaking into patterns as he flew past. The structure expanded and contracted, reacting to his speed. Lightning cracked. Electricity sizzled. He ignored the light show and scanned the sky beyond his hidey-hole. His senses narrowed. He expanded the cosmic net, hunting for Hamersveld north of the city.

His sonar pinged again.

The spikes ridging his spine rattled and—

Flying in formation, four dragons rose over treetops.

Shark-gray scales flashed in the gloom.

Forge bared his fangs. Fantastic. Better than he hoped. Hamersveld, leading the pack in all his water dragon glory. In no hurry, the male rolled into a wide turn and headed toward the Sound. Forge's muscles tightened. His talons flexed, readying for the fight and . . . bloody hell. Could it be any more perfect? Unaware of his presence, the enemy had turned toward him instead of away, putting the enemy pack on a collision course with the illusion he hid behind.

Wings spread wide, jagged spine swaying, Hamersveld slid into a low glide, coming up over building tops toward Puget Sound. Forge started the countdown. Not yet. Almost in the sweet spot. Wanting to go, knowing he couldn't, he hauled on his reins, waiting for the window of attack to open and . . .

Three. Two. One—

Liftoff!

With a growl, Forge turned hard. He wheeled into the wall. The seam split, shattering the illusion. The air sizzled. Blue swirl exploded across the night sky. As the boom went supersonic, rattling windows in apartment buildings, his brothers-in-arms took flight.

Nightfuries roared.

Enemy dragons screamed.

The Razorbacks surrounding Hamersveld put on the brakes. Ahead of the pack, Hamersveld shrieked in fury. The snarl ripped through the air as a wall of water blew sky-high. With a quick shift, Forge banked around the barricade. His wing tip cut through the waterfall as he moved to intercept. On the other side of the cascade,

Hamersveld wing flapped, trying to compensate, struggling to adjust, determined to alter his flight path.

Too little, too late.

Divide and conquer. Split Hamersveld from the group. The plan was already in full swing as Bastian and Rikar ambushed the other rogues, cutting Hamersveld off, leaving him alone and unprotected.

"Go!" The snap of bone came through mind-speak. A male screamed in pain as Bastian yelled, *"Wick . . . Gage—move it. Forge—bring him down."*

Forge growled. Like he wasn't trying? But . . . shite, the male was fast. Parrying his thrust. Using water to keep him at bay. Baring his fangs, Forge twisted into a quick flip. He feigned left and broke right, smashing through another water barrier. Hamersveld backpedaled. Talons spread, Forge lashed out with his paw. His claws caught smooth gray scales. Muscles along his side pulled. Warm blood splashed up him forearm. Hamersveld howled. Forge hissed in pleasure. Fuck, that felt good. Just right. Perfect in every way as, spiked tail flying, he whirled around. His razor-sharp tail followed in a vicious arc and . . .

Wham!

Bone cracked. Dragon blood flew, disintegrating into ash as Hamersveld's head whiplashed. The brutal crunch echoed. He nailed the big male again. And again. Talons slashing. Claws deployed. Spiked tail flying. Showing no mercy as he pushed him out of the city, back toward the forest, and away from the water. Hamersveld countered, spun fast, and lashed out with his jagged tail.

Forge ducked.

Razor-sharp spikes clipped one of his horns. Agony pulsed through him. Blood gushed over his forehead. Forge ignored the running stream and whirled right. The move put him behind the enemy. In prime takedown position. Not wasting a second, he grabbed the male's hind leg. His claws dug in, cleaving through muscle to reach bone. Hamersveld screamed. Forge yanked and, wings pulling hard, hauled him backward through the air.

Bringing his tail around, he slashed the bastard's wing. Thick webbing ripped. His prey grunted in pain and lost altitude. Still locked onto the enemy, the added weight wrenched his arm. Muscles stretched, threatening to rip his shoulder from its socket. A water club slammed into his face. His teeth rattled. Hamersveld clawed at him, leaving wide, bloody tracks on his scales.

Battling to stay in the air, Forge scanned the sky. Where the hell was his backup? He needed some—right now. No way he could hold Hamersveld much longer. Even with his wing torn, the big male was strong. He might make it to the Sound if Forge let go. Once in the water, he'd never be able to catch him and . . . goddamn it. Where the hell was—

Hamersveld stabbed him with a water spear.

A gash opened on his ribs. *"Fucking hell!"*

"Hold on to him, Forge!" Bronze scales flashing, Gage rocketed into view. He pointed the Taser, aiming for Hamersveld's flank. *"I've got the bastard lined up."*

Seeing reinforcements arrive, Hamersveld shrieked in alarm. "Fen!"

The cry for help reverberated.

The tattoo bracketing Hamersveld's spine shimmered. The glimmer turned to red glow. Gray smoke misted the air in front of Forge's face. Yellow eyes peered out from the strange fog. Vertical pupils narrowed on him. Dual-clawed forepaws struck, slashing at him from inside the brume. Forge reared, trying to get out of range and—

Small fangs flashed in the gloom. An earsplitting shriek tore the night wide open.

The devastating sound blasted through his head. A boom detonated inside his skull, hammering his temples, blurring his vision, shaking him like an earthquake. The wren screamed again, using his death cry to debilitating effect. His body seized. Forge jerked as his grip loosened. His claws slipped, releasing his hold on Hamersveld as the wren emerged, fully formed, from the tattoo.

Turning tail, the water dragon fled, flying fast toward Puget Sound.

"Nay!"

His scream of denial blasted through the forest. Treetops rocked in reaction. Head and ears ringing, muscles still seizing, Forge refused to cry defeat. Reaching out, he grabbed hold of Fen's tail. The miniature dragon whipped around. Raptor-like claws slammed into his shoulder. More blood rolled over his scales. Forge didn't care. No way was he letting Fen go. He tightened his grip instead, relishing the burn as spikes cut into his palm.

He yanked Fen sideways.

The wren screamed again, hammering him with sound waves.

The barrage slammed into him. His eyes crossed. "You little bastard."

Fear bloomed on Fen's face. He called for his master. Hamersveld roared. Magic slithered on the night breeze and—

Fen disintegrated in his hand.

Smoke drifting between his fingers, Forge froze, hanging in midair. What the hell had just happened? Nothing natural was his guess. But as he watched the wren shoot toward Hamersveld in a messy scramble, rocketing through the sky in a tumble of wispy black smoke, he frowned, struggling to understand. Eyes glowing from inside the fog, the miniature dragon looked back at him. The little freak hissed once more, then disappeared, merging with the male's tattoo, becoming one with his master as Hamersveld escaped into the water.

Time slowed.

The other Nightfuries cursed, flying in to surround him.

Sloan thumped him with his tail. "*What the hell happened? We had him. We—*"

"Shut up," Forge murmured without an ounce of ire. *"Let me think."*

The pack paused, growing silent, circling him like vultures around a fresh kill.

Forge didn't notice. Brow furrowed, he hovered in place and stared at the spot where Hamersveld had disappeared, letting the effect of the wren's death cry dissipate. A headache took its place, hammering his temples as he assembled the facts. Understanding arrived in a hurry. Water dragon, wren, magical tattoo. The three were connected, an intricately woven story no one had ever bothered to tell and . . . bloody hell. He should've realized earlier. Nothing happened in a vacuum, and as realization struck, the way forward hit him like a clawed fist. All of a sudden, he knew how to help his best friend.

"I need tae revisit the library."

Flipping into a somersault, Venom eyed them through glowing red eyes. *"Why?"*

"A book," he murmured, ignoring his pack, searching his memory. *"I read something in one of the tomes. Something I think will help Mac."*

"Go," Bastian said. *"Explain on the way."*

With a nod, Forge ignored his injuries and wheeled around. Leaving the other Nightfuries in his wake, he flew hard for Black Diamond. He didn't have a second to lose. The answer lay in the underground vault, the library full of ancient tomes. Within easy reach. As long as he moved fast and perfected the setup in time, Mac stood a chance of surviving. But first, he needed to get home and talk to Hope. Telling her the truth so soon hadn't been part of the plan, but the time for hiding was over.

Circumstances changed.

Time frames got moved up.

Females ended up shocked along the way, but that couldn't be helped. Not this time. Not with Mac's life on the line, so . . . fuck it.

He would come clean and be honest with her. It was only fair given he needed her help.

He would've done it anyway . . . eventually.

Mating a female without sharing the truth of Dragonkind simply wasn't done, but as the forest fell away, giving way to the river, worry got the best of him. Hope might hate him afterward. She might never accept him as her male, but . . . Forge clenched his teeth . . . no help for it. He needed every female inside the lair on board for his plan to work. Otherwise, he didn't have a chance in hell of saving Mac's life, and he'd lose his best friend forever.

Chapter Twenty-Three

Folding his wings, Ivar fell out of the sky. Dropping through thick clouds, he aimed for the break between rooftops, pointing his paws toward the expansive lawn below. Wind blasted over his scales. The rattle and shake soothed his temper, the chatter from the guards landing behind 28 Walton Street did not.

Multiple paws set down, crushing frozen grass under-talon.

A spiked tail clipped one of the rusty oil tanks sitting in his appalling excuse for a backyard. The quiet clank annoyed the hell out of him. Bad form, he knew. He swallowed a growl along with his irritation. His soldiers weren't doing anything wrong. In fact, each male was doing it just right. Getting a gold star. Receiving an A-plus in the procedure department—whatever (who the fuck cared?)—as the pack went about the usual business of arriving home: folding wings, shifting into human form, gathering at the rear entrance . . . waiting for him to set down.

Different night, same routine.

No one entered the lair until he did.

On a normal night, Ivar would've approved. Given his warriors a big thumbs-up. Right now, he just wanted them gone.

Five feet from the ground, he spread his wings, slowing his descent. His talons touched down without making a sound. The warriors in his personal guard stopped talking and turned to look at him.

"Inside—all of you," he murmured, tucking his wings. As the webbing brushed his flanks, Ivar rolled his shoulders, trying to shed the tension. *"I think I'll stay outside awhile."*

Rampart, the bravest of the four, stepped forward. A frown on his face, he shook his head. *"It isn't safe outside, commander. The Nightfuries—"*

"Don't know where I sleep."

The guard opened his mouth again.

Ivar's eyes narrowed.

Without saying another word, Rampart snapped his yap closed and, with a flick of his fingers, ushered the others into the lair before stepping over the threshold himself. The door closed with a soft click. Ivar released a pent-up breath. Finally—some relief. A little peace and quiet. Tipping his head back, Ivar glanced up, into the night and inky darkness. A clean slate. No stars tonight. Nothing but thick clouds in a stormy sky. With a shrug, he pressed his chin to his chest, stretching sore neck muscles. Just as well. He didn't need any witnesses, celestial or not, when he crossed the street to visit Sasha.

Calling on his magic, he transformed into human form and conjured his favorite pair of Lucky Sevens. A T-shirt went over his head as motorcycle boots settled on his feet. His leather jacket made an appearance next, hugging his shoulders, smelling of home, making him recall better times . . . like when he'd lain in a sex kitten's arms and listened to her sigh his name.

The image prompted his get-up-and-go.

Checking none of his warriors lingered, he glanced toward the door. Nothing. Nobody. All quiet on the home front. Without looking back, he crossed the backyard and walked around the corner of the old firehouse. Kicking a beer bottle out of his way, he jogged up the flagstone path flanking the building. Boot soles cracking over shattered glass, he stepped onto the city sidewalk and veered left, heading toward the bungalow sitting across the street.

An ancient Jeep sat in the driveway.

Ivar huffed. Fucking rust bucket. Sasha needed to invest in a new vehicle. Something more reliable, preferably one with a working warranty. Skirting the back bumper, he kicked one of the tires. Rust fell from the undercarriage, leaving a lump of corroded steel under the driver's side door.

Ivar scowled at it. "Jesus fucking Christ."

Forget about letting her in on the purchase. He'd buy a new Jeep for her himself. Wouldn't be too much trouble. Step one—lift and carry, dump the POS into the deepest lake he could find. Steps two, three, four, and five—purchase, plate the Wrangler in her name, wrap it with a red ribbon, and set it in her driveway. Easy as breathing. End of story. No need for her to know who'd KO'd the old and given her the new.

Still glaring at the thing, he strode up her front steps. Wood creaked beneath his weight. He switched focus. His gaze landed on the door and—

Her keys were in the lock.

Right out in the open for anyone walking by to see . . . and enter.

Concern burned through him. His brow furrowed, Ivar scanned the street over his shoulder. Searching for threats, he reached out and grabbed the leather keychain. Metal jangled against his palm. Finding no one in the shadows, he turned the key, then clenched his teeth. Not even locked. Sasha had entered, forgotten to pull the key free, and not flipped the dead bolt on the door behind her.

"What the hell?" he whispered, worry turning to fear.

Sasha might live in the suburbs, but it was still the city. Females weren't always safe. Danger lurked around every corner and—Jesus. She needed her gorgeous little ass spanked. Or, at the very least, a lengthy talking-to, one that would no doubt devolve into a lecture about personal safety.

Turning the knob, Ivar pushed the door open. Stagnant air rushed out to greet him. His fear evolved into terror. Oh Jesus. He knew that smell. Had scented it less than an hour ago at Cascade Valley Hospital inside the quarantine area. Heart pounding, boots thumping, Ivar crossed the threshold into the house. He scanned the darkness. One large room, three functions—kitchen, living, and dining—but no Sasha.

Sidestepping the peninsula, Ivar swung left, walked down the narrow hallway, and turned into her bedroom. The smell of sickness grew stronger. His heart shuttered inside his chest as he spotted Sasha. Curled in a ball, buried under a mound of blankets, she lay in the center of her bed.

"Sasha!"

She moaned in answer.

His heart started beating again. Alive. She was *alive*—in pain sure, but still breathing. Guilt struck, eating him whole as he stopped beside the bed and sat down. The mattress tilted. Sasha rolled toward him. Ivar reached for her, peeling the quilt away, needing to see her face. His hand brushed hot skin. A fever, a dangerously high one in need of treatment and a high dose of antiviral.

Something he could give her. Right now. Before she sickened further and ended up beyond help.

The thought sent rage racing through him. Compulsion—his need to protect her—did the rest, centering him as he reached into his mental vault. The lifesaving formula came when called. Preparing the compound, he calibrated the dose to her exact needs. Height. Weight. Blood type. He hit all the markers, ensuring what he intended to give her would kill the bug he'd created . . . and she'd somehow caught.

Frowning, Ivar filled a syringe inside his mind. Where the hell had Sasha been? He kept track of her movements, stalking her from afar, ensuring she stayed safe while out in the wilds doing her research. None of the reports had placed her anywhere near Granite Falls.

Not that it mattered. Not anymore.

She was sick. He was here to help. Thank the goddess he possessed what she needed.

"Kitten?"

Her eyelashes flickered before she opened her eyes. "Ivar?"

"*Da,* I'm here."

A tear rolled over the bridge of her nose. "You came back."

Wiping the droplet away, he nodded as her eyes drifted closed again. "I have medicine for you."

"Doctors said they couldn't help."

"I know, but I can," he said, stroking the damp hair from her temple. "Trust me, kitten. It'll help."

"Okay," she whispered, so trusting that guilt ate him alive.

Son of a bitch, it was his fault, every bit of the mess. He'd created the problem, and now carried the blame . . . was the reason Sasha lay feverish in her bed. His throat tightened. Fucking hell. His arrogance knew no bounds. The fact he'd fixed it—designed the antiviral, delivered the drug, and given it to sick humans—didn't wipe his slate clean.

She suffered, and now, so did he.

Biting the cap, he pulled the plastic off the needle. The work of seconds, he unwrapped her. Sasha whimpered in protest. He murmured, soothing her as he pulled the last blanket away and her oversized T-shirt above her hips. Pale skin glowed in the low light. His dragon half seethed, wanting to be let out of its cage. Ivar reined in the inclination and, conjuring an alcohol swab, disinfected a patch on the curve of her bottom.

"A little pinch," he murmured, voice deep enough to reassure her. "Breathe in, little one."

Sasha inhaled.

Pushing the needle into her skin, he delivered the dose.

She flinched. "What is it?"

"An antiviral. You'll feel better in a day or two."

"I hope so." She coughed, the hacking sound making him hurt for her. "'Cause this sucks."

"I know, kitten."

Desperate to soothe her, he cupped her cheek. The contact settled her and helped him. Although, her feverish skin still bothered him. She was too hot for his liking. Maybe she needed a couple of ibuprofen. He didn't have any, but humans seemed to always have some on hand, so perhaps Sasha kept some in her medicine—

"Will you stay?" she asked, wrapping both her hands around his.

His thumb brushed over her cheek. Her bio-energy flared, catching magical fire around her. Her aura flamed, turning a deep scarlet red. Ivar froze as the burning rush slid along his arm, over his shoulder, and up the side of his throat. Pleasure pricked through him. He caressed her again. Her energy fired hotter, tempting his inner beast, forcing hunger to the surface. Ravenous need took hold, arousing him so fast his grip on her tightened. The slight show of force shut Sasha down. Between one breath and the next, her bio-energy retreated and her aura cooled, settling back into normal ranges.

Staring at her in disbelief, Ivar shook his head. Holy fuck. Incredible. Sasha was high energy, a *zinmera*, a female so rare most males never saw her like in their lifetime. Power personified, females of Sasha's caliber manipulated the Meridian, lowering energy levels when uncertain—or faced with a threat—disguising the power, camouflaging themselves, fooling a male into believing her beneath his notice.

A great defense mechanism. A necessary one given Dragonkind's track record with high-energy females.

Ivar drew in a deep breath. No wonder Sasha turned him inside out. His reaction to her made all kinds of sense. Despite being hidden from view, his dragon half had sensed the power, scenting her bio-energy even when she muted it.

Curling closer to him, Sasha tugged on his arm. "Will you stay with me?"

The request clogged his throat the first time. Her second appeal nearly slayed him where he sat. God help him. He wanted to stay—he really did—but instinct told him he shouldn't. Her status as a high-energy female changed everything. And not for the better.

An image of cellblock A rose in his mind's eye.

A month ago, he would've scooped her up and carried her home. Found a never-before-used cell and locked her inside it, but . . .

The thought turned his stomach.

No matter how unwise, he refused to strip Sasha of her freedom. She was a gorgeous female with an indomitable spirit, a wildlife ecologist with a burning desire to heal the planet. No way could he cage her. She belonged in the world, out doing her job, not in a state-of-the-art jail cell waiting to be bred.

The realization stunned him. The emotion behind his certainty scared him. His world had shifted, setting him adrift in a sea of confusion. Now he didn't know what to do—embrace the changes taking hold inside him or cling to his old way of being.

A fork in the road. Two different directions to go, and for the life of him, Ivar couldn't figure out which way to turn.

An ache bloomed in the middle of his chest. Rubbing the tight spot, he returned his focus to Sasha and raised his hand. Fingertips hovering above her head, indecision took hold. Impatient to claim her, his dragon half settled the matter, making him give in and stroke his fingers through her hair.

The light caress caused her to stir. Opening her eyes, she met his gaze, all soft brown eyes and pretty pink cheeks. "Ivar—please?"

"I'll stay for a little while. Just until you fall asleep."

"I don't like that plan."

"Play your part in it anyway, Sasha," he murmured, walking a fine line, caught between what duty demanded and his need to keep her safe. "The rest will take care of itself."

A nice sentiment. If only that were true.

But as he twirled her blond hair around his fingertips, Ivar recognized his words for what they were—a lie. Things rarely worked out in a female's favor. Not with Razorback warriors involved. Something always went wrong. So only one conclusion to draw. If he kept visiting her, his pack would discover the truth—that he protected an HE female outside of cellblock A. No one would understand his reaction to her. Ivar huffed. Hell, *he* didn't understand it, and as Sasha snuggled closer, trusting him with her safekeeping, Ivar turned toward a hard truth instead of away.

He couldn't continue to see her.

Every minute he stayed endangered her life. Which meant he needed to get up and go. Walk away from Sasha and never look back. Right now, before his guards came searching for him, and the female he wanted but knew he could never have ended up trapped.

Chapter Twenty-Four

Head bowed, dressed in his ceremonial robe, Zidane knelt in the middle of the sacred chamber. Hewn from solid granite, the circular room lay at the heart of the mountain. Hot water flowed through channels carved into the rock wall, streaming into a pool flanked by ancient stone stairs. Steam writhed around him, dancing like ghosts as sweat trickled over his nape, down his back, making the heavy fabric stick to his skin. His fire dragon loved the attention, all the inferno-like heat. His mood, however, continued to deteriorate.

Hands fisted at his back, Zidane gritted his teeth. *Kristus* help him. He hated religious ceremonies. The shit-show always went on forever. And now, after an hour of being locked in the chamber, he couldn't stave off the discomfort. Or his annoyance. Everywhere he turned, something else irritated him—the stone floor digging into his shins, the cloud of jasmine clogging the air, the burn in his lungs, the ritualized chant making his temples throb and his head ache.

Impatience stabbed at him.

A snarl rose at the back of his throat. He swallowed it at the last second. No matter how uncomfortable, he refused to make a sound and show weakness. Not while his sire stood watching. Not while Dragonkind priests circled like sharks. Not when he was so close to achieving his goal—free rein in his quest to annihilate the Nightfury pack. But as the discomfort mounted, the urge to move and stretch overwhelmed him.

His thigh muscles quivered in fatigue.

Grinding his back molars, Zidane pushed away the pain. Fucking Archguard. The idiots never did anything with expediency. He understood the drill. Had spent his life surrounded by the absurdity, but—*hovno*, what idiocy. Dragonkind elite needed to pull their heads out of their asses. All the pomp and circumstance wasn't necessary. Say a few words. Have a few drinks. Anoint him with holy water. What was so difficult about that? And why was it taking so fucking long? The question banged around inside his head. A second later, the chant came to a close.

The chamber went quiet.

Praying it was over, Zidane lifted his head. The idiot priests started up again, male voices rising in unison, baritones thick with promised blessings. With a sigh, he bowed his head again. His neck muscles whined in protest. The rest of him did too, screaming in pained silence as, long robes swishing over the stone floor, the priests walked a circuit around him. One revolution, then another as each doused him with blessed water. Droplets rained down on his skin, merging with sweat as the holy males widened the circle to include the warriors kneeling at his back.

He sensed his warriors shift, moving from knee to knee, behind him.

Hands still pressed to the small of his back, Zidane flicked his fingers. The signal settled his pack, quieting the group as he refocused on the ceremony. Might as well commit every detail to memory. Paying attention never hurt. And honestly, much as it pained him to admit it, he wanted to remember the ritual. Be able to recall the ancient rite word for word, syllable by syllable, one sentence after another when he was old and gray. The details mattered. Being selected to command a kill squad, after all, didn't happen every night.

Satisfaction curled through him.

Finally . . . an edict made in his favor. Signed, sealed, and delivered by the Archguard.

The vote had taken longer than expected. A whole forty-eight hours of waiting and watching—of hoping and praying—but in the end, his sire had gotten the job done. The decision to exile the Nightfury pack hadn't been unanimous. Far from it. Bastian was too well loved to throw to the wolves without question.

Split down the middle, elite members of his kind had argued in favor of the Nightfuries. Many still grumbled, taking Bastian's side, disagreeing he deserved death for defying the Archguard's order to deliver Forge to Prague. The introduction of new evidence—namely, the attack on Rodin's pavilion by Bastian's warriors . . . a fantastic lie presented at a critical juncture of the assembly—shoved the vote over the edge, leaving Rodin to win by a narrow margin.

Ah, the manipulation of the masses.

Zidane hummed in enjoyment. Lucky for him, his sire knew how to fight dirty . . . and some males could be bought like common whores. Money changed minds—was a powerful motivator under the right circumstances. Not that he cared about Rodin's methods. The politics of it wasn't his problem. His sire could deal with the fallout if the truth ever surfaced. Right now, only the outcome mattered.

Xzinile for the Nightfuries. A preapproved hunting license for him.

Pressing his chin to his chest, Zidane suppressed a smile. Start a running tally. Put one down in the win column. Zidane—one. Bastian—zero.

The priests stopped chanting.

Zidane held his breath, hoping, praying, waiting for the moment when—

The bell tolled, ringing once, twice, a third time before the chamber fell silent.

Wooden legs scraped across the stone floor as a male rose from his chair. "Rise, Commander. Stand and be recognized."

Bringing his arms forward, Zidane pressed his hands flat against the floor. Cold granite cooled his palms as he pushed to his feet. Stiff muscles squawked. Uneven stone met the soles of his bare feet. Burying the discomfort, he raised his head. Spread over the altar at the front of the chamber, a thousand candles burned bright. He squinted, allowing his eyes to adjust to the sudden burst of light. Leveling his chin, he squared his shoulders and met his sire's gaze from across the room.

Rodin's dark eyes flashed with yellow fire. "Do you accept the responsibility given you? Will you carry out your task with honor?"

"I do," he said, saying the words expected of him, even though he didn't believe any of it. Honor belonged to the weak, not him. Never him. He was a destroyer of warriors, the methods he employed never involved a code. Morality had no place in his world. "I will."

"Then let it be so." Raising his hands, Rodin turned his palms up and, holding each one high, bowed his head. "Go, Commander. Take your warriors. Make good on your promises. May the goddess guide you on your quest."

Zidane nodded. "The will of the Archguard be done."

"Iazen," the priests shouted in Dragonese, giving a final blessing, voices rising like a thunderclap against the high ceiling.

Fisting his hand, Zidane placed it over his heart. He thumped his chest three times. The drumbeat woke his dragon half. The beast seethed in its cage, begging to be set free as the males in his kill squad struck their own chests. The thud echoed, reverberating inside his heart as he turned to face them. His gaze landed on the last warrior in line. His first in command raised a brow, asking for orders without words.

"Ready the plane, Yakapov," Zidane murmured. "We leave for Seattle within the hour."

"Very good, Commander."

Zidane hummed as his warriors moved to obey. *Seattle*, the Emerald City, where Bastian still thrived, but wouldn't for long. The place he planned to make his new home. His mouth curved. *Very good* was right. Indeed, nothing could be better. Without looking back, he left his sire behind and strode across the chamber toward enormous double doors, already dreaming of dead Nightfuries and the battles to come.

Chapter Twenty-Five

The chocolate mousse tasted so good, it nearly killed Hope when her spoon scraped the bottom of the bowl. Alone in the kitchen, elbows planted on the massive center island, she peered into the empty dish. All gone. None left. She frowned. Well, mostly. A few streaks of dark chocolate remained, marring white china, taunting her with the promise of another bite. God, that would be good. The absolute best given the guilt banging around inside her head . . . and her heart.

Death by chocolate. The proposition sounded fantastic right now.

Giving her spoon a lick, Hope glanced around the kitchen. Pale walls gave way to designer cabinets and an ocean of Carrara marble countertops. A host of halogens spotlit the six-burner gas stove and all the details most people missed. But not her. Hope saw every little thing: the quality of the construction, each perfectly mitered corner, the precision of the paint job. Everything in its proper place. Nothing to provoke criticism. The kind of room that invited a person to sit down and stay awhile. A place where honesty reigned and secrets came to die.

The idea made her tense.

Nothing she'd done at Black Diamond resembled anything close to perfect. Not that she expected perfection. Far from it, but as she looked around, getting stuck on the details, she realized what she was doing—falling into old habits, critiquing everything in sight, fighting to regain control of her environment after feeling so out of control with Forge. The thought made her chest tighten and memories rise. Hawkeyed observations—a top-notch defense mechanism, a throwback from a lifetime spent trying to please her father. Details mattered to him, and so, as a child, she made them matter to her too.

Not a bad thing. Precision suited her personality and being observant helped her excel as a therapist. But only if she stayed true to herself. Honesty was key. A willingness to acknowledge her flaws and see her mistakes played a role too, but . . . God. So many mistakes. Too many missteps. She'd made all the wrong moves with Forge. Now, she didn't know how to reset her strategy.

Or even if she could.

Particularly since she wanted to make love to him again. Then maybe once more—or fifty times—after that.

Playing with her utensil, Hope scowled at the chocolate streaking her bowl. Frigging Forge. What was it about him? Why did he send her into such a tailspin? Why did her heart ache and her mind hurt whenever he left her? The last question made her growl. *Left her.* Talk about using the wrong words. Forge hadn't abandoned her. He'd gone to do his job (whatever that entailed), yet even knowing that, she felt . . . yes . . . *abandoned.* Left behind. Out of the loop, as though she lacked crucial information—the kind she required, but he hadn't shared.

Mind churning, she examined the thought. Ridiculous assumption or well-founded suspicion? Instinct at its best or insecurity at its worst? Hope frowned. She couldn't say for sure. Couldn't prove he withheld information, but for some reason, she sensed the evasion. She could see the gap in her knowledge base and didn't like it. He was hiding something from her. A big something, a *something* she needed to know in order to help him.

"The evasive jerk." Eyes narrowed, Hope glared into her empty dish.

"Go ahead. Lick the bowl." Standing under the archway leading into the dining room, Angela grinned at her. "I know you want to."

Did she ever, but somehow, it didn't seem prudent. Or even close to polite, and given all the lines she'd crossed since arriving at Black Diamond, stepping over another one seemed unwise. Setting her spoon down, Hope pushed the bowl away. Fine china slid across smooth marble and bumped into her coffee cup. "Where have you been?"

"Sorry I'm late. I got held up on a video conference." Hazel eyes pinned to her, Angela crossed the kitchen. Skirting the massive island, she headed for the coffee maker. A mug got pulled from an open shelf. Glass clinked against metal as coffee got poured into it. Caffeine fix in hand, her friend turned, leaned her hip against the countertop, and gave her a good once over. Hope tensed. Taking a sip of coffee, Angela raised a brow. "What's bothering you, Hope?"

She wanted to say, "Everything." Somehow, though, admitting the weakness out loud felt like defeat. She should be able to figure out Forge on her own. Was trained to deal with difficult situations, to help when no one else could. So instead of telling the truth, she tossed her far-too-observant friend an annoyed look. "Always the detective."

"Always the evader," Angela said, countering with a jab of her own.

Playing it cool, she rolled her eyes. No need to come clean. No need to admit a thing, but as she opened her mouth to reply, her brain derailed, making her blurt, "I slept with Forge."

Angela blinked.

Hope froze. A second later, she cringed. Dear God, why had she said that? Such a stupid thing to admit given her purpose inside the house. Silence beating on her like a baseball bat, she stared at her friend, waiting for the reprimand, the shock and disapproval, her inevitable firing and—

"Good for you," Angela said, calm as you please.

"What the hell?" Her friend should be taking her to task, not giving her approval. Drawing a deep breath, Hope pulled her wayward brain back onto the tracks. "How can you say that?"

"Maybe because it's true?"

"No answering a question with a question." Off balance, struggling to find mental equilibrium, she glared at Angela. "That's one of our rules."

Cupping her mug in both hands, Angela huffed. "We have rules?"

"Shut up." Agitation reaching new heights, Hope pushed away from the countertop. She crossed her arms, then shuffled her feet. When that didn't help, she pointed her finger at her friend. "You know we do—unspoken ones."

"And whose fault is that?"

Crap. Cornered. Nowhere to go, even fewer places to hide. Hope sighed. Her friend was right. No sense denying it. "Mine, I guess."

"You're good at keeping people at bay," Angela said, taking a sip of coffee. "You've always boxed out really well."

"Part of the job. I can't help people if I don't remain objective. Emotion clouds judgment and—"

"Forge is making things cloudy?"

"Yes . . . goddamn it. He's driving me nuts. I can't get a read on him. One minute I think I know him better than anyone I've ever met, and the next, he's confusing me. It's all screwed up, Ange. Everything's murky. I can't see a clear path through any of it." Frustration spun her around the lip of hopelessness. How could she help if nothing made sense? Forge blew her off course at every turn, and with her itching for him, the situation seemed unlikely to improve anytime soon. Deflated, Hope sighed. "I think I may be in over my head here."

"You're not."

"What?"

"In over your head."

Hope frowned. "How can you tell?"

"Your reaction to him might feel extreme, but his need for you is just as powerful, and that's a good thing."

Uncertainty sank deep, dragging Hope back into confusion. "I don't understand."

"I don't think we're meant to," Angela said, amusement in her tone.

"Gee, thanks. That's so helpful."

Her friend laughed. "These guys aren't like any others you've met, Hope. I warned you it wouldn't be easy, but I think you're on the right track."

"Sleeping with him is considered the right track?"

"Absolutely." Turning her mug in her hand, Angela treated her to a thoughtful look and . . . uh-oh. Hope knew that expression. She'd seen it countless times whenever her friend launched an argument she planned to win. "You've worked with a lot of people, right?"

"Yes."

"Okay, so, tell me—when does therapy stop being about someone going through the motions and start to be what you would consider successful?"

Good question. Only one answer. Elbow on the counter, Hope met her friend's gaze. "When a patient trusts me enough to share their truth."

"Good. Now, let's turn this on its head," Angela said. "Think of it this way—the closer you get to Forge, the more you touch him skin-to-skin, the better he'll respond. The more he responds, the safer he'll feel and the more deeply he'll trust you. The instant that happens, he'll stop hiding his truth. Get it?"

No . . . not really. The argument bordered on convoluted. Backassward in every way. One hundred percent bizarre in a field full of weird things, and yet, the words *stop hiding his truth* resonated. She wanted him to trust her. Hell, she wanted him . . . period. So instead of brushing Angela's advice aside, Hope did as suggested and turned it on its head, examining the idea from all angles. Instinct told her the approach made sense—touching him as often as she could would work. It went against everything she'd been taught, all of her considerable experience, but . . . Forge was unlike anyone she'd ever treated.

She sensed his struggle. Along with the secrets he kept.

Oh sure, he stood more than ready to jump into bed with her, but he had yet to talk about his past. She needed those details, for him to open up and be honest with her. Hypnotherapy worked well when she understood a patient's personal history. When she knew what psychological pressure points to push and which to leave alone. It was a process, an intricate dance between her and the person she was trying to help. Which left her with a problem, one Angela suggested she held the power to solve. So . . .

Time to decide—put up or shut up.

Taking a deep breath, Hope reached for her coffee cup. As she pulled it across the countertop, dark liquid swirled against white ceramic, making her mind spin and her heart race. Holy crap. Was she really going to go against convention and do this? The question hung in the void less than a second before the answer pushed it aside. YES. Without question. She was diving in headfirst—going to embrace the illogical, let go of the guilt, and make love to Forge again.

"Helluva way to help him," she whispered, startled by the idea even though she knew it was the right way to go. Shaking her head, she glanced at Angela. "You realize everything here is upside down and backwards, right?"

"You'll get used to it," Angela said, an instant before her attention snapped toward the hallway leading out of the kitchen. The movement spun her friend around, into a 180-degree turn. Surprised by the sharp pivot, Hope stilled with her mug halfway to her mouth. Skirting the end of the island, Angela glanced over her shoulder. Intent hazel eyes met Hope's. "Along with the tingle."

"The what?"

The second she asked, a prickle danced up her spine. Heat shimmered across her lower back, chasing the vibration, lighting fire to the need banked but still burning in her blood. A second starburst streamed over her skin, heating her body until the pinpricks morphed into pleasure. Her heart started to pound: harder, faster, hammering the inside of her chest.

Hope quivered as another round hit.

"Holy crap," she gasped, not understanding. Nothing new there. Every time she turned around something inside Black Diamond confused her. "What is that?"

"Rikar . . . or in your case—Forge." Feet already in motion, Angela jogged toward the exit. "Oh, and Hope?"

"Yeah?"

"Get ready."

"For what?" she opened her mouth to ask.

Angela made herself scarce, disappearing from view on the way to God only knew where. Hope scowled. Blast it all. Now what? Every time she thought she might be getting somewhere, someone pulled the rug out from under her. Or rather, she got left standing in a kitchen with all kinds of questions and no one around to answer a single one. With a grumble, Hope set her mug down with a bang. Flummoxed again. Beyond annoying. Practically rage inducing and—

"Jalâyla."

The deep voice stroked over her skin. Her head snapped toward the dining room. Lust blazed into an inferno, causing a needy sound to escape her, and . . . oh, thank God. Forge. Hope sucked in a quick breath as her gaze ran over him. Boots planted, stance wide, he stood beneath the timber-beam archway like a hard-bodied dream. Leather jacket on, dark hair mussed with a bruise marring one cheek, he looked good enough to eat. Like salvation wrapped into an ultrasexy package. Violet eyes on her, he growled. The sexy sound vibrated inside her like a tuning fork, setting off a chain reaction. Unbearable need tightened her muscles, the onslaught fogging her mind until only one thought remained.

She wanted him. This instant. No waiting. No compromises. Just him deep inside her.

Nostrils flaring, he breathed deep. "You smell fantastic, lass."

"I need you," she said, overwhelmed, unable to hide her desire.

"I know." Lifting his hand, Forge held it out, palm up. "Come here."

A wave of yearning rolled through her.

Her greed for him added to the urgency, propelling her around the corner of the massive island. The closer she got, the tenser Forge became. She quickened her pace. He flicked his fingers, impatience in the movement, demanding her touch. Skin against skin. Oh baby. Hope bit back a moan. God, she needed him that way. No rhyme. No reason. Throw all her questions into the nearest garbage bin.

She stepped into range.

Forge murmured her name.

Ignoring his outstretched hand, Hope pushed into his arms. Her breasts met his chest. Her hands delved into his hair. He groaned as she took hold of the thick strands and tugged his head down. Cheek to cheek now, she inhaled, filling her lungs with him, allowing his scent to soothe her. A heartbeat passed, then two. Anticipation a throb in her veins, she raised her head, set her mouth to his and, tasting him deep, took what she wanted.

Flat on his back in the middle of the rotunda, Forge stared up at the fresco. Painted by Wick, the image depicted dragons on the hunt. Brilliant with color. Alive with movement. Majestic in composition. Each scale, every spike and sharp fang accounted for as dragons took flight across the domed ceiling. Fitting decoration for a sacred room;

a place so special the mated Nightfury warriors used it more as chapel than chamber, choosing to say their mating vows and claim their chosen females beneath the spread of dragon wings. But no matter how magnificent, the painting didn't compare to the female he held in his arms. Hands roaming her back, he kept Hope right where he wanted her—draped over top of him, cheek pressed to his heart, her beautiful body on display and within easy reach.

He should do something about that: conjure another blanket, cover her up, preserve her modesty in the event one of his brothers entered the sacred space. But as he caressed her, enjoying the smoothness of her skin and decadence of her scent, adoring the amount of trust it took for her to fall asleep in his arms, Forge couldn't make himself move. He loved her this way, open to his touch, unabashed and immodest, all soft female and generous curves.

A tidal wave of contentment washed through him.

Beautiful female. Sweet, sweet lass. She'd loved him so well over the last hour, egging him on, coming back for more, her need so complete she laid him bare, exposing his heart—all his wants and needs—without even trying. Any other time, with any other female, the vulnerability would've triggered the opposite response. Made him balk and want to bolt. But not Hope. His dragon half thought of her as his. His human side agreed, claiming her with silent conviction instead of loud fanfare.

Although, that would come . . . eventually. After he worked up the courage to show her the truth of his kind.

The idea made him nervous.

Settling his palm against the small of her back, he smoothed the other over the tangle of her long hair. The thick strands clung to his fingertips as though trying to stroke him back. His worry settled. Unease disappeared. It always did when he touched her, making him believe it would be all right. Hope might not know it yet, but she belonged to him in the same way he belonged to her. The bond grew by the moment, strengthening the connection he shared with her, twining around her heart, just as it had taken hold of his. Which meant he should wake her.

Time was running out.

Almost set up in the gym, Bastian and the others wouldn't wait much longer.

Sighing, Forge smoothed his hands over her bottom. His grip on her firmed. She twitched, grumbling in her sleep. He set his teeth to the curve of her shoulder and bit down gently. Her nose crinkled. He licked over the small mark, jostling her a little, and whispered her name.

"No." Hope growled, her voice an octave lower than normal. The muscles bracketing her spine tightened. Hands curling into fists, she snarled. "No retreat."

Forge frowned and, raising his head off the floor, peered down at her face. Air stalled in his throat. Jesus. The dream. She was lost inside his dream again, about to—

With a shriek, she exploded into motion. Eyes closed, rising like a viper above him, she raised her fists, hissing in her sleep. "Rodin—you bastard. I should have known."

His heart paused mid-beat. The string of words slammed into his mind, and suddenly, he knew who spoke them. It wasn't Hope. The voice belonged to his father. She might be inside the dream, right in the middle of the battle, but she was reliving his experience, drawing the poison from his mind and projecting it into her own.

Bloody hell. Energy-fuse in all its glory. He'd never imagined it capable of such things, of coaxing his dragon half to give his mate information he couldn't access himself. Unable to move, he listened to Hope snarl at Rodin again. The name resonated, shaking him inside, hammering the barrier he sensed around the memory.

Her bio-energy spiked.

With a quick shift, he sat with her straddling his lap, putting him face to face with her. Hope growled and raised her fist. He grabbed hold, trapping her knuckles against his palm with one hand and cupping the back of her neck with the other. With them connected at three points—nape, hand, and groin—the Meridian whiplashed, opening a channel deep inside him. His magic sparked as his mind expanded, reaching for hers. Hope quivered against him. Folding the cosmic band, he looped it over and around them, taking the excess energy, protecting Hope from the onslaught as he sank into the powerful stream.

"Stay with it, Hope." Leaning in, he set his mouth to the corner of hers. "I need tae see all of it."

Spellbound by his voice, still fast asleep, Hope froze against him. He tightened his hold on her. The energy stream intensified. As her lips parted on a gasp, he banged on the mental barricade, requesting entrance into the memory. Her brow furrowed. He pleaded his case, asking for help. She responded without hesitation and, relaxing her guard, opened her mind. He slipped through. Mind meld took hold, fusing his consciousness with hers. His dragon half hummed and—

Mental walls began to crumble and . . . fucking hell. There it was, on the horizon inside his mind—perfect recall. With a powerful thrust, Forge flew toward it.

The surge made Hope flinch. Her eyes popped open. "Forge!"

"Donnae move, *jalâyla*." Deep inside her mind, surrounded by her body, he held her gaze. Pupils unfocused, she stared back. "Stay with me."

Unblinking, she obeyed, sharing the memory. The tempest expanded. The battle played out. Claws ripped through scales. Males screamed in pain. Someone attacked him from behind. Forge whipped around, desperate to protect his flank but . . . too little, too late. An orange dragon with black-tipped scales held the upper hand. With a vicious swipe, the bastard knocked him out of the sky. As he tumbled toward the ground at breakneck speed, his sire roared his name and, banking hard, went after Rodin.

His mental screen flickered.

He lost sight of his father as he hit the ground. Bones snapped. One of his wings shattered, tearing apart the webbing. Tasting his own blood, agony ripped through and—

The frame went dark.

Sorrow filled him, raging into a river inside him. Forge closed his eyes as he relived the loss. God help him. His sire and brothers—gone in the blink of an eye. And Rodin was to blame. He saw it clearly now. The leader of the Archguard had murdered his family. But why? Forge frowned. Why take the risk? What the hell had made his sire so dangerous to the bastard? Excellent questions. No real answers, but one thing for sure? He possessed what he needed now—what he'd waited over fifty years to find: a modicum of closure, a direction to move along with the information Bastian required to bury Rodin and protect the Nightfury pack.

Exhaling in a rush, Forge turned his attention to the female quivering in his lap. He murmured her name. Hope whimpered, the tears in her eyes telling. Regret punched through, making him hurt for her. She didn't deserve to carry his pain, but as he cupped her face, desperate to soothe her, Forge knew he didn't hold the power. Compelled by energy-fuse, his dragon half shared everything with her: the good, the bad, and all of the ugly.

Throat gone tight, he shook his head. "I'm so sorry, Hope. I never would have shared the memory if given a choice. Sweet lass, please forgive me. I never meant tae hurt you."

"Me? It's not—forget about me!" Her breath hitched. "He got you. Rodin killed you. Forge, he—"

"Nay, Hope," he rasped, battling pain inflicted over fifty years ago as he withdrew from her mind. Using his magic, he retreated a little at a time, smoothing down ragged mental edges, soothing her fear, clearing the shock away. Hugging her tight, he nuzzled her cheek, kissed her mouth, then turned to lick the tears from her face. "He didn't kill me. I'm all right, lass. Alive and well—right here with you."

Trembling, she gripped his shoulders. Fingers searching for old wounds, she stroked his skin, pressed her hands over his heart, assuring herself he still lived. She drew in a choppy breath. "What was that? What just happened?"

"You met my dragon half."

She blinked. More tears fells. Forge brushed each away, waiting for her to react to the news. It didn't take long for her to recover. He felt her mind sharpen, then start to whirl.

Confusion in her gaze, she searched his face. "Your what?"

"Difficult to explain."

Her brow furrowed. "Try anyway."

"How about I show you instead?"

Aye. Without a doubt. Showing her would be better. More advisable all the way around, except . . . shite. She'd already suffered one shock today. Mind meld took some getting used to, after all, and as he lifted Hope from his lap and stood, worry jabbed at him. Again. Like always when he thought about telling Hope the truth. So many unanswered questions. Very few reassurances. But as he set his female on her feet, drew a blanket around her shoulders, and met her gaze, Forge knew the time had come. No more hiding. Enough with the lies. She needed to know the truth. He needed to tell her. Now came the difficult part, pulling back the veil to reveal Dragonkind. All while praying his act of faith drew her closer to him, instead of pushing her away.

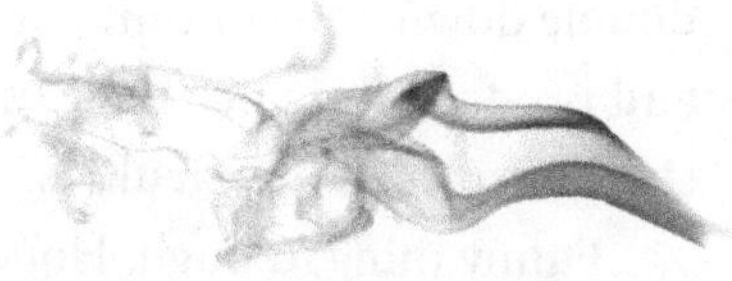

Chapter Twenty-Six

Bare feet cooling on mosaic tile, Hope pulled the blanket over the tops of her shoulders as Forge backed away. Her focus on his face, she crisscrossed the corners, gathering the wool in her fists, and pressed the soft fleecy side to her skin. The preemptive strike against the chill didn't help. Without his warmth surrounding her, cold air attacked, shivering up her spine. He took another step away. And then another, leaving her standing alone in the center of the circular room. Unease slithered in, winding her so tight she felt fragile. Almost brittle. Seconds away from breaking.

The internal turmoil clued her in, jump-starting her brain.

Her mind spun, hopping from one thought to the next. Something was wrong. Terrible, in point of fact. After what she'd witnessed—and how he'd made her feel: close and connected, needed and valued, loved and cherished—his retreat signaled trouble. All right, so the dream sequence (dragon attack . . . whatever!) worried her. So did her reaction. Waking in his arms that way had been strange. Beyond startling, but odd as it seemed, in that moment riding out the storm with him had felt right too. As though she'd belonged there—flying alongside him, fighting in that battle while she struggled to protect his blind side.

Which, safe to say, placed her on the wrong side of sanity. Made her certifiable, or something. Label it crazy, then call it a day, 'cause . . . every professional in the field of psychology would agree with her assessment. No one would argue. Each one would double down and commit her to a psych ward without delay. Poke and prod, analyze her to death in the hopes of figuring out where she'd misplaced her faculties.

Funny thing, though. Hope frowned. She didn't feel the least bit crazy. She found clarity instead, liking the idea of sharing a connection with Forge. What she didn't appreciate was the distance. She hated that he was walking away. Pulled by an invisible tether, she stepped forward, following his retreat.

"Nay, lass—stay there." Expression serious, gaze intent, he tipped his chin. "Better yet, back up a few paces."

"Why?" She didn't understand. Couldn't begin to guess the problem. "Why are you leaving?"

"I'm not leaving. I just need more room."

"For what?"

"Stubborn lass." He sighed, the sound so full of exasperation Hope smiled. Show-off. The big faker. He didn't mean a second of it. He enjoyed baiting her. Relished her reactions, maybe even delighted in teasing the sharp edge of her temper. The realization helped her relax. It was all right. Whatever he wanted to show her couldn't be all bad. Releasing her white-knuckled grip on the blanket, she gave him what he wanted—the best mock death stare she owned. He chuckled in appreciation. "Back up, bad girl, and I'll show you."

"Okay." Doing as he asked, she retreated. Her butt bumped against the opposite wall. As she glanced over her shoulder, the picture behind her came into focus. Crafted from tiny mosaic tiles, the dark-purple dragon rose between two huge columns, taking up the entire section of wall. Hope blinked. Wow. Impressive work from an insanely talented artist. She ran her gaze over the image, appreciating the time it must have taken to create it, before dragging her attention back to Forge. "But this had better be good."

He snorted. "Somehow I donnae think that's going tae be a problem."

The wariness in his tone set her back on edge. The worry she saw in his eyes strengthened the feeling. Intuition sparked, giving her a bad feeling. "Ah, Forge?"

"Remember something for me, lass," he said, rolling his shoulders. "Whatever happens, know I will never hurt you."

Hope's brows collided. *Never hurt her.* Of course not. Forge wasn't the type of guy to—

The air warped around him, cutting her off mid-thought.

Heat rolled off him and into the room. The warm blast blew the hair off her face a second before his eyes started to glow. A blinding pulse of light burst through the rotunda, painting everything in purple wash. Breath locked in her throat, she watched him transform. His body changed, lengthened, grew into a . . . holy crap. A dragon. He was . . . had changed into . . .

A huge, towering dragon.

Shock blasted through her. Her brain derailed, flying off mental tracks. Dark-purple scales glinting in the low light, he tilted his head and gazed down at her. Unable to move, she stared up at him, mouth hanging wide open.

He lifted his paw and flexed enormous talons. The hooked tips of razor-sharp claws clicked together. The sound propelled her out of stunned stupefaction. Brain cells fired in rapid succession. Her body jerked as she inhaled hard and—

"Donnae scream," the dragon said, sounding exactly like Forge.

His command caused air to jam in her lungs. Unable to breathe, Hope shuffled sideways.

"Donnae run either, *jalâyla*. Just stand still and look at me for a moment. See me, Hope."

See him? Seriously? Feeling lightheaded, Hope forced her muscles to unlock and sucked in much-needed breath. Oxygen filled her lungs. She snapped her mouth closed. Had he gone mad? Completely crazy or . . . no, wait. Strike that last thought. The insane one must be her. Mental incapacity explained everything. Gaze locked on him, Hope quivered. All right. Good. She was making perfect sense. Only a psychotic person, after all, remained unmoving when faced with a dragon.

"Take another breath, Hope." Her lungs expanded—oxygen in, air out, moving in time with the dragon's scaled chest. A glint of approval in his eyes, the dragon dipped his horned head. His scaled nose even with her head, he smiled, revealing huge fangs. "You're doing fine."

"Holy crap," she wheezed, unable to believe what she was seeing. Or that she stood with her feet in the fictional fire. Literally. Everyone knew dragons belonged in books, scaring the hell out of fairy-tale princesses, not hanging out in rotundas with their horned heads brushing the roof. "You're not supposed to exist."

Forge snorted. Flames sparked in his nostrils, heating the air in front of her face. "Do I look fake tae you?"

"No, but . . . ," she said, tugging the blanket back over her shoulders. "What are you?"

"Dragonkind," he said, as though one word explained everything.

She scowled at him. "I need more of an explanation than that, Forge."

"We're a different species, lass. A hidden one," he said, moving one of his talons in her direction.

Hope tensed but, afraid to move, stood still and silent as Forge nudged the edge of her blanket aside. The back of his claw skimmed the outside of her thigh. Smooth as polished glass, harder than granite, his nail caressed her skin. She drew in a shaky breath, waiting for fear to rise, but . . . it never came. She recognized his touch, cleaved to the familiar vibration, knowing to whom it belonged.

Watching her closely, he stroked her again. "I'm the same male you made love with earlier, Hope, just wrapped in a different package. The magic in my veins allows me to shift from human to dragon form, and back again."

Disbelief bombarded her. "Magic?"

"Aye." His familiar brogue washed over her. "Just because you donnae see it, doesn't mean magic isnae real."

All right. She bought that. Might even believe it. Probably should, given she stood in a room talking to a dragon. "You can use it . . . shift . . . whenever you want?"

"Of course."

Shock faded, giving way to curiosity. All kinds of questions surfaced, spiraling through her mind, resurrecting her intellect, and a healthy dose of awe. She looked him over again, her gaze touching the horns on his head, the spikes along his spine, and the huge knife-like blades gracing the tip of his tail. Jeez, those looked nasty. Super dangerous. He could no doubt slice her in half with nothing more than a quick flick of that thing. Hope knew it but, guided by instinct, inched closer to him anyway. She wanted to touch him. To get a better sense of him in dragon form.

Standing between his paws now, she raised her hand. Forge didn't move. He waited instead, staying perfectly still as she pressed her palm to his chest. The hard ridges of his scales scraped over her skin. Hope released a pent-up breath. Incredible. He was alive with heat, so warm she didn't need her blanket anymore. She hung on to it anyway and, wrapping the fleece a touch tighter, continued her exploration. He dipped his horned head. A tingle slid over her nape as he murmured her name.

Surprise made her exhale. God, how incredible. He was real, not imagined. The dragon was Forge; Forge was the dragon. No disputing it. No sense denying it either. She recognized his voice, knew his touch and the scent of his skin. But it was the unique vibration he emitted that held her captive. She felt it every time he reached for her, and she slipped into his embrace.

"Can you change back—right now?"

Forge didn't answer. In the space between one heartbeat and the next, he shifted, moving from dragon to man so fast Hope jumped in alarm.

"Jeez!" Losing her footing, she tripped and bumped into his chest.

Big hands landed on her shoulders. He held her still a moment. The instant she looked up and met his gaze, Forge pulled her into his arms. "All right?"

"I have no idea," she said, being honest. "I think I may have lost my mind."

"Nothing wrong with your brain, lass," he murmured, wrapping her closer, encouraging her to snuggle in. Hope didn't argue. Nor did she fight it. Needing a steadying hand, she tucked her head beneath his chin and burrowed in, making a home inside his embrace. "You handled seeing me in dragon form very well."

Nestled in his arms, Hope shook her head. Had she handled it well? She didn't know. Even after touching his scales, she still couldn't say for certain. Her mind wouldn't settle, jumping all over the place, causing her senses to trip over what remained of her brain. Instinct said nothing had changed. He was the same guy. She was the same girl. And yet, red flags kept flying, ringing internal alarm bells. She'd known he'd been hiding something. An important something. A something she'd been determined to unearth, but . . .

Hope swallowed, working moisture back to her mouth.

She never suspected his secret would stun the stuffing out of her. Or throw into question everything she held to be true. An image of Forge in dragon form flashed across her mental screen. God help her. A different species—both human and dragon, able to shift form at will. Her mind stumbled over what he'd shown her. Over the facts. Over everything she'd believed to be true and must now discard. And as Forge picked her up, strode through an open archway and down some stairs, murmuring something about a shower, Hope didn't know what to do—keep trusting him and stay. Or run screaming all the way home.

~

Palm to palm, his fingers entwined with Hope's, Forge led the way out of his bedroom and turned into the deserted corridor. Quiet reigned supreme in the long white-walled space. No rumble of voices from down the hall or inside the kitchen. No females laughing inside J. J.'s music room. No shuffling of papers from the office Evie now worked in either. Just him and Hope and her continued silence.

With a gentle tug, he reeled her in, needing her close as he strode past the collection of fine art hanging on the walls. Forge didn't see a single frame. He was too focused on Hope. Beyond worried by her reaction. Sick with the idea he might be losing his female.

Her silence rubbed him raw.

Her confusion wrenched his heart.

He needed her to stop the silent routine and start asking questions. Open a dialogue. Tell him what she was thinking. Request his aide in helping her understand all he'd shown her. Impatience clawed at him. Forge shut it down and, stopping in front of the elevators, shook his head.

Oh, so not the right reaction. Rushing her wouldn't work. Poking at her would only push her away. He knew it. Sensed deep down where intuition lived and logic made a home. It was her turn to engage. He'd done enough talking in and out of the shower: telling her of his kind while he washed her, explaining energy-fuse and the bond she now shared with him, showing her how he drew nourishment from the Meridian, source of all living things, through her. So aye. Time to shut up. Time to be patient. Watch and wait. The ball lay in her court. Nothing for him to do now but hope she picked it up and ran with it.

Squeezing her hand, he summoned the elevator with his mind. Magic hummed in his veins. Gears ground into motion, bringing the cage up from seven floors down.

The snap of magic in the air made Hope shiver. Her hand twitched in his. She shuffled closer to him, and Forge waited. Would she turn to him for comfort? Would she trust him with her thoughts? Would she allow him the privilege of—

She cleared her throat. "So . . . what are we doing, again?"

Relief spun him around the lip of gratitude. His knees went weak. Thank fuck. Finally. About time her inquisitive nature kicked back into high gear. "An energy circle."

"And you think it will help Mac?"

Good question. Only one answer. "I donnae know, lass. I'm praying it works. If it doesn't, I'm out of options."

"He's that sick?"

"Aye. And worsening by the moment."

"Is the circle thing dangerous?"

Probably. He didn't know. Not for certain. He'd never participated in an energy circle before. Had never seen one either. He'd read about the practice years ago, in an ancient tome housed in the Scottish pack's library . . . thanks to his sire. A big believer in education, he'd made Forge and his brothers study the annals every day. Prep school, Dragonkind style. For his sire, the old adage had held true: knowledge equaled power, and power saved lives.

Manipulating the Meridian, drawing huge bursts of power, was always tricky. Add five high-energy females to the mix and the risks approached perilous.

"Crap," she muttered, when he didn't answer right away. "It is, isn't it?"

"I willnae let anything hurt you, Hope."

The softly spoken promise brought her chin up. Green eyes full of gratitude met his. He sucked in a deep breath. She flexed her fingers, realigned her palm with his, and, leaning in, wrapped her arm around his biceps. The press of her body made his hum in pleasure. She gifted him with a smile, making his heart somersault inside his chest. The first one he'd seen from her in what seemed like forever.

"I believe you, but you know . . ." Her brow furrowed, she trailed off. A second passed, tumbling into more as she gathered her thoughts. "All this Dragonkind stuff, well . . . it's pretty scary."

"I know. I've shown you a lot today." He frowned. Maybe too much. Christ. Perhaps he'd done it wrong. Shocking the hell out of Hope twice in one morning—first with the dream and mind meld, and second by showing her his dragon—might've been overkill. He stifled a snort. *Might have.* Christ. Replace it with *absolutely, no doubt about it.* He needed to have his head examined. Lifting his free hand, he cupped the side of her throat. Fingers spread wide, he touched as much of her as he could, playing with the wispy hair at the nape of her neck. "It will get better. You'll become accustomed tae me in time and—Hope, you donnae have tae participate. If you're not comfortable with—"

"I call bullshit. Don't tell me that." Temper flaring, her eyes narrowed on him. "This is for Mac. He's my friend too, Forge. I'll do whatever it takes to help him, and besides . . . you need me to complete the circle."

True enough. He needed at least five high-energy females inside the energy circle. Otherwise, he wouldn't be able to draw enough power from the Meridian. Mac needed a jump start, a blast of energy so strong it put his dragon half into overdrive. The idea made perfect sense. After what he'd witnessed with Hamersveld, he understood what plagued his best friend. Mac was struggling to pull a wren into their world from the other side—from the ether, a mystical realm protected by the Goddess of All Things. Only one way to solve that problem—overload Mac's magical side, pump him full of so much healing energy it pushed the wren from the confines of the tattoo.

A beautiful theory, unproven but poetic.

But as the elevator doors slid open and Forge stepped inside, pulling his female along with him, his need to protect Hope shifted gears. He didn't want to put her in the circle. He wanted her to stay out of it—safe from all harm. But with Myst pregnant and unable to participate, excluding Hope left him one HE short.

Without her, Mac would die. Then again, if anything happened to Hope, Forge would too. He wouldn't survive losing her. He loved her too much already. The admission jolted through him, shocking him as it sank in and settled deep, fusing with the core of him. Aye, it had happened fast, but the truth couldn't be denied. He loved Hope. The words rang true, no reason to deny or question the way he felt about her.

Which put him in an untenable position. Damned if he did. Damned if he didn't. Not that it was his decision to make anymore. His female had a say. Forge knew he would never change her mind. True to her generous nature, Hope wanted to help. She refused to turn away from a friend in need and would resent him if he forced her onto the sidelines. Not the best way to begin a relationship, so . . .

No help for it.

He couldn't stop the plan he'd set in motion now.

But as the doors closed and the elevator began its descent, instinct sparked, and Forge couldn't shake the awful feeling something terrible was about to happen.

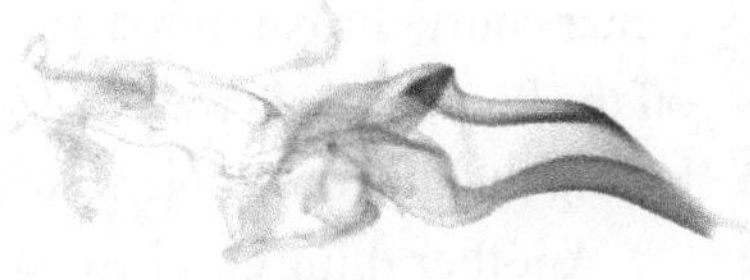

Chapter Twenty-Seven

Boots planted on the edge of the basketball court inside the gym, Forge searched for his female in the chaos. His gaze jumped over Sloan and Bastian. Heads together, bent over a computer, the pair commiserated, yakking about God knew what and . . . shite. He didn't care. Not right now. Not with Hope in the wind and—fucking hell. He turned his back for one second and she disappeared. Scampered from view. Made herself scarce . . . whatever. His brow furrowed, he leaned right, looked past Haider and Nian, ignored Wick's raised brow and Venom's knowing grin. He scowled. Where the hell—

The sound of her voice cranked his head around.

He found her in less than a second.

Back to being quiet, she sat cross-legged on an exercise mat with the other females. Chin tilted down, she dragged her hands through her strawberry blond hair. A quick twist of her fingers. A faster flash of an elastic, and she tamed the unruly mass, imprisoning the strands in a messy bun atop her head. Angela said something to her. His female grinned, a huff of laughter escaping as she gave Rikar's mate a playful shove.

The muscles roping his abdomen clenched.

Christ, he adored watching her. Would never get tired of seeing her smile and her eyes spark in pleasure. Running his gaze over her one more time, ensuring she was all right, he turned his attention back to the center of the gym. The designated workhorses, Venom and Wick saw to the setup. Large wrestling mat already pressed flat at center court, the pair lifted a padded hip-high table. Stout legs levered off the floor, the lads walked it sideways and set it down in the middle, hiding the dragon emblem stamped into the rubberized surface.

Another thing checked off his list.

The last link in his mental chain.

One more step toward making Mac well.

Eyes roaming, he swept the scene again. Everyone here and accounted for, not a single soul missing, the entire pack on board with his idea and the energy circle. The unconditional acceptance should've made him feel better. Eased down his tension and helped him breathe easier. It didn't. Worry acted like a poison pill instead, making him twitch with unease, winding his muscles so tight he struggled not to snap . . . at everyone in sight.

Swallowing a snarl, Forge rolled his shoulders.

The soft thud of footfalls sounded to his left. Glancing sideways, he glowered as Rikar strode toward him. The Nightfury first in command's lips twitched. The urge to haul off and hit the male thumped through him. Forge flexed his hands. Bloody hell. Nothing about the situation approached funny. Not after all he'd put Hope and himself through today. Not Mac's worsening condition. Nor the potential clusterfuck of an energy circle he was in charge of initiating.

Rikar came abreast of him.

"Screw off, laddie," he said, more growl than actual words. "Go bother someone else."

"Now, now." Stepping alongside him, Rikar slapped the back of his shoulder. The solid tap rocked him forward. "Settle down, big guy. You've got it well in hand and . . ." He glanced toward the exercise mat. Pale eyes settled on his mate, glowed in pleasure, then skipped over to Hope. "Don't worry. Angela's got her."

Shite. He hoped so. No matter how close at hand, leaving Hope with others when she needed him most didn't sit well. But he couldn't do two things at once. He needed to supervise the setup. Make sure everything went just right. No mistakes could be made. If he screwed up, even a bit, Mac would suffer along with every female in the room.

"Where are Mac and Tania?"

"On the way," Rikar said. "Myst took the IV out like you asked. She's monitoring his vitals. Gage is rolling them in."

"All right, then," he murmured, taking a deep breath. No more stalling. Time to set his plan in motion and pray it worked. Sending a quick word in the goddess's direction, Forge released the lungful in a long, slow rush and glanced at Rikar. "Get everyone into position."

With a nod, Rikar brought two fingers to his mouth. A sharp whistle pierced the air. Everyone's attention snapped in his direction. Raising his hand, he flicked his fingers, signaling the roundup. A cacophony of sound erupted. Chairs scraped against the wooden floor. A computer clicked closed. Heavy footfalls echoed against the gym ceiling as his brothers-in-arms moved as one, interrupting the buzz of industrial-size lights overhead. Dressed in flowing ceremonial robes, Angela, Evie, Hope, and J. J. followed the males. Bare feet padding over the wooden floor and onto the rubber mat, each female took her position next to the table.

Hope met his gaze.

Forge nodded in approval, his pride for her almost leveling him where he stood. Beautiful female. His mate was so damn brave. She crossed all boundaries and ticked every box on his wish list, exceeding all expectations. His eyes holding hers, he tipped his chin. She smiled back—not a lot, a slight lifting of her lips—but it was enough to calm him as Gage pushed Mac's hospital bed through open double doors and into the gym.

Wheels squeaked across the floor.

Dragging his focus from Hope, Forge stared at Mac. Christ help him. His friend looked terrible. Tattoo glowing bright red, skin the color of ash, he lay unconscious, belly down on the narrow mattress. Curled around her mate, Tania didn't look much better. Exhaustion lined her pretty face, and as her dark eyelashes lifted and she met his gaze, his heart sank. Fucking hell. It was worse than he thought. If the energy circle didn't work, if he couldn't calibrate the frequency, if the tiniest thing went wrong—

"Tania," J. J. said, voice wobbling, heartbreak in her eyes as she moved toward her sister.

"Don't, baby J. No more tears," Tania whispered as the bed stopped at the edge of the wrestling mat. Weakened by energy drain, her muscles quivered as she planted her hands on the mattress, curled her legs beneath her, and pushed herself upright. "Forge?"

"Aye, lass."

"You can do this." Exhaustion lining her features, thinner than a few days ago, she met his gaze. "I'm trusting you to see it through . . . no matter what happens."

Throat gone tight, unable to speak, he nodded.

"Let's go." With more determination than strength, Tania swung her feet over the side of the bed. Her bare feet touched down. Using the bed rail for balance, she stood, looked from Gage to him, then gestured to the table. "I need help moving him, guys. Could you—"

"You're not lifting a finger. Up onto the table, Tania," Gage said, stepping around the end of the metal footboard. "Forge and I will move him."

"Please be careful. Don't touch his tattoo," she said, entreaty in her tone. "He's in a lot of pain."

Doing as she asked, he and Gage muscled her mate over to the padded tabletop. But shite, it wasn't easy. Mac was heavier than hell. Stood to reason. Packed with muscle, standing well over six feet tall, none of the Nightfury warriors were lightweights, but . . . Jesus. An unconscious Mac tipped the scale, and as Gage grumbled and he growled in exertion, struggling not to brush against his best friend's tattoo, uncertainty crept into view. Faith swept it aside. Tania trusted him. The rest of the pack was counting on him. Hope needed him to guide her through the process, so . . .

Fuck his insecurities.

Settling Mac on the table, Gage stepped away.

Forge stayed and, leaning down, grasped the back of Mac's neck. He squeezed gently. "Hold on, brother. I'm going tae make it right. Get you what you need."

Still unconscious, Mac bared his teeth on a growl.

He nodded. Good enough. Mac's dragon half had heard him. Even now, the beast would be readying, preparing for whatever Forge threw at him. Releasing his friend, he nailed Tania with a serious look. "You too, lass. Hold on tight. Whatever happens, donnae let go."

Astride Mac's hips, Tania settled in, taking her position on the tabletop. "Thank you."

With a nod, Forge turned to the other females clustered around the table. Heart in his eyes, he held Hope's gaze and unleashed a stream of magic. The bond he shared with her sparked. She shivered. He strengthened the connection, lending her his strength, warming her with his heat, flooding her with all the love he felt for her. He felt her link in, grab hold, accepting all he gave her. Tears sheened her eyes as he touched her mind. He murmured in reassurance. Her shoulders square, she leveled her chin and drew a deep breath. Forge did the same, then looked away, struggling to stay calm as he tipped his chin and gave Angela the green light.

Taking his cue, Angela moved into position, leading the group.

He backed away and stepped off the mat. As they formed a semicircle around the table, Angela reached out and clasped Hope's hand. J. J. and Evie followed suit, reaching out, linking up until all four women held hands. Connected now, energy started to hum, supercharging the air as J. J. closed the circuit and locked palms with her sister. Taking a deep breath, Tania offered her free hand to Angela. The last in the chain, Angela glanced at Rikar and, taking a deep breath, grasped Tania's wrist, covering her pulse point.

The snap of combined energy buzzed in the room, raising the fine hairs on his skin.

The females breathed in, breathed out, and acting as one, tapped into each other's bio-energy. Electricity arced among the five. With a deafening crack, the door into the cosmic stream blew open. Magic bled from the portal, pouring into the gym. The Meridian rose in a monstrous wave. Bio-energy thundered, overtaking the room. Light-filled rings appeared around the table. Burning bright, each one pulsed as the Meridian screamed. The blue bands throbbed once, twice, a third time, throwing explosive heat into the room and—

The rings detonated.

A deafening crack ripped through the air.

The blast blew Forge off his feet. He slammed into the hospital bed. Metal groaned as the bed tipped over, banging against the floor. He landed on his ass in a heap beside the bed. Ears ringing, light fixtures creaking above his head, he struggled to his knees. His gaze landed on the circle.

Bleeding energy in the center of a cosmic storm, long hair whipping in circles, Tania threw her head back. Lips parted on a gasp, she became the conduit, funneling all the energy into Mac.

Arching beneath her, Mac roared.

Angela yelled, telling everyone to hold on.

Mac's tattoo pulsed, beating like a heartbeat, then . . . stilled. Time slowed. The energy expanded and contracted. Red drained from the tribal marking on his friend's skin, smoothing out, turning the color of polished silver. The cosmic storm stilled as an eerie fog rose above Mac's chest.

Silence descended. No one moved. He could hardly breathe.

A mind-splitting shriek tore through the gym.

Pain ripped across Forge's temples. His vision blurred. Pressing his hands over his ears, Forge fell back on his ass. Fuck, that hurt. So much he couldn't make himself move. Getting his feet under him seemed an impossibility, but Christ, he needed to reach Hope. She was over there . . . somewhere. All the females were and—

A form materialized inside the brume.

Vertical pupils aglow, the wren pushed outward, materializing over Mac. Blue-gray scales gleaming, the miniature dragon bared his fangs. He hissed, the daggerlike spikes around his neck rising like hackles as he screamed again.

Nightfury warriors cursed, the sound bringing each one to his knees.

Fear joined the agony throbbing through Forge's veins. "Hope—move! Everyone—move back! Get the hell—"

The wren screamed a third time.

More groans echoed inside the gym.

"Stop it—right now," Tania said, her tone clipped. "You're hurting everyone's ears."

Grabbing the overturned hospital bed, Forge pulled himself off his ass and looked across the gym. Shite. Nothing but haze. He couldn't see a fucking thing. Blinking rapid-fire, Forge cleared the blur away and forced himself to focus.

On her feet beside the table, Tania faced off with the wren.

His scaled lip curled, exposing a fang.

Tania held her ground, refusing to retreat, and stared down the miniature dragon. "Now, you listen here. Back off until Mac—"

"Motherfuck." With a snarl, Mac rolled off the table. His feet landed with a thump. Aquamarine eyes aglow, his friend stepped in front of Tania and, using his body to shield her, reached out. His hand caught hold, curling around one of the wren's horns. "Exshaw, settle down."

Faced with a command given by his master, the miniature dragon turtled, rolling onto his back, exposing his belly, playing submissive to Mac's dominant. Relief grabbed Forge by the balls. Thank God. It was over. The energy circle had worked. Mac was alive. Gratitude tightened his throat. He watched his friend sway on his feet for a moment. But as Tania came to his rescue, slipping beneath Mac's arm to lend support, reaching out to introduce herself to the wren, a different worry struck Forge.

Scanning the mat, he searched for his female. "Hope?"

"Here," she said, crawling out from behind a table leg.

His heart clenched, then released as another round of relief hit him. Ears still ringing, a blinding headache forming, he planted a hand on the floor and pushed to his feet. His knees threatened to give out. Forcing strength into his legs, he wove an unsteady path toward her. Unwilling to wait for his arrival, she scooted across the floor. Halfway across the mat, she reached for him. Forge didn't hesitate. He let his knees buckle. The second his arse hit the floor, he lifted her into his lap.

His hands moved over her.

She started to tremble.

With a rumble of reassurance, he caressed her everywhere, stroking her skin, searching for injuries, settling his fears. "I'm okay, I'm okay," she whispered over and over, burrowing into him, trying to get closer, asking without words to be held. He didn't deny her. Couldn't deny himself. It was as it always would be—she was the center of his universe. His sun and moon, every star in his sky. And as he tucked her close, listening to the hum of mated males soothe their own females, he thanked the goddess, not only for Mac's safe return, but also for the female nestled like a gift in his arms.

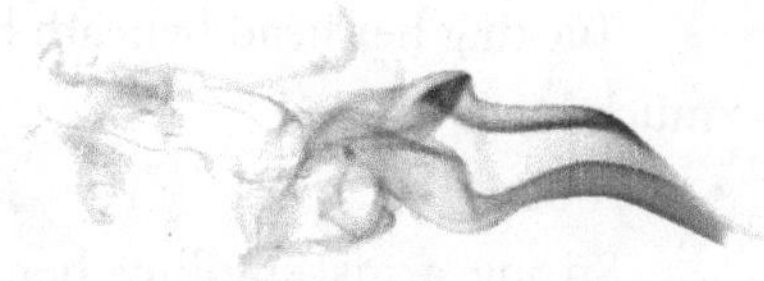

Chapter Twenty-Eight

Tucked against Forge's side, Hope stepped off the elevator. The movement jarred her. Her senses jangled, making her temples throb and her whole body hurt. Clenching her teeth, she took a deep breath and looked around, trying to get her bearings, allowing Forge to lead, struggling to stop the blinding whirl inside her head. But nothing she tried worked. The tumbling force inside her tightened its grip. One mental revolution spun into another. Now her mind burned and the awful buzz spread, infecting muscles and bone, bringing tears to her eyes.

Hope blinked each away, but . . . God. She couldn't stop the mental blur. The whiplash slashed her. No relief in sight. No safe port in the storm. Just the roar in her veins and the splinter of once-organized thoughts.

"F-forge?"

"Shh, *jalâyla*. We're almost there."

Almost where? She wanted to ask him, but as her vision blurred, the hardwood floor beneath her feet warped. Her knees dipped. She stumbled. Forge cursed and, without breaking stride, picked her up and kept walking. Her whole body sighed in relief. Thank God. She needed the contact—skin-to-skin would be best, but any part of him touching any part of her would do. His grip grounded her. His voice soothed the chaos inside her head. Although, the pace didn't help.

Each of his footfalls knocked through her, making her cling to him harder.

Tucking her head beneath his chin, Hope stifled a shiver. "How much longer?"

"Soon."

Strong arms cradling her, long legs carrying her down the deserted corridor, Forge dipped his head. His mouth brushed her temple, making her crave more contact. She whispered his name. Murmuring in return, he adjusted his grip and kept going, putting distance between her and the others. A good plan. She needed the space. Needed to get away from the gym and chaos still ruling inside it.

The second he'd gotten his feet under him, Forge recognized the problem. She was in overload: overwhelmed, awash with sensation, unable to close the connection and stem the raging flow of the Meridian. Now she bled energy, body being buffeted by the powerful stream and the driving bite of the other women's bio-energy. Removing her from their presence seemed like the smart move. Hope knew it. So did Forge. She could practically see his thoughts inside her own head. Was tapped in somehow, reading his worry as he hurried past her bedroom door, taking her God only knew where.

Not that she cared, just as long as he stayed with her.

Teeth chattering, Hope tightened her grip on him.

Hugging her closer, he set his mouth to her temple. Her senses expanded. Her mind contracted. The nasty burn moved from mind-torquing awful to somewhat manageable. Awareness came back online. Opening her eyes, Hope stared at the wall as Forge strode past. White paint. Expensive artwork. A chunky chair rail. Okay. Good. She had her bearings. Glancing down, she stared at her bare feet. The hem of her ceremonial robe fluttered against her ankles. Cold air washed over her toes. Forge growled against her cheek.

A soothing wave of heat washed through her.

Hope sighed as the intense vibration lessened, dragging her from the edge of mental meltdown. She inhaled again, filling her lungs, forcing her body to calm. Good. Better. Almost there. She could do it. Accept what he offered: absorb and release, take it in, let it go, and . . . *breathe*.

"That's it, *jalâyla*," he said, the rumble of his voice against her skin reassuring her, allowing her to listen. "Easy now. You're all right."

His voice washed the last of her tension away. Her vision cleared. Her brain came back online. Exhaling another shaky breath, she shuddered in his arms.

Lifting his head, he peered down at her. His eyes roamed her face. "Better?"

"Yes," she whispered, sounding surprised. "Thank you."

"For what?"

"The energy thing. You just fed me, didn't you?"

"I did."

"Wow," she said, awe making her stare at him in wonder. Crazy, she knew. The idea of an energy exchange—of him feeding her and her doing the same for him—should've freaked her out. At least, a little. But after the energy circle and the intensity of her reaction, allowing Forge to soothe her that way didn't seem strange anymore. It felt right. *He* felt right. "Does it always feel like that?"

He shrugged. "No clue. I've never fed a female before."

Hope blinked. "Not once?"

"Nay."

"I don't know what it says about me, but . . . good," she said, feeling small minded, but . . . God. She couldn't help her reaction. The idea of him with another woman did strange things to her. Provoked all kinds of nasty thoughts—mostly having to do with murdering any woman who dared touch him. "I'm glad I'm the only one."

"You are at that, lass . . . you are at that." Pleasure in his eyes, he levered her in his arms and set her down on something. Her butt connected with smooth stone. Hope jolted and stared down at the expanse of white marble. She frowned at it a second before she realized where she sat—inside the kitchen, as far away from the gym as the house allowed. Smiling at her, he leaned in for a kiss. His mouth brushed hers—a soft touch, teasing pressure—before he retreated to glance over his shoulder. "Can you dish up some soup, Daimler?"

"Of course, Master Forge," a guy said, British accent ringing crisp and clear from somewhere inside the kitchen. "Two bowls or one."

"One for now." Big hand on her nape, he played with the hair, twirling it around his fingertips, keeping her steady with his touch. "She may want a second later."

Her stomach balked at the suggestion. She might feel better now, but eat something? Hope wrinkled her nose in protest. "Thank you, but I'm not hungry."

Forge gave her a stern look. "You need tae eat."

"But—"

"You expended a lot of energy in the circle, lass." Purple gaze full of worry, he scanned her face. "You need tae replenish your reserves. Food will help do that."

She'd rather have him, but instead of arguing, she caved. Gave up and gave in without a fight. His concern did her in, crushing her ability to deny him. No way she could say no. Not now. Not in the face of his need to take care of her. Not if it meant causing him undue stress.

"Soup sounds good," she said, throat so tight she could hardly get the words out.

Cupping her cheek, Forge stroked her once and nodded in approval. A second later, she went airborne in his arms as he picked her up. A quick swivel. A faster sideways step, and he set her down on a stool next to the island. The clang of metal on glass echoed. Footfalls sounded. A moment later, a bowl full of chicken noodle soup landed in front of her. The elegant hand retreated. Hope glanced up and met Daimler's gaze. She whispered, "Thank you." Pointed ears peeking out from a crop of dark hair, the corner of his eyes crinkled, showing approval, as steam curled from the bowl and . . .

Her attention snapped back to the soup. Holy God. It smelled delicious. Her mouth started to water. A second later, her stomach growled, surprising her.

A knowing twinkle in his eyes, Daimler tucked a spoon beside her bowl. And Hope dug in. The first bite closed her eyes. The second made her hum in bliss. The hot broth spread warmth through her body, the noodles filled her empty stomach, banishing the ache and . . . hmm. Comfort food shouldn't taste this good. The elf was more than just the Nightfury go-to guy. He was a culinary wizard, one who took chicken noodle soup and elevated it to an art form.

Hope hummed her gratitude around a spoonful.

Daimler chuckled.

She took another bite.

Seated beside her, watching like a hawk, Forge encouraged her to eat more. As she neared the bottom of her bowl, he reached out and caressed the underside of her chin. She turned to look at him. Intense purple eyes met hers. "Have another bowl after you're done."

Her instincts twanged. Hope's focus on him sharpened. "Where are you going?"

"I need tae check on Mac and Tania," he said as Daimler set a plate of homemade bread in front of her. "I won't be gone long. Half an hour at most."

Angling her spoon, Hope set it inside the bowl. "I could go with you."

Forge shook his head. "Exshaw is shaken . . . still hostile after a difficult birth. Until Mac has the wren completely under control, you aren't tae go anywhere near him—all right?"

"Okay." No sense arguing. Endangering her life wasn't something she wanted to do with Forge around. He took protecting her to a whole new level, and something told her he wasn't above bending her over his knee. She cringed and . . . yeah. Not going to happen. Getting her butt warmed—so not on her list of things to do anytime soon. Or ever. "You're sure Mac's all right?"

"Aye."

"Tania too?"

"Donnae worry, lass. Both are already on the road tae recovery." Tucking a strand of hair behind her ear, he traced her bottom lip with his fingertips. Need zipped through her. His eyes heated an instant before he turned and looked at the elf trying not to eavesdrop across the kitchen. "Will you be all right on your own for a few minutes?"

She wanted to say no. Independent spirit refused to let her. She was a big girl. Rock solid. No need to go weepy over a few minutes without him. "Go, Forge. I'll be fine."

He studied her a moment, making sure, then turned to Daimler. "May I leave her with you?"

Gold front tooth flashing, dimples out, Daimler smiled, charming her without even trying. "It would be my pleasure to keep her company until you return, Master Forge."

"Stay here, *jalâyla*." Giving the end of her nose a playful tap, he pressed a hard kiss to her mouth and got up to go. "I won't be long."

She nodded, but as he skirted the island and headed for the door, the harsh zip of energy came back. Pressure built inside her head. Her temples started to throb . . . crap. It wasn't fair. She should be able to keep it together. Had been okay—comfortable and relaxed—with him seated beside her, but the greater the distance between her and Forge grew, the more intense the vibration became. Now she sat on the edge of panic once more, heart thumping, hands flexing, so tense she wanted to scream for him to come back. She squirmed in her seat, set to snap, ready to run, needing to—

"Think of your mate, my lady," Daimler said, breaking into her thoughts, giving her someone to focus on. "Hold a picture of Forge in the center of your mind."

"Will it help?"

"Yes."

With the burn flaring through her, Hope didn't argue. She did as he asked, refusing to question the advice. An image of Forge formed in her mind's eye. She clung to it, remembering the sound of his voice and the way she felt when he held her. The vibration ebbed. Her body calmed—not much, but it was enough. Better than losing it and flying headlong into a panic attack. Taking a deep breath, trying to channel the excess energy, she turned wide eyes on Daimler. "I think I may be losing it."

"You're in shock, my lady—in energy overload. You need Master Forge close. Only natural after all you've been through today," Daimler said, sounding so reasonable—as though what she suffered happened every day. She didn't know what to do: ask for a hug or let frustration out of the bag and smack him upside the head. "Most females are brought into the fold more gently, but you've been thrown right in and—"

"You're kidding, right?"

He blinked. "Of course not. I would never tease you in such a manner."

Hope stared at him as though he'd lost his mind. Daimler must be joking. She frowned. *More gently,* her foot. Was he insane? Nothing about the Nightfury warriors meeting their mates ever happened *gently*.

She'd heard about it in the gym, while sitting cross-legged on exercise mats with the other girls before joining the energy circle. Each had recounted how she met her husband (mate . . . whatever!). The only scoop she didn't have was Mac and Tania's. At least, not yet. But it would come, just as soon as the pair landed on their feet again.

"Daimler," she said, trying (and failing) to match his reasonable tone. "You can't be serious. I mean . . . Bastian airlifted Myst off the road while she drove her car. Angela was kidnapped and held captive before Rikar rescued her. Wick broke J. J. out of prison, and Evie nearly got blown up inside a hospital before Venom got to her."

He pursed his lips. "Well, it has been exciting."

"Exciting," she said, incredulity growing. Well, that was one way of putting it. *Insane* might be another. The thought stole her air. Without Forge to channel it, a raging claw of excess energy upped the ante, threatening to overwhelm her. Battling sensory overload, Hope shook her head. "I can't . . . I don't think I can . . . I need to go. I can't stay here."

"My lady—"

"Will you take me home?" she asked without thinking. Leaving was a bad idea. Hope knew it. Felt it. Sensed it deep down the second she opened her mouth, but . . . God. She needed space, a safe place to process and think things through. "Would you do that for me?"

"No," he said, dashing her hopes with a single soft-spoken word. "I'm sorry, my lady, but I won't allow you to leave the lair. Not without Forge's permission."

"But—"

He held up a finger. The words dried up, refusing to leave the tip of her tongue. She watched him pivot toward the fridge, mind spinning, mouth silent as regret made a home inside her heart. Goddamn it. Daimler was disappointed. She could see it written all over his face, and as he pulled the freezer open, Hope wanted to apologize. For so many things. For being afraid. For not being able to handle the energy overload. For making him believe she didn't want to stay with Forge.

"Daimler?"

"You will not apologize to me, Hope," he said, tone uncompromising. "You will save that for your mate when you tell him what you asked me to do. In the meantime . . ." Returning to the counter, he set a glass dish full of chocolate mousse along with a clean spoon in front of her. "Off you go."

Hope stared at the dessert, not understanding. "Where am I going?"

"To your room," he said, his stern expression making her feel like a wayward child in heaps of trouble. "You've some thinking to do, and you need to do it alone."

Chastened by an elf. Hope swallowed. It was surprisingly effective.

Cheeks burning, she picked up the dish and slid off the stool. As her feet touched down, she turned toward Daimler and opened her mouth, trying a second time to apologize. He wagged his finger at her. Hope closed it again and, feeling like a four-year-old reprimanded by her father, did as she was told. She rounded the island, left the kitchen, and scurried down the hall toward her bedroom, heart in her throat, a bowl full of chocolate mousse in her hands, the words *when you tell him what you asked* echoing like a warning inside her head.

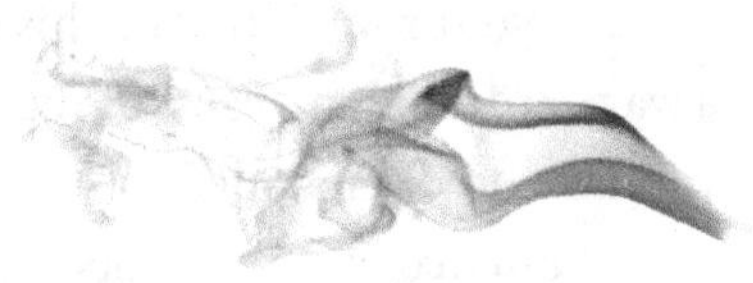

Chapter Twenty-Nine

Crouched in front of the dresser in her room, Hope reached into the bottom drawer. She nudged her boxing gloves aside. Bypassed her favorite skipping rope. Shoved a pile of workout clothes out of the way. Her fingertips brushed the box she'd hidden at the very back. Heartsore, still reeling from Daimler's disapproval, she hesitated a second, palm pressed to the warped wooden top, wondering if she should just leave well enough alone. Some things deserved a quiet death. Her childhood was no doubt one of them, but as memories called to her, she couldn't resist.

Or turn away.

She pulled the box out instead and, with a slow pivot, turned toward the bed. The thick duvet with pretty blue stars lay flat and smooth, the picture of perfection with its mound of pillows as she walked toward it, and into the teeth of her future. A funny thought, particularly since the past lay heavy in her hands. Not that it mattered. The juxtaposition, the span between then and now had shrunk. Now, the past and present stood side by side, forcing her to relive that day in the cemetery when she'd watched Adam's casket be lowered into the ground.

Sorrow struck like a barbed fist.

Old wounds opened, imaginary blood pooling as she hopped up and crawled onto the bed. Settling cross-legged in the middle of the mattress, Hope stared at the horse carved into the box top, wondering what Forge would have to say about it all. A lot, no doubt. Smart. Aware. More intuitive than most, the guy never seemed to lack for words.

The thought made her smile.

Taking the lid off her treasure box wiped it from her face. She tipped the container over. Mixed emotions spilled out along with the contents—so many photographs, too many memories. Tears pricked the corners of her eyes as she picked up the first one. Wearing a grin the size of Rhode Island, her six-year-old brother stood on a dock, fishing rod in one hand, a tiny fish in the other. She remembered that day. Adam had been so proud. Her father, however, had not. Par for the course. Not much pleased the vice admiral outside of his work, and as always, when away from the naval base, he was present in body, but never in spirit.

Blowing out a heavy breath, Hope continued on, flipping through the pictures. Stopped to examine one. Laughed out loud at another. Choked back a sob as she came to a photo of her and Adam grinning from the steps of the campus library. Freshmen year. Hope huffed in wonder. Good lord, look how young they'd been: fresh faced and enthusiastic, optimistic in every way. The world had been so bright and shiny then, oysters in the palms of their hands. Her fingertip ghosted over the glossy surface of the photograph, tracing the contours of his face.

"Oh, Adam," she whispered, talking to her dead twin as though he could still hear her. "Why did you do it? It couldn't have been that bad."

But Hope knew it had been.

No one understood better than her that Father never let up. She'd been able to cope, get by, avoid the worst of his scrutiny. Being born a girl had saved her, removing her from Father's notice. As his only son, Adam hadn't been so lucky. Staring at a photo of her brother dressed in cadet blues, Hope shook her head. So much pressure. Too many expectations. Little to no approval. The vice admiral excelled at the equation—at manufacturing unachievable goals and all the self-doubt that went along with them.

After years of soul-searching, she knew it had been a recipe for disaster. One her brother had chopped up, sautéed, and thrown into a proverbial pan. Exploding with such violence, he'd shattered lives while he lost his own. It wasn't an excuse. She would never be able to excuse his actions. Not then, not now. But as she peered into her past, remembering the good times, Hope thought, perhaps, she understood him better. She hoped so, anyway. It was the only way for her to put Adam to rest. Forever. For always. Like any normal person would.

Shuffling through another stack of photos, Hope pulled one free, flipped it over, and—

A tingle prickled along her back.

Hinges sighed. A second later the door swung open.

Serious violet eyes met hers. Forge raised a brow. "Hiding?"

"Kind of," she said, her heart giving a happy hop at the sight of him.

Stepping into the room, Forge gestured to the box resting beside her. "What's all this?"

"Pictures. My past in one messy pile." Picking up a photograph, she held it out to him. "Come see."

Forge didn't hesitate. He took her invitation, crossing the room to sit down on the edge of her bed. He held her gaze a moment. The worry in his eyes drew her tight, making her wonder what he was thinking before he accepted the photo. His eyes moved over the glossy surface. "Your brother?"

"Yeah," she said, smiling as she stared at the image of her and Adam on shiny new bicycles. She pointed at the one she sat on. Her fingertip traced the colorful tassels hanging from the handlebars. "I'd just turned ten. We spent the whole summer riding around the naval base. It drove the soldiers at the gate nuts, but . . . God, I loved that bike."

His mouth curved. "You were a pretty wee lass."

With a huff of laughter, she handed him another picture. And then another, recounting stories, heart growing heavy at turns and lightening at others, telling Forge everything she could remember about Adam. About herself, sharing her past the only way she knew how . . . by being as honest with him as he'd been earlier with her. He'd talked nonstop after showing her his dragon half (in the shower, in the bedroom, while they'd both gotten dressed), explaining his world, why Rodin wanted him dead, and how important linking the Archguard leader to the murder of his family was to the dragon pack inside Black Diamond.

She'd listened then, taken it all in without interrupting.

Now he did the same, his focus on her absolute. More patient than anyone she knew, he absorbed all she said, asked a question here or there, but mostly let her talk, as though he knew she needed to exorcise her past in order to move on.

At length, he reached over and pulled a photograph from the bottom of the pile. "This him? Your da?"

Her eyes settled on a picture of her father. Throat gone tight, she nodded.

"You ever see him?"

"No."

"Why not?"

"He won't answer my calls, never mind let me visit." As Forge's brows collided, Hope tensed, knowing she needed to explain. Not a happy proposition. She never spoke of her father . . . to anyone. Not even Angela knew how toxic the relationship with him had become. But as confusion rose in Forge's eyes, she knew avoidance was no longer an option. Trusting someone meant opening up, shining a light on the untidy parts of life as well as the good. "He blames me for Adam's death. Thinks I should have known about the attack and stopped it."

"With what, lass—your psychologist superpowers? Your magical ability tae read people's minds?"

Hope blinked in surprise.

He raised a brow, challenging her father's unfairness . . . and her guilt. "Sounds like I need tae pay your sire a visit. The male needs some sense knocked into him."

She huffed. No doubt, but . . . jeepers. *Psychologist superpowers?* Seriously? Forge had just stepped off the reservation. In a funny, totally adorable, God-he-filled-her-heart-to-the-brim kind of way. Even so, she treated him to a no-nonsense look. "You are not allowed to hit my father."

"Can I scare him?" he asked, tone playful, face full of hope. He held his hand up, thumb and forefinger an inch apart. "Just a wee bit?"

His hopeful expression made her laugh. A second later, tears pooled in her eyes, the pain pouring out before she could stop it. With a sympathetic murmur, Forge reached out and drew her in, pulling her across the bed. His arms wrapped around her. Hope didn't fight him. Turning into his embrace, she let herself cry—for the first time in ages—allowing him to comfort her, to see her weakness and soothe away the heartache.

Being pulled outside her comfort zone—out of her life and into Black Diamond—had smashed through her defenses. Now her foundation lay cracked and crumbling, nothing but rubble around her, the destruction making room for a new start. Forge was right. She wasn't a mind reader. She couldn't have known what Adam intended. Which meant she needed to forgive herself for missing the signs and move on. She might feel responsible, but she wasn't at fault. Adam had made his decision and carried it out. No way for her to know . . . or stop him from hurting all those people.

For some reason, the simple truth turned the tide, shifting her way of thinking. To heal, she must let go and make room. For something good to enter her life. For someone new—a man-dragon who'd made it clear he wanted her to stay.

The realization scared her a little. And stunned her even more.

"Hey, Forge?"

"Aye, luv."

She sniffled into his shoulder. "Thanks."

"For what?"

"For being here. For listening."

"There is nowhere else I would rather be, Hope, than with you."

God help her, he was awesome. The absolute best. Everything her heart had hoped to find, but her mind had refused to believe existed. Which meant . . .

She needed to tell him what she'd done. Why she sat on her bed instead of in the kitchen with Daimler. Hope grimaced. Crap. She really didn't want to admit she'd been sent to her room like a naughty four-year-old. Hope wanted to grumble at the unfairness—about the urge to open up and tell Forge everything whenever he got anywhere near her—but well . . . hell. She couldn't fight it. Might as well get it over with and come clean.

Steeling herself for his reaction, she lifted her cheek off his chest and took a fortifying breath. "I asked Daimler to take me home earlier."

"I know. He told me."

Her mouth fell open. "Seriously?"

"Aye."

She frowned. "A total tattletale, isn't he?"

"Only where wayward females are concerned."

"Yeah, well, not to worry." Throwing him a disgusted look, she tossed the photo she held onto the messy stack. The pile shifted, sliding across the duvet. "He had your back."

Adjusting his hold on her, Forge wiped a tear from her cheek. "What did he do?"

"Not much." Which qualified as annoying. Or really embarrassing depending on the point of view. "He gave me a stern look, handed me a bowl of chocolate mousse, and sent me to my room."

"Could've been worse." His gaze tracked to the empty dish sitting on her nightstand. Amusement sparked in his eyes. "At least he banished you with chocolate."

"Thank God," she muttered, glad Daimler epitomized fantastic. "I might have murdered someone on the way here otherwise."

The lighthearted comment fell flat, making her nervous. She figured he would laugh and the tension she sensed in him would ease. Neither happened. His hand flexed against her back. Serious purple eyes searched her face. The scrutiny made her twitch. The trace of fear she saw on his face caused her throat to tighten. God forgive her. She'd screwed up. By asking to be taken home, she'd shaken his confidence . . . and hurt his feelings.

Gaze locked on his face, she smoothed her hand over her thigh. She needed to explain. Hadn't intended to hurt him, but . . . God. After all the Dragonkind drama, she'd craved familiarity, something she recognized to ground her.

With a quick shift, Hope slid further into his lap. She needed to get closer, touch him more, put her hands on his skin. Cupping his face, she looked him straight in the eyes. "I wasn't trying to run away."

A muscle twitched along his jaw, against her palm. "Why then, lass?"

"You left to make sure Mac had what he needed, and I—"

"I was gone less than twenty minutes."

"I know, but without your arms around me, I panicked. I can't explain it, but the second you left I needed to replace you with something familiar. I thought my house . . . being surrounded by my things . . . would work." Tears clogged the back of her throat. With a murmur, he pressed his cheek to hers. Day-old stubble scraped across her skin. Hope sighed in relief when he hugged her tight, sharing his affection, accepting her without question. "I'm sorry if I worried you."

"You did at that, Hope." Lifting his chin from its perch on top of her head, he leaned away. She tried to hold on. His big hand landed on her nape. Heat from his palm spread through her like wildfire, chasing her chill away. He held her there, then shifted his grip and forced her to look at him. "But now, I need tae ask—"

"Is this normal?" she asked, the bond she sensed, but couldn't see, flexing deep inside her.

"What—you interrupting me?" Lips twitching, he shook his head. "Sad tae say, lass, but I think it might be."

"No, I mean . . ." Hope frowned, trying to get her bearings. He'd told her a lot, but it wasn't enough. She needed to understand how Dragonkind relationships worked. A bond was one thing, being enthralled (fascinated, captivated, delighted . . . pick a word, any word) by him was quite another. "Sorry about interrupting, but really, I need to know—is what's happening between us normal, 'cause I gotta say, how I feel about you is freaking me out a little."

His expression softened. "*Jalâyla.*"

"It's insane." Struggling to fit the pieces together, Hope ignored the endearment. "I've fallen so hard for you. Way too fast. My brain is telling me to slow down—that it can't possibly be real, but my heart . . ." Chest aching, she rubbed her hand over her breastbone. "My heart—God, it's telling me to trust what I feel, but . . . is it real, Forge? Am I imagining the connection with you or—"

"Nay, Hope, never think it. Donnae ever doubt it." His grip on her firmed. Hard muscles flexed around her as he lifted her off his lap. She went airborne a second before being set astride him. Her knees sank into the mattress on either side of his hips. Big hands bracketing her waist, he dipped his head and pressed a kiss to the corner of her mouth. "The bond we share is powerful. Like magic, it's as real as the air we breathe. We may not be able tae see it, but we feel it all the same."

His explanation circled inside her head. Gripping his shoulders, Hope pulled in a breath. All right. Good enough. His explanation made sense to her. It wasn't based in logic. It wasn't anchored in anything concrete, and yet, as she cupped his face and reached out with her mind, she found him. Could see Forge clear as day. Felt him every time her heart beat. Saw his need for her each time he met her eyes.

"It's so strange," she whispered. "Even when you're not with me, I sense you. I feel you with every breath I take."

"I feel you too." Stroking the hair from her face, Forge kissed her again. It wasn't much, a simple brush of his mouth, but Hope registered the resonance along with the worship in his touch. "The fall has been fast and furious for us, without any sort of warning, but lass, love doesn't care about convention. It doesn't hold tae human timelines or care what others think. Love has a mind all its own—and settles when and where it chooses. You are my female, Hope. I am your mate. I will love you for a lifetime if you let me."

His promise poured through her, healing old wounds, filling her so full she couldn't contain it. Tears pooled in her eyes. "I'll let you. And I'll love it, Forge . . . almost as much as I love you."

"Sweet lass," he murmured. "You make me so proud. I love you. I'll cherish you too, and just so you know—you'll be moving into the lair and sharing my bed, sleeping in my arms every day from now until forever."

"So bossy," she said, teasing him as the tension eased. "I may have some demands of my own, you know."

"Tell me."

Tilting her head, she considered. "I want you to take me flying at nightfall. We'll go to my place and get some of my things."

"No problem." He growled and, flashing teeth, nipped at her bottom lip. "What else?"

"I don't want to close my practice. I'd like to continue counseling trauma victims."

"I'll make it happen. Go on."

"And lastly . . ." She trailed off.

He picked up the thread. "Aye?"

"I'll need you to keep your promise."

He raised a brow. "Which one?"

"The one that says you'll love me forever."

"Already done, lass," he murmured, tumbling her back onto the bed. "Already done."

Done. Such a simple word: quick, concise, as charming as the man-dragon kissing her blind. Stroking her hands through his hair, Hope hummed against his mouth. He murmured in welcome. She smiled in pleasure. Uh-huh. No doubt about it. She was *done.* Done running. Done hiding. Done pretending she hadn't been waiting for Forge to come along and shine his light into the dark corners of her world. She hadn't known how much she needed him. Or realized the damage closing herself off from others would do, but now, she couldn't deny the truth. She'd been so lonely. He might turn her inside out, upside down, and backwards, but that was all right. Fine by her. No problem at all, just as long as he loved her always and she got to spend a lifetime in his arms.

Acknowledgments

It took awhile for me to write *Fury of Surrender*, the sixth novel in the Dragonfury Series. Longer than I expected. I ran into one roadblock after another in the writing of it. Sometimes, I've learned, that happens to a writer. Life gets in the way, on purpose, forcing us to refocus, shining a brighter light on all we strive to accomplish. I learned a lot from Forge and Hope. Most of it about forgiveness and being as kind to yourself as you've been taught to be to others. Time well spent. Lessons well learned. And a book I absolutely adore. I hope you enjoy *Fury of Surrender* as much as I have and still do. Hugs, and happy reading!

Tremendous thanks to my literary agent, Christine Witthohn: for your patience and encouragement over the last year, for shepherding me when I thought I'd lost my way. You are, without a doubt, the best of the best.

Many thanks to my editors, Anh Schluep and Jennifer Glover, for taking the words on the page and making *Fury of Surrender* into a flesh-and-blood book.

To Melody Guy—thank you. The book is better for you having been part of it. Your astute observations, commitment to a great story, and getting the details right challenged me to make the book better at every turn.

To my friends and family—thank you for your smiles and laughter, for the patience you show when I'm deep in Storyland. Your sunny faces brighten my days. I love you all.

Last, but never least, to Kallie Lane, fellow writer, critique partner, and friend. Thank you for all the BS sessions, chats on the phone, and being so honest. You make me better. You always have. Thank you!

I raise a glass!

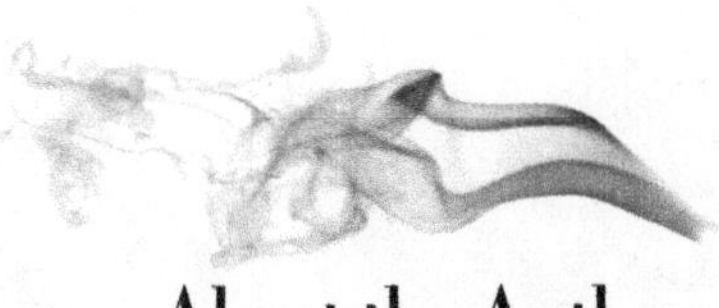

About the Author

Photo © 2009 Julie Daniluk

Coreene Callahan is the bestselling author of the Dragonfury novels and Circle of Seven Series, in which she combines her love of romance and adventure with her passion for history. After graduating with honors in psychology and taking a detour to work in interior design, Coreene finally returned to her first love: writing. Her debut novel, *Fury of Fire*, was a finalist in the New Jersey Romance Writers Golden Leaf Contest in two categories: Best First Book and Best Paranormal. She lives in Canada with her family, a spirited Great Pyrenees mix, and her wild imaginary world. Visit her online at www.CoreeneCallahan.com and on Twitter @coreenecallahan.